THRALL

DAUGHTERS OF LILITH:
BOOK I

Jennifer Quintenz

SECRET TREE PRESS

Printed in the United States of America

First Printing, 2012

ISBN-13: 978-0615655765
ISBN-10: 0615655769

Secret Tree Press
www.JenniferQuintenz.com

This is for you, Dad.

CONTENTS

ACKNOWLEDGMENTS

This is my first novel, and to say I have many people to acknowledge for its existence would be a bit of an understatement. Thanks to my family, friends, writing groups, teachers, cheerleaders and champions—your constructive criticism and encouragement gave me both the strength and the desire to push through the rough patches and resist the temptation to stop at "good enough."

A few special acknowledgments. To my unflagging manager Marc Manus for his insight, determination, and faith. To Alex Glass, Kate Crockett, and David Baird for their laser-focused editorial suggestions and for helping me see the unexplored potential in this story. To the amazing band of writers that read and offered feedback on various stages of this project; Davah, Bethany, Amy, Liz, Kristin, Kelly, Josh, (the other) Josh, Ali, Ann, and my sister Amanda. To Steven Fiedler for sharing his ninja-like editorial skills (I owe you a box of red pens).

And finally, to my husband James for his overwhelming love and support.

Her house sinks down to death,
And her course leads to the shades.
All who go to her cannot return
And find again the paths of life.

- Proverbs 2:18-19

1

The night of the dance was crisp and clear, one of those desert nights when the world seemed to be holding its breath. Fall was giving way to winter and there was an edge to the breeze. It kept most of us inside, which was a shame because the sky was perfectly cloudless. Coronado Prep was perched on the outskirts of town, far enough away from the city lights that anyone who looked up could have traced the dusting of the Milky Way across the inky expanse of space. Not that any of us were stargazing. It was Homecoming; there was more than enough glitter for us inside.

The gym had been transformed from the open and airy space we knew. Rich velvet curtains cascaded down the bleachers and lights ringed the dance floor, giving the whole place a funky elegance. Someone flipped on a black light and a flood of bubbles swirled into the air, glowing weirdly over the crowd. Dancers screamed in exhilaration. Strobe lights kicked on, turning everyone into silhouettes, making us anonymous in an instant. No more jocks, no more prima donnas, no more losers. In that moment, we were one. The feeling was intoxicating.

I spend a lot of time in high school trying to blend into the background. It isn't usually hard. People look past me like my skin is some kind of social camouflage. Except for my two best friends, Royal and Cassie. They see me. Most of the time, that's all I need.

But tonight, lost in the crowd, I felt like I was part of something bigger. The thrumming music seemed to drive away the differences between us, and all that was left was this primal, pulsing crowd. Yes, I knew everything would go back to normal soon. That doesn't mean I wanted it to end.

We were dancing when the power cut out, plunging our insulated world into darkness. I couldn't make out anything in the gloom, except for the pools of light cast by the emergency exit signs. The sudden absence of sound left a ringing in my ears.

Headmaster Fiedler's voice cut through the silence. "Just a second, folks. We've got someone checking the breakers."

There were a few groans, and then someone moaned out a goofy *ooooooooo!* A nervous titter passed through the crowd. Someone else made a loud raspberry, earning a few more snickers.

"Lovely." Royal's tone was dry. "I was just thinking what I really wanted tonight was to be trapped in a dark room with the cast of 'Lowest Common Denominator: The Teenage Years.'"

Cassie and I weren't the only ones who laughed at this, but that sense of belonging I'd had was already starting to evaporate. The power came back on, and the dance floor was once again bathed in swirling colored lights. People stood, breathing hard, aware of the sheen of sweat beading across their faces. A few of us glanced around self-consciously—it felt weird to just be standing on the dance floor. I curled my hands around my bare arms reflexively. I felt conspicuous standing in this strapless dress. Just like I'd known I would. The random growth spurt I'd hit a few years ago had left me tall and lanky and paranoid about my bony shoulders. Definitely not something I was keen to show off, no matter how pretty the satiny, pearl-gray material of this dress was. Royal and Cassie had worked hard to talk me into buying it. For the hundredth time that night, I wished I'd had the extra 40 bucks to buy the matching shrug.

"All right!" The D.J. called over his microphone, voice a little too bright. "Let's kick it up a notch!" Another song poured out of the speakers; his attempt to electrify the crowd. Dancing erupted around us, but I wasn't in the mood anymore. The onslaught of noise felt suddenly overwhelming.

"I think I'm going to sit this one out."

Cassie breathed out a sigh of relief. "Seconded."

Royal shook his head, resigned. "You can lead the ladies to the dance, but you cannot make them rock."

"Says the one of us who hasn't been wearing high heels for the last four hours," I said.

Royal shrugged. "Blame the shoes if you must. And for the record, I don't care what you think. You look dazzling." When I opened my mouth to argue, Royal laid a finger across my lips. "Don't speak." I couldn't help it; I smiled.

Cassie noticed a kid walking by with a cupcake in hand. "I'm so hungry I could pass out."

We pushed out of the crowd and found the refreshment table. Cassie zeroed in on a chocolate cupcake, grinning like a mischievous pixie—her smile was infectious. Her long black hair, done up in spiky knots for the dance, framed her face like a punk-rock crown and her dark eyes sparkled. Cassie's parents had moved here from China right before she was born. She had inherited her mom's willowy figure and her dad's artistic talent, but the genuine sweetness that made her seem almost naïve—that was 100 percent Cassie. Under the shifting lights, the material of her dress shimmered between green and purple. She called her style "fashion forward," and she'd designed and sewn the dress herself. If I'd tried something like that, I would have been walking around in a glorified toga. Cassie was a magician with her needle and thread. Not that she got to flaunt her skills very often. We wore gray and burgundy uniforms every day at school.

Next to her dress, Royal's deep crimson jacket seemed almost subdued. He looked like he owned the place, but he would look that way in jeans and a t-shirt. Royal had grown up with a kind of bulletproof self-confidence which I envied daily. He was shorter than me by an inch or two, and rail-thin with a jaw that could have been sculpted by one of the old masters. He regarded the world through dark brown eyes that could be warm or inscrutable, depending on his mood, but they always gleamed with sharp intelligence. His brown hair somehow managed to look perfectly tousled at any time of day. Objectively, Cassie and I could see that Royal was good-looking. But we never saw him *that* way, even before we knew he was gay. He was Royal. He'd always been one of us.

Royal caught Cassie's hand and twirled her around, making her laugh. They looked so vibrant. Next to them I felt bland. I was quite possibly the only student at Coronado Prep who actually preferred uniforms to street clothes. Considering that, it made sense that one of the few times a year we got to wear practically anything we wanted to school, I'd ended up in a gray dress. I hugged myself again, longing for that shrug.

Royal noticed the movement while picking up a chocolate frosted cupcake. "Cold?"

"No." Quickly turning my attention to the table, I selected a promising cupcake with white frosting. I had to set down the delicate silver clutch Cassie had made me to peel back the cupcake's foil wrapper. My hopes were rewarded. Red velvet. I eyed the side door. It was propped open, inviting. "Actually, I could use some fresh air."

As we walked across the gym, Royal turned to me. "We still have to finish The Birthday Conversation. Don't think you're getting off that easy."

"What's wrong with samurai movies, pizza, and Red Vines?"

Royal glanced at Cassie. "Do you want to field this one, or shall I?"

"Braedyn. It's your 16th birthday," Cassie said, looking exasperated.

I felt an inward sigh but smiled. "It's not for another month, guys." Before Royal and Cassie had brought it up, I'd planned to spend my birthday like I'd spent the last three or four: hanging out with them at my house. But they'd gotten it into their heads that I needed something bigger this year.

Cassie reached for Royal, eager for backup. "Which gives us plenty of time to plan something spectacular. What about the Raven? If there's ever a time for a big party, this is it."

"You do realize that my dad is never going to let us go to a club?"

"People can surprise you," Cassie said.

We walked through the door and into the late September night. I stopped in my tracks. Three couples were hanging out on the wide side steps of the gym, sneaking sips from metal flasks, looking bored. The glitterati of Coronado Prep. One girl had her arms twined around a guy, kissing him against the side of the building. My stomach twisted unpleasantly. Amber Jenkins. The iron-straight curtains of her perfect sun-bleached blond hair gleamed like ice in the moonlight.

Amber had turned middle school into a custom-made nightmare for me. As an awkward, gangly kid with frizzy hair and braces, I'd been an easy target for Amber and her genetically blessed posse to hone in on. Isn't there some team-building exercise where you unite a group by focusing their energy on a common goal? Tormenting me became their pet project. Middle school was the reason I'd cultivated the ability to blend into the background. Since then my braces had come off, I'd figured out a few tricks to tame the chaos of my hair, and everyone else was catching up height-wise. But while Amber hadn't acknowledged me since we started high school, the memories were still fresh enough that I didn't want to draw her attention. I turned, flustered, and stumbled into Royal.

Someone snickered, and Amber's cold eyes flicked over to us. "Enjoying the show?" I'd always thought her thin, straight nose gave her face a pinched look when she frowned, but the rest of the student body seemed to worship her. Eager to flee this scene, I turned to re-enter the gym. Cassie caught my eye, just as ready to get away from them as I was.

But before we could retreat into the gym, another student appeared in the door behind us, blocking our escape. He nodded a greeting to Amber. "Hey, Amber. Fiedler asked me to tell you they're starting in five minutes."

"Right," Amber said.

The boy she'd been kissing glanced at his watch. Derek Hall was the celebrated captain of the Coronado Prep soccer team. He had dark gray eyes and short, pale blond hair that looked even paler against his soccer tan. "How much longer are we stuck here?" He leaned his forehead against Amber's, smiling into her eyes. "I want to get to the after-party."

Amber traced a finger down his chest and pushed him away coyly. "After the ceremony." She glanced over her shoulder, at the other two girls in her group. "Time to turn it on, ladies." Missy and Ally fell into step with Amber as usual, following her back to the gym door. Missy, a cute and curvy strawberry-blond, followed Amber through the door and flashed me a quick smile. I think Missy and I could have been friends in a different life. Ally, not so much. She fished a mirror out of her clutch and ran manicured nails carefully through her hair, shouldering me roughly aside as she passed.

Royal steadied me with a hand. "Do not let those jockubines into your head," he said.

"Dude. That's my girlfriend you're insulting." I saw a flicker of interest penetrate Derek's boredom.

Royal shrugged. "Shouldn't you boys be polishing your tiaras for the big entrance?"

The other two guys pushed away from the wall and moved to flank Derek. The dark-haired, olive-skinned boy was named Rick. He was in a few of my classes, but we'd never spoken to each other that I

5

could remember.

The other was Parker Webb, co-captain of the soccer team. Cassie was standing so close to me I could feel her breath catch. Even in the moonlight, I could spot the rosy blush spreading across her cheeks. She'd been nursing a crush on Parker since we were all in middle school together. Okay, with his pale blue eyes and jet-black hair, he wasn't exactly hard on the eyes. But there was a coldness in Parker that had always set my teeth on edge.

Derek took a step toward us. "This is a private party. Are you going to go back inside, or do I have to move you?"

Royal's stare was icy. "If you want to dance, Derek, you just have to ask."

A dangerous smile bloomed on Derek's face. "You want to repeat that?"

"We just wanted to take a walk," Cassie said.

"So pay the toll." Derek plucked the cupcake out of her hands. Cassie stood, eyes downcast, while Derek wolfed her cupcake down in three big bites. "Saved some for you." Derek wiped a finger full of frosting across Cassie's lips. She recoiled while the boys laughed. "Oops. You've got a little something on your face there."

Without pausing for thought, I shoved my cupcake at Derek. He caught my wrist and hoisted it up over my head, crushing the cupcake in one smooth motion. Bits of cake and frosting cascaded down, leaving creamy splotches across the light gray satin of my dress. I wrenched my hand out of his grip, gasping.

Royal planted a hand on Derek's chest and shoved him back. "Keep your hands off her."

"It's okay, Royal," I mumbled. My heart beat wildly. All I wanted was to turn and run.

There was an unmistakable glint in Derek's eyes. He was brewing for a fight. "You know," he said, taking a step closer to Royal, "since you mentioned it, I do feel like dancing." Parker's eyes flicked from Derek to Royal as he took another sip from his flask. Rick just shook his head, grinning.

"Let's go," I said, catching Royal's hand. Reading my growing panic, Cassie helped draw Royal back toward the building.

"Whatever." Derek turned back to his friends. Parker pointed at a drop of frosting on Derek's tux. Derek frowned, glancing at me once more before we pulled the gym door closed behind us.

Safe inside the dance, it took a minute before I could settle my nerves. I was only vaguely aware of Royal and Cassie venting about Derek and the soccer jocks. Their tirade washed over me as I focused on calming down.

With a fresh jolt of adrenaline, I realized I'd left my clutch on the refreshment table. Cassie had given it to me on my birthday last year. It was pearl-gray and covered in tiny glass beads that she'd sewn on by hand. The lipstick and the 20 bucks inside were nothing compared to its sentimental value.

"I'll be right back," I told Royal and Cassie.

Halfway to the refreshment table I saw Derek. He was standing at the table, scrubbing his tux with a napkin. My clutch glittered on the edge of the table behind a row of glasses. I edged closer to the wall, preferring to lurk in the shadows until he left rather than risk another confrontation. Derek reached for a glass of clear soda, turning toward me. I held still, willing myself to blend into the darkness. Something caught Derek's eye. He straightened, staring across the gym with an odd expression on his face. I followed his gaze. That was the first time I saw her.

She moved through the crowd with a sensual, hypnotic confidence. Definitely not a high school student. Long, honey-blond hair hung in loose curls halfway down her back. Her dress flowed around her like mercury, swirling daringly around her thighs with every step. In her wake, dancers stopped and stared. Guys craned their necks to watch her pass, as though she was the only light in a world of darkness. One boy held a drink half-tipped toward his mouth, unaware of the soda dribbling down the front of his shirt. His date jerked the cup out of his hands, startling him out of his trance. Only then did he notice his shirt was sopping wet. It looked like he was waking up from a dream.

Headmaster Fiedler moved to intercept her with a distinctly "students only" look in his eyes. She saw him coming and shook her head slightly, a little knowing smile playing over her face. The headmaster's steps slowed, then stopped. The honey-blond turned away from him and glided to a stop in front of Derek. Derek's eyes bulged. She ran her fingers lightly over his tux.

"Looks like you've been up to no good," she said. "My favorite pastime." Her voice was rich, taunting. If I'd been any farther away, the music would have drowned her out. But separated from them by a few yards at best, I heard her clearly. Satiny red lips quirked up at the corners. Derek licked his lips, unable to gather his thoughts well enough to form any words. She tilted her head to look into his eyes. "I couldn't help noticing that little fight you had with your girlfriend."

"Fight?" Derek shook his head slightly. "Who—You mean Braedyn? She wishes." His laugh wavered, sounding a little strangled.

"Then this should make her crazy jealous." The honey-blond snaked her fingers up into Derek's hair and drew his face down toward hers. He melted into the kiss. His hands reached for her waist, but she caught them with a light laugh.

Derek breathed out, stunned.

The newcomer played at straightening his collar. "Can you spare a minute? I need your help with something. Something private." Her eyes slid over his shoulder, locking with mine. My heart gave a sickening lurch and I turned away, mortified. It was like she'd known I was staring, eavesdropping on their conversation. I started to walk back to Cassie and Royal, then stopped when I remembered my purse still on the table behind me.

When I turned back, both Derek and the newcomer were gone. I edged closer to the table, scanning the area, but couldn't spot even a glimmer of that silver dress. I scooped the clutch up, grabbed a fistful of napkins, and retreated back to Cassie and Royal.

"She returns," Royal said, eying my haul. "With enough napkins for an army."

"Thanks for trying to cream Derek for me," Cassie said. "Sorry about your dress. I'll make it up to you."

"You want to make it up to me?" I asked. "Grab a napkin. I prefer red velvet in my mouth, not in my hair." Royal and Cassie grabbed some napkins and started cleaning bits of frosting and cupcake out of my hair.

Royal turned his attention to a clump of frosting on my shoulder and grinned. "Standing up to the soccer jocks. Who knew you had it in you?"

"What are the odds he'll forget about it and leave me alone on Monday?"

"About the same as a bull not charging for the flapping red cape," Royal answered. "Olé, my little matador."

"This is not comforting," I said.

Cassie giggled.

The music faded. We turned back to the dance floor as people began clearing a space for Headmaster Fiedler. Time for the annual ritual of announcing the Homecoming Court.

"Amber is finally getting the crown to match her attitude." Royal's tone was sour. "Don't ever let them tell you it doesn't pay to be evil."

On stage, Fiedler held his hands up for silence. "Coronado Prep, it gives me great pleasure to announce your Homecoming Court! Ally Krect and Parker Webb!"

A spotlight flooded the double-entrance to the gym as Ally and Parker emerged. Ally beamed in the spotlight. She was oblivious to Parker who was squinting in irritation at the glare. They arrived at the stage and Fiedler placed a tiara on Ally's head. She adjusted it quickly, then her hand shot up in victory. The gym roared with approval.

Fiedler gestured back to the gym entrance. "Missy Jefferson and Dan Buchannan!" More wild cheers as Missy and her date emerged. Missy looked pleased and a little embarrassed by the screaming. She hustled Dan through the crowd and accepted the tiara from Fiedler with a quick smile and wave. Fiedler gestured and the music changed. Everyone turned as a spotlight snapped onto the far gym doors, sparkling with the half-ton of glitter the Dance Committee had covered them in. "And now for your Homecoming Queen and King!"

Royal sighed with distaste. "I hope he trips and breaks his neck."

"It's a little early, but I do have a birthday wish coming," I said.

Royal pretended to consider this idea for a moment before dismissing it. "Mm... Save it for something important."

The screaming built as Fiedler threw his arm toward the waiting doors. "Amber Jenkins and Derek Hall!"

The glittering doors opened. Amber emerged into the spotlight. Alone.

"Huh. He missed his big entrance." Cassie wasn't the only one craning her head for a better look at Amber. Amber forced a smile and headed toward the stage. You could practically feel the fury radiating off of her as she passed.

Royal shrugged. "Maybe we'll get lucky and Amber will skin Derek alive."

I found myself glancing back at the refreshment table. Something tugged at my conscience, but I brushed it off. I told myself Derek was Derek, and he'd clearly made his choice. Why should I care if it landed him in hot water?

Looking back, I think some part of me sensed things were about to go terribly, terribly wrong.

2

M onday morning dawned soft and cold, as if the day was as reluctant to wake up as I was. I closed my eyes, burrowing farther under the comforting weight of my blankets. Someone knocked on my bedroom door.

"Rise and shine, pumpkin. I'm making breakfast." Dad could be aggressively chipper in the morning. I pulled a pillow over my head. There was another knock on the door. Chipper and relentless. "You awake in there?"

"Yes," I said, tossing the pillow aside. "I'm awake."

"Excellent. See you in 10."

I yawned and rolled out of bed. My feet found their way into slippers and I headed for my closet. It was a small walk-in, but all of my clothes fit pretty comfortably on one side. I didn't have Royal's interest in buying clothes, or Cassie's talent for making them. I pulled a burgundy skirt and a white button-up shirt off their hangers.

As I got dressed, my eyes strayed to the other half of the closet. It was a history, in objects, of my life to date. Old shin guards from my one season trying soccer. A few pink and white tutus Dad bought for the handful of recitals I danced in. A stack of sheet music I'd learned over seven years of piano lessons. And here it was, sophomore year of high school, and I still hadn't demonstrated a natural talent for anything. Of course, getting good at anything takes practice and hard work. I knew that. I had just never found anything I was so excited about that it seemed worth the effort it would take to master it.

I grabbed my gray Coronado Prep sweater from a hook and turned off the closet light.

As I ran a brush through my hair, my reflection stared back at me from the little mirror hanging over my dresser. If I had to pick one word to describe myself, I would probably say "average." Tall and skinny, mousy brown hair, pale skin. I had the kind of nice-but-not-exceptional face that never earned any double takes, unless you saw my eyes. The irises were shot through with colors that ranged from sky to a blue so deep it looked almost purple. My dad had brown eyes and brown hair, so whoever my mother was, these startling eyes must have come from her.

When I was little, maybe three or four, I had this sudden epiphany that other kids had a dad *and* a mom. So I asked Dad where my mom was. He got quiet for a long moment, and then he was explaining how sometimes people have to leave us—even if they don't want to—and sometimes they can't come back. When I said I didn't understand, Dad said I would in time. And that's all he would say about her. If he had any pictures of her, he wasn't sharing them. He never said it, but I got the impression that she died giving birth to me. Whenever I brought her up, I could see the pain in his eyes. Over the years, I must have asked thousands of questions about her, but Dad always deflected them. I never stopped wondering who she had been, or if she'd known me long enough to love me.

The acrid scent of burning batter pulled me downstairs. Morning light flooded into the kitchen. Of all the rooms in our house, I loved this one the best. It was open and inviting. From the kitchen you could see through the dining room to the gorgeous picture window taking up most of the far wall. The cabinets were a rich oak wood and the Spanish tile floor was a warm terracotta. There was something comforting about the combination.

Dad stood in the dining room, lost in his own world, absently setting the table. He was an interesting mix of rough and refined. He owned a company that handled security systems for homes and businesses. Although he was a businessman, to me he never seemed entirely at ease in a suit. His short brown hair was speckled through with gray, but he moved with the muscular ease of a guy who looked like he'd be more comfortable in a fight than an office. At 42, he kept himself fit, although he was starting to get a little bit of a belly.

Dad's given name was Alan, but he preferred it when people called him Murphy. I think that might have been a hold over from his soldier days, but he didn't talk about them much. Whenever I asked about that part of his life he changed the subject. Whatever he'd seen or done, it must have been bad enough that he wanted to protect me from it. He wanted to protect me from all the grim things in this world.

I looked around for the source of the burning smell. A perfect stack of golden pancakes sat on a plate, ready for the table. Next to them, another pair of pancakes smoked on the griddle, forgotten. I grabbed a spatula and quickly flipped the burning pancakes onto an empty plate. "Hey, Iron Chef. I think your pancakes are done."

Dad looked up, startled. "Oh, no." He joined me at the griddle, frowning at the ruined pancakes. Pancakes were one of his specialties. "That's what I get for daydreaming."

"At least there were only two casualties," I offered. "The rest look amazing."

Dad kissed the top of my head and handed me the plate of golden pancakes. "We should eat before they get too cold. Grab the orange juice, would you?"

I pulled a carton of orange juice out of the fridge and poured two glasses. "So what's the special occasion?"

"Who said there was a special occasion?" he asked. "Why can't a dad just decide to cook a questionably nutritious breakfast for the apple of his eye?"

I followed Dad into the dining room and sat at the table. He set a plate in front of me. A few pats of butter melted into creamy puddles on top of the golden pancakes. Exactly the way I like them, just butter, no syrup. They smelled fantastic. My stomach rumbled eagerly. I took a bite. They were delicious—light and fluffy with a hint of cinnamon. "Mmmmm."

Dad's eyes twinkled at my reaction. "Bon appetite."

I took another bite and savored it. Dad watched me. His own plate of pancakes sat before him, untouched. I glanced at the kitchen clock. "Aren't you going to be epically late to work?"

"They can manage without me for one morning," he said. "How is it possible that you're almost 16 years old?"

He said this so wistfully that I laughed. "Dad, I'm still the same me."

"Well, the government disagrees with you. Apparently they only make these appointments..." He slid a piece of paper onto the middle of the table. "...for mature young people ready to take on the responsibilities of legal drivers." I saw the New Mexico MVD logo.

My official driver's license application.

"The same me, but also mature, law-abiding, and totally responsible!" I said, snatching up the application. After all the driver's ed classes and supervised practice in Dad's truck, I was finally going to get my actual license. "When do we get the car back?"

"In a week or two," he said. He was letting me drive his old Firebird. It had been sitting in the storage garage in our back yard for years, so he'd sent it out for a tune-up. It was kind of a rust-bucket, with cracked seats and a layer of grime it would take hours to scrub off the dashboard. But it was still a car, and in a few weeks it would be *my* car.

"I've got the perfect stickers for the back window already picked out."

Dad smiled. "Mature responsibility is a good look for you."

I glanced up, sensing my opportunity. "Speaking of growing up, maybe this year, since it's my 16th and everything, Cassie and Royal and I could celebrate my birthday at the Raven?"

Dad actually choked on a bite of pancake and had to wash it down with a swig of coffee. "The club?"

"They have an underage section and it's totally cool. It's not like we can get into any trouble. Please, Dad?"

"Hang on. First of all, you're turning 16, not 21. I don't think a club—"

"Wait, just—would you think about it before you say no?"

Dad frowned, but after a moment—and very reluctantly—he nodded.

"Thank you!"

Dad arched an eyebrow. "I'll *think* about it."

I took another bite of pancake, envisioning the look on Royal and Cassie's faces if Dad actually said yes.

"Oh, honey, could you come straight home after school today?" My mouth was too full to ask, but he saw the question in my eyes and answered me. "Just a couple of things we need to talk about. And if someone delivers a package, don't open it. I special-ordered something for your birthday and it should be arriving soon."

I swallowed. "Mmm. This special-order thing intrigues me. What's the talk about? Notice how I caught that little distract-her-with-the-present thing you did?"

Dad drained the last of his coffee and ruffled my hair, something he hadn't done for a couple of years. "As usual, your gift of perception awes and amazes me. Look, nothing to worry about. It's just that you're growing up now, and there are some things we need to—"

I clamped my hands over my ears. "Agh! LA LA LA LA LA! If this is the sex talk, you should know that they covered all the pertinent stuff in health class, so, you know, no potentially mutually emotionally scarring father-daughter talk necessary."

"Right." Dad leaned back in his chair, amused. At that moment, we saw Royal's car pull into our driveway out the bay window. Dad stood, finishing his coffee. "After school, okay? Don't keep your friends waiting."

I ate the last bite of pancake off my plate, then stood and gave him a quick peck on the cheek. "Thanks for breakfast. I'll clean up when I get home." I hurried out the front door, scooping up my school bag on the way out.

Fall mornings in the high desert can be bracing. I took a breath and shivered. It must have rained last night; an unusual humidity gave the air an extra bite. I drew my sweater tighter around me as I walked out of the house. Pretty soon I'd need to start wearing my winter coat again. Our house had a wide front porch (Dad called it our portico) framed by hand-carved wooden pillars. It had been built in the 1930s in the old New Mexico Territorial style. Our front door and window grids were all painted a pale turquoise, which stood out dramatically against the sand-colored stucco of the house's exterior. The windows were still framed with the original Victorian details and painted a dark chocolate brown. There was something that felt handcrafted about our home. Lived-in. Safe.

Royal's convertible idled in the driveway. Cassie was already sitting in the back seat, waiting for me.

Royal gestured over my shoulder. "Looks like you've got new neighbors."

I followed Royal's gaze to the house next door. We lived in a pretty little neighborhood. Like ours, most of the houses on our street had been built in the 1930s. I didn't know a lot about the Great Depression other than what they cover about the dust bowl in school, but I knew that Puerto Escondido had become a center for artists under the New Deal. Because some of those artists built up our neighborhood, a lot of homes on our street were registered as historical landmarks. Most of them were meticulously maintained.

The glaring exception was the house just to the left of ours. It would be charitable to call it an "eyesore." It had stood, empty and neglected, for as long as I could remember. But Royal was right. A moving van was parked on its cracked front drive. I turned back to Royal.

"Wow. Someone actually bought that crap hole?"

Royal's eyes widened a fraction. "Uh..."

I was too mystified to read the warning in his face. "I thought the city condemned that place. I heard the roof collapsed. How cracked do you have to be to move into a roofless deathtrap?"

Someone spoke behind me. His voice was quiet but warm. "I can think of worse things than falling asleep under the stars."

I clamped my mouth shut, mortified. Royal smiled helplessly; the damage was already done. I cleared my throat, doing my best to salvage the moment. "Stars. Sure. Now that you mention it, I can see how that would be..." I turned to face my new neighbor. When I saw him, I almost lost my train of thought. "Kind of... romantic."

He stepped out from behind an overgrown hedge at the edge of the property. He couldn't have been much older than me, but there was something about him that made him seem infinitely more experienced—a gravity in his eyes, like he'd been living with a deep pain. He had an athlete's build and dark hair that fell across his face, long enough to cover his eyes. He brushed a lock back and I found myself staring. His eyes seemed to shift colors between light green and tan in the dappled morning light. They crinkled warmly as he smiled. I felt a heat rising in my face and knew I must be blushing.

Behind him, a compact man emerged from the house and picked a box up off the creaking porch. When he spotted us, his steps slowed.

"Lucas," he called. "Give me a hand."

The boy acknowledged this with a half-hearted wave, shrugging for our benefit. "Have fun at school." His eyes lingered on mine for a moment, then he turned and walked back into his new home.

I stood in awkward silence for a moment.

Cassie spoke first. "Huh. I never really understood 'drop-dead gorgeous' before."

Royal laughed, and the spell was broken.

I opened the passenger side door and slid into Royal's car quickly. "If you love me, get me out of here." Royal grinned, hitting the gas and pulling away from the curb.

Cassie leaned over my shoulder and whispered, "And right next door to you, Braedyn. Talk about an early birthday present from the universe."

The first half of the school day passed uneventfully. Royal caught up to me after math and we made our way to the dining hall for lunch.

"Did you ask your dad about the Raven?"

"It could go either way," I said. "He almost choked to death when I brought it up, but he did promise to think about it."

"So there's hope." Royal's eyes lit up. I could almost see the plans forming in his head. Someone shouldered past me, knocking me into Royal. Royal turned after them, incredulous. "Um, excuse you?"

It was Amber and Ally. They looked back at us, eyes wide with feigned innocence. Ally snapped her compact mirror shut. "Oh, sorry, I totally didn't even see you." I rubbed my shoulder, seething. Ally was the best athlete on the cheerleading squad—an actual gymnast. She was the principal reason they'd won regionals last year. But she took all her cues from Amber.

"What's your problem?" I asked, struggling to rein in my anger.

"Seems like you're the one with the problem," Amber said. "Maybe you should get an orange vest or something." Her eyes shifted to something behind me and she smiled. I turned.

Greg Pantelis was walking through the crowd. He had dark olive skin, dark curly hair, and a dazzlingly white smile. Rumor had it he'd been born on a small Greek isle that had been in his family for generations. He was the star of the swim team, and take my word for it—that had nothing to do with athletic prowess. Girls would line the bleachers at swim meets to catch a glimpse of Greg with his shirt off. He was a daily topic of conversation in the girls' locker room.

Amber slicked a hand through her perfectly straight hair and pulled Ally down the hall after him. "Hey, Greg. Wait up." Greg turned and gave Amber a friendly smile. She and Ally flanked him as they disappeared into the crowd.

"There's never a vomitory around when you need one," Royal said sourly.

I smiled, trying to shake off my anger. "I don't think that word means what you think it means."

"I don't care," he said. "It *sounds like* what I think it means."

I was still laughing as we made our way into the dining hall. Cassie was already seated at our customary table by the back wall. She looked up from a math book as we joined her.

"Quiz?" Royal asked.

"I'm tutoring after school," Cassie answered. "Just wanted to brush up on differentials."

Royal put on a mock-disapproving voice. "No advanced math at the table, young lady."

Cassie closed her book with an exaggerated sigh, playing along. "You never let me do anything fun."

Lunch at Coronado was served family style. Generous portions of lasagna and broccoli sat steaming on the table. We started serving ourselves.

Royal nudged me. "Look, it's the return of the little lost king." Cassie and I turned to look where Royal pointed. Derek, Parker, and three other guys from the soccer team entered the cafeteria, pausing to hang their jackets on a row of coat hooks nearby. Derek looked exhausted and distracted.

Parker frowned at him. "Dude, snap out of it. We have a game tonight."

Derek shook his head, as if to clear his vision, and unzipped his jacket. "I'm sorry, man. She was one frisky little pussycat. I got zero sleep on Saturday night."

Parker looked disgusted. "Hope it was worth it. Amber's gonna gut you when she finds out you ditched her to hook up with some random hottie."

Derek glanced over his shoulder, paranoid. "Dude. Keep it on the DL. We're getting together again tonight." Derek hung his jacket on a free hook. His friends traded amused glances as they turned to head for their usual table in the center of the dining hall.

Cassie and I traded a look. Cassie imitated Derek's irritating swagger. "I'm like cat-nip for babes," she murmured. I clapped a hand over my mouth to muffle my laugh.

"Hold up." Parker put a hand out, stopping Derek. I glanced up and saw Parker staring directly at me. I turned back to my plate as a tight knot formed in my stomach. Behind me I could hear Parker asking, "How much was that bill?"

Out of the corner of my eye, I saw Derek turn in my direction. Cassie spotted him, too. We were so focused on Derek that we didn't notice as another person stopped at our table.

"Mind if I join you?"

I looked up. My new neighbor was standing beside me with his hand on the back of an empty chair. He wore a Coronado Prep uniform, and somehow made it seem almost casual. He smiled into my eyes, waiting. I realized I was staring and grasped for something to say. "Yes." Cassie kicked me under the table and I heard my mistake. "No. No, we don't mind."

Cassie and Royal traded a quick look and Cassie gestured to the table in welcome. "The more, the merrier."

He sat down with a self-deprecating smile. "Thanks. I hate first days." His smile took in all of us. "I'm Lucas."

Royal pushed the lasagna tray over to Lucas. "Welcome to the Gulag. I'm Royal. This is Cassie. I'm sure you remember Braedyn."

"I do. Nice to make it official." In the light of the dining hall, his eyes looked greener than they had this morning—a light, rich green flecked through with gold. I felt a shivery thrill passing over my skin.

Derek planted his hand on the table between us, snapping me out of the moment. He smiled at me coolly. "You owe me for dry cleaning," he said. His friends stood behind him, ready for the show.

Royal frowned. "I thought you soccer guys spent lunch practicing your ball handling."

Derek glanced over at Royal. "Keep your personal fantasies to yourself. This is between me and cupcake here." Derek turned back to me. I looked helplessly around the table. Cassie, never good with conflict, stared at her plate. Royal's jaw was tense. And Lucas... Lucas's eyes had gone flat, hard. "50 bucks ought to cover it. You have expensive taste in icing."

I stood, looking for any way out. "Anyone else feel like eating on the quad?"

Cassie followed my lead, pushing her chair out. Too late, she realized she had just blocked my escape around the back of the table. I tried to slip past Derek.

He trapped me with his arm. "Um, where do you think you're going? We have business to settle."

I felt my face grow hot again. "Move your hand, Derek." Derek slid his free hand around my waist and pulled me snug against him. I heard someone chuckle behind us. I jerked away from Derek, humiliated.

Derek smirked. "Be more specific next time."

"You want specific?" Lucas hauled back and punched Derek in the face. Derek staggered backwards. Parker and the others stared, too shocked to move for a moment. Lucas glanced at me, calm. "You okay?"

I nodded woodenly.

Two of Derek's friends tackled Lucas. Cassie screamed. That got everyone's attention. It only took a second for the dining hall to process what was happening. Somebody bellowed "Fight!" and students rushed to surround us in a mob. I was dimly aware of a teacher sprinting for the phone. Within moments, everyone in the dining hall was clustered around us.

The guys who tackled Lucas pulled him upright, yanking him off the floor by his arms.

Cassie stared in horror. "We have to do something!"

The boys turned Lucas to face Derek, each pinning one of his arms tightly behind his back. Derek cracked his knuckles, putting on a show for the crowd. The skin over his jaw was turning red where Lucas had hit him. His eyes narrowed in anticipation, hungry for revenge. Lucas watched him, focused. Derek gripped the front of Lucas's shirt and raised his fist to strike. My heart leapt into my throat, but Lucas twisted at the last second and Derek's punch landed across his teammate's face.

The crowd screamed encouragement. Lucas scrambled back, his eyes locked on Derek. Derek turned on him, surprise giving way to fury. Lucas shrugged slightly, smiling as if to say, *we can stop this anytime you like*. Derek's scowl deepened.

Parker joined Derek, clapping a hand on his shoulder to let him know he had backup. Lucas pushed his shirtsleeves up, ready for more.

I heard Cassie's sharp intake of breath. I glanced at her and saw her concern deepen. Her attention seemed split between Lucas and Parker. I didn't share Cassie's divided loyalties. I just wanted someone to intervene before Derek and his friends took Lucas apart.

Parker dove first. Lucas surged forward. His movements were fluid, almost formal. His fist connected and Parker staggered back with a growl of pain, clutching his nose.

Cassie covered her mouth, cringing and shutting her eyes, tight. I couldn't look away from the fight.

Derek turned to his teammates. "Come on!" Parker and the other boys ringed Lucas. Lucas glanced around at them, calculating. Only the slightest tension seemed to enter his eyes. But Derek—he was a different matter all together. His customary swagger had vanished. His mouth was twisted in determination. Everything about him seemed taut, ready to spring. Panic raged in the back of my mind. This wasn't just a fight anymore. Derek wouldn't stop until Lucas was seriously hurt. I scanned the dining hall for a teacher, but saw only the mass of students grouped around the fight.

I saw Derek glance at Parker, who edged back behind Lucas.

"Careful—!" I warned, but I was too slow. Derek feinted, and Lucas took the bait. When Derek pulled back, Lucas ended up swiping thin air where he thought Derek would be. The move cost him; Lucas stumbled, losing his balance.

Parker, seeing his opening, drove a fist into Lucas's side. Lucas recoiled, eyes watering, but he kept his hands up. Derek threw a savage punch at Lucas's face. Lucas twisted out of the way, caught the punch, and jerked Derek off-balance. As Derek careened wildly forward, Lucas twisted Derek's arm and shoved him face-first into the crowd. The two other boys charged Lucas from behind.

"Behind you!" I shouted.

Lucas turned and dropped, kicking out a foot to trip one of the boys while he shot a fist up into the other boy's stomach. His attackers both hit the ground, groaning. Lucas rolled to his feet, but Parker was ready for him. Parker's fist smashed into Lucas's mouth with a sickening crack. For a minute it looked like Lucas might fall, but he shook his head, found his footing, and turned to face Parker unsteadily. A trickle of blood traced a thin line from the corner of Lucas's mouth down to his chin.

Before either boy made a move, the whole dining hall heard

Fiedler's voice, harsh with anger. "Where? Where are they?!" The crowd parted. The headmaster approached, furious. He stopped in the center of the chaos.

Lucas lowered his fists and glanced at me. In that moment, he looked almost vulnerable, as if afraid of what I might be thinking.

Fiedler glared at the boys as the assembled crowd buzzed with excitement. "All right. Who started it?"

Everyone's gaze shifted to Lucas. Lucas straightened. His eyes lingered on my face for a long moment, and then he turned to face the headmaster.

3

The wind was starting to pick up as we left the dining hall. Headmaster Fiedler led Lucas and the other boys straight to his office. I followed, along with half the school. People would be dishing about this fight—and the new kid—for weeks. The buzzing crowd dropped away as we crossed the quad. By the time we reached the administration building, I was the only one who followed Fiedler and his charges inside.

Fiedler stopped outside his office and gestured to the benches resting against the walls. "Sit." Derek opened his mouth but Fiedler held up a hand, furious. "Not a word, Derek. I'm going to speak with Ms. Fitch, and then we'll start calling your parents."

Ms. Fitch must have been the teacher I'd seen run to the phone as the fight was beginning. She glared at Lucas, arms crossed. She'd clearly already decided who was to blame for the fight. Fiedler held the door open and Ms. Fitch disappeared into his office. Fiedler shot one more disapproving glare around the room, and then followed her inside. The door swung shut behind them with an ominous thud.

Derek and his friends collapsed on one bench, muttering angrily to one another.

I sat beside Lucas on the other bench. "Let me go in with you," I said quietly. "I can explain what happened."

"I think he probably already knows what happened." Lucas smiled dryly. Mid-day sunlight flooded the administration hallway, kicking up off the white floor. It made everything achingly bright.

"But he doesn't know why," I said.

"In my experience, they don't care why a fight got started. They're more concerned about finding out who started it."

I didn't know what else to say. "I'm sorry."

"I'm not." Lucas's eyes were clear of any resentment or blame. "That guy had it coming," he said. "I'd do exactly the same thing if it happened again."

Warmth bubbled up through my chest. The door opened and Fiedler appeared. "Don't tell him that," I whispered into Lucas's ear. He smiled.

Fiedler scanned the faces of the boys sitting outside his office. "Lucas Mitchell? Not a great way to get started at Coronado Prep. Come on in." I watched Lucas follow Fiedler into the office. "Ms. Murphy," Fiedler said, spotting me. "Shouldn't you be getting to class?" Lucas gave me one last smile, and then the door closed behind them. The bell rang, marking the start of the next period. I had to run to class.

I skidded into the gym after throwing on a pair of burgundy gym shorts and a gray t-shirt. I expected to get chewed out by Ms. Davies for being late, but she hadn't arrived yet. Cassie and Royal waved from the bleachers. I joined them. All the magic of Homecoming was gone; the gym was back to normal, just like the rest of us.

"What happened?" Cassie asked in a hushed voice. She'd tied her hair into two silky black corkscrews on top of her head, but she was sucking on one long tendril that had escaped.

"I wish I knew," I said. Cassie heard the frustration in my voice and squeezed my hand.

P.E. had never been my favorite subject, but it was the one class that I didn't have to share with soccer jocks or cheerleaders. Usually, this was something to celebrate, but today I was dying for any word about Lucas's fate, even if it came from the enemy.

Our gym teacher, Ms. Davies, entered carrying an old boom box. Some of the students groaned. She waved this off cheerfully. "Change of plans, kids. After Saturday night, it became evident how desperately you all need some formal dance tips. Pair up. We're going to start with a waltz."

Cassie might have been the only kid in the whole gym that brightened. "Ooo, dancing!"

Royal fished in his pockets and drew out a small piece of paper.

Royal's older brother was a doctor. Occasionally he took pity on Royal and wrote him a few fake doctor's notes to excuse him from class. Royal called them his "get out of jail free cards" and tried to save them for emergencies. "Cassie," Royal said. "Waltzing is not dancing. Dancing is about letting the music inspire you. It's about freeing all those things we carry inside that can't be expressed in words. It's about—"

Cassie grabbed the doctor's note right out of Royal's hands.

"Hey!" Royal tried to snatch it back but Cassie was too fast.

"Very inspiring." Cassie said, tearing the note up. Royal's eyes widened with horror.

"What was it this time?" I asked. "Sprained ankle? Dehydration?"

"Pre-migraine," Royal said. "But now—" he looked at Cassie, irritated. "I guess I'm dancing. Okay, girls. There are two of you and only one of me. Who's the lucky lady?"

The gym door opened and Lucas walked in, looking a little lost. I stood, my heart leaping into my throat. "I should—I should make sure he's okay."

Royal turned to Cassie. "Looks like Fate is smiling on you."

"Don't I know it," she said.

Royal gave me a little "shoo" gesture.

I met Lucas in the middle of the gym, more than a little surprised at the relief flooding through me. "Whatever you told Fiedler must have been good if you're still here," I said.

"They usually let you off with a warning your first week at a new school." Lucas looked so calm you'd never guess he'd been fighting five guys less than an hour ago. What would it take to shake this guy?

"Spoken with authority," I said.

"I have some experience with this."

Ms. Davies clapped her hands for everyone's attention. "All right. Guys. Arms up like this, one for her hand, one for her waist. Lead with your left foot. Watch me."

Lucas and I glanced at the class. Everyone else had already paired up for dancing. Which meant we were now partners. I looked back at Lucas, suddenly tongue-tied. He offered his hand, and I took it gingerly. He slipped his other hand around my waist. I could feel the warmth of his palm radiating through my shirt into the small of my back. It was hard to pull my concentration away from the sensation.

My heart was beating so hard I felt sure Lucas would feel the pulse through my fingertips.

After a moment, Lucas took my other hand and placed it on his shoulder. "I think that's the general idea," he said.

"Right." I was keenly aware of lean shoulder muscles under my hand. Part of me wished the floor would open up and swallow me. The other part hoped this class might last forever.

Ms. Davies hit a button on her boom box. The full orchestral strains of a waltz echoed through the gym. "If you can count to three you can dance the waltz," she said. "All right, gentlemen. You're leading this party. Let's go."

Lucas guided me forward with the lightest possible pressure. There was something so confident about the way he moved, I found myself relaxing into his arms. We glided over the slick gym floor as though we'd been fashioned one for the other, made for this dance.

"Watch your form, people! You've got to learn the rules before you can break them." Ms. Davies swept through the crowd. She passed us and nodded. "Excellent, you two." Ms. Davies moved onto the next couple, but I stumbled, suddenly self-conscious.

"Whoa," Lucas said. "You okay?"

"Yeah." I cleared my throat, casting about for something to say. "So. You have a lot of experience with first days?" I suddenly remembered the muscular man on Lucas's porch this morning. "Let me guess," I said. "Your dad's in the military, right? My dad was a soldier. A long time ago. They have that same look."

Lucas regarded me strangely for a moment. "Hale's my guardian, not my father. I haven't seen either of my real parents in years." He lowered his voice. "But I know you know how that is." There was an odd tone in his voice; he sounded almost conspiratorial. I didn't know what to say. Taking my silence for some kind of confirmation, Lucas carefully danced us a little farther away from the class. "You have no idea how long I've waited to meet someone else who gets it," he murmured. "Someone under the age of 25," he added sheepishly.

An uncomfortable tingling sensation shot down the back of my neck. Whatever Lucas was talking about, I wasn't in on the secret. I pulled slightly away from him to get a clearer look at his face. "I don't—I'm sorry, what does that mean?"

Lucas read the genuine bewilderment in my eyes and faltered.

Ms. Davies clapped loudly for the class' attention. "All right, everyone. Good. Gather around and we'll talk about some variations."

Students started to collect in a group around Ms. Davies. Lucas and I stood rooted to the floor, facing one another. Questions pulsed through my thoughts. Before I could find the words to ask, Ms. Davies interrupted us.

"Braedyn? And, I'm sorry, is it Lucas?" Ms. Davies gestured. "Come join us."

Lucas moved first. As he passed me, his expression became a little more guarded, his smile a little less personal. I followed him over to the group, but I couldn't catch his attention for the rest of the period. It was like he'd become completely absorbed in Ms. Davies' lecture.

Royal slid up next to me with an appraising look. "Details. After class."

My head was still spinning as Royal and Cassie walked with me to English. Cassie danced in front of us, grinning.

"So? What did you and Lucas talk about on the dance floor?" she asked.

"Just... stuff," I said.

Royal arched an eyebrow. "You two had your heads together for a solid five minutes. Please tell me you at least made plans to go out for coffee or something."

"Coffee?" I asked.

Royal turned to Cassie for backup. "Cassie? Help me. This is like remedial dating lesson one."

I looked at Royal and Cassie, suddenly getting what they were implying. "Dating? We just met this morning. I don't even know if he's interested in coffee."

Royal gave me a pointed look. "He's interested."

"How can you tell?"

"Braedyn, honey, he was eyeing you like a caffeine junkie eyes a hazelnut macchiato," Royal said.

Cassie looped her arm through mine. "Royal's right, Braedyn. He's into you."

When I hesitated, Royal rolled his eyes in exasperation. "He took on half the soccer team to defend your honor. Make it easy on the poor guy." Royal opened the door to the humanities hall for us. "Ball's in your court."

I walked into our English classroom turning this thought over in my mind. I replayed the day, remembering the amused twinkle in his eyes in front of his house this morning. The terrifying adrenaline-rush of the fight. The warmth of his hand on my back. And then the strangeness of our last conversation.

When we took our usual seats near the front of the room, I was no closer to sorting out the jumble of feelings in my mind. Royal opened his book and started scanning the chapter.

"Didn't do the reading again, huh?" Cassie asked.

Royal didn't look up from the pages. "Concentrating." Cassie shook her head, smiling.

Amber, Ally, and Missy entered and took the seats directly behind us. They were mid-conversation.

"I'm calling dibs," Amber said.

Ally scoffed, irritated. "What is this, elementary school? You can't call dibs on a boy."

"I think I just did."

"What about Derek?" Missy's voice was edged with concern.

"What about him? He left me standing alone in the spotlight at Homecoming. He can go screw himself."

"Are you seriously interested? Or are you just looking to make Derek jealous?" Ally asked.

"If Derek gets jealous that's his problem," Amber said. "Right now, all I'm looking for is some alone time with Lucas Mitchell."

"You're so bad." Ally laughed.

I felt frozen.

Mr. Young entered and started writing on the blackboard. "All right, welcome to the world of Jane Austen, people. I suspect you'll find it has much in common with Coronado Prep. So, 'Pride and Prejudice.' First thoughts? Amber?"

Amber straightened behind me. Mr. Young might have thought he'd caught her off guard, but Amber was a competitive student. She practically purred her answer, but I couldn't focus on what she was saying. I'd overheard enough high school boys describing which limb they'd be willing to trade for a date with Amber to know I was outmatched. If she'd set her sights on Lucas, I didn't stand a chance.

Amber didn't waste any time putting her plan into action. That day after school, I arrived at the edge of the parking lot where Cassie, Royal, and I usually met for the ride home. Royal was already there, twirling car keys around his finger absently.

"Cassie had to go back for another math book," he said.

I heard Amber's high laugh cutting through the afternoon. I turned. As soon as my eyes found Lucas, it felt like an icy balloon burst in my chest. Amber had her hands looped around his arm, hanging onto him, staking her claim. She said something to him and Lucas chuckled.

Cassie joined us, clutching a pile of books to her chest. She'd noticed Amber and Lucas, too. I saw her eyes dart quickly to my face, checking to see if I was okay.

But then Lucas spotted us. He extricated himself quickly from Amber's grasp and left her standing on the sidewalk as he headed toward us. Her mouth fell open with outraged surprise.

Lucas's eyes gleamed, more gold than green in the afternoon light. His smile thawed the ache in my chest, warming me from the inside.

"Hey guys," he said. "I was hoping I could get a ride home with you."

Royal grinned. "Done and done," he said. "Let's roll." Royal led the way to his car and we followed. I snuck a glance at Lucas. He seemed at ease again. I couldn't detect any trace of the confusion or tension I'd seen in him at the end of gym. We reached Royal's car and Cassie gave me an encouraging smile. She took the front passenger seat wordlessly.

"After you," Lucas said, offering a hand to help me into the back seat.

"Thanks," I said, taking it. His skin was warm and soft. It was hard to let his hand go as I settled into my seat.

Once we'd all buckled in, Royal pulled out of the parking lot. I stole another sidelong glance at Lucas. The wind was toying with his hair. He sensed me watching and I dropped my eyes quickly.

"Listen," he said, facing me. "I didn't mean to come on so strong in gym class."

"No apology necessary," I said. "I just hope we'll get to finish that conversation at some point." I'd meant it to sound teasing, but Lucas grew solemn.

"Yeah."

I could have kicked myself. We spent the rest of the ride home in uneasy silence. Royal caught my gaze in the rearview mirror, urging me to make a move with his eyes. I shook my head pointedly, warning him to back off. When we finally pulled up in front of my house, Cassie turned around to face me.

"I'm going to need you for a fitting session soon," she said. Cassie had made a tradition of sewing my birthday presents. Every year she topped herself. I couldn't wait to see what she'd come up with next.

"You just say the word and I'm there," I said.

Royal caught my hand as Lucas and I climbed out of the back seat. "Remember," he said. "Easy does it. You don't want him making a decision about the Raven tonight. Just plant a few seeds; it's a safe place, no alcohol allowed, etcetera, etcetera, etcetera. Call me if you need advice. These negotiations can be delicate."

"Got it."

Cassie crossed her fingers. "The club would be so cool. But even if we end up watching Kurosawa movies in your living room, it will still be an awesome party."

"We'll burn that bridge when we come to it," Royal said. "In the meantime, think positive." He shifted into reverse and pulled back onto the street. Cassie waved goodbye as they disappeared down the street. Suddenly, Lucas and I were alone together for the very first time. Neither of us spoke for a moment.

"So," Lucas started. "I guess I'll see you—"

Before he had a chance to say goodbye, I blurted, "Do you like coffee?"

"Coffee?" He looked a little startled at the question.

"I thought—maybe we could get some sometime."

"You like coffee?"

"Sure?" I lied. If it meant getting to know Lucas a little better, I could learn to like it.

The door to my house opened and Dad walked onto the portico. "Braedyn?" he called. "Hey. I thought I heard Royal's car."

"Yeah." I waved him off, stalling for a few moments of time.

"That's my dad," I said to Lucas. "He's got this talk planned, so I should probably go."

"Coffee would be nice," Lucas said. To my surprise, he walked with me up the flagstone path. "Mr. Murphy," he said, offering a hand to my dad. "It's an honor to finally meet you, sir."

I grinned at Lucas. "Finally? You moved in like 12 hours ago." I expected some kind of reaction from Dad, but he wasn't smiling.

"Why don't you head home, Lucas?" Dad said. "Braedyn and I have to talk."

I felt the skin on the back of my neck prickle. I hadn't introduced them. "You know him?" Dad and Lucas traded a strange look. I was suddenly aware that I was out of the loop. My stomach gave a sickening lurch and I turned back to Lucas. "You—what you said earlier—?" My eyes flicked to Dad's face.

Dad glanced at Lucas, suddenly intent. "What did he say?"

Lucas straightened. "I'm sorry, sir. I thought she—"

"I know what you thought. Go home." Dad turned to me, softening his tone. "Inside. I'll explain everything." He held the door open for me. I walked inside, scared. Behind me, I heard Dad address Lucas one more time. "Tell Hale I need a minute."

Lucas's voice wavered. "I don't really tell Hale things so much as—" but Dad closed the door on Lucas, ending the discussion.

I stood in the foyer, afraid to follow Dad into the living room. I had this strange sensation, like I was standing in quicksand. I'd lived here my whole life, but all of a sudden it felt different. My eyes landed on the staircase, and memories flooded into my head. I used to play hide and seek with my dad. My favorite hiding place was the closet under the stairs. The door was camouflaged by wainscoting—it looked just like part of the wall. When I was a kid I thought this was the coolest thing in the world. I probably ended up hiding there 80 percent of the time. Of course, Dad always knew where I was, but he acted like he couldn't find the door. It made me feel safe and clever.

"Come and sit down," Dad said. I entered the living room and lowered myself onto the couch. "I have to explain something that's going to be hard to wrap your head around, but I need you to hear me out." He took a deep breath, steeling himself. "Honey. I'm not your biological father."

I felt my breath catch. The room seemed to tilt and I gripped the arm of the chair. My life, everything I thought I knew, was sliding away. Deep down, I'd suspected this talk was serious, but I wasn't prepared for this. I looked at him and saw a stranger for the first time. Things started falling into place. He knew almost nothing about my mother. That's why we didn't have any pictures of her. Of course I didn't look anything like Alan Murphy; we didn't share any biological connections. This special talk he wanted to have, it was so obvious. I was growing up. It was time for me to know the truth about my real parents.

"If you're not my father," I said, my voice shaking, "Who are you?" My head started to throb dully.

"Your father and I were soldiers together," he said. "Friends." Dad pulled a photograph out of his wallet and handed it to me.

The photo depicted two men, sitting on a muddy jeep. I recognized my dad... Murphy. He must have been in his early twenties at the time. He had the same barrel chest as he did today, the same warm brown eyes and close-cropped hair. He wore a cocky smile as he lounged against the jeep with easy confidence. The other man stared straight out of the photo at me, composed and thoughtful. He was equally fit, but smaller, trimmer. His hair was a lighter brown, and his eyes were blue. I'd never seen this man before, but there was something familiar about him. The line of his nose. The arch of his eyebrows. I saw these features everyday—every time I looked into a mirror. "That's him," I said. "That's my father, isn't it?"

"Paul Kells," Dad said, nodding. "He was one of the best men I've ever known. Smart. Brave. And his sense of humor—" He smiled in memory, but the smile didn't last. "You have a lot of him in you. So many times I've wanted to tell you about him."

"Why didn't you?" I asked.

Dad started to say something, but stopped himself. Before he could gather his thoughts, his phone rang. He checked the caller ID, frowned, and turned the phone off.

"Why didn't you tell me about my real father?" I pressed.

"It's complicated," he said.

I looked back at the picture, studying the stranger who shared so many of my features. I swallowed a surge of emotion and looked up. "So I'm adopted," I said quietly. "That's why you wanted to have the big talk?"

"No," Dad said, his eyes crinkling anxiously. "I mean, yes, you're adopted. But no, that's—that's not what we need to talk about."

I stared at him, processing this. "You're telling me you're not my dad, but that's not the big news?" Dad shook his head no. I felt a strange tingling in my head, like the onset of a fever. When I spoke, the words came out in a whisper. "What do we need to talk about?"

"Paul, your father, he died just before you were born." But here Dad stopped and lifted a hand to rub his temples. He was struggling with something, something he didn't want to tell me.

"What happened to him?" I asked faintly.

"He was killed."

I felt my mouth go dry. "Killed... by who?" I asked.

"It's... He was killed by a Lilitu, Braedyn." Dad watched me closely, gauging my reaction. But I barely had one; that word meant nothing to me at all.

"What's a Lilitu?" I asked.

Dad ran a hand through his hair, changing tack. "What you need to understand— we're in a war that most people can't even see. The battles are hidden, the enemy wears a near-perfect disguise. They look human. That's what makes them so dangerous."

"What's a Lilitu," I asked again.

Dad took a deep breath and let it out. "A demon."

I thought I'd misheard him. "Sorry, what?" I asked. Dad just watched me, worried. "Did you say—?"

"Yes. Lilitu are demons."

"Demons. Just... walking around." My voice sounded strange in my ears. Too far away. Somewhere in the back of my mind I wondered if this was what it felt like to be in shock—like a big fuzzy blanket was wrapped around an alarm inside my head, and even though the alarm was blaring its heart out, I could barely hear it. I could barely think.

"No. Not just walking around. They're on a mission, Braedyn. If we don't stop them, they'll make the earth their home. Trust me, that's not going to work out so well for humankind."

I forced a sick smile. "You're joking, right?"

Dad shook his head wearily. "No. No, Honey." He reached for my hand, but I jerked it out of his reach. I was starting to get angry.

"So my father is some stranger I've never heard of before, and now you're telling me you think a demon killed him?" My voice was growing shrill.

"I know," Dad said. "I know you must think I'm nuts. This sounds insane. But it's real, Braedyn. I'm dead serious. Lilitu, they can look human when they need to. They can be quite beautiful, actually. And they use that beauty to seduce people. They—they need to forge a connection with their victim in order to feed. Physical intimacy—it gives them access to a person's essence. Their soul." He looked me straight in the eye. "Do you understand what I'm telling you, Braedyn?"

I shook my head.

"A Lilitu's embrace can be fatal. Paul, your father..." He struggled for the words. "By the time I figured out what was happening to him, it was already too late to stop it. The thing is, Braedyn—"

The front door opened without ceremony, and the man I'd seen that morning on Lucas's porch walked in.

Dad stood, startled. "Hale."

Hale was in his early thirties. His face was free of wrinkles, except where they pooled at the corners of his eyes. He exuded intense, unconscious authority. He was wearing a dark t-shirt, which stretched over a broad chest and strong arms. A thin scar divided one eyebrow and kicked down onto his cheek below. The scar drew attention to his crisp gray eyes, alive with intelligence. He moved with the same kind of focus as Dad. I knew that look instantly. Another soldier.

"You turned your phone off. Let's go, Murphy. Gretchen's waiting for us."

"I need a minute with Braedyn," Dad said.

"We can't spare it. Gretchen's tracking one right now. She thinks it attacked a high school kid."

Dad's jaw tightened with concern. "She's sure about that?"

Hale gave Dad a wry smile. "You want to question her, be my guest."

Dad looked at me, torn. "I know this is terrible timing," he said. "I promise we'll finish this when I get home. But I have to take care of something first."

"You're leaving me?" A rising panic made my voice sound shrill.

"I want to help," Lucas said, stepping into the foyer.

Hale nodded. "Good. You can stay with Braedyn. Fill her in."

"But I'm ready to fight," Lucas said.

"I know," Hale said. He clapped Lucas on the shoulder as he headed for the door. "You'll get your chance, Lucas. Just not today." Hale walked out of the house.

Lucas frowned. "That's what you keep saying," he muttered to himself.

"Lucas," Dad said quietly. "Keep her out of trouble." He followed Hale out the door. I watched him leave, shell-shocked. Lucas eyed me. The silence stretched for a long moment.

"I really thought you knew," he said. When I didn't respond, Lucas sighed. "I know it's hard to accept. When I found out—"

I spun on Lucas, interrupting. "Do I look stupid? I don't believe in demons. Just, please, go home. I want to be alone." I walked toward the stairs, but as I passed him Lucas caught my hand and held it firmly. I tried to pull free but Lucas wouldn't let me go.

"Why do you think your dad and Hale just ran out of here?" Lucas asked. "They're not chasing an ice-cream truck, Braedyn. They're demon hunters. It's what they do."

"How do you know?" I spat back. "Aren't you the one they leave behind?" Lucas released me, stung, but I was angry. I'd meant it to hurt.

"The Lilitu are real," he said. His eyes held mine, unwavering. "Whether or not you believe in them."

"Prove it," I said, my voice like ice.

"All right," Lucas said, grim determination settling into his eyes. "I will."

4

Twenty minutes later Lucas and I were walking through the heart of Old Town. The mayor had made a big push to redevelop the former town center of Puerto Escondido about a decade ago. The Plaza had been paved in terracotta cobblestones, and local artists had been commissioned to paint a variety of lush murals around the area. The land to the west of the square had been transformed into a park to preserve a few ancient catalpa trees planted there by the old missionaries. Royal, Cassie, and I had spent many weekends in Old Town eating green chile chicken enchiladas from Madrigal's and roaming the shelves at the old bookshop. It was one of a handful of stores that had thrived here even before the redevelopers rolled through the neighborhood.

Walking down the cobblestone street with Lucas, I didn't even see the displays in the windows of my favorite shops. My head was full to bursting, and I was startled when Lucas suddenly pulled me against the side of a building behind an ornamental tree. He pointed to a woman lounging against a brightly painted wall across the Plaza.

I eyed her, uncertain. In slim dark jeans, an edgy t-shirt, and steel-tipped boots, she could have been a drummer for an indie rock band or a bartender at a biker club. Her short, spiky hair looked effortlessly cool, and her expression was calm and collected.

"Gretchen can track them," Lucas said. And as we watched, Gretchen straightened, shoving her hands into her pockets. Lucas leaned forward, intent. "There." He pointed at a woman gliding out of a boutique dress shop. She moved like she was made of liquid grace. Like she wasn't constrained by the same laws of gravity as the rest of us. She paused by a table full of businessmen when she noticed them staring. Lucas sat back on his heels, grim. "There's your proof.

A soul-sucker in the flesh."

"A pretty blond flirting with a bunch of suits?" I asked. "How is that proof?"

Lucas lowered his voice. "Not flirting. It's called enthralling. It's like a spell that makes it harder to resist their advances. Not that most guys try."

"Oh. A spell," I said. "Well, when you put it that way..." Lucas heard the sarcasm in my voice.

"You're not taking this seriously."

"You think?"

"I get that she looks harmless," he started.

"You mean the terrifying blond who's maybe 115 pounds soaking wet?"

"She's a killer," Lucas said flatly.

The beautiful woman turned toward us in the sunlight. As soon as I saw her face, I recognized her. It was the same woman who'd approached Derek at Homecoming. The one who'd pulled him away right before he and Amber were supposed to be crowned. She brushed her honey-blond hair back over one shoulder. The air seemed to shimmer around her. I suddenly noticed that almost every guy in the Plaza was watching her. She basked in the attention, smiling. One of the businessmen started to stand up before he caught himself and returned to his seat. I shook my head, unable to match what Lucas was saying with what I was seeing.

"She's a killer," he said again.

I waited for more, for some kind of explanation that made sense. He didn't offer one. "Just take your word for it?" I asked, frustrated.

Lucas didn't bat an eye. "Yes."

"Why?"

"Because." Fed up, I started to walk away. Lucas grabbed my hand. The anguish in his voice was real. "Because one of them murdered my brother." Raw emotion ran unchecked over his face. I suddenly knew: this was the source of the pain I'd sensed in him earlier.

Empathy warred with logic in my head. There was no doubt that Lucas believed what he was saying. But I couldn't. There had to be some other explanation. "How do you know?" I asked softly.

A cloud seemed to pass behind his eyes and Lucas shuddered.

When he answered me, his voice was so quiet I almost couldn't hear the words. "I was there." The fight seemed to go out of him. He sagged against the wall behind us, reliving some nightmare in his mind. When he reached up to wipe away the moisture gathering in his eyes, I looked away.

The blond turned in the plaza, smiling a greeting as someone exited the shop behind her. I recognized his swagger, but it took a moment for me to believe it was really him.

"Derek?" I didn't intend for my voice to come out as shrilly as it did. The blond turned toward us, her eyes sharp. Lucas whipped me back around the corner and out of sight.

"I didn't think you two were friends," he said.

"We're not. It's just..." I swallowed hard and changed the subject. "You don't think she would hurt him?"

Lucas didn't answer me. As one, we edged closer to peek around the corner. The blond was scanning the Plaza. Her eyes swept over Gretchen. Stopped. Gretchen straightened, alarmed. I saw movement behind the blond. Dad and Hale slipped into the Plaza, flanking her. She saw them and ran— directly toward us.

Lucas shouldered in front of me protectively. But the blond darted into alley on the other side of the building we were crouched against. We watched as Hale signaled to Dad and Gretchen. They split up and darted out of sight. Lucas waited a moment longer, then pulled me forward.

"Come on," he said. He led me down the alley the blond had just disappeared into.

"What are you doing?" I hissed. The alley opened into an enclosed courtyard lined with the backdoors to half a dozen different shops. Lucas and I crouched behind a set of old stone steps leading up to the closest shop. From this hiding place, we had a clear view of the courtyard.

The blond had stopped in the center of the space, unsure which door to try. She made a decision and moved toward a dark blue door. As her hand connected with the doorknob, it opened from inside. Dad was there, blocking her escape. Something metallic gleamed in his hand. The blond stumbled back in alarm.

An inky shadow boiled up from the ground at the blond's feet, despite the full sun beaming into the courtyard. It spiraled up her body, wrapping her in a cloak of darkness— and she disappeared.

"No," Lucas breathed. "Where's Gretchen?!"

"What—what was that?" I stammered. "She disappeared. How did she disappear?"

"Shh!" Lucas's eyes were fixed on my dad, creased in worry. In the courtyard, Dad tensed, as though preparing for a fight. He gripped a wicked looking knife in one hand and sliced it through the air in front of him.

Gretchen burst through another door, breathless.

"Gretchen?!" Dad growled. "Where is she?!"

Gretchen scanned the courtyard and shook her head, frustrated. "Too late. She's gone. I don't get it. It's like something tipped her off."

Lucas hunched lower. "We should go back," he whispered.

"Get up," a man growled behind us. We turned. Hale towered over us, his gray eyes crackling with anger. Lucas and I jerked, startled.

"Hale," Lucas said. "I was just—"

Hale's expression didn't soften. "Home. *Now.*"

"What is it?" Gretchen said, approaching with Dad.

Lucas and I stood. Dad frowned when he saw us. Gretchen's eyes slid over me quickly. They were a deep chocolate brown, and seemed startlingly dark against her fair skin. Up close, I noticed her spiky hair made her angular features seem even sharper.

"I guess the definition of 'out of trouble' has changed since my day," Dad said. I felt Lucas stiffen beside me, mortified. I stepped forward quickly.

"It's my fault," I said. "I—I didn't believe. I asked him for proof."

"It's okay, Braedyn," Lucas murmured.

Gretchen lowered her voice dangerously. "Oh no. We're about two state lines away from okay."

"Gretchen. Get them out of here," Hale said.

Another shop door opened behind us. Derek emerged. "What the hell is going on?" he asked. His eyes looked slightly wild. "What'd you do to her? How—" he swallowed, scared. "How'd you make her disappear?"

Dad traded a grim look with Hale. Gretchen turned to Derek, composing her features.

"You better come with us," she said.

The inside of Lucas's house was different than I'd pictured it. It wasn't as badly damaged as the outside suggested. I'm not saying it would make any magazine covers, but it was homey and comfortable. I stole glances around the living room while Gretchen tried to explain things to Derek.

He wasn't taking the news any better than I had. "No way. No way is she a—"

"You've seen a lot of grown women disappearing into thin air?" Gretchen asked. Derek looked extremely creeped out. He didn't answer her. "She leave you with any souvenirs?" Gretchen asked, trying a different tactic. "On your back, maybe?"

At this, Derek looked up sharply. I glanced at Lucas. Lucas met my gaze unhappily.

"Claw marks," Gretchen said.

Derek looked sick. "How do you know that?"

"It's what they do," Gretchen said. "Except they usually go after soldier-types. I don't know what she wants with you, Derek, but you're in trouble." Derek sat in uncomfortable silence as this started to sink in. Gretchen turned to Lucas. "Tell him."

Lucas looked up, startled. "Me? I'm not sure I'm the best one to—"

"You want to be involved?" Gretchen interrupted. "It's not all hunting and fighting. This part, dealing with the victims, is just as important." Gretchen sat back, watching Lucas. He rubbed his hands together nervously.

"Right." Lucas turned to Derek. "It's basically three strikes and you're out."

Derek gave Lucas a frosty glare. "I hate baseball."

"It's a metaphor, dude," Lucas said. "Do you want to hear this or not?" Derek glared but didn't answer. Lucas collected his thoughts for a moment. "The first night you spend with one of them weakens you, but you can recover. The second night, it's a lot worse."

"Define worse," Derek said. I leaned closer, curious.

"She'll turn you into a Thrall." Lucas read the blank look in Derek's face and elaborated. "Physically you'll look the same but it won't be you inside anymore. She could tell you to do anything, and you'd obey without question."

"Anything," Derek said. "Like running down the street naked?"

"This isn't a game of truth or dare," Lucas said. "She could get you to rob a store." He paused. "She could get you to murder someone and you wouldn't even bat an eye. Everything you are, everything you value or believe, it all fades away. That's what it means to be a Thrall."

Derek glanced at Gretchen. She nodded slowly, seconding Lucas's explanation. After a long moment, I spoke up.

"Why Derek?" I asked. Lucas glanced at Gretchen, but she waited for him to answer.

"I don't know," Lucas said. "Mostly, the Lilitu use Thrall as guards when they're sleeping, so they tend to pick tougher guys." He glanced at Derek. "No offense."

There was another stretch of silence. Then Derek shifted in his seat.

"What's strike three?" he asked. Lucas's expression was all the answer he needed. Derek blanched, starting to lose it. "You're saying I could *die?*"

Gretchen leaned forward, stepping in. She put a comforting hand on Derek's shoulder and nodded to us. "All right. Why don't you two give Derek and me a minute?"

Lucas and I stood and walked into the foyer. We stopped at the base of the staircase.

"I can't believe it," I said quietly. But enough had shifted in my world in the last few hours that I couldn't *not* believe it, either. Lucas seemed to read my thoughts.

"I know," he breathed. We stood, just staring at one another for a few heartbeats, then Lucas shrugged. "Grand tour?" he asked.

He said it so casually I couldn't help but laugh. "Lead on."

Lucas led the way upstairs. When we reached the landing, I studied the second floor hallway curiously. It was lined with doors, each opening into a room that was large enough for a twin bed, a dresser, and not much else.

"It's an old barracks," Lucas said, noticing my look. "The Guard has owned this place for ages." Lucas pushed open the door to one of the small rooms. "This one's mine." I followed him inside. It was a little more than twice the size of my closet. Aside from a twin bed and a modest chest of drawers, there was a small desk and chair. A leather jacket hung on a hook by the door. "Home sweet home," he said. "At least for a little while. This makes the fifth time Gretchen and I have moved since Eric—" Lucas didn't finish the sentence.

I walked into the room, running my fingers over the old wood surface of the desk.

"So, you and Gretchen," I asked neutrally. "Are you guys a thing?"

Lucas grinned, amused. "Uh, no. Big, emphatic no. Gretchen was in love with my brother. They were engaged forever before they got married. Seriously, it was like five years. Then, just a few months after they finally tied the knot, Eric died. Gretchen's pretty much the only family I have left. She's also the reason I'm here." He saw my curiosity and bit his lip. "Gretchen can see them," he explained. "When Lilitu cloak themselves, Gretchen can see through their shields. You can't learn how to do it," he added. "You're either a spotter or you're not."

"That's..." I shivered. "Creepy."

Lucas looked away from me for a moment. "Yeah. She didn't know she was a spotter until Eric was attacked. She—she saw him die."

I couldn't think of anything to say. After a moment, Lucas looked up at me again.

"At least we know the truth," he said. "That's more than a lot of people ever get. It was just a matter of time before we found the Guard. So no, we're not a thing. I mean, I love Gretchen." He smiled again, fainter this time. "But I love her like a really tough, really bossy big sister."

I don't know why it made me feel so much better to hear it, but it did. "What exactly is the Guard?" I asked.

Lucas sat on the edge of his bed. "We're humanity's only real defense against the Lilitu."

I turned to look at him, skeptical. "What about the police? What about the army? Why don't you just tell people what's going on so we can prepare?"

Lucas smiled humorlessly. "The Guard has tried for centuries to get the word out," he said. "Come on. You didn't believe until you saw one cloak herself in front of your own eyes. What makes you think anyone else will?"

43

"Cloak—you mean when she turned invisible?"

"Yeah."

"How do people not know about this?" I asked incredulously. "I mean, we can't be the only people to ever see a lady disappear and think, 'Hmm, that's extremely unusual.'"

Lucas sighed. "The Lilitu don't want the world to know about them. It would screw up the hunt if people got wise. Lilitu spend a lot of time covering their tracks. Thane says a really powerful Lilitu can make an unguarded mind believe whatever she wants him to believe."

"They can mess with our heads?" I asked. Lucas nodded. "So that's why I've never heard of them before?"

"You've heard of them," Lucas said. "Most people call them succubae, and take them about as seriously as vampires and werewolves. But the truth is, they're all over history. You know Helen of Troy, right? Started the Trojan War back in ancient Greece? The face that launched 1,000 ships?"

"Sure. We studied Greek mythology last year."

"Lilitu."

"You're serious?" I studied his face for any sign of amusement. Found none.

"That was the last big battle between us and them. It ended with the Truce, which was supposed to separate humanity and Lilitu forever. But the Lilitu keep slipping back into our world, and the Guard keep chasing them down. Every century or so the fighting gets bad and a lot of people die, but the Lilitu always make sure the general population walks away believing it was war or plague or some natural disaster."

"Natural disaster?"

"Like an iceberg sinking the Titanic," Lucas said. "No one wants to believe Lilitu had the run of the ship, or that when they were done playing they caused the crash. And they got first shot at the lifeboats, by the way. Women and children, right? You want another example? The Salem Witch Trials started over a Lilitu."

I shook my head, trying to keep up. "The Titanic, the Salem Witch Trials, the Trojan War. How long has this battle been going on?" I asked.

Lucas shrugged. "Since the beginning."

"The beginning of what?"

"The beginning. The garden of Eden."

"Eden?" I was surprised to find I had any skepticism left.

"Believe me, I know." Lucas said wearily. "This story is old. Older than history. Take it with a grain of salt. It goes like this: God created Adam and Lilith out of clay. Lilith was supposed to be Adam's wife, but she wasn't interested, so she runs away from the garden. Three angels are sent to bring her back. Senoy, Sansenoy, and Semangelof—"

"Seriously?" I asked. "Angels?"

"I'm just telling you what they told me," Lucas said. "Anyhow, these angels chase her down but Lilith refuses to go back, even though the future of humanity is at stake. So God creates Eve out of Adam's rib, which turns out pretty good for Adam. Things are great for a while, until they get curious about this special tree—"

"And eat the apple."

Lucas smiled. "And get themselves expelled from the garden forever. That's when they become mortal. And by 'they,' I mean 'we' as in all of humanity. Lilith was never technically expelled from Eden—she left of her own free will. So she and her children are still immortal." I made a face. "Look, I'm not saying I believe the whole thing. But there are two creation stories in Genesis, and the Lilitu—I know they're real."

Lucas's eyes shifted almost imperceptibly, looking at something behind me. I turned. On the desk was a picture of a charismatic guy in his twenties. He was wearing a leather jacket and had his arms wrapped tightly around a girl. She snuggled up against him territorially. Her wide eyes were framed with thick dark lashes, and wild, curly dark hair spilled down her back. Her face seemed to shine in the dark picture. It was the only photo in the room. I turned to the jacket hanging on the wall. It bore the same creases along the arms as the jacket in the photo. "That's your brother in the picture, isn't it?"

"And that's the demon who killed him." Lucas picked up the photo, letting his hair fall forward, obscuring his eyes from view. The weight of his sadness pressed down on us both.

"Lucas," I said gently. "Maybe you shouldn't keep—I mean, don't you have any other pictures of your brother?"

Lucas looked up. Dark anger roiled in his eyes. "I'm not keeping this because of Eric."

I suddenly understood. "She's still out there. The Lilitu that killed

45

him."

"I'll catch her. Someday." Lucas reached past me to set the photo down. "Like Hale always says, they're only immortal until you kill them." We were suddenly face-to-face, just inches apart. "It's strange," he murmured.

I felt my mouth go dry. "What's strange?"

"Explaining this to Murphy's daughter." He looked into my eyes and I felt a jolt pass through me. After a long moment, Lucas straightened and I found I could breathe again. "You're taking this a lot better than I did when I found out," he said. "You want something to drink? I think we have some soda downstairs."

We came down the stairs and saw Gretchen and Derek still talking quietly in the living room. Now that I knew about her and Eric, I saw Gretchen differently. She was leaning close to talk with Derek, and she looked almost gentle. I thought about how long she and Eric had been engaged, and then—just as they were starting their life together—how she lost him. That hard-as-nails exterior she projected, it must be hiding a devastating grief.

Lucas led me through the foyer to the dining room. Like our house, the dining room opened into the kitchen. But this kitchen was colder than ours, less welcoming. Lucas opened the refrigerator and pulled out a few cans of generic soda.

"Gretchen must have done the shopping," Lucas said with a sigh. "She's got this personal crusade going against sugar."

"Sugar and demons," I murmured.

Lucas smiled. "So what's he like as a dad? Murphy?"

"You keep saying his name like he's some kind of legend," I said.

"He is," Lucas replied. "At least in the Guard he is. And not just because he caught more Lilitu than guys with careers twice as long as his. Most guys join up because they lost someone. Like Gretchen and me. Like Hale. But Murphy—your dad— They say he had a dream about the Guard and volunteered the next day."

I shook my head, mystified. "It's just been the two of us forever. I thought we knew everything about each other. Now, I feel like I don't know him at all."

"That's not true," Lucas said. "You know what makes him laugh, what makes him proud. You know the man he is now. The guy that made the decision to leave the Guard behind so he could raise a little girl on his own."

I felt a lump rise in my throat and nodded.

Lucas seemed to war with himself for a moment before coming to a decision. "Come on. I want to show you something."

"What?"

"You want to know about the Guard?" he asked.

I nodded.

"Then you have to see this."

5

Lucas led me back to the foyer. Trying not to draw Gretchen's attention, we slipped quietly along the side of the stairs and stopped in front of a door. It was in roughly the same place as the crawlspace under the stairs at my house. But when Lucas opened this door, he revealed another set of stairs leading down to some kind of basement. A light glowed beneath us, warm and inviting.

"What is this?" I whispered, eyeing the narrow staircase.

"The heart of any Guard outpost," Lucas answered. He flashed a smile full of mischievous anticipation. "The armory." He led the way down the steps.

At the base of the staircase I stopped to take it all in. The basement was much larger than I expected. It must have covered most of the property. Support posts dotted the cavernous space, keeping the high cement wall from crashing down. One wall was lined with weapon racks. A large collection of swords and daggers gleamed under spotlights. I could pick out a few stranger weapons among them as well. There was something that looked like a spear, something else that looked like a machete, and several quivers full of different kinds of arrows.

I moved forward, curious. Lucas watched as I picked up a dagger. The metal of the blade was shot through with strange waving lines that shifted colors as I turned the dagger in the light. It reminded me of an oil spill on water, a kind of shimmering dark rainbow of colors swirling together. I moved to touch the blade with my thumb, but Lucas caught my hand, stopping me.

"Careful," he said. "It's sharper than it looks. And cuts from these things take a long time to heal. Trust me."

I held the dagger more carefully. "What kind of metal is this?"

"It's not the metal that's special," he said. "It's the forging process that makes it different from other blades."

"Different how?"

"Well, for one thing, these are the only weapons we know of that can actually hurt a Lilitu. I mean, you can shoot a Lilitu with a gun, but you'll just piss her off."

"You make it sound like all Lilitu are girls," I said.

"Not all of them," Lucas said. "Just most of them. Male Lilitu are incredibly rare. I mean, I've never met anyone who's ever met anyone who's even seen one. Thane swears they exist, but I've only ever seen female Lilitu."

It was the second time he'd said that name. "Thane?"

"He's an archivist. And a bitter old grouch." Lucas shrugged, smiling. "But he knows his stuff."

I turned my attention back to the dagger in my hand. "Have you ever killed one?"

Lucas got quiet for a moment. "No. I've never killed anything. The truth is, when I think about it, when I picture actually doing it—" He stopped, unable to finish the sentence. "If Eric was still alive, I wouldn't even know they existed. But because that Lilitu was free to hunt, my brother is gone. Every one of them we kill means lives saved. If I don't fight, who will?"

I looked at the weapons again, wondering what I would do if I ever had to use one of them in a fight. I gripped the dagger tighter and sliced an imaginary line through the air slowly. Lucas was watching me with a strange look on his face.

"What?" I asked.

"What I said in gym class was true," he said. "I've never been able to talk about this with someone my own age. I know your world was just turned upside down. But, I'm glad you know. Does that make me a terrible person?"

I met his eyes. They were full of empathy. The basement was cool, and standing this close to him I could feel the subtle heat radiating from his body. "Yes," I said. "A truly horrible, grotesque, mockery of a human being. I can't believe I'm even breathing the same air as you." A sheepish smile spread over Lucas's face. I punched him lightly in the shoulder with my free hand, grinning.

"All right," he said, gesturing for the dagger. "Hand it over. I want to show you something." He exerted pressure and the dagger sprang apart into two interlocking blades. I hadn't detected any seam in the metal when I'd held it a moment ago.

"Fancy knives," I said, impressed.

"Shh." Lucas walked into the empty space in the middle of the armory, one dagger in each hand. One moment he was standing still, and the next he was in motion, daggers flashing in his hands. It was some kind of martial arts form, aggressive and powerful. Suddenly I understood how he'd managed to take on five guys at lunch and walk away. His movements were precise and quick. When he finished, I burst into applause.

"That was awesome. What is it, some kind of kung-fu?"

"It's an old Mesopotamian fighting style," Lucas said. "I've been studying with Hale."

"Looks complicated."

"Here." He transferred the daggers to my hands and moved close behind me, curling his hands around mine over the daggers. "This is the basic form." He guided my hands, moving us through the form in a slow, deliberate rhythm. After a moment, he released my left hand. "All movement comes from your center. Focus here." He placed his left hand on my stomach. I felt a flutter of sensation at his touch. Pressed against him, I was aware of every movement of his body. We swept across the floor in unison. The rest of my world seemed to fall away; only the warmth of his touch and the gentle pressure of his hands remained. I turned my head toward his, brushing his cheek with mine. I heard his quick intake of breath, felt his arm tighten around my body. We finished the form and for a moment, neither of us moved. Then Lucas stepped back, releasing me.

"A natural," he said. His voice sounded almost hoarse.

"No. Just following your lead." I handed him the daggers. He snapped them together and returned them to their shelf. I brushed the hair back from my face, recovering.

"I'm serious," he said, turning back to me. "You could have a bright future in demon hunting. All it would take is a decade of dedicated combat training and the end of your social life."

I laughed. "Mm. Tempting as that sounds, I'm going to have to pass."

Lucas shrugged, faking disappointment. "It's a shame. We've got all this equipment to train with, just languishing, unused."

"Well, teach me something else," I said. "Something useful, that won't require carrying a huge knife everywhere I go."

"Fine. You want boring, we can do something boring." Lucas considered me for a moment, and then walked behind me again. "Let's say someone grabs you." He put his hand on my shoulder. "You can't run away if they're holding you, right?"

"Right."

"Okay. I'll show you how to get away. You grab me." He turned his back to me. I put my hand on his shoulder. Lucas's head turned slightly at my touch. "No, *grab* me. Like you mean business. Summon your inner warrior princess." I giggled and tightened my grip. Lucas moved. He gripped my wrist and twisted it while turning to face me. The movement forced my elbow to point up at the ceiling and I had to spin away from him; it was that or let my elbow snap. Lucas put a slight pressure on the back of my hand, pushing it toward my wrist as my arm locked straight. With a gasp of surprise, I was on my tiptoes, pin-wheeling for balance. Lucas's voice wasn't even strained. "From here you could turn and run. It'd buy you a few seconds, at least." He released me.

"Show me how you did that!"

Lucas worked with me for half an hour until I felt comfortable with the move. It all depended on gripping the wrist correctly, controlling the elbow twist, and not letting up on the pressure. After I'd successfully repelled him 10 times in a row he stepped back, rubbing his shoulder.

"Nice. I think you've got it."

"What's next?" I asked.

"I thought you were a pacifist."

"This is self-defense, right?" I turned my back to him. "So?"

He came up behind me and caught me in a bear hug. "I can show you how to get out of this, too, but if we're going to start doing throws we should really put some mats down."

"Where do you keep the mats?" I turned to face him, and suddenly the bear hug became an embrace. Lucas looked into my eyes, startled. My hands were resting lightly on his chest. When I didn't pull back, Lucas adjusted his arms, pulling me a little closer. His gaze moved to my lips. I tipped my head up as he leaned forward.

I think it would have been a perfect kiss.

Above us, the door to the basement burst open and footsteps pounded down the stairs. We turned, startled, as Dad appeared at the bottom of the basement stairs.

"Braedyn?"

Hale and Gretchen entered the basement behind Dad. Every one of them looked grim.

Lucas released me. "I was just showing her the—"

"Out," Dad growled. Lucas glanced at me, bewildered, and left the basement. Gretchen's eyes burned with unmistakable hatred.

"You," she hissed. "Never touch him again."

I was baffled by her anger. "What did I do?"

"Braedyn." Dad took a step toward me. "I love you. Nothing's ever going to change that." Gretchen grabbed Dad's arm and jerked him around to face her.

"You knew. You knew and you raised her anyway. What the hell is wrong with you?"

Hale spoke up. "We need her, Gretchen." When she turned her rage on Hale, he didn't flinch. "This is the assignment. Are you in or out?"

Gretchen glanced at me, incredulous. "You can't be serious...?"

All of a sudden I felt cold, like ice water had flooded into my veins. "Someone tell me what's going on." Gretchen faced me, her eyes full of venom.

"Gretchen," Dad warned. But she shrugged past him to get in my face.

"The demon that killed your father was your mother," Gretchen said. "That makes you a Lilitu, just like her." Dad grabbed Gretchen by the shoulder and spun her around to face him.

"That's my daughter," he growled.

"She's the enemy," Gretchen hissed back. "And if you were half the Guardsman you're supposed to be—"

"*Enough.*" Hale's voice rang with authority, cutting Gretchen off. "Gretchen. Wait upstairs. And Gretchen, Lucas stays in the dark. Are we clear?"

For a moment, it seemed like Gretchen might refuse. Hale just watched her calmly, waiting for her to make a move. Gretchen finally nodded sourly. She turned and marched back up the stairs. I heard the door at the top of the stairs slam shut.

I shook my head. "That's insane. I can't be what she said." I turned to Dad, pleading. "Tell him."

"Honey." Dad's gaze didn't waver. In his eyes I could read the truth. I turned away from him abruptly.

"I want to go home."

Hale pulled two chairs out from under a worktable. He sat in one and gestured at the other, offering me a seat. I didn't move. "Braedyn," he said. "You're going to be very powerful very soon."

"Powerful? Look at me. I—I'm getting a C in phys ed."

Hale gave me a brief smile. "Lilitu powers present at 16. If you haven't felt them yet, you will."

I looked him in the eye. "What do you want from me?"

Hale sat back in his chair, watching me levelly. "Murphy says you could be a powerful ally. Most of the Guard won't see it that way. If they knew you existed, they'd want to eliminate you before you grew any stronger." He said this so casually it took a moment for me to realize what he meant.

With great effort, I kept my voice steady. "And what do you think?"

Hale considered this. After a moment, he spoke. "In your DNA, you are the enemy. But Murphy raised you. He taught you empathy and love." Hale leaned back in his chair. "The plain truth is, we need your help, Braedyn."

I glanced around at the weapons surrounding us. "How can I help you? You're the ones with the arsenal of demon-killing crap."

"We're losing ground against the Lilitu. We know they're planning something big for winter solstice. We need your help to figure out what."

"Sure," I said, keeping my voice level. "Just let me grab my special demon decoder ring and I'll get right on that."

"Braedyn." Dad spoke quietly, but I saw fear in his eyes.

Hale stood. "It's okay, Murphy. Let's give her some time. This is a lot to digest." He turned back to face me. "You want to know what I think? I think you have a choice to make. You can take lives or you can save them. So I'm reserving judgment until you let me know whether Murphy was right about you." Hale studied my face almost gently. "Don't keep me waiting too long." With that, Hale stood and walked up the basement stairs, closing the door on his way out.

When we were alone I turned to Dad. Stricken. "Why didn't you tell me? Dad?" He didn't respond, and a searing rage rose up in me. "Oh, right. I forgot. I'm not your daughter. I'm your *ally*."

"You are my daughter, and you know it," he said softly. I felt pressure building behind my eyes.

"Did you kill her? Did you kill my mother?"

He shook his head. "As far as I know, she's still alive."

I needed fresh air. I tried to brush past Dad but he caught me and held me tightly. "Braedyn, you have to nip this thing with Lucas in the bud. Any feelings you have for him put both of your lives in danger." I tried to pull away, but he held me tighter. "What I said earlier, about the way Lilitu kill—it's not a choice for them. It's part of what they are. What you are. I need to make sure you understand. You can't get romantically involved. Not with Lucas. Not with anyone."

I struggled out of his grip and glared at him.

He held my gaze. "Hate me if you need to. But please hear me. Be careful with Lucas. He hates the Lilitu, and his grief is still fresh. We're not keeping the truth from Lucas to protect him. We're doing it to protect *you*. Lucas knows how to fight. He's good enough that if he decided to hurt you, he could do it. We don't want to give him a reason to. Do you understand?"

"Yes, *Murphy*," I said coldly. "I understand."

Something seemed to break inside Dad; the light in his deep brown eyes faded. He bowed his head. Nodded.

I fled the basement before the swelling dam inside me had time to burst.

6

I awoke the next morning, groggy. My thoughts were slow to collect. For a few moments, I lay still, enjoying the warmth of the bed. And then everything came crashing back, and the world seemed to tilt on its axis.

A sharp crack sounded outside my bedroom window. I slipped out from under the covers, shivering in the early morning chill. The wood floor was cold as stone to my bare feet. I walked to the window and edged the curtains apart, peering into Lucas's backyard.

Lucas was pulling a rotted plank off his back porch with a crowbar. Gretchen leaned against the rail behind him, giving orders. A stack of new lumber rested on blocks in the lawn behind him. When Lucas had wrestled the rotted plank up he glanced at Gretchen. She made a sweeping gesture that seemed to cover the entire back porch. Lucas nodded glumly. Gretchen entered the house, leaving Lucas alone. He waited a moment, and then shot a furtive glance up at my window.

I stepped back quickly, letting the drapes fall closed. My heart pounded. After a night tortured by indecision, I still didn't know how I was going to face him. I walked to my closet and pulled some clothes out with leaden fingers. I dressed numbly, unable to shake this sense of dread.

Downstairs, Dad was waiting for me at the dining room table. I ignored him, fixed a bowl of cereal, and ate it leaning against the kitchen island. Dad pushed back from the table and walked into the kitchen.

"I was worried about you last night," he said. I ate the cereal wordlessly, refusing to acknowledge him. He took the hint and sighed. "All right. I'm going to miss dinner tonight, but there's an enchilada for you in the fridge. We're watching Derek in shifts."

I looked up as a wash of guilt swept over me. I'd forgotten about Derek. "Is he going to be okay?" I asked.

Dad hesitated. "We're doing everything we can for him."

"That's not exactly a yes."

"It's complicated."

"What's complicated about it?" I snapped. "If he spends another night with her, he turns into a Thrall. You think he'd risk that, now that he knows?"

Dad bit his lower lip, something he did when he wrestled with a decision. "Lilitu have formidable powers," he said. "Derek may know what's at risk, but that doesn't mean he'll be able to resist her. She's already weakened him; he'll be more susceptible to her now." Dad reached out and smoothed a lock of hair back behind my shoulder. "I am sorry about yesterday," he said. "I should have told you sooner. I know that now. But I didn't want to hurt you. For the last 16 years, my whole life has been about protecting you."

I lowered my spoon, no longer hungry. "What happens now?"

"What do you mean? With Derek?"

"With me." I asked the question that had kept me up half the night, and my voice quavered. "If the Guard is depending on me...?" I looked up. "What happens if I mess up? What happens if they decide they don't need me after all?"

"Braedyn," he said, his voice heavy with emotion. "If it ever comes down to a choice between the Guard and you, I won't hesitate. We'll be gone before they know we're running." Hot tears stung my eyes. Just hearing those words unknotted some of the muscles in my back.

Royal honked outside. I ran my hands under my eyes, brushing away tears.

"I should go," I said.

"About Lucas—" Dad said.

"Don't," I interrupted, as some of the anger from last night rekindled. "I already told you. I understand." Dad nodded and I walked out of the kitchen.

"Braedyn," he called after me. "Let me know if anything strange happens, okay?" I stopped in the dining room, glancing over my shoulder at him.

"Define strange."

"You'll know it if you see it."

I hesitated. "The Lilitu you were tracking in the Plaza yesterday. She was at my Homecoming dance."

Dad's eyes locked onto my face, suddenly alert. "You're sure it was the same woman?" I nodded. "Did she approach you?"

"No."

"She didn't say anything to you? Didn't try to make contact?"

"No," I repeated. "She was there for Derek."

Royal gave his horn another quick beep outside.

"Go ahead," Dad said, lost in his thoughts. "You don't want to make your friends late for school."

It was a grueling day. Trying to stay away from Lucas was easier said than done. We didn't have any morning classes together, but I saw him in the halls between every period, trying to catch my eye. I managed to make it all the way to lunch without trading words with him. As Royal and I walked toward the dining hall together, I stopped.

"I'm going to spend lunch in the library," I said. "English paper." I hurried away, before Royal had the chance to unravel my excuse. There was a vending machine in the library foyer, but I didn't have any change. I sighed. If I was going to make a habit of ditching lunch, I'd have to start packing something to eat.

I sat by a library window with a good view of the dining hall. As the lunch hour drew to a close, students began trickling out onto the quad. I made my way to the gym and slipped into the girls' locker room before anyone else had arrived. I was already changed into my gym clothes when Cassie walked in. She didn't attempt any subtlety.

"What's going on with you and Lucas?"

I feigned nonchalance. "What do you mean? Did he say something?"

"No, but it's pretty obvious he's worried about you." Cassie opened her locker and started changing. "Are you avoiding him?" She studied me, concerned. "Did something happen?"

I turned away from Cassie so she couldn't read my face. "No. I'm just busy with school."

"Uh huh." It was clear from her tone Cassie didn't believe me. She finished changing and closed her locker. "Well, he's eager to see you.

He spent most of lunch with his eyes glued to the clock." Cassie started walking toward the gym entrance. I didn't move. She stopped and looked at me. "Are you coming?"

"Actually, I'm not feeling so good," I lied. "Will you tell Ms. Davies I went to the nurse?" Cassie's eyes looked troubled, but she nodded. "Thanks."

Cassie and the other girls left for the start of class. I sat on the locker room bench for a long time. My hands were trembling. I was scared of facing Lucas. Scared that if I let myself get close to him, it wouldn't matter what Dad had said. The memory of his arms around me... I clasped my hands together to keep them still, but I couldn't stop my mind from spinning. What would that kiss have become? I changed slowly back into my school clothes and walked to the administration building to visit the nurse. All the while, Lucas haunted my thoughts.

By the end of fifth period I was distracted and irritable. My stomach rumbled unhappily, unwilling to let me forget the lunch I'd skipped. I walked to English in a stormy mood. Cassie and Royal traded a worried look but left me alone.

"I have a plan." I heard Amber's voice behind me as the class settled into their seats. "I saw his sister dropping him off at school today."

Mr. Young entered the classroom and picked up a piece of chalk, writing "IRONY" on the blackboard. "Let's continue our discussion from yesterday," he said.

"He doesn't drive?" Ally whispered behind me, scoffing.

"Not everyone has a car," Amber replied.

"Ladies," Mr. Young warned. But as he turned back to the blackboard, Ally lowered her voice.

"So what's your plan?"

"I'm going to offer to be his ride," Amber said. Rick, sitting on the other side of Amber, snickered. She turned on him, scowling. "You're demented, Rick. Get your mind out of the gutter." She turned back to Ally. "Think of all that alone time to and from school. Just me and Lucas. He's going to be wrapped around my little finger in a week."

"Shut up," I said, turning around in my chair to face Amber. "I'm trying to learn something here." The class burst into laughter. Amber's nostrils flared. Mr. Young turned from the blackboard, surprised.

"Thank you, Braedyn." He glanced around the room. "All right. Irony. Who's got an example?" Royal raised his hand. "Yes, Royal."

"The Homecoming Queen brags about her plan to get a guy to fall in love with her in front of the girl this guy actually wants." The class burst into laughter again.

"From the book," Mr. Young said. "But good example." That set off another round of laughter before Mr. Young could get people to focus on the lesson at hand. Amber slid down in her chair, eyes smoldering.

After class, I hung back, waving for Royal and Cassie to leave without me. I wasn't good company today. As I walked out the door, Amber shoved past me, knocking the books right out of my hands. I dropped to the floor to collect them, and someone bent down beside me to help. Lucas. We gathered everything off the floor and stood, facing each other awkwardly. Lucas handed me my English spiral and my copy of *Pride And Prejudice*.

"Thanks," I said.

"You're avoiding me." It was a statement, not a question. I made the mistake of meeting his eyes, and felt my heartbeat surge. "I can talk to Murphy," Lucas offered quietly. "I'll tell him whatever he's mad at you about, it's my fault. I'm the one who took you to the hunt. I'm the one who showed you the armory."

"He's not mad." I bit my lip, but this was the opportunity I needed. I took a quick breath, before I lost my nerve. "He just doesn't want me hanging out with you."

"Gretchen doesn't want me hanging out with you, either," Lucas said. His eyes held mine, steady.

"Then why are you talking to me?"

"No one asked what I wanted." Lucas brushed a lock of hair back behind my ear. I felt his touch like a line of golden fire across my cheek. It took all my strength to look away from him.

"I don't think this is a good idea."

"Why not?"

"The Guard," I said. "It's your life. Not mine." The words came out of my mouth in a hoarse whisper. "I'm late for class." I turned away. Lucas caught my arm.

"Wait. We're going to need each other." He swallowed, looking suddenly vulnerable. "Yeah, okay. I *like* you like you. But if you don't feel the same, I'll never bring it up again. We can hang out as friends. Throw a Frisbee around. Whatever. So long as we have each other to talk to when things get bad. And they do. They will." He took a steadying breath and smiled. "So. What do you say? Friends?"

"Lucas," I started. But I couldn't finish the sentence. Every part of me longed to give in. And that's what finally gave me the will to shake my head no. I couldn't control my feelings for Lucas. That was the whole problem. "No," I whispered.

"No you don't want to be buddies, no you don't like Frisbee...?" He was trying to win a smile. I didn't give him one.

"No to all of it."

He leaned back, his smile fading. "I'm— If you're saying you don't want me around—?"

I looked down the hallway. A few stragglers were slipping into class. The bell would ring any second. "That's what I'm saying."

Lucas froze, his eyes searching my face for a long moment. "Okay. I'll leave you alone." Lucas turned and walked down the hallway. He didn't look back.

After school, Royal and Cassie found me at the edge of the parking lot, staring. They followed my gaze and saw Amber, smiling into Lucas's eyes possessively.

"What does she think she's—?" Cassie started.

"Come on," I said, interrupting. "Let's get out of here." Royal glanced back at Lucas, uncertain. "Lucas is getting a ride with someone else." Amber was already leading Lucas to her car.

As we pulled out of the parking lot, fury and grief battled within me, alternating stabs of fire and ice. Cassie watched me in the rearview mirror.

"Okay, seriously. What is going on with you and Lucas?"

"Nothing." I stared out at the passing scenery.

"Clearly," Royal said. "But we want to know why."

I couldn't tell them. I couldn't tell my best friends why I had just asked the first guy I really liked to leave me alone permanently. Cassie saw the tears brimming in my eyes and shook her head at Royal, warning him to let up.

When they finally dropped me off at home, Cassie squeezed my hand. "If you want to talk," she said.

I nodded and forced a smile. "Thanks. See you tomorrow." I watched as Royal pulled back onto the road, then turned to go home. The front door was unlocked. I pushed it open, unsettled. "Hello? Anyone home?"

"In here," Dad called from the dining room. I found him sitting at the table with Hale.

"What's wrong?" I asked, feeling a knot forming in the pit of my stomach.

"I want you to start training," Dad said.

"Training for what?"

"Self-defense," Hale answered. "We'll start with hand-to-hand combat. I won't transition you into bladed weapons until you're ready." The memory of Lucas in the basement came back in a powerful rush. I turned away from Hale, flushed.

"I'm—I don't want to fight."

Hale nodded, calm. "I see. What happens if you meet another Guardsman one day? If he doesn't know you're on our side?" His tone was mild, but his eyes burned. "Do you know what Guardsmen do when they capture a Lilitu?" I glanced at Dad.

"Okay, Hale," Dad said. "I think you've made your point."

Hale's eyes didn't leave my face. "You've seen our armory. Not all of those weapons are used to kill."

Dad stood up. "That's enough."

"She needs to understand what's at stake," Hale said. He turned to me. "I'll see you in 15 minutes." Hale left. I faced Dad, pissed.

"Did it even occur to you to ask if I wanted this?"

"I would do anything in my power to protect you," Dad said. "But I'm not always going to be around. Let Hale help you. You may need to know this stuff some day."

Something in his voice chilled me.

15 minutes later I was walking into the Guard's house in yoga pants and a long sleeve t-shirt. Lucas sat at the round dining room table

doing his homework. He looked up as I entered. When he saw me, his expression grew stony.

"Training," I said by way of explanation.

He watched me cross the foyer to the basement door, then turned his attention back to his homework. His hair fell forward, shielding his eyes from view. It hurt more than I'd expected, getting the cold shoulder from him. I slipped quietly into the staircase and pulled the door closed behind me.

Hale was waiting for me in the basement. "Have you ever studied any martial arts before?"

"No." I shifted self-consciously, feeling like a fool.

Hale didn't let this bother him. "Not a problem. We'll keep it simple at first. Sound good?" he asked. I shrugged. He ignored my lack of enthusiasm and began the lesson. He taught me three basic punches to start. For the next four hours I practiced them against a punching bag while Hale watched, correcting my form, encouraging me. By the end of the session I was exhausted and my arms felt like lead weights hanging from my shoulders.

"Good work," Hale said. "Same time tomorrow."

"But I can barely move now," I complained.

Hale smiled, incorrigible. "Just think how strong you'll be in a month."

We settled into a routine. Every day I'd come home from school, change into yoga pants and a t-shirt, and spend the next four hours in Hale's windowless basement working out my frustration on a punching bag until dinnertime. Lucas watched me come and go, but he was as good as his word; he left me entirely alone.

By the time winter solstice was two months away, none of the powers Hale seemed to think I should be developing had appeared. He and Dad grew more anxious by the day. I didn't have time to worry about powers or solstices or whatever the Lilitu had planned. I was too busy trying not to care about what Lucas was doing. It hadn't taken long for him to end up as a semi-permanent fixture on Amber's arm. He joined her lunch table. He made friends with her friends. He let her hang all over him. And he ignored me. It was cold comfort knowing he was doing exactly what I had asked him to do. Lunches were the worst. Amber's laugh was high and shrill. Each time it cut through the lunchtime chatter I'd look up and catch sight of Lucas smiling at her, or laughing at something she'd said, or sitting with his arm thrown casually around her shoulders.

On Halloween, Amber was extra giggly. In honor of the holiday, the school was serving French fries with lunch. Amber dipped a long fry in ketchup and dotted the end of Lucas's nose. He smiled and moved to wipe it off, but Amber caught his hand, stopping him. She leaned forward and licked it off. Their friends laughed at the show, and Amber grinned, satisfied. I turned away, feeling hollow inside.

That night, I was spreading newspaper out on our portico when Amber pulled up in front of Lucas's house. She got out of her car wearing a skin-tight black costume and bounded up to Lucas's front door, adjusting a pair of cat ears perched on top of her head. I drew back behind one of our carved wood columns to watch surreptitiously. She knocked on the front door and waited. When Lucas answered, Amber looped her arms around his neck and kissed him casually. I drew back sharply, feeling a pit open up in the bottom of my stomach. Amber took Lucas by the hand and led him back to her car. Before they pulled away, I thought I saw Lucas glance in my direction.

"I've got the pumpkins." Royal emerged from my house, carrying three fat pumpkins. "Who's got the knives?"

"Here," Cassie replied, following him out of the house. "Oh, we need a bowl for the guts."

"There's one in the kitchen," I said, rising. "I'll get it." Cassie's eyes shifted to something over my shoulder. I turned. Derek was walking up the flagstone path to my house. He nodded a greeting to Royal and Cassie.

"Can I talk to you for a second?" Derek asked me. Dark circles marred the skin under his eyes, giving his face a drawn, sickly look. "It's important."

Royal's eyes narrowed to unfriendly slits. "I sincerely doubt that."

"It's okay," I said, standing. "I'll be right back." Royal's mouth dropped open in astonishment. Cassie handed him a carving knife, but her eyes were full of questions.

I followed Derek back to the sidewalk. We huddled together against the crisp autumn breeze. The sky was a blank gray slate that seemed to draw the color out of everything around us. Derek faced me.

"You don't look so good," I said.

Derek smiled humorlessly. "Didn't sleep so good." He was quiet for a moment. "You remember when we were kids and Scott Legant's gang whaled on me every day after school?"

"Of course I remember," I said. "It was because of me. You stood up to them when they tried to take my field trip money."

"Yeah. Pretty stupid of me."

"I thought it was pretty decent," I said. "You were a decent guy, briefly."

Derek shrugged. "I was weak. I went home with bloody noses four days in a row, and my parents never said a word about it." A deep bitterness filled his voice. "My dad didn't believe in coddling weakness. He expected us to take care of our own problems. When I finally went to him for help, he says, 'In this life, you're a predator or you're prey. You decide which it's going to be.' So I decided. And it's been like living someone else's life ever since." He kicked at a clump of brown grass. "I know I've been an ass to you these last couple of years. You guys, trying to help with this—" He stopped, frustrated, and shoved his hands into the pockets of his pants. "I'm not good at this stuff, but... For real. I appreciate it." He looked up, meeting my eyes. "And I'm really sorry."

I didn't know how to react. I'd never seen him like this before. He looked sincere. I nodded, and Derek gave me a half-hearted smile.

"So. Do you think I'm screwed or what?"

"I don't know," I said. He deserved the truth.

Before Derek turned back to the clump of grass at his feet, I saw a flash of something in his eyes. I realized he was terrified.

"Okay, cool. I'll just..." He shrugged again. "Wait and see."

A patch of air seemed to darken over Derek's shoulder. It took a minute for me to realize what I was seeing. A thin ribbon of shadow coalesced in the air, like a line of ink spilled into water. The twisting blackness edged toward Derek, curled around his face. It stroked his cheek, then seemed to dissipate. Derek did not react to the touch. I stared.

"What is it?" Derek asked. "You look like you just saw a ghost."

"Nothing," I stammered. "I should get back. They're waiting for me."

Derek gave me a strange look, then shrugged. "Happy Halloween," he said, and walked down the street.

I turned away from Derek and pulled my cell phone out of my pocket, dialing Dad. He was with Hale tonight. Guard business.

He picked up on the second ring. "Braedyn? What's wrong?" I described what I'd just seen. Dad listened silently. When I finished, I heard him take a deep breath. "Okay."

"What do you mean okay? What was that thing?"

"The Lilitu that attacked Derek is trying to keep their connection alive. She's making sure he doesn't forget about her."

"He didn't even react," I said.

"He couldn't see it," Dad said. "Most humans can't."

A jolt of panic speared through my stomach. "So my being able to see it, this is a Lilitu thing?"

"Stay calm. Remember, we knew this was going to happen."

I hugged myself tightly, trying to calm down. "What do I do now?"

"Go about your evening. Have fun with your friends. I'll talk to Hale." He hung up.

I heard the shrill laughter of a group of elementary school kids and glanced up. Trick-or-treaters darted along the sidewalks, chaperoned by smiling parents. Kids walked past me, talking and laughing.

"Braedyn," Cassie called. "It's getting dark!"

"Coming." I shuddered, and this time it wasn't because of the cold October air. There must have been 100 people walking the street, admiring costumes, collecting candy. Not one of them sensed a demon in their midst.

The following Monday in gym class, Ms. Davies announced we'd be starting volleyball.

"I'm going to split the class into four teams of four," she said. "You'll each play a three-game set."

"I call Cassie and Braedyn," Royal said.

"Not so fast." Ms. Davies held up a sheet of paper. Instead of letting us pick teams, Ms. Davies had randomly assigned them. She read off the teams. As more and more names were called, I felt a growing sense of unease. Royal and Cassie were sent to the other side of the gym to face off on opposite teams. And Lucas and I were assigned to the same team on this side of the gym.

I could barely look at him as we took our positions. I'd never been a fan of volleyball, but I threw myself into the game, trying to focus on anything but Lucas. He seemed to be trying just as hard to ignore me. Our team won the first game of the set and lost the second. As we started the third game, I noticed the other half of the class gathering; they must have finished their set already.

It was an intense match. After 15 minutes, we were up one point, with one point left to win.

"Bring it home!" Royal shouted. "The sooner you end this, the sooner we can go and change." The class laughed, but a few other students started cheering. Ms. Davies watched from the sidelines, smiling at the enthusiasm.

Lucas and I stood at the net while the other team served. One of our teammates bumped the serve forward to Lucas. He crouched, setting the ball perfectly. Without thinking, I leapt up and spiked the ball over the net decisively. Even Ms. Davies looked shocked.

The class erupted in sound. Lucas threw his arms around me. I laughed, startled. He pulled back quickly, but his smile was intoxicating.

"You're getting stronger," he said. "Must be all that practice with Hale."

"At least it's good for something," I replied. His grin deepened. For a breathless moment, I let myself look into his eyes. There were so many questions I wanted answers to, so many things I wanted to say. Lucas watched me, waiting, as though he could sense me summoning the nerve to speak. I opened my mouth to say something, but at that moment the bell rang and I lost my nerve. Something like disappointment flickered through his eyes. Lucas nodded a goodbye and walked away, leaving me feeling chilled—like someone had just turned off the sun.

After school I stood at the edge of the parking lot, restless and sad. For a month I'd tried to stay away from Lucas, but that one touch was enough to undo all my self-discipline. I looked around for Royal or Cassie. But instead of seeing them I caught Lucas staring at me. Amber came up behind him and snaked her arms around his chest. I saw his shoulders tense. Amber's eyes cut toward me, glinting. I wasn't the only one who'd seen him staring. Amber took Lucas by the hand and pulled him into the parking lot. Lucas let her draw him away, but his face was troubled. At her car, Amber kissed him lightly on the cheek. Lucas barely reacted. Amber glanced back at me, suspicious, before slipping into the driver's seat. I watched them drive away and let out a long, frustrated sigh.

Cassie put a hand on my shoulder, startling me out of my stormy thoughts.

"Tomorrow will be better," she said.

"How?" My voice sounded rough, cold.

"It has to be," Cassie said. "It's your birthday." Her words left me breathless. My birthday. I'd completely forgotten.

Tomorrow I would be 16 years old.

7

My birthday dawned, unwelcome. I was startled out of a formless dream when Dad knocked sharply on my door.

"Up and at 'em, kiddo," he called. "We've got a date with the MVD. Don't want to keep them waiting."

I mumbled something in reply and tried to open my eyes. Waking was hard, like rising toward the day from a deep pool of dark sleep. By the time I threw the covers back and got out of bed I was well behind schedule. I ran the shower while undressing, then stepped into the warm cloud of steam with my eyes half-lidded. The shower wrapped me in sheets of hot water and I relaxed into the sensation, losing track of time.

"Braedyn," Dad called outside the bathroom door. "We need to leave in five."

I turned the water off, feeling a jolt of adrenaline. I quickly toweled off, headed to my room, and pulled a few things out of my closet. I dressed in record time, but as I fastened up my shirt, the fabric started straining against the buttons alarmingly. The shirt must have shrunk in the laundry. I wrestled it off and grabbed another one out of my closet, but found the same problem. I glanced at myself in the mirror, surprised. It wasn't the shirt.

"Honey?" Dad called outside my bedroom door.

"One second!"

"Okay. I'm going to pull the car out. Come down when you're ready."

"Yeah." I heard him leave. My heart hammered. I tried to convince myself it was just a growth spurt. I fished a white tank top out of my dresser and pulled it on, then buttoned my school shirt up to my sternum. I elbowed my way into the only Coronado Prep v-neck

71

sweater vest I owned and checked my reflection again.

The girl in the mirror could have been a stranger. She had long slender limbs, pale skin, deep blue eyes—and graceful, feminine curves. I stared, breathless. My hair, which had always seemed mousy to me, had developed a rich sheen overnight. I reached up to touch the dark waves. My reflection mimicked the motion with a fluid grace that was uncomfortably familiar. I looked away, unsettled.

A present sat on my dresser; a small square box wrapped in elegant silver paper. There was a tag on the box that read, *Happy Birthday, Braedyn. Love, Dad.* I stared at the signature for a long moment.

As I held the present in my hand, I heard Dad honk the horn out front. I felt like a wolf that had been raised by dogs. I'd grown up thinking I was human. Maybe I didn't look all that different from them, but they recognized there was something wild and dangerous about me. The Guard was here to control the threat I posed, one way or the other. I let the present drop out of my hand into the trashcan by my dresser. Numbly, I headed downstairs.

As I walked out the front door I froze, unprepared for what greeted me.

Dad's breathtakingly restored 1968 Pontiac Firebird sat on the driveway. It gleamed with a new coat of sky blue paint. He'd said he was getting it tuned up, not... this. The last time I'd seen the car, rust had been gaining ground over the sun-dulled black paint, making it look like a mottled orange-and-black bruiser of a car. This car looked sleek and retro and gorgeous.

"Care to drive?" Dad had been watching me from the porch bench. When I turned to face him, a strange expression flitted over his face— like a mixture of sadness and resignation. But whatever he was feeling, he brushed it aside and stood, holding out a set of car keys wrapped with a big red bow. I took the keys gingerly and walked to the car. Opening the door, I slid into the driver's seat. He'd even had the car reupholstered in a soft, pale gray fabric. Dad sat in the passenger seat and buckled his seat belt. "Whenever you're ready," he said.

I turned the key and the engine jumped to life, humming. I'd logged a bunch of hours in this car, taking practice drives with Dad all over the city. But none of the dozens of times I'd turned the key in the ignition felt quite like this. Now, it was my car. I shifted into reverse and gave it a little gas. The car glided out of the driveway and onto the road. When I depressed the clutch and tapped the gas pedal, the newly tuned engine roared in challenge.

"There's a sound that takes me back," Dad said.

I let up on the clutch, curious to see what the Firebird was capable of. The car shot forward and my hair whipped back in the sudden wind gusting through the open window. I battled a sudden urge to gun it out of town and just leave the whole crazy situation behind. Would the Guard come after me? Would they stay behind to try to help Derek? Dad threw a hand on the dashboard reflexively, bringing me back to my senses. I pulled my foot off the gas and the Firebird relaxed, coasting easily down the street.

"I'm changing, aren't I?" I asked. Dad glanced at me quickly. He didn't say anything.

He didn't have to. His silence answered the question for him.

45 minutes later I stood at a chipped Formica counter, watching while a middle-aged bald man checked the results of my written driver's test. Fluorescent lights thrummed overhead, putting my nerves on edge. Dad sat in the waiting area behind me, but I could feel his eyes on my back. Finally, the bald man looked up.

"Okay, Ms. Murphy," he said. "Written test, vision test, everything looks good. That just leaves the driving test. Ready to hit the road?"

I felt a flutter of nerves in my stomach but nodded. He picked up a set of car keys and gestured for me to follow him outside.

I'd thought there would be more to the test. After I adjusted the seat and the mirrors, I started the engine and pulled carefully out of the MVD parking lot. At the bald man's direction I drove around the block. I had to stop at one light. It was the shortest drive I'd ever made. I didn't even have to parallel park. I just pulled right back into the parking space I'd pulled out of.

Dad was waiting on the curb for our return. He walked over to us as I parked. The bald man gave me a smile and handed over a piece of paper.

"Excellent work, young lady. Passed with flying colors. Just hand this over when they take your photo for your new license. Drive safe and congratulations!"

"Thanks," I said. Dad opened the car door for me, eager for the verdict. "I passed," I told him.

"I'm so proud of you, honey," he said, squeezing my shoulder as I got out of the car.

I shrugged his hand off. "I've got to get my picture taken," I murmured. I was still thinking about the hurt look on his face as the MVD photographer snapped my driver's license photo.

I made my first solo drive to school after dropping Dad off at home. Pulling into the school parking lot, I found a spot and killed the engine. Students hung out on the quad, savoring their last few moments of free time before the school day started. I spotted Cassie and Royal near the administration building. Cassie saw me and waved. I got out of the car as they headed over.

Royal gave me a shrewd once-over. "Someone's been drinking her V-8."

Cassie eyed the Firebird, awed. "Is that your Dad's old car?" Over her shoulder, I saw Parker and a few other guys from the soccer team approaching. Derek trailed after them with this lost look, like a starving puppy desperate for a scrap of food.

"Yeah." I ducked back into the car to grab my book bag, hoping Parker would pass us by. No such luck. I heard him give a low wolf-whistle as they got a clear view of the Firebird.

"Damn," Parker said admiringly. "Get a load of..."

I stood up, book bag in hand, and Parker's voice trailed off strangely. Wind teased my hair across my face. I shook my head, meaning simply to flip my hair back over my shoulder. In that same moment, a new gust caught my hair, streaming it out behind me as if someone were running their fingers through the strands. Parker and his friends stared.

Parker's tone grew almost husky. "That."

Cassie was still admiring the Firebird. "Wow, Braedyn... Wow. Last time I saw that car it was—he must have spent a fortune to restore it!"

I closed the door, eyeing Parker and his friends uneasily, then turned my back on them. "Yeah. I figured I'd have to slum around in some rust bucket through college. Guess not."

74

Royal glanced at me. "Honey, when someone gives you a car for your birthday, you get excited. When someone gives you a freshly-painted classic car, you flip the freak out." I heard the disapproval in his voice and winced.

"I—I know. Things have been..." I decided sticking close to the truth would be easiest. "I'm having some trouble with my Dad."

"Does that mean he said no to a party at the Raven?" Cassie looked at me, disappointed. She and Royal had been pestering me to get an answer from Dad for weeks. I'd kept telling them he hadn't made his mind up yet, but the truth was, I'd been so distracted lately I hadn't pressed him. Considering everything else that was going on, a birthday party was pretty low on my list of things to worry about.

But as I looked at Cassie, I felt a surge of rebellion. If my old life was about to end, this might be my last chance to have a normal birthday. I wanted to celebrate it with my friends.

I smiled at Cassie and lied. "He's totally up for it. We're on."

"Um, next time lead with that," Royal said, his whole face lighting up. "We have to get the word out. Party at the Raven tonight!"

"I hear that place is the bomb," Parker said. I turned around. Parker and his friends were still standing there, admiring my car. Cassie finally noticed him, blushing.

"Hi, Parker," Cassie said shyly.

Parker ran a finger over the hood of my car. His ice-blue eyes mirrored the Firebird's new paint job. "That's a lot of car for a girl." Parker didn't even acknowledge Cassie. His eyes were glued to me. "I could teach you how to handle it, if you like." Cassie looked at me quickly, stung.

I gave Parker a chilly smile. "I'm sure you have a lot of practice *handling it*, Parker," I said. "But I don't need your help." Royal snorted a surprised laugh. I didn't wait around for Parker's response. "Come on," I said to Royal and Cassie. "I want to get something to eat before first bell." I looped my arm around Cassie and led her away. Royal followed us, frowning. Like me, he didn't understand Cassie's thing for Parker. Neither of us wanted to see her get hurt.

I shot a quick look back at Parker. His blue-black hair stood out in sharp contrast against the morning sky. Without taking his eyes off me, Parker elbowed one of his friends. He dropped his voice, but I could have sworn I heard him ask, "You ever been to the Raven?"

"What are you going to wear tonight?" Cassie asked me that day at lunch, handing over the serving bowl of asparagus. I spooned a generous portion onto my plate.

"Well," I said, thinking out loud. "I've got some new jeans that would look great with—"

Royal didn't let me finish. "No jeans. Bad Braedyn."

"What about that black dress you wore to Winter Ball last year?" Cassie asked.

"Isn't that kind of formal for a club?" I asked.

"You have to dress up," Cassie said.

"I've got it," Royal said, leaning forward. His eyes gleamed. "Break out the ultra-swanky sky-blue dress I got you at the Plaza last summer for your birthday. You still haven't worn it outside your house."

I set down the bread roll I was buttering. "You're kidding, right?"

"It'll match your new ride." He said this like it was the only logical thing to do.

"I distinctly remember telling you not to buy that dress," I said, pointing my butter knife at Royal. "Cassie, you were there."

"It is kind of spectacular," Cassie said. "I think I'm with Royal on this one."

"Judas." I finished buttering my roll.

"Let's make this easy." Royal pulled a quarter out of his pocket. "Heads, you walk on the wild side and repay my birthday generosity by wearing the sky-blue gorgeousness. Tails, you play it safe and wear whatever your little heart desires. Just to be clear, that does not include jeans. Deal?"

I glanced from Royal to Cassie. Cassie clasped her hands together, in eager anticipation. I sighed. "Fine. Deal."

Royal flipped the quarter up. It glinted in the sunlight streaming into the dining hall. Royal deftly plucked it out of the air and slapped it onto the back of his hand.

"And fate has decreed..." he lifted his hand revealing the quarter. Heads.

"Score!" said Cassie.

"Well, well, well." Royal looked extremely satisfied.

"Um, excuse me?" I almost didn't recognize Amber's voice. It was pitched an octave higher than her normal register. I turned to find her glaring, arms crossed, behind my table. Ally and Missy stood with her. "What the hell do you think you're doing?"

"Eating lunch," I said. Out of the corner of my eye I could see Cassie and Royal trading a look.

"Tonight is Desert Fest," Amber said. Behind her, Ally nodded grimly.

"So?"

"So? You're throwing a party at the Raven!" Amber's shriek travelled across the dining hall. More than a few heads turned to see what was going on. Her iron-straight blond hair quivered with rage.

I stared at her in astonishment. "How do you know that?"

Amber's eyes darted to her lunch table. Parker and his friends were watching us with interest. Question answered. And then I noticed Lucas. Our eyes connected, and he didn't turn away. A slow warmth spread through my chest— until Amber stepped in front of me, breaking our eye contact.

Amber's eyes were narrow slits. "Postpone. Ally and I have been planning this for two months."

"Today is my birthday," I said, smiling coldly. "I'm not postponing my party because it's inconvenient for you."

"I hope you're not relying on this glam-tramp makeover to win friends and influence people," Amber hissed. "If you force people to choose between us, you'll be disappointed."

I pushed my chair back from the table so abruptly that Amber took an involuntary step back. I stood, facing her.

"Then let's give them the choice and see." I turned my back on Amber and stepped onto the middle of our dining table. Royal and Cassie reacted, jerking back, startled. I turned to face the crowded dining hall. A sea of faces looked up and I flashed my brightest smile, feeling a swell of confidence. It was a rush, standing before the expectant crowd. I had everyone's undivided attention, and I only needed it for a few seconds.

"Hey, party at the Raven tonight," I shouted. "It's my birthday and everyone's invited!" I wasn't prepared for the resulting cheer. When I looked back at Amber, her lips were pressed into a thin line of fury. Behind her, I saw Headmaster Fiedler making a beeline for my table.

Oops. The noise died down to a dull roar as people turned away, talking excitedly with their friends.

"Ms. Murphy," Fiedler said, arriving beside the table. "Down."

I moved for my chair, but someone had pushed it in, leaving me nothing to step down on. Amber watched from a few feet away, her eyes smoldering with glee. Seeing my predicament, Fiedler pulled the chair out for me. He gave me his hand to steady myself as I climbed down.

"Sorry," I said. "I got a little carried away." When he didn't answer, I looked at his face. Fiedler was giving me a strange look. He cleared his throat and released my hand.

"Well. Just don't stand on any more tables and I think we can let this slide." Fiedler straightened his tie. "Happy birthday." He walked out of the dining hall.

Amber stared at me, open-mouthed.

"That was... forward," Royal said. His expression was guarded, but I detected uneasiness in his eyes.

I glanced back at Amber. Her astonishment had been replaced by a look of unsettling calculation.

At the end of the day, Cassie walked me to my car. It felt a little strange, parting ways with her in the parking lot instead of getting a ride home with her and Royal. The Firebird gleamed in the afternoon sun.

"Amber is on the warpath," Royal said, joining us. "You should have heard her in Geometry. She's threatening to shun anyone who comes to the Raven tonight."

Cassie looked worried. "Maybe I should get some party favors or something."

"Don't waste the money," I said. "I hate to admit it, but Amber's right. No one's going to show up to a party for a girl they don't even know when they could be getting smashed in the middle of nowhere with a bunch of cheerleaders."

Royal didn't look convinced, but Cassie smiled, relaxing a little. "More dance floor for the rest of us."

"Looks like you have another admirer," Royal said. I looked up.

Greg Pantelis, star of the swim team, was hovering at the edge of the parking lot. He'd never looked in my direction before, but when he caught my eye he walked over to us.

"I hear the Firebird belongs to you," he said. "Nice ride." Greg's eyes slid over my face. Out of the corner of my eye, I noticed Amber and Ally approaching, engrossed in conversation. They hadn't seen me yet. "Is anyone taking you to the party tonight?" Greg asked.

"I'm not going to Desert Fest," I said, distracted.

Greg laughed. "I mean your party."

Amber grabbed Ally's arm, stopping both of them in their tracks. She turned to look at Greg and me, eyes wide with disbelief.

Greg's words finally sunk in. "What?" I asked. Beside me, Royal and Cassie watched us.

"Your party," he repeated. "At the Raven. Do you have a date?"

I could sense Amber hanging on his words. It wasn't much of a secret that she'd been angling for Greg before she and Derek started dating. If I wanted to stick it to Amber, I wouldn't find a better opportunity than this. I beamed up at Greg, playing naive for Amber's benefit. "No. Why do you ask?"

Greg, solely focused on me, had no idea Amber was listening to every word he said. "You're... different than the other girls at school. There's something special about you." I could see Amber stiffening in my peripheral vision. This was the first time in our lives that I had the upper hand and Amber was the one on the outside looking in. I'll admit, I relished the turnabout.

I stepped closer to Greg, putting a hand lightly on his chest. "That's really sweet," I breathed. The touch affected Greg more than I anticipated. He lowered his head toward me and I felt my breath catching in my throat. With a tingling sensation, I knew he would kiss me with the slightest provocation. Aware of Amber standing nearby, devouring us with her eyes, I tipped my head up and let my lashes flutter closed. In answer, Greg cupped the back of my head with one warm hand. He pulled me slightly forward and kissed me.

"Braedyn," Cassie said. I heard something in her voice. Shock, maybe.

Greg's lips were soft and warm. It was pleasant enough... but something was missing. When Lucas had held me in his basement— when my eyes had fluttered shut of their own volition—I'd felt a longing so intense it had left me breathless. As soon as I thought of Lucas, I was overwhelmed with a sort of sick emptiness. I pulled away, breaking the kiss, flustered. I saw confusion fill Greg's face.

"Is something wrong?" he asked.

"I— It's my fault," I whispered. "I'm sorry." I glanced away from Greg and saw Lucas staring at us from across the quad. His face was drawn, pale. Amber was already moving to greet him. She reached him quickly, but Lucas didn't seem aware of her existence. He didn't look away when I met his stare. Shame flooded through me and I turned away from Lucas. "I—I need to go home."

"So, about tonight?" Greg asked.

"She's coming with us," Royal said, ending the conversation.

Greg looked from Royal to me, bewildered. "Well," he said. "Maybe I'll see you there."

I nodded, but I couldn't meet his eyes. Greg left, and Cassie and Royal turned on me.

"I didn't even know you liked Greg," Cassie said in a small voice.

"I don't," I answered miserably.

"So what the hell was that?" Royal asked.

"I don't know," I moaned, feeling sick. "How much did Lucas see?"

"Enough," Royal answered. "All the juicy bits, for sure."

"You do like Lucas," Cassie said. It sounded like an accusation, and I didn't deny it. "I don't understand. Why don't you tell him that? Can't you see he likes you, too?"

"You're right," I said glumly. "You don't understand."

Royal frowned. "As long as we're making a list of things we don't understand, how about adding the part where you invited the whole school to your party to piss Amber off."

"Yeah," Cassie added, hurt. "I thought this was going to be our special thing."

"Does this mean you guys aren't coming?" I asked in a small voice. "It won't be any fun if you aren't there."

"As if we don't know that," Royal scoffed. But after a moment, he softened. "Of course we're coming. It's your big day."

Cassie watched Amber and Lucas walking across the parking lot, twirling loops of long black hair between her fingers. "So what's the plan?" she asked. "Do you want to get ready together? I could bring my stuff over to your place after dinner." She glanced at Royal. "If you can give me a ride."

"At your service," Royal said.

"Dad's taking me out for dinner," I lied quickly. "I don't know when I'll be back. It might just be easier if we all meet at the club at nine." I was going to have to sneak out of my house to go to this party. That wouldn't be possible if Cassie and Royal showed up at my doorstep.

Cassie shrugged. "Okay."

Royal's eyes narrowed suspiciously. "If this means you're trying to get out of wearing—"

I cut him off. "No," I said. "A deal's a deal."

Royal looked slightly mollified. "You know, a little mascara might bring out those eyes."

I drove home, pulling up as the sun dipped low on the horizon. The days were getting shorter and shorter as we edged closer to the longest night of the year—winter solstice. I pushed the thought out of my head, doggedly determined to enjoy my birthday if it killed me.

When I got to the house the driveway was empty. Dad was out again. I parked my car on the street leaving the driveway clear for Dad's truck. I wouldn't be sneaking out anywhere if he boxed me in. I locked my car and headed into the house.

I went up to my room and tossed my book bag on my bed. I had about four hours before I had to start getting ready for the party, so I sat down to outline my term paper for English. By the time I had finished the first draft of my outline, it was a little after eight o'clock. Dad still wasn't back. He must have gotten the late shift watching Derek. I decided to start getting ready for the party.

I flipped my closet light on and thumbed through hangers until I found the sky-blue dress. I pulled it out, eyeing it nervously. It was the most daring dress I owned. The hem fell six inches above the knee and the back plunged open to the waist. I slipped it over my head and zipped it up at the side. It fit perfectly, fluttering prettily with the slightest movement. I had a pair of delicate silver heels with tiny rhinestones across the straps. They had just peeked out beneath the long black dress I'd worn to last year's Winter Ball. Tonight they'd be on full display.

I glanced at myself in the mirror. The dress was surprisingly flattering. I played with my hair for a few minutes, but it looked best down. I was just starting on my makeup when I heard the front door open downstairs. I felt a rush of panic and hurried to my bedroom door to lock it. Dad's footsteps sounded on the stairs. When he reached the second floor, he knocked on my bedroom door.

"Braedyn?" Dad called softly through the door. "I'm sorry it's so late, but I thought we could celebrate. I've got a cake here with your name on it. Literally. 'Braedyn' in bright red frosting. Very bold."

"I'm not hungry," I said.

"Can I come in?" he asked. "I'm dripping wax all over this delicious cream-cheese frosting. I know you're angry with me, but do you really want to take it out on the cake? It's red velvet." I kicked off my shoes and pulled my bathrobe over the dress, belting it tightly. I opened the door a crack.

Dad held a small, lushly frosted red velvet cake on a plate. 16 candles flickered happily, reflecting in Dad's warm brown eyes. "Happy birthday, sweetheart."

I blew the candles out and the hallway darkened.

"Still not hungry," I said.

"I know you must be overwhelmed," he said gently.

"That's a bit of an understatement. I barely recognize myself in the mirror. And now, all these people who barely even noticed me before..." I shook my head, remembering Greg with another wash of shame.

"I wouldn't blame you if you're mad at me."

"You could have prepared me," I said, letting some of the tension I'd been carrying around since morning into my voice.

"I know," Dad sighed. "But I didn't know what to—I didn't want you to feel any different from the other kids."

"Turns out, I'm pretty different."

"You're the same girl you've always been," Dad said firmly. "You're smart. You have a good head on your shoulders. None of that has changed." I struggled to keep my composure. I wanted to stay mad at him. It felt like I needed that anger to keep me grounded. But it was hard when he was standing there, saying all the right things, looking so worried.

"Can we do this tomorrow?" I asked. "I'm tired."

"Sure," Dad sighed. He lifted the cake with a half-hearted smile. "Red Velvet and I will be waiting for you downstairs if you change your mind."

I smiled faintly and closed the door. I could hear him moving back down the hall. After a moment, I slipped the robe off and stepped back into my shoes. I looked at the clock. 8:47 P.M.. If I didn't get out of here soon, I was going to be late to my own party.

I shoved a lip-gloss into my purse, slipped into a coat, and put my hand on the doorknob. But then I hesitated. Trying to sneak past Dad downstairs was a recipe for disaster. I walked to my bedroom window instead. It squeaked as I slid it open. I looked down and felt my stomach twinge. I edged one leg out of the window and let my foot find the sturdy trellis that supported a climbing rose. The trellis felt solid under my hands and feet. I climbed down it like a ladder, picking my way carefully around the twisting vines. Thorns pulled at my coat but I managed to make it to the ground mostly unscathed. I made a quiet dash to the Firebird.

I tossed my coat behind the driver's seat and got into the car, slipping my key into the ignition. Before I turned it on, someone knocked on my window. I felt my heart leap into my throat and turned, expecting to find Dad glaring at me furiously. Instead, I saw Lucas, wearing Eric's black leather jacket over shirt and jeans.

I rolled down my window. "Lucas?"

"Can I get a ride to the club?" At my blank stare, Lucas's smile faltered. "Cassie invited me to your birthday party. I thought that meant you wanted me there."

I glanced at my house feeling more and more exposed. Dad could look out the window and see us at any moment. "Get in." Lucas shrugged out of his jacket as he walked to the passenger side. He tossed the jacket into the back seat beside mine and slid into the car. I turned the key and hit the gas as he closed the door. Lucas hurried to buckle his seat belt as we flew down the road.

"Whoa," he said. "I'm pretty sure they're not going to cut the cake without you."

I gave him a cool look. "Where's Amber?"

"She doesn't own me," Lucas said.

"Does she know that?"

Lucas laughed ruefully. "Not so much. She likes to think she can bend the world to her will." After a moment, he shrugged. "She thinks she wants me, but she doesn't. Not really."

"What makes you so confident?"

Lucas shrugged. "Amber wants a guy that's going to drop everything for her. That's not me."

His words soothed my agitation like a balm. The tension in my shoulders eased. "What about you?" I asked. "What do you want?"

"Isn't it obvious?" he asked, looking straight at me. I had to force myself to keep my eyes on the road. My head felt dangerously light. After a moment, Lucas looked at his hands, folded in his lap. "So Cassie... she made up that invitation, didn't she? You don't actually want me at this party."

I gripped the wheel so hard my hands started to ache. I knew what I should say. I should tell him nothing had changed, I still wanted him to stay away. But I couldn't make myself say the words.

"Exactly how much trouble did I get you into?" he asked, pained. "Sounds like you've got it even worse than I do."

"Why?" I asked, glancing at him. "How much trouble are you in?"

"I'm pretty much under house arrest. They let me out for school, and that's it."

"And Halloween," I corrected. I couldn't keep the tinge of jealousy out of my voice.

Lucas sighed. "Yeah." He leaned his head back against the seat. "Gretchen keeps trying to encourage this thing with Amber. Which is pretty funny, considering Amber's the kind of girl Gretchen used to eat for breakfast." He shrugged. "What can I say? It was nice to have a break from the house projects. I've already plastered and painted the walls, fixed the front steps, replaced the back porch, and re-caulked the windows. I'm even learning to grout."

"Sounds like you're in pretty hot water," I said.

"I broke one of the cardinal rules," Lucas said glumly. "No outsiders in the armory. Period. I'm in the doghouse until Hale decides I've paid for my crimes and gives me back my social life."

"So why are you in my car?"

Lucas gave me an amused smile. "Well, Braedyn, I noticed you climbing out the window and decided to follow your lead. I'm guessing if Murphy knew you were having a birthday party, he'd have let you walk through the front door."

I smiled back, caught. "Fair enough."

"You look amazing, by the way," he said.

"Thanks," I murmured, blushing.

"That's what I don't get about you," Lucas said softly. "You ask me to stay away from you, then get mad when I hang out with other girls. You tell me you don't want to be friends, then look totally crushed when I leave you alone after a game of volleyball." Lucas turned to study me in the light of my dashboard. "And if I didn't know better," he said. "I'd think you blushing at my compliments actually meant something." He looked out the window. "I wouldn't have come if I'd known you didn't want me here," he murmured. "It's too hard to be around you anyway."

My nose stung as an onslaught of emotion rolled over me. I bit my lip, fighting off tears. If I started crying now I would die from shame. The Raven came into view and I drove into the crowded parking lot, gliding into the first spot I could find and killed the engine. We sat for a moment in the dark silence of the car.

"I'm sorry," I said hoarsely.

"Why? You didn't do anything wrong. It's not like you made me feel this way. And it's not like you can help it if you don't feel the same." Lucas unlatched his seatbelt and reached for the door handle. Before he opened it I caught his hand. Lucas looked at me, startled.

"What?" I said, battling the hope that surged in my chest. "What do you mean?"

"You want me to say it again? Because it feels kind of crappy to tell someone you like them and..." He studied my face, mystified. "Braedyn? Are you crying?"

"I like you," I whispered. "I *like* you like you."

The tension in Lucas's face evaporated. Without another word he slid toward me, slipped his arms around me, and drew me forward into a kiss. Our lips met and the jolt of electricity I felt in my stomach dwarfed every kiss I'd imagined us having. My willpower broke, swept away by the force of my feelings. For one moment, nothing was real beyond this kiss. After a long moment, Lucas pulled back to look into my eyes.

When he spoke, his voice was husky with emotion. "You have no idea how badly I've wanted to hear you say that." I lifted a trembling hand to his face. His eyes closed, savoring the touch.

"What are we going to do?" I asked. "Gretchen... my dad...?" Lucas caught my hand and kissed my fingers. I took a deep breath, dizzy. "I want to be with you," I said. "I want to be with you more than anything."

"We can deal with Gretchen and your dad tomorrow," Lucas said. "Let's just enjoy tonight."

"That sounds good." I leaned forward shyly. "Do we have to go in?"

Lucas chuckled. "I'm good with staying right here," he said. "But Cassie and Royal—?"

"Right." Reluctantly, we got out of the car. Lucas offered his hand and I took it, feeling his fingers close around mine warmly. We turned to the club. That's when I noticed the crowd.

"Of course," I sighed, frustrated. "The one night people decide to mob this place would have to be my birthday." Lucas gave me a strange look but didn't say anything. "Keep an eye out for Royal and Cassie. Maybe we can still get a table."

We reached the edge of the crowd. I started to recognize faces from Coronado Prep.

"There she is!" someone shouted. An excited thrill ran through the crowd. People stepped aside, forming a path to the club. I clung to Lucas, startled.

"Hey, you invited them," he said with a small smile.

"But...? There's no way all these people are here for my party?"

Missy waved from the crowd. "Oh my gosh, Braedyn, I love your dress!"

"Thanks," I said with a sinking sensation. If Missy was here, what had happened to Desert Fest?

A breeze kicked up, swirling around me. I felt my dress fluttering around my legs, acutely aware of the eyes of the watching crowd. "Come on," I whispered. "Royal and Cassie are probably waiting inside." We made our way to the front door and the crowd closed up behind us. By the time we reached the entrance, we were in the heart of a noisy mob.

Lucas felt my hand trembling. He gave it a comforting squeeze and leaned close. "Don't worry," he said. "I've got your back."

Together, we walked into the club.

8

"Holy wow," Lucas breathed out. That summed up my thoughts exactly.

We came to a dead stop inside the club's entrance. Ripples of silvery material covered the tables while strands of tiny lights twinkled across the ceiling. Elegant bouquets of white roses adorned the tables. Mingled with the velvety petals were gleaming crystalline icicles. More crystals lay scattered across the tabletops, sparkling like loose diamonds. Ice statues stood guard around the room, lit dramatically in pillars of white light, while cool blue lights shifted on the dance floor. The effect was devastating. The place was packed. I felt like we'd crashed a party for an A-list celebutante.

Half the soccer team lounged by one of the tables. Parker noticed me walking in. "Yo, the Birthday Girl!" he said, a wide grin splitting his face.

"Happy Birthday," someone said to my right. I turned and saw a perky woman in her twenties holding a delicate tiara in her hands. She slipped the tiara onto my head and stepped back, admiring her handiwork. "Perfect." She turned me to face the assembled crowd and a cheer went up. I wanted to shrink into the floor. A new song pumped into the club and people started dancing.

"Who are you?" I asked, turning to the perky woman.

"I'm Rachel, the party planner," she said, beaming. "Your friends said this was a last-minute surprise, so since we couldn't talk to you about it, we decided to go with 'Ice' as a theme. I love a double-entendre. Enjoy."

Lucas guided me into the club and let out a low whistle. "I guessed Royal was loaded, but this is insane. You have some devoted friends."

"There's no way I'll ever be able to make this up to him," I said, uncomfortable. I looked around for Royal or Cassie but couldn't see them anywhere. As we made our way through the packed club, random people kept calling my name. We came to a stop beside a table holding a massive, silver fountain. Soda poured from one tier to the next in a shimmering curtain. This table also held the largest of the ice sculptures: a beautiful young woman in a traditional Japanese kimono, holding two slender swords.

I grabbed Lucas's arm, stunned. "I think that's Tomoe Gozen," I breathed.

"Which means—?"

"She was a samurai from the twelfth century," I explained. Lucas gave the statue a second glance, interested.

Parker slid up next to me. "Someone said you loved that stuff. We told Rachel and she had this carved for you."

"Why?"

Parker smiled with his signature confidence. "We wanted to do something memorable for your birthday."

I looked around with a growing sense of dread. The honey-blond demon in Old Town had mesmerized tables full of suits. Lucas called it enthralling. Everywhere I looked, I saw boys smiling in my direction.

"It's happening," I whispered with a rush of fear.

"What was that?" Lucas asked, leaning closer.

A slow song filled the club and Parker took a step toward me, trying to edge Lucas to one side. "How about a dance?" Parker asked, giving me a smile.

"Took the words right out of my mouth," Lucas said. Parker seemed to see Lucas for the first time. He frowned as Lucas offered me his hand. I let Lucas guide me onto the dance floor. "I kind of hate that guy," he murmured. "Although I guess I should feel bad for him."

"Why's that?"

"I know what it feels like to want someone who doesn't want you back," Lucas said simply. The dance floor was dimly lit and warm in the press of bodies. Lucas held me close. I let go of my worries, leaning into him, resting my head on his shoulder. His hands curled tighter around me. There was something lovely and anonymous about the darkness of the dance floor. The slow song came to an end far too soon, replaced by another throbbing dance song. As the floor flooded with eager dancers, I pulled Lucas to one side.

"I should find Royal and Cassie," I said.

"Sure. I'll get us something to drink." Lucas turned away and started pushing through the crowd toward the bar.

As I turned to search the crowd, Parker found me. "Perfect timing. This song was my request." He offered me his hand, clearly hoping to lead me back to the dance floor.

"Actually," I said. "I'm kind of here with someone, Parker."

"One dance isn't exactly cheating." Parker took my hand.

"No, thanks," I said firmly. "But I bet Cassie would love to dance. She's got to be around here somewhere. You should find her."

"I didn't arrange all this for Cassie." Parker wouldn't let my hand go. "Come on. One dance, then we'll call it even."

"Even?" I said, irritated. "I didn't ask you to do this."

"Didn't you?" He smiled, as if catching me in a lie. "You made sure we heard the details of your party, then practically challenged me with that look this morning."

I stared at him, dumbstruck. "What?"

"This morning," he repeated, getting impatient. "By your car."

"Parker," I said, wrenching my hand away from him. "I think your imagination is playing tricks on you."

Parker's eyes narrowed. He glanced at his friends, watching curiously at the table behind us, then turned back to me, suddenly cold. "If I'd known what a tease you were I never would have wasted good money on you."

"Forget what I said," I spat. "Cassie's way too good for you."

Parker looked like he wanted to say something else but I pushed away from him into the crowd. I noticed someone moving through the dancers out of the corner of my eye. I turned to see who it was and my stomach turned to ice.

A smoky shadow swirled lazily around a sensual brunette. I'd never seen her before, I was sure of it; she didn't have the kind of face you'd forget. She danced riotously in the center of the room, throwing her head back with wild abandon. I blinked, staring. The shadows ringing her weren't as formless as I'd first thought. They were smoky wings, draped like a cape around her shoulders, hard to make out in the darkness.

"No," I breathed. I suddenly knew what I was looking at. No one else was reacting to the wings, because no one else could see them.

The Lilitu smiled seductively at her dance partner and turned in his arms. He led her around the dance floor and I caught sight of his face. It was Greg. The demon gave her smoky wings a little snap. They shook off a dark mist and Greg unknowingly breathed it in. He shook his head and stumbled, grinning at his slip like an intoxicated idiot. The Lilitu leaned close to whisper something into Greg's ear and his smile deepened. She took Greg's hand and started to lead him off the dance floor. Dancers moved out of their way without acknowledging them at all.

I was too frozen by fear to move. Greg had no idea what kind of danger he was in. I needed Lucas. He would know what to do. I turned to look for him and came face-to-face with Amber.

"Pretty pleased with yourself?" Amber asked, her lips pulling back in a sneer. "Fair warning. I'm not letting Lucas go without a fight."

I scanned the room over her shoulder, too desperate to take her bait. I couldn't see Lucas anywhere.

"You wrecked Desert Fest," Amber growled. "You owe me!"

I pulled the tiara off my head and shoved it into her hands. "Here," I said. "Keep it." I pushed past her into the crowd.

A few moments later I spotted Lucas, moving toward me with two blue drinks in hand. We met in the crowd and he offered a glass to me.

"Better drink this fast," he said. "Look." I followed Lucas's gaze and spotted Derek moving through the crowd as if he was searching for something. "If one of the Guard followed him here, it's going to be a short party for us."

"We're in trouble," I said. "I saw a Lilitu on the dance floor. With Greg."

Lucas stared at me, suddenly serious. "How do you know she was a Lilitu?"

"I *saw* her," I repeated. He read the full depth of my meaning in my eyes.

"You're a spotter?" Lucas set his drink down, took my hand, and wove us through the crowd toward Derek. Derek looked up as we cornered him near the club's entrance. Lucas pushed him back against a pillar. "You shouldn't have left your house, man." Derek looked foggy, like he was half-asleep. Lucas grabbed his face and looked into his eyes. Derek's pupils were so large the irises looked almost completely black. Lucas glanced at me sharply. He pulled his cell phone out of his pocket and dialed.

"What is it?" I asked, seeing Lucas's fear.

"She's drawing him to her," he said. "I think she plans to attack." Lucas bent his head as someone answered his call. He had to shout into the phone. "Gretchen, it's me. I'm at the Raven club with Derek. There's a Lilitu here." Lucas met my eyes grimly. "Because Braedyn can see it." His eyes tightened slightly. "Yeah, I know what you said. You can skin me later. Get down here. This place is packed." Lucas hung up, urgent. "We have to get him out of here."

I glanced around the club, full of laughing, dancing people. They were completely unaware of the danger in their midst. "What about everyone else? What about Greg?"

"Derek is vulnerable," Lucas said, frowning. He didn't like this any more than I did. "He's one mistake away from becoming a Thrall. He has to be our priority. Derek, you're going to have to come with—" But when we turned back to the pillar, Derek was gone. "Damn!" Lucas scanned the room. Spotting Derek in the heaving crowd wasn't going to be easy. "Can you see the Lilitu?"

I looked back at the dance floor. I couldn't spot any trace of the smoky shadow I'd seen before. "No."

"Okay," Lucas said, tense but determined. "I'll check the back, you take the dance floor." I nodded and Lucas slipped into the crowd, headed for the back hallway.

I moved toward the dance floor, feeling useless. Someone screamed behind me and I turned—but it was just a girl, laughing as her boyfriend spun her in his arms. On edge, I moved forward without looking where I was going. I crashed into someone and turned to apologize. The words died on my lips.

Two Lilitu stood before me, regarding me with eyes like deep pools. The first had short red hair, cut in an elegant bob. She turned, deferring to the second.

This Lilitu had long blond hair so pale it was almost white. Her limbs were a study in grace, from the perfect curve of her shoulder down to each immaculately manicured fingernail. She held my gaze with mesmerizing power, but underneath her beauty she looked... alien. She stared into my face and tilted her head to one side.

"Welcome, little sister," she said. Her voice rang with a metallic edge. It seemed to mute the noise around us. Wings of shadow rose up behind her, unfurling majestically. I jerked back as a swell of terror rose in me. I'd never been this close to something so clearly other.

The redhead studied me impersonally. "This one?" Her lilting voice sounded puzzled. "She's so... new."

As I stared at the Lilitu, I suddenly had an odd sensation that their beautiful features hovered over something deeper, like the reflection of the sky on water. As I made this realization, I was able to see beneath the surface beauty. Under their human faces, cold white skin stretched over angular bones. Inky lips parted to reveal pointed gray teeth. And their eyes... I let out a frightened breath. Their eyes were black, unfeeling, like the eyes of a shark. The eyes of a predator.

The white-blond Lilitu raised one of her hands. I saw with a shudder that hovering under the illusion of human fingers, her fingers ended in bony, pitch-black claws. The inky color stained her fingers, but faded to a bone white by her wrist. She brushed the tip of one dark finger against my forehead. I jerked back, repulsed. A chill lingered where she'd touched me.

The redhead glanced at her, waiting. The white-blond Lilitu looked almost disappointed.

"What..." My throat was dry. I swallowed. "What do you want?"

"She is not ready," The white-blond Lilitu said. She turned back to the dance floor and melted into the crowd. The redhead followed, shooting me one last curious frown before they disappeared in the press of bodies.

My heart beat wildly in my chest for a long moment before I could summon the courage to flee. I backed out of the crowd and pressed against the back wall.

"Hey." I heard Royal's voice and turned. He looked me over, irritated. "We've been stuck outside for half an hour. You walked right past us on your way in. Didn't you hear us?" Royal's hair was perfectly tousled, as always. He looked amazing in a fitted black shirt with thin threads of silver running through it.

Still reeling from my encounter, I only half-understood what he was saying. "What?"

Cassie was taking the club in. Her eyes gleamed with excitement. "Cool ice sculpture! I can't believe all these people showed up." Cassie's homemade dress clung to her willowy figure expertly. A half-dozen black braids crisscrossed over the top of her head like an elaborate headband. She'd curled the rest of her long black hair, letting it spill down around her shoulders in playful waves.

"Something's happening," I whispered, feeling a sudden stab of fear for my friends. "I can't explain right now, but you need to leave."

"I don't think you have to explain." Royal's eyes shifted from me to the packed club.

I knew what he was thinking but I'd have to apologize later. "Please. Get out of here."

"Cassie brought your Red Vines," Royal said, ignoring me.

Cassie glanced at the paper bag in her arms with a sheepish smile. "There's not enough for everyone. Maybe if we cut them all in half—"

Another sweep of smoky shadow caught my eye. "Just take them with you and go!" I snapped. Cassie jerked back, hurt. Royal draped a protective arm around her shoulders.

"More Red Vines for us," he said. "Come on. We can break in my dad's ten-point-two sound system." Royal led Cassie away, shooting one last glare at me. I watched them walk all the way to the exit before sagging in relief.

I eyed the dance floor but couldn't move. The white-blond Lilitu had looked at me with a casual familiarity that made my skin crawl. They weren't surprised to see me, which meant they'd known I would be here. I shuddered, suddenly cold. What did it mean?

An earsplitting siren cut through the music. Lights flooded the space, killing the ambience instantly. Someone had pulled a fire alarm. People scattered off the dance floor, grimacing and clamping hands over their ears. Some moved toward the emergency exits, others huddled by the bar trying to figure out what was going on.

I saw Dad pushing through the crowd at the entrance. He strode into the room, furious, and spotted me. Another coiling swirl of smoky shadow moved toward him from the empty dance floor. I focused on it and saw the redhead Lilitu sprinting toward Dad, her claws extended, her face warped in fury.

"Dad! Behind you!" I screamed, pointing reflexively.

Dad spun around, unsheathing two gleaming daggers in one smooth motion.

The people huddled at the bar saw the daggers. Screams rang out, and the rest of the crowd fled from the club. I saw a bouncer trying to push through the mass exodus out of the corner of my eye, but I didn't have time to watch him. I was focused on the Lilitu. At the sight of the daggers, she had stopped her charge. Now she edged around Dad warily.

"I can't see it," Dad said, tense. "I need your help, Braedyn."

The Lilitu charged. "Left!" I shouted.

Dad moved, sweeping through an advanced version of the form Lucas had showed me all those long weeks ago in the basement. Watching him, I saw the fighter Lucas might become after decades of practice. Dad's movements were strong and focused; the blades blurred in his hands. He pressed toward the dance floor and the Lilitu edged away from the daggers in his hands, glancing at me uneasily.

"What the hell are you doing, man?!" the bouncer roared. I turned, startled. With the last of the crowd escaping out of the doors, the bouncer was able to enter, eyes fixed on Dad. Dad ignored him. "Hey! I'm calling the cops!"

"Dad?" I said, uneasy.

"Focus, Braedyn!"

I turned back, but the Lilitu had taken advantage of my distraction. She leapt for Dad and I only had time for a strangled gasp. It was enough. Dad heard me and dropped to one knee, slicing out with his daggers. One of the blades pierced the Lilitu's shadowy wing. Dad adjusted instantly, twisting the blade and pulling. The dagger somehow turned the smoky wing solid, ripping through the tough membrane with a meaty sound. The Lilitu's shriek drowned out the fire alarm. The illusion of beauty surrounding her fell away and she was revealed in her other form. Her wings beat the air with a leathery sound and she ripped herself away from Dad. Instead of blood, a gleaming, pearly ichor streamed from her wounded wing, spattering the floor. The Lilitu hissed in fury. Dad moved back a step warily.

"Holy—" The bouncer staggered back into a wall, and then turned and ran out of the club. Every instinct I had urged me to turn and run after him, but I couldn't leave Dad alone.

Across the dance floor, I saw Lucas emerge from the back hall with Derek. Derek's eyes were dull, unseeing. But Lucas's face went rigid with shock. I wondered if he'd ever seen a Lilitu unmasked before. The Lilitu retreated from Dad and glanced at Derek. Lucas's grip on Derek tightened uneasily.

Gretchen burst through the club entrance with Hale close on her heels. I saw Hale's eyes widen slightly when he saw me, but Gretchen was focused on the Lilitu.

She joined Dad, drawing her own daggers. They moved, flowing through the steps of the fighting form with lethal power. I had a vision of an army of soldiers trained like this. Suddenly the fight seemed a little more even. The redhead stumbled back in the face of their attack. After a moment's fury, she turned and fled to the back hallway, knocking Lucas and Derek hard against the wall as she passed. She was gone.

I felt my knees go weak with relief.

Gretchen turned toward me, but her eyes focused on something behind me. Her face tightened with determination. "Another one! By the bar!" Hale spun around, daggers in hand, ready to fight. I looked over my shoulder. The brunette Lilitu, wrapped in her shadowy cloak, was preparing to spring.

"Get the boy out of here! We've got this covered!" Hale shouted to Lucas.

Lucas pushed Derek into a run. They raced across the dance floor. Lucas grabbed my hand as they passed, pulling me toward the main entrance. "Come on!"

"My dad—"

"He can handle this! Move!" Lucas half-dragged me out the club's front door. As we fled, we heard another terrible shriek behind us.

Outside, the night air seemed colder than it had been when we'd arrived, just half an hour ago. It bit at my eyes, stung when I breathed it in. People huddled by their cars, confused and disoriented.

"The bouncer," I said. "He saw her."

"It won't matter." Lucas said, glancing back at the club bitterly. "You'll see."

Derek swayed on his feet between us. Lucas and I steadied him. Derek didn't look good.

"Best thing we can do is get him out of here," Lucas said, seeing my worry. The three of us made it to my car. I tossed the keys to Lucas and helped Derek around to the passenger side. Lucas opened the driver's door and grabbed his leather jacket, pulling it on against the cold. The Firebird had a fold-down back seat. I crawled into the car and pulled the back seat down, then got out to make room for Derek.

"In," I said, expecting resistance. To my surprise, Derek got inside wordlessly.

"He'd walk off a cliff if you told him to," Lucas murmured. "His will has been compromised. We need to get him out of here. Come on."

Lucas drove back to our houses. When he parked, I helped Derek out of the back of the Firebird and pulled him toward the Guard's house. "No," Lucas said. "I'm working on the back door. It doesn't lock."

"You have all the weapons," I whispered.

Lucas scanned the area, thinking fast. "Okay. Get inside your house and lock the doors. I'll be right back." Lucas ran into the Guard's house. I led Derek up the front walk to my house. The porch light was out. It made the portico—which usually felt welcoming— seem dangerous. Derek tripped on the flagstone path. I caught him and we made it to the front door.

"You're going to be okay," I said, more for my benefit than for his. I pulled the keys out of my purse and fumbled to open the front door. I felt the lock click and relief washed over me. I opened the door.

She was standing on the other side, smiling. The honey-blond Lilitu I'd seen with Derek at Homecoming. She'd never been at the club; she'd been waiting for us here. Semi-transparent ebony wings folded gracefully behind her. They shimmered even blacker than the darkness of the house.

"You," I stammered.

"Hello, Braedyn." She smiled, and her green eyes gleamed. I only saw a hint of the other form behind her face. "I think you have something that belongs to me." I felt the keys drop out of my hand but I didn't hear them hit the floor. She grabbed my arm and jerked me into the house. I skidded across the floor and fell.

Looking up, I could see Derek and the Lilitu silhouetted in the doorway. The streetlights outside edged them in a cold gray light. She pushed Derek into the house. Unresisting, Derek staggered to the floor next to me. Instinctively, I grabbed his hand. It was shaking. I gave his hand a squeeze I meant to be comforting and his eyes found my face. Maybe there was still a flicker of Derek inside.

Then the Lilitu slammed the front door and everything was dark.

9

I heard the door lock, felt it like a jolt in the marrow of my bones. The Lilitu took a step forward into the darkness. My eyes, adjusting, could make her out against the windows.

"Who are you," I asked.

"I'm Karayan."

As I focused, details rose up out of the shadows. I could see my house clearly, but everything was rendered in shades of gray. I sucked in a sharp breath. Night vision. If this was another symptom of my disease, that meant she could see us, too. I shifted my gaze and sure enough, Karayan was staring at me from across the foyer.

"I've been waiting a long time to meet you," she said.

I grabbed Derek's arm and pulled him to his feet with a strength born of desperation. "Stay with me," I hissed into his ear. He didn't argue. I had to guide him; I don't know what he could make out in the dark house, but it couldn't be much.

"Really?" Karayan called from the foyer. "You're going to make me chase you?" I ducked into the guest bedroom with Derek. He pressed against the wall, breathing fast. He wasn't winded from our dash down the hall—this was sheer panic. I heard Karayan walking down the hall. When she spoke, she sounded amused, confident. "Okay, but you should know I've never lost a game of hide-and-seek."

I struggled to open the window into the backyard. It was stuck fast—we weren't getting out this way. I grasped for a plan, but my mind was blank. I pulled Derek down behind the bed and crouched beside him.

"That's her, isn't it?" Derek asked.

"Quiet," I whispered. Derek nodded. We waited.

I heard Karayan stop just outside the guest room and cursed myself for the obvious choice. We were sitting ducks in here. But instead of entering, Karayan turned and continued on. I didn't buy for a second that she'd missed us. She knew exactly where we were. She was toying with us. But it bought us time. I heard her voice down the hall. It sounded like she was entering the kitchen.

"Oh, by the way," she called merrily. "I've decided what I'm giving you for your birthday present. I hope you like it." I heard the click of a light switch. A warm glow spilled out of the kitchen into the hallway before us. I looked at Derek, who had his eyes squeezed shut. "It's a story, so pay attention."

I edged forward and peeked out of the room. The hall was empty. I didn't waste any time. I pulled Derek into the hall. He resisted, but I shoved him around the staircase back toward the front of the house.

I heard the refrigerator open in the kitchen. "Ooo, red velvet." Derek and I reached the foyer, staying pressed against the living-room side of the main staircase. If Karayan walked into the dining room, she'd spot us as soon as we left the shelter of the staircase to move toward the front door. We'd have to risk it. It was the only way we were getting out of here.

"We're going to have to run," I whispered to Derek.

He shook his head. "No. No. She's right there."

"Derek, this might be our only chance." I pulled on his hand, but Derek planted his feet, refusing to budge.

"She'll see us," he moaned.

It was no good. I looked around, trying to come up with another idea. And then I felt it—the seam to the door of the crawlspace under our stairs. My old hiding place. I found the hatch and opened the door. The crawlspace was a lot smaller than I remembered, but there would be room enough for two people to hide if we crammed in.

"Inside," I commanded quietly. Derek scooted into the closet without a word.

Karayan must have finished taste-testing my cake, because she started talking again. "Okay, story time. In the beginning, God created two beings out of clay. Adam and Lilith. They were equals in Eden."

I slipped into the closet after Derek and eased the door closed. The hatch made a tiny click as it latched. I almost screamed when the stairs creaked overhead. Karayan must have been in the foyer as I was closing the hatch. I felt an icy wash of fear. We listened as Karayan walked up the stairs. Her voice reached us clearly, even through the wood paneling.

"But Adam, you probably know the type. He didn't want an equal, he wanted a groupie." We listened as Karayan reached the top of the steps and walked into the upstairs hallway. I glanced at Derek in the dark. He hugged his knees tightly, eyes staring blindly in the darkness of the crawlspace.

I heard Karayan's voice, muffled but intelligible. She was in Dad's room. "And then one day, Lilith saw the Archangel Samael in the garden. For the first time, she understood love. She left Adam for Samael, even though it meant disobeying God."

Derek reached a hand out to me. "Will she find us here?" he asked. I shook my head no, pretending a confidence I didn't feel.

Karayan's voice sounded at the top of the stairs. "Samael was afraid of God's wrath, so turned her out. Brokenhearted, Lilith refused to return to Eden. To punish her, God sent three angels to kill one of her children every day until she went back to Adam. Does that seem fair?" The stairs creaked above our heads.

I felt a fervent hope that she'd go back to the guest room. Maybe she thought we were still hiding there. My thoughts raced ahead, trying to predict her next move. If she went into the back hallway, we could still make a break for it.

"Lilith let the pain of Samael's betrayal temper her will," Karayan continued. "Instead of crawling back to Adam like a broken thing, she chose to fight for her children, for her birthright. Some of us are still fighting. An eye for an eye..." Karayan had reached the bottom of the stairs. I didn't hear her for a moment. I couldn't tell where she'd gone. Then a shadow broke the line of light edging the closet door. I didn't have time to scream.

Karayan ripped the door open, splintering the hinges. She jerked me out into the living room with a strength that belied her delicate form. She smiled. "And a life for a life."

"Don't hurt him." My voice trembled.

"Weren't you paying attention?" Karayan asked. "It's us against them, sweetie." I shook my head helplessly. Karayan studied me. "The Guard wants to put you on a leash. Come with me. I can teach you how to use all those shiny new powers you're starting to develop. I've seen you with those schoolboys. You're a natural. Now," she said, smiling. "This is the part where you ask me to take you under my wing. Sort of a big-sister little-sister thing."

I stared at her. "You've been watching me?"

"You think I scope out high school dances for kicks?" Karayan laughed. "Teenage boys are fun, but they can get a little clingy." Her eyes glinted cruelly, and I knew. She wasn't going to let Derek go.

"Derek, run!" I shouted. Derek obeyed me, gathering all his courage to scramble out of the closet and race for the door.

Karayan didn't take her eyes off my face. *"Derek. Stop."* There was a new quality to her voice, a sparkling resonance, as though it was underscored with a throaty chime. It froze Derek in his tracks.

"Derek?!" I shouted, feeling panic rising in my throat. "What are you doing? You have to get out of—!" Karayan drove a fist into my stomach, hard. I felt my knees buckle and fell against the wall. I caught myself, doubling over. A searing pain spread across my belly. I felt like gasping and retching at the same moment. I dragged in a ragged breath. Karayan grabbed my hair at the nape of my neck and pulled me onto my feet. I hissed in pain. All the defiance I'd felt three seconds ago was gone, replaced by stinging terror.

Karayan forced me to the front door. I was still gasping. Every step sent a new stab of pain down my side. We passed Derek. He stood, still as a statue. Only his eyes, wide with animal terror, gave him away. Karayan unlocked the door and opened it. The cool night air greeted us. She shoved me over the threshold. I fell to the porch, cradling my side. Karayan towered over me, the soft waves of her honey-blond hair framing a grim expression.

"You don't know the Guard yet," she said softly. "I think it's time for you to see exactly what they're capable of." Karayan reached a hand out to Derek, not even bothering to look at him. He took her hand, all resistance gone. Karayan gave me a look full of pity, then kicked the front door shut in my face.

"Don't hurt him," I screamed at the door. There was no answer. I scrambled to my feet, grabbing the doorknob, but it was locked. I dropped to my knees, searching the porch for my keys. Even with my heightened vision, I couldn't see them anywhere. I stood and threw my body against the door. It didn't budge.

I saw my purse on the front porch where I'd dropped it. My cell phone was peeking out of one corner. I snatched it and speed dialed

Dad.

It only rang once before he answered. "Braedyn? What is it?"

"Dad? She's here! She's got Derek in the house!"

There was a fraction of a moment of silence, and then Dad cursed. "Get away from there. We're on our way." The line went dead. They were coming, but they wouldn't get here soon enough to help Derek.

Forcing myself to move despite the burning in my stomach, I raced across the lawn to Lucas's house.

The front door was standing ajar. I hurried inside and went straight for the basement stairs. Lucas was charging up with a sack full of weapons. When he saw me, he froze.

"Braedyn?"

"She's in my house," I said. "With Derek."

Lucas's whole demeanor changed. He dropped the sack and pulled out a set of the daggers I'd seen him training with. The difference between the way Lucas and Dad handled the daggers was as stark as night and day. With a sick sense of dread, I knew we were no match for Karayan. She'd already beaten me, and he was just a kid. That thought didn't seem to cross his mind. He raced past me, out of the house.

"Lucas, wait for me!" I ran out of the house after him. The pain in my stomach kept me doubled over, slowed me down. Lucas raced across the lawn up to my front porch and slammed into my front door, but it wouldn't budge for him either.

"The Guard is coming," I said breathlessly, reaching our portico and leaning heavily on a wooden column. "We just have to keep her from attacking him until they get here. I know where the spare key is for the backdoor. We can get in that way."

Lucas's eyes fell on a large terracotta pot housing a spray of flowers. He picked it up and slung it at the living room window. The window shattered in a spray of glass. Lucas ran the arm of his leather jacket over the frame, knocking out the last jagged bits of window. He vaulted through the window.

"Lucas, wait!" I lunged after him, trying to catch him before he disappeared into the house, and landed hard against the window frame. Red and gold stars bloomed in front of my eyes. I lurched to one side of the portico and threw up. After it was over, I straightened. My throat burned, my nose and eyes were running, and all I wanted to was to curl up and hide. I scanned the street. No sign of the Guard. My stomach churned with panic. I turned back toward the open window, but heard only silence from inside. I couldn't leave him to face this alone.

"Lucas?" My voice came out in a grating whisper, but it was too weak to travel far. I climbed through the window, eyes wide for any sign of Karayan.

Lucas came out of the kitchen, daggers in hand. "Where did she take him?" Something moved in the hall behind Lucas.

"There!" I said, recognizing Derek's silhouette. "Grab him and let's go!" I turned to the front door, unlocking the heavy bolt and pulling the door open. When I looked back, I expected to see Lucas and Derek running to join me. Instead they faced each other, frozen.

"Derek?" Lucas asked, tense. "What's going on, man?"

Derek stepped forward. Lucas hesitated. That was a mistake. Derek picked a ceramic vase up off the hall table and hurled it. Lucas dodged out of the way, and lost his balance. Derek jumped Lucas from behind, knocking one of the daggers halfway across the living room and running Lucas's head into the wall.

"Derek!" I screamed. "Stop! What are you doing?!"

Derek ignored me. Lucas went limp in his hands. The other dagger fell to the ground at their feet. Derek dragged Lucas back into the foyer before Lucas could summon the strength to jerk out of his grasp. Blood coursed down one side of Lucas's head from a fresh cut. I ran into the foyer. Lucas half-turned to face me. Behind him, Derek grabbed a wooden chair next to the hall table. Derek swung the chair for Lucas's head with lethal force.

"Get down!" I shouted.

Lucas dropped to his hands and knees. The chair exploded against the wall where Lucas's head had been seconds before. Splintered wood rained down on him. Lucas lunged for Derek, driving a fist into Derek's throat. Derek wheezed, a horrible wet sound, but didn't otherwise react.

"No," Lucas said. He clearly expected to have dropped Derek with that blow. Lucas backed into the dining room table. Derek grabbed Lucas by the front of his leather jacket and punched Lucas across the face. His fist connected with a sickening crunch. Lucas fell back against the table hard, but Derek didn't release his hold. Derek pulled his fist back for another shot. I darted forward and grabbed Derek's upraised arm. Derek turned on me, releasing Lucas, who dropped limply onto the table.

"Braedyn, careful!" Lucas cried, struggling to his feet. "He's a Thrall!"

I looked at Derek and saw his eyes. They were flat. Emotionless. Derek moved. It didn't seem like any effort at all for him, but the blow sent me flying across the foyer. I hit the wall and slumped to the floor.

Lucas stumbled toward me, terrified. "Braedyn? Braedyn, get up. We have to get out of here." Derek walked up behind Lucas, expressionless.

"Lucas," I tried to warn him, but my voice sounded thick.

Derek grabbed Lucas by the collar of his leather jacket, and wheeled him around. Lucas's arms pin-wheeled for balance. Derek tightened his grip, and then ran Lucas straight through the bay window of our dining room. I saw Lucas curl his arms protectively around his face just before he impacted with the glass.

I heard an earsplitting scream and realized it was coming from me. Derek turned to face me. There was no flicker of thought in his eyes.

I heard tires squeal outside. Gretchen's voice cut through the night. "Lucas? Lucas?! God, Hale, call 9-1-1!"

Dad burst through the front door. Derek turned to face him, and a glimmer of recognition came into Derek's eyes, as though this was what he had been waiting for. They squared off, and the contrast was plain. Derek was fit and well muscled for a high school guy, but Dad had never lost his soldier's physique. His chest was half again as broad as Derek's, and the muscles along his arms tensed like knotted ropes beneath his shirt.

Dad risked a brief glance at me. "Are you all right? Can you stand?"

"I don't know," I said. I rolled to my knees and stood, holding onto the wall.

Dad turned his attention to Derek. "Get out of here, Braedyn."

"Something's wrong with Derek," I said, worried. "Lucas tried to—"

"I've got this, honey." Dad circled Derek, cautious. Derek tensed. "Easy, son. I don't want to hurt you." Dad stopped and lowered himself into a crouch. He didn't take his eyes off Derek, but his hand drifted to the ground. I followed the movement and realized Dad had spotted one of the daggers Lucas had dropped. Derek's lips pulled back in a grimace. He lunged before Dad had a chance to pick up the weapon.

They connected. Derek moved with unbelievable power, but Dad was faster than I would have thought possible. Dad managed to dodge most of the swings, but Derek caught him across the jaw with a left-handed swipe. Dad took the punch like a boxer, dancing back quickly.

"Dad!" I stood frozen in place.

"Outside, Braedyn!"

"She's supposed to see." Derek's voice came out like a growl.

Dad turned to me, wild panic in his eyes. "Braedyn, go!" Derek moved, caught Dad by the shoulders, and twisted, throwing Dad to the ground. Dad tried to roll free but Derek kicked him savagely in the ribs. Dad rolled to his side, gasping.

Derek pulled a gun out of the back of his jeans. With a sick sense of realization, I suddenly knew what Karayan had been doing in Dad's bedroom. He'd kept that gun in a box in his closet since I was a little kid. He took it out to clean and check it once a month without fail. He'd taught me what I needed to know about gun safety. Looking at the weapon, I saw that the safety was off. No emotion flickered in Derek's face. He leveled the gun at Dad's head. Dad grew still. I saw Dad swallow, but otherwise he made no move. Derek's finger tightened on the trigger.

I felt a pressure building inside, fueled by helpless fury and the desperate need to control this situation. "*Stop.*" It was as though all other sound was snuffed out. As though my voice tunneled through the space between Derek and me, connecting us with a filament of sound. I could feel the word pushing toward him, cracking the air between us with a sound like little chimes. I was vaguely aware of Dad staring at me, his expression stunned. Derek froze and I felt a swell of triumph. Whatever she'd done, I could do it, too. I could speak and make Derek listen. I could reach him. Maybe it wasn't too late. Derek's hand trembled faintly, and I felt my triumph melt away. I felt the connection between us start vibrating, and I knew that if it snapped Derek would shoot my dad.

Dad seemed to realize this as well. "Focus," he said softly. Derek's hand twitched again as contradicting desires raged within him. I reached for the mysterious power, desperate to solidify the line.

"*Put the gun down*," I said. Again I felt the words pushing through the space between us and felt the connection surge, growing in strength.

Gretchen edged into the foyer, clearly aware of the tension in the room. "Hale, hurry."

Hale entered the dining room from the kitchen, coming up behind Derek. Hale moved quickly, catching Derek in a chokehold. When Derek's gaze shifted off of Dad, Dad knocked the gun out of Derek's hand. It skittered across the floor. Derek was struggling in Hale's grip. He tried to throw an elbow into Hale's side but Hale shifted easily to avoid the blow. Derek's face was turning bright red.

Hale's piercing gray eyes met Dad's. The scar bisecting his eyebrow seemed paler against his flushed skin—it was taking all his effort to hold onto Derek. "Thrall?"

"Yes." Dad sounded haggard. Hale's face seemed to harden. He glanced at me and back at Dad. Unspoken communication seemed to pass between them. Dad stood and crossed the distance to me in a few quick steps. Derek's struggles were becoming more frantic. Dad pushed me toward the front door.

I couldn't take my eyes off Derek. "He—he can't breathe."

"Come with me." Dad's voice was firm. With a shock I realized Hale was killing Derek. I turned back, trying to break away from Dad. Dad caught me against his chest and half-dragged, half-carried me onto the porch. I fought him like a wild thing, trying to claw my way past him back into the house. I could hear the horrible scuffing of Derek's feet on our dining room floor.

"No! Dad, no!" I heard my voice, high and shrill. Dad held me in a grip like a vise. He clamped his free hand over my ear, pinning me to his chest, muffling the sound of Derek's death.

"I'm sorry, baby. I'm sorry. He's gone. He's already gone. There's nothing we can do for him." Dad held me until I stopped fighting him. When he released me, the silence was ominous.

I looked into Dad's worried face and the edges of my vision started swimming. Dad's concern changed to alarm. I was aware of the world tilting, and suddenly I was looking up at the ceiling of the porch. The last thing I felt was Dad catching me before I hit the cement. I saw his lips moving but no sound made it through the haze. My thoughts were snuffed out by a welcome peace, and I gave in to unconsciousness.

10

I found myself standing in a field of white roses, under a wide, silver disc of a moon. I took a deep breath and was instantly aware of the absence of pain in my side. It was a welcome relief. Someone moved beside me and I turned. Karayan was only inches away, studying the flowers.

I jerked away from her. "What did you do to me? What is this place?"

"I didn't do this. You did." Karayan wrinkled her nose in distaste. "White roses? Not exactly my style." I stared at her in bewilderment. "It's a dream, Braedyn. You pulled the ripcord of reality to escape."

In my mind's eye I saw Hale's face again, grim as he tightened his grip around Derek's throat. I heard the horrible noise of Derek's feet scuffing against the floor, and then the silence. I lifted a hand to my face, feeling sick.

Karayan read my expression. "So. They killed him." Her green eyes softened. "Now you've seen how the Guard operates. Care to reconsider my offer?"

"What?" I whispered, numb.

Karayan tilted her head, eyeing me shrewdly. "Clearly I picked the wrong pressure point. If not Derek... then who? If you tell me who he is, I'll show you how to find him in his dreams."

The pieces started falling into place. "You picked Derek... because you thought I liked him?" I asked. Karayan's eyes flickered. "You knew they would kill him."

"I had to show you what the Guard is capable of," Karayan said, crossing her arms defensively.

"You're telling me," I said quietly. "You let Derek die to prove a *point?*"

"You saw what they did to him. You think they'd hesitate to kill you if they had even the smallest reason to doubt you?" Karayan's gaze was piercing. I swallowed. "You're Lilitu. You belong with us." Karayan reached a hand out toward me. I jerked back out of reach. Karayan bit her lip, frustrated. "Let me show you how good it can be. I have the perfect life. The food—it'll blow your mind what a gifted chef can do. And once you move into a penthouse suite, you'll never go back to life among the ants." Karayan gestured broadly. "The best part? I'm in charge. Guys throw themselves at me, I have a little fun, I get bored, I move on. No obligations. No rules. No one owns me."

"Sounds like quite a party," I said softly.

Karayan allowed herself a small grin. "You don't know the half of it," she said.

"All those guys. Did you feel anything for any of them?" Karayan looked up at me, surprised. I saw a flicker of something—conflict?— pass over her face.

"You're thinking about this all wrong," she said, but her easy smile didn't reach her eyes.

"What happens if you fall in love?" I asked. I needed her to have the answer. I needed her to show me a path forward with Lucas.

"Love is a distraction," Karayan said, shrugging. "Who needs love when you have power?"

"I do," I whispered.

Karayan turned away from me abruptly, but not before I saw a flicker of pain in her eyes.

"So that's that," I murmured. The disappointment was crushing. "You can fall in love, but it doesn't change the fact that your touch is poison. If you act on your feelings, you'll destroy the one you love." I stared at Karayan, but she wouldn't meet my eyes. I felt a surge of anger. "Now tell me again how you have the perfect life."

Karayan was silent for a long moment. Her hand drifted out to stroke a beautiful white rose. "You're a clever girl," she said. "So think about this: like it or not, you're exactly the same as me."

"I'm nothing like you," I spat. "I don't want to hurt anyone."

Instead of answering, Karayan bent and touched the ground. A pool of dark water grew in the grass at our feet, full of brilliant flickers of light. Karayan watched them, fascinated.

"Look at all those dreams," she said. "You could spend all night every night with a boy in a dream and the worst thing that happens to him is he wakes up tired but happy. No harm, no foul."

"Then, why did you...?" I hesitated and Karayan laughed again. Her smile was knowing. It made me feel foolish and inexperienced.

"Let me put it this way," she said. "Relying on dreams for sustenance is like being a vegetarian for ideological reasons. Sure, it'll keep you alive, but after one too many tofu burgers, you'll do just about anything for a steak."

My head was spinning. "Sustenance?" I asked.

Karayan looked at me closely. "Interesting. The Guard really is keeping you in the dark. You're Lilitu, Braedyn. If you want to grow up to be healthy and strong, you're going to need a more balanced diet than most girls."

"I don't—what are you talking about?"

"Ask your daddy," Karayan said, her voice taking on a bitter undertone. "I'm sure he'd love to explain it to you. We have more important things to discuss. I'm here to give you the chance to join us."

I looked at her sharply. "Join you for what?"

"The daughters of Lilith have the same right to be here as the sons of Adam," Karayan said. "We were created from this earth in the beginning, just like they were. It's time we reclaimed our birthright. It's time to tear down the Wall between our worlds."

I felt a prickle of intuition at the base of my neck. "On winter solstice."

Karayan regarded me cautiously, a calculating look in her eye. "I told Ais you'd be worth our time."

"What if I don't want to join you?" I asked.

Karayan picked a single white bloom, turning it in the moonlight. It gleamed in her hand. "Think about it carefully. You've got a big decision to make. You can embrace what you are, join your sisters, and live forever. Or..." Karayan tossed the rose to me. I caught it reflexively. In an instant it was yellowed with age, scattering petals, a wilted, dead thing. Karayan's voice grew colder, quieter. "You can play at being human, betray your sisters, and die. It's your choice. Any questions?"

"Just one." I peered into Karayan's dark green eyes. "Who is Ais?"

Karayan's expression faltered. The next moment, she had vanished without so much as a sound. I glanced back at the rose in my hand. A maggot crawled out from behind one of the remaining petals. I flung the rose away with a jerk of disgust—

—and felt a throbbing pain in my side. My eyes opened. I was lying on our living room couch. Someone had draped a blanket over me. The lights were off, but plenty of warm light spilled in from the foyer. I saw Hale and Dad standing in the dining room, talking quietly. Gretchen stood beside them, staring out through the shattered dining room window, arms crossed.

My eyes caught on something in the doorway to the kitchen: Derek's unmoving feet. His sneakers were scuffed and one lace had come undone. My heart turned over in my chest. I tried to sit up, but the throb in my side grew into a stab of pain. I fell back weakly.

"Careful," Lucas said nearby. "Hale thinks you've got a cracked rib." His voice kindled a warmth inside me. I turned and found him sitting in a chair across the living room. His right hand was wrapped in a small towel, and an angry red mark darkened half of his face.

Lucas stole a quick glance at the grownups in the dining room. As he turned, I saw the hair matted with blood along the side of his head. I eased off the couch and went to him, ignoring the throb of protest in my side.

"You're hurt," I whispered, kneeling by his chair to look into his eyes.

"I've had worse." Lucas raised his good hand and traced fingertips across my cheekbone. His hand lingered to sweep a lock of hair behind my ear. Then he lowered his hand to brush my side gingerly. I sucked in a sharp breath at the touch. Lucas's eyes tightened with misery. "I think I got off easier than you did."

"You got thrown through a window," I said. "Why aren't you at the hospital?"

In answer, Lucas nodded to something behind me. I turned. Eric's leather jacket was draped over a chair. Long scratches marred its surface. If Lucas hadn't been wearing the jacket when he'd gone through the window, the glass would have shredded his skin.

"Derek almost killed you," I whispered, finally realizing how lucky we were to have survived.

"About that." Lucas tilted my face up gently. "I haven't had a chance to thank you for stopping him."

"All I did was give him another target."

"Don't do that." The look Lucas gave me was so intense my breath caught in my throat. "I'm alive because of you." He still held my chin lightly in one hand. As if he read my thoughts, Lucas leaned forward, lips parted.

"Lucas," Hale called from the dining room. His voice sounded tense. "Go home."

Lucas and I turned. Hale was moving toward us. Behind him, Dad and Gretchen stood close together, watching us. Lucas dropped his eyes, smiling sheepishly.

"Busted," he said quietly to me. "I'll see you later." He stood, picked up Eric's jacket with his good hand, and left.

After Lucas left, Dad stepped away from Gretchen. I saw what he'd been hiding from us. Gretchen held a gleaming Guardsman's dagger in one hand. Dad's hand was wrapped tightly around her wrist, immobilizing her.

"Drop it," Dad said quietly. The hairs on the back of my neck stood on end. Gretchen glared murder at me, but she let her hand open. The dagger fell, thunking into the wood of our dining room floor.

"This is exactly what I said would happen," Gretchen said. "I called it as soon as you told me what she was." Her eyes never left my face. Grief and rage washed over her features.

"You don't make the calls," Hale said. "Drive Lucas to the hospital. We'll talk about this later."

Gretchen didn't move. "This isn't just about Lucas," she said. "If you put your faith in her, you put us all at risk. The cause—"

"She's made her choice, Gretchen," Hale interrupted. "She proved that tonight." Hale gave me a brief nod of approval before turning back to Gretchen. "You don't have to like it, but she's part of the team."

Gretchen stewed, but didn't argue. She turned on Dad. "Keep her away from Lucas." With another glare at me, she stormed out into the night.

Dad finally relaxed. He bent to retrieve the dagger. I stood, gasping at a severe twinge in my side. Dad's eyes creased with worry. "We should get you to the hospital, too."

"Wait," I said. "There's something I need to tell you." I glanced at Hale, uneasy. "Both of you," I said.

Dad helped me back to the couch as Hale joined us in the living room. Dad sat beside me on the couch, while Hale perched on the edge of the coffee table. "I know what they're planning," I said. Their eyes widened in surprise. "They're going to tear down the Wall separating our worlds on winter solstice."

"How...?" Hale's eyes were full of questions.

"Karayan. The Lilitu who killed Derek. She found me in my dream." Dad and Hale looked at one another. The revelation seemed to leave them breathless. For a long moment, no one spoke.

"Did she say anything else?" Hale asked. "Anything about how or where—?"

"No. But she told me—" I swallowed, uncomfortable. "She told me to ask you about Lilitu... sustenance." Dad nodded slowly. "I guess we're going to have that sex talk after all," I said, trying to smile. Dad reached out and squeezed my hand. We heard the thin sound of a siren growing stronger by the moment.

Hale stood. "All right. The police will be here soon. We should prepare."

"There's one last thing," I said. "She mentioned someone called Ais." Hale and Dad turned to me, eyes suddenly sharp.

"Are you sure," Dad said, his voice strained with tension. "You're sure she said 'Ais?'"

"Does that mean something to you?" I asked.

Hale turned to my dad with a grim look.

"No," Dad said, answering an unasked question. "Don't even think about it."

"We need him," Hale replied. "And you know it."

"Hale, please." Dad glanced at me, eyes tight with anxiety.

"Can you think of anyone else?" Hale asked. Dad dropped his eyes, silent. Hale stood. "I'm going to make the call," he said.

Two hours later, Dad held my hand as I was wheeled back into the St.

Stephen's hospital emergency room. I'd been examined and x-rayed, and they'd given me something for the pain before taping my middle tightly. The medication was making me a little loopy, but at least it muted the pain. As an orderly steered my bed into a curtained partition, I spotted Lucas sitting on another hospital bed across the aisle. He smiled at me faintly. Gretchen noticed and pulled their curtain closed.

"All right, young lady," the doctor said, giving me a kind smile. "Why don't you rest. I'll be by with the results in about an hour. Sound good?" When I nodded, he turned to my dad, lowering his voice. "The police are waiting to talk with her."

"Can you give us five minutes before you send them in?" Dad asked. The doctor nodded and pulled the curtains closed around us. Dad sat on my bed and lowered his voice. "Listen, honey," he said. "The police are going to interview you about tonight. I want you to stay as close to the truth as possible. You snuck out of the house, you went to the club, tell them all of it just like it happened."

"Minus the demons," I murmured.

Dad nodded. "When you get to what happened in our house, tell them you and Lucas and Derek came home after the club and found a masked man robbing the place."

"Why can't we tell them about Karayan?" I asked, uneasy. "Not that she's a Lilitu, but—"

"The police aren't equipped to deal with a Lilitu," Dad whispered urgently. "Please trust us on this. Hale's already briefed Lucas. Your stories need to match."

I nodded unhappily. The curtain parted and two detectives came in, a woman and a man.

"Hello, Braedyn," said the woman. She looked older than her partner. Seasoned. "I'm Detective Kerns, and this is Detective Bierson. I understand you had a pretty traumatic night." She flipped open a notebook and took out a pen.

I nodded.

"Why don't you take us through your evening. Everything you remember. No detail is too small. Okay?"

I took a deep breath and started talking. As I talked, Kerns wrote down everything I said. She stopped me periodically to ask a question. Bierson watched me the entire time like a hawk. I did what Dad wanted. I talked about sneaking out and heading to the club. I told them about my birthday celebration, and described the confusion when someone pulled a fire alarm.

"Do you know who pulled the alarm?" Kerns asked.

"No," I lied. Bierson jotted something down on a piece of paper. "I only remember people running off the dance floor."

"Did you see any weapons?" Kerns asked.

I glanced at Dad. He nodded imperceptibly. "Knives," I murmured.

Kerns nodded. "That's consistent with what some of the other kids are saying, but no one stuck around long enough to get a good look at the suspects," she said. "All the bouncer could tell us was there were two armed men fighting."

"Like a gang fight?" Dad's expression was 100 percent concerned father. Lucas was right. It didn't matter that the bouncer had seen them; the Lilitu had covered their tracks.

"I'd rather not speculate on that just now," Kerns said to my dad, then nodded for me to continue. I described leaving the club with Derek and Lucas, and getting home to find someone in our house. I described the punch to the ribs, and running to get Lucas's help. But then I switched to Dad's version of events. I described the killer as male and wearing a mask. In this version of events, the masked man threw Lucas out of the window, and I watched helplessly as he killed Derek, then fled when my dad arrived.

"All right." Kerns stood, gesturing to Bierson. "We may have some follow up questions for you later. In the meantime, you focus on healing, okay? We'll do everything we can to catch this guy."

I mumbled a thank you and they left.

Dad put a hand on my shoulder. "Why don't you try to get some sleep?" he said. I shook my head wearily. Exhaustion made my whole body feel three times heavier than normal, but I was too freaked out to sleep. After about half an hour, Kerns and Bierson returned. They had fresh coffee with them. The smell made my stomach queasy.

"I don't feel so good," I said. Dad felt my forehead, concerned.

"Just a few more questions, Braedyn," Kerns said, flipping through her notes. "You said Derek was still alive after the intruder threw Lucas out of the window?"

"Um, yeah," I said, groggy. "The killer got him in a chokehold. I heard his feet scraping on the floor. His hands—he was trying—" I saw it all again, vividly. Hale with an arm around Derek's face. Derek, mad with rage, ready to kill us all. "He was trying to pull the guy's arm away from his neck. He couldn't breathe—" I couldn't stop the flood of memory. The smell of coffee was way too thick. I turned and snatched up a plastic bucket, retching for the second time that night. My stomach heaved, but it was empty. The spasm sent a new wave of pain through my side and I sobbed out a moan. Dad was on his feet in an instant, taking the bucket out of my hands and helping me lay back.

Kerns stood quickly. "I think that's all we need for tonight." Bierson nodded and closed his notebook. "Mr. Murphy, can I have a quick word?" Kerns gestured for Dad to follow her out. I sank back into the gurney, curling onto my good side. I felt my thoughts swimming, and noticed absently that the over-washed hospital sheets seemed to have no smell. They were stiff and cool against my face. I stayed curled on my side until Dad came back.

"Good job," he murmured, stroking my hair. "I think they bought it."

"Knock, knock," my doctor said, pulling the curtains open. "I've got your x-rays." He flipped on a light board over my bed and Dad and I turned to look. Hale had been wrong. My rib wasn't cracked. It was broken. "There's not too much we can do for you," the doctor said. "It's just going to take some time for you to heal. Keep them taped for a few days, but no longer. You need to be able to take deep breaths or you could develop lung problems down the road."

By the time the hospital released me, it was dawn. I gingerly changed back into my blue dress. It felt strange walking into the morning light. The police left a patrol car behind to give us a lift. We couldn't go home because the crime scene investigators hadn't cleared it yet. So Dad asked the police to drive us to the Guard's house.

Hale opened the door for us. He'd anticipated us; he'd made up beds in two of the vacant rooms upstairs. As Hale led us up the stairs, I saw Lucas in his room. Gretchen was in there with him, talking. Lucas stood as I passed, his face full of concern, but Gretchen caught his arm before he could come to me.

"Give her some space," Gretchen said. "She's never seen anyone die before." She glanced at me, her expression ice.

But Lucas's face was alive with feeling. His eyes held mine, steady, until Hale stopped in front of two doors at the end of the hallway. Each small room had a twin bed, curtains on the window, and nothing else.

"Let me know if you need anything," Hale said. He clasped Dad's hand, then glanced at me. My eyes traced the thin scar from his eyebrow down onto his cheek. Sometimes, like now, it almost disappeared against his skin. "She's a credit to you, Murphy," Hale said quietly. A warm smile spread over Dad's face. Hale put his hands on my shoulders. "Rest for now. We'll talk about what comes next when you're feeling stronger." Hale walked back to the stairs and down into the house below.

"Are you hungry?" Dad asked.

"No," I said. "I just want to sleep."

"About the club—"

Guilt twisted in my gut. "I know. I'm sorry."

"I'm not trying to make you feel bad." Dad's voice dropped. "Considering everything that happened, it might be lucky that you were there. I'm bringing it up because..." He smoothed back my hair, and I realized he was fighting tears. My eyes started stinging in response. "I can't protect you if I don't know where you are," he said simply. I leaned into him and he wrapped his arms carefully around me in a tender hug. I yawned, and Dad released me. He pressed the bottle of pain pills we'd picked up at the hospital pharmacy into my hand. "I'll get you a glass of water."

"Thanks." I walked into one of the featureless rooms and closed the door. I eased the dress off, trying to move my ribs as little as possible. Someone had left a t-shirt for me. I lifted it off the bed. A slip of paper fluttered onto the bed. I picked it up. As I read the words, a giddy lightness filled my chest.

I left this shirt for you, in case you'd like something fresh to sleep in. It's as close as I can get to holding you myself. —L

Someone knocked softly on the door. I slipped the note quickly under my pillow. "Yes?"

The door opened and Dad handed me a glass of water. "Good night," he said.

"Thanks." I looked at the window. The sun was starting to come up. Dad kissed me on the forehead and left.

I took one of the pain pills and washed it down with a gulp of water. Then, glancing nervously at the door, I pulled Lucas's note out and reread it. His t-shirt smelled like clean laundry, but under that, it smelled like Lucas. I slipped it on and wrapped my arms around myself, breathing in his scent. I was still smiling as I climbed into bed, pulled the covers tight around me, and fell instantly and deeply asleep.

I slept like a rock until Dad woke me up, shaking my shoulder gently. The ever-changing marquee of my dreaming mind hadn't made the nap very restful. Fragments of dreams, most full of anxiety and paranoia and fear, blended one into the next.

"I thought you were going to let me sleep," I said, rubbing my eyes. I glanced at the window, confused by the afternoon light streaming through a crack in the curtains. "What time is it?"

"It's nearly three o'clock."

I did the math, and sighed. "Can I have just a few more hours?"

"Braedyn, it's Sunday. You've been asleep for two and a half days."

"What?" I sat up, blinking to clear my vision.

"You need to eat something."

At the mention of food my stomach growled.

Dad nodded decisively. "Get dressed. We're going out for lunch." He tossed me a pair of my jeans and a fresh shirt. "I grabbed these for you." He said, keeping his voice neutral. "I just got word from the police. We can go home tonight."

I looked up sharply. Dad pulled the door closed as he left. I got out of bed and pulled Lucas's t-shirt off. It wasn't until I glanced down that I remembered my broken rib. Only, the pain in my side was almost gone. I peeled back part of the tape from my ribs. The skin beneath looked almost normal, just slightly discolored. I left the rest of the tape in place, unsettled. I fished Lucas's hand written note out from under my pillow and slid it carefully into the pocket of my jeans.

I walked down the hall to Lucas's room with his t-shirt in hand. His door was closed, so I knocked softly. Gretchen opened the door.

"And they keep telling me not to worry about you," she said coolly.

"I was just returning this," I said, holding out the t-shirt. Gretchen grabbed the front of my shirt and pulled me in close. "Hey!"

"You may have the rest of them fooled, little demon," she whispered in my ear. "But if I ever find you alone with Lucas, I will kill you."

Anger coursed through my body as I pulled out of her grip. "I would never hurt Lucas."

"You're everything he's training to fight against," Gretchen said. "And he trusts you. What do you think that will do to him when he finds out the truth?" She looked me straight in the eye, keeping her voice low. "You've already hurt him. He just doesn't know it yet."

11

S tanding at the head of the flagstone path leading up to our house, my courage failed.

"Are you ready for this?" Dad asked, noticing my hesitation. I forced myself to nod. Sheets of plastic had been taped over the broken windows. Someone had cleared all the broken glass off the porch, but a few bits still glittered in the yard.

Dad opened the door. We walked into the foyer. Sunlight streamed in through the plastic and flooded the space with bright light. I saw the marks on the wall where Derek had swung the chair for Lucas's head, but the splintered chair was gone.

I looked at Dad. "You cleaned everything up."

"I didn't want you to have to relive it any more than you're already doing," he said, squeezing my hand. "You're my girl. You know that, right?"

I felt tears brimming in my eyes. I hugged him. "I know." So what if he wasn't my biological father? He was everything else. His arms tightened around me, then he released me.

"What are we eating?" he asked. "I can pick something up or," he looked me over, worried. "If you don't want to be alone, we can go out."

"I'd rather stay here," I said. "I should probably shower. It's been a few days."

"Are you in the mood for anything in particular?"

"Green chile chicken enchiladas," I said. "With extra sauce."

Dad smiled. "Well, your appetite has definitely recovered. I'll be back ASAP."

I watched him go, then headed upstairs to my room, locking the door. He didn't need to know how hard it was being back in this house. Leaning against the door, I noticed a bit of bright paper in my trashcan. I bent and pulled out the birthday present I'd thrown away.

I opened it gingerly. Inside the box I found a note. It read, *I've always known which side you're on.* Underneath the note there was a beautiful cameo carved with the image of an angel. She stood boldly, head held high, wearing an armored breastplate over the long folds of a voluminous robe. Graceful, sculpted wings draped down her back like a feathered mantle. She was both serene and powerful. The cameo hung from a short velvet cord. I swallowed against the sudden lump in my throat and fastened the cameo around my neck.

I noticed Lucas standing at his open window, resting his arms on the sill. When his eyes found mine he straightened, smiling warmly. His right hand was bandaged, and the red marks covering the left side of his face were darkening into sullen bruises. I moved to my window for a clearer view of him.

Lucas suddenly turned, speaking to someone behind him. He gave me a quick look, then closed his window and moved into his house. I saw Gretchen's silhouette behind him, and drew away from the window quickly.

A few minutes later, I heard the door open downstairs. "That was fast," I called, heading out to join dad for our meal. Three steps from the bottom of the stairs, I stopped.

A stranger stood in our foyer.

He was older than Dad, thin and wiry. His shaved head bristled with a spray of gray and white stubble. "You must be the demon Murphy thinks he's tamed," he said. I felt a chill pass over my skin. The stranger's hand moved, brushing open the thick trench coat he wore. Metal glinted as he withdrew a Guardsman's dagger. "Come closer."

"Who are you?" I didn't move from my place on the stairs.

"Someone you'll learn to obey before the day is out," he said simply. "Don't make me ask again." I glanced at the door behind him, judging my chances. The old man moved. Before I had time to register what was happening, I was sprawled on the floor of the foyer at his feet, gasping in surprise. "Get up," he said, his voice measured. I picked myself up, wincing at the twinge in my side. The stranger walked around to face me. "I assume you know what happens when a Lilitu attacks a man?" He waited, but I only glared at him. "I've asked you a question."

"Yes," I said, bristling. "I know what happens."

"Tell me."

I answered through gritted teeth. "The first attack makes him weak. The second attack turns him into a Thrall. The third attack kills him."

"You've left something out," he said. I looked at him blankly. "So," he murmured. "Murphy has spared you the full truth. A Lilitu only attacks the same man three times in order to have a child." His eyes bore into me. "Do you understand what I'm saying? A human has to die in order for a Lilitu to be born."

"I didn't ask to be born," I whispered, stricken.

The stranger's eyes did not soften. He walked to the plastic-covered window and glanced out. "A few decades ago, the Guard realized our recruitment numbers were dropping off. We'd done our job a little too well. How do you make people join a fight against an enemy they don't believe in?" He looked back at me and smiled a bitter smile. "Leadership decided we needed a Lilitu on our side. An ally with the enemy's powers, someone who could help us keep an eye on them, someone who could prove the threat was real. And so they let an innocent man die in order to capture the pregnant demon who'd killed him." He walked back toward me, raking his eyes over my body impersonally. "Lilitu biology is different from ours; it takes your kind less time to gestate. Within a few weeks, we had an infant Lilitu under our control."

I stared at him, stunned. "What are you saying?" I breathed. Was this the story of my birth?

"They named the infant Karayan. As the best lucid dreamer in the Guard, I was charged with raising her."

"What?" My eyes bulged in surprise.

"You may have fooled Murphy," he said quietly. "But I know what you are. Your humanity has a limited shelf-life."

"You don't know anything about me," I hissed. The stranger slapped me, hard enough to knock me back a step. Hot tears burned in the corners of my eyes. I glared at him.

"You will address me with respect," he said mildly.

The door opened and Dad entered, carrying our lunch. It took him all of two seconds to take in the scene.

"The hell I will," I growled at the stranger. He lifted his hand to

123

strike me a second time. Dad caught his wrist before he made contact. The stranger turned on Dad, outraged.

"You brought me here to train her," the stranger said. "Let me do my work."

I looked at Dad, horrified.

Hale burst through our front door. He stopped when he spotted the stranger pulling his hand free of Dad's grip. Hale's eyes darted to my face and he frowned. "Thane. I asked you to wait for us."

"Why didn't you tell me he'd arrived?" Dad asked in a tight voice.

"Gretchen picked him up from the airport 15 minutes ago," Hale said.

Dad brushed my cheek with his fingers. "He hit you?" His voice was quiet, but an undercurrent of rage ran through it.

"You've coddled her for long enough," Thane said. "Do you want her prepared to face what's coming or don't you?" Dad turned on Thane, fist balled to strike. Hale threw himself between the men.

"We've gotten off on the wrong foot here," Hale said. "But Thane is right about one thing, Murphy. Someone has to help Braedyn prepare." Hale turned on Thane, his jaw tight with anger. "And I don't care how you've done things in the past. You lift a finger against the girl again, you'll answer to me."

Thane's eyes flicked from me to Hale. He didn't look pleased. With obvious effort, Dad stepped away from Thane.

"Maybe we'd all better sit down," Hale said. He faced Dad, grim. "Thane's brought some news you need to hear."

Ten minutes later we were seated around the coffee table in the living room.

"So? What news?" Dad asked Thane, hostility thick in his voice. Thane glanced at me, hesitating.

"She's part of this unit," Hale said. "She needs to know."

Thane frowned. "Last summer, a Lilitu killed one of the Three." Thane said this with almost no emotion. A thick silence descended. Dad and Hale stared at Thane.

"One of the three what?" I asked numbly. No one answered me. "Are you—?" I stared at Thane. "Are you saying the angels are real?"

Thane's eyes flicked over to me. Hale put a hand on my shoulder. When I looked at Hale, he nodded, his eyes shining with grief.

"Which—which one was killed?" Dad asked, shaken.

Thane's eyes cut to the choker around my neck. "Semangelof," he said.

"It was Ais," Dad said. "Braedyn says she plans to break through the Wall at winter solstice."

Thane nodded. "Semangelof's death will have weakened it substantially. The tomes are unclear on a lot of this, but my research seems to indicate a strong Lilitu might be able to create a hole in the Wall the night of winter solstice—a hole big enough to bring a new army through."

"If we're looking at another major battle with the Lilitu..." Hale glanced at Dad, unsettled. "We're not ready."

The room grew quiet. I looked around. "Who is Ais?"

Thane answered me. "One of Lilith's first daughters. An Ancient One. Powerful. It's rumored that she can read the conscious mind."

"We have to find her and stop her before she acts," Hale added. "It's the only way to preserve the integrity of the Wall."

"Agreed," Dad said.

Hale turned to me. "You need to start training with Thane tonight."

"This is a bad idea," Dad said. He glanced at Thane. "How do we know he won't do more harm than good?"

"We're out of time, Murphy," Hale answered. "You know the longer we wait, the stronger Ais is getting."

"I'm not comfortable with this."

"Braedyn may be the only one who can find Ais in time to make a difference," Hale said. "And Thane is the only one of us who can teach her. We have just over a month left before winter solstice."

"You know what happened with Karayan," Dad said. Thane made a sound and dad turned on him. "You treated her like a loaded weapon from day one."

"I made sure she knew what she was, and why we needed her."

"She was a child, Thane. She needed a father, not a drill sergeant."

"I raised Karayan honestly," Thane snapped. "She never had any illusions about her destiny."

"And I'm sure that had nothing to do with why she ran away."

Dad's voice was dry.

"Don't congratulate yourself too soon," Thane snarled. "This one obeys you now, but how long do you think it will last? One year? Five?"

"Go home, Thane." Hale looked tired. Thane opened his mouth to add something but Hale didn't give him the chance. "Now." Thane stood and walked out of the house. "Let him cool off," Hale said, turning back to Dad. "I hadn't realized how deeply his failure haunts him." He was silent for a moment. "But she is going to have to study with him." Dad didn't answer.

"I don't know the first thing about any of this stuff," I said. "How am I going to learn anything useful in a month?"

"Remember," Hale said gently. "You were born to do this. No one had to teach you how to breathe, right? It should be the same with dreaming. When it's time, your instinct should take over."

"Instinct." My doubt must have shown on my face.

"When you fell into the dream just a few nights ago," Hale said. "Did anyone teach you how to do that?" I shook my head. "You see?" he said.

"Maybe you should start at the beginning," I said. "Pretend I don't know anything."

Hale nodded. "We're all connected. Most of us are never consciously aware of it, but as long as we are living, we share the same dream space. It's what the psychologist Carl Jung called the Collective Unconscious. Most people dream in little pockets of constructed reality within this larger dream world. If you can break free of your own dream, you have access to the unconscious minds of all of humankind. Humankind and beyond."

I met his eyes, uneasy. "And you think I'll be able to break free of my own dream?"

"You're a Lilitu," he said in answer. "With practice, you won't even need to fall asleep to access the dream world. For now, you should focus on the basics: learning how to escape your own dream, learning how to locate someone else's dream, communicating with a dreamer. I'll make Thane explain how he senses the connections between Lilitu and their victims, but we can deal with most of the advanced stuff later."

"Advanced stuff, like what?"

"We're a little sketchy on the details," Hale said. "But some Lilitu powers extend beyond the dream. For example, we know that Lilitu can influence people's thoughts. They also seem able to predispose people to make certain decisions or take certain actions. Which brings us to the other side of the equation. All of these things take energy." Dad and Hale exchanged a look. An uneasy feeling pooled in my stomach.

"What kind of energy?" I asked. There was an awkward pause.

"I can handle this," Hale said, turning to Dad. "It might be easier for you both if I do it." Dad looked at me, clearly uncomfortable.

"This is The Talk, isn't it?" I asked. Dad let out a long breath and nodded. I glanced at Hale. We'd been training together in his basement for weeks now, and he'd proven to be a patient, compassionate teacher. I nodded assent.

"I'll leave you two alone," Dad said. "But if you have any questions—"

"I know, Dad." Dad turned and walked into the kitchen. I stared at my hands.

"This energy," Hale said. "It's a spiritual energy, and it's very powerful. It can aid Lilitu with healing, replacing the need for sleep, and other things we barely understand."

"Am I immortal?" I asked quietly.

"We think so. Provided you take care of yourself. As your powers get stronger, they'll drain more and more of this spiritual energy from you. You'll need to replenish that energy somehow."

"When you say 'replenish...?'" I felt my cheeks grow warm with embarrassment. "Lucas... he called Lilitu soul-suckers." I looked up at Hale, sick. "Is that what you mean?"

Hale took my hand in his. "No. What Lucas was talking about, that only happens when a Lilitu attacks someone in the physical world. Most Lilitu replenish this energy by visiting human men in their dreams."

My face was burning. "And if I don't replenish it?"

Hale leaned back, releasing my hand. "If you don't replenish this energy, your Lilitu powers will weaken you and—eventually—kill you. We don't know much about this, but a while back the Guard captured and held a Lilitu who... starved herself to death this way. She grew more and more exhausted. She slept longer, but woke up just as tired as she'd been when she went to sleep. In a few weeks, her body was twisted with pain and weakness. She ate everything we gave her, ate herself sick, but she never felt full. The soldiers who were there said it was like watching someone starving to death, only it was her spirit that withered away to nothing." Hale met my eyes, worried. "I think that's why you slept through the entire weekend. You used *the call* for the first time, and followed that by leaping straight into a dream from full consciousness."

I stared at Hale, struggling under an avalanche of new questions.

"We need you to learn, Braedyn," Hale said quietly. "If we can't find a way to stop Ais, we will lose the war. We will lose the earth."

"What about the Guard?" I asked.

"I hate to disappoint you, but what exists now is just a scattered remnant of the force we used to be. There are maybe 100 Guardsmen left in the world, but we've only managed to make contact with two other groups. An army of Lilitu could hunt us down easily and there would be no one left with the knowledge of how to fight them." Hale looked me directly in the eye, unflinching. "I'm asking you to take care of yourself. We can see to your physical needs, but only you can feed the Lilitu part of yourself."

I looked away from Hale, light-headed.

"One last caveat." Hale dropped his eyes, equally uncomfortable. "Please stay away from Guard members. We don't want to risk— You'll be around us all a lot. So." He cleared his throat. "It would be best if you sought out some other young men to visit in your dreams." He couldn't have been clearer if he'd just said *stay away from Lucas.*

"I—I've never even gone on a real date," I said.

"I'm not talking about romance, Braedyn."

"I am. You wanted Murphy to raise me like a human girl. Congratulations, he succeeded. It's a little too late to decide you want me to act like a demon."

Hale stared at me, startled. "We're not asking you to— Even a simple kiss could replenish your energy."

"There's nothing simple about a kiss," I said.

"Maybe this can wait a little while," Hale said, unhappy. "It's not like you're going to be folding space anytime soon."

"Folding space—?"

"It's not something you have to worry about." But when he saw my confusion, Hale explained. "There have been rumors for centuries that some of the most powerful Lilitu can use the dream world to make a hole from one physical place to another, in effect folding space. It was one theory to explain how some of the Lilitu were able to get here after the Wall was built. But we have no proof this is possible."

I considered this, intrigued. Finally, someone mentioned a Lilitu power that had nothing to do with hurting people.

"The truth is," Hale continued, "there's very little we actually know about them, other than that they're weakest at dawn, strongest at dusk, and vulnerable to our daggers." He smiled ruefully. "I'm learning new things about Lilitu every day." It sounded like an apology. "All right. This has turned into a regular lesson, hasn't it? And what's a lesson without homework? Your first assignment is to find me in a dream, and tell me something I don't know about you."

"Something you don't know about me? You mean, like—?" I started.

He cut me off. "Save it for the dream. Just ask me to remember whatever it is you tell me. Sound simple enough?"

Simple, right. I just had to figure out how to get myself into a lucid dream, search the vast dream world for Hale, tell him some secret about myself, and make sure he remembered what I told him. "Sure."

Hale stood. "We're going to do everything we can to help you," he said. I nodded, and Hale walked out the front door, closing it gently behind him. My head was churning through everything I had just learned. I wandered into the kitchen and found Dad pouring himself a cup of coffee.

"Coffee? Isn't it kind of late for that?" I asked.

"This is your first attempt at lucid dreaming," Dad said. Which meant he'd been listening to our conversation. "I figured, maybe you'd want your dad there, you know, for moral support."

I nodded, moved. "What if I can't do it?"

"Then we'll try again tomorrow." He stood, steaming coffee in hand. "You ready to give it a shot?" I felt a nervous jitter in my stomach. Time to see what this dream thing was all about.

Getting into a lucid dream wasn't as hard as I expected. Dad had dragged his desk chair into my room and talked me through a relaxation exercise Hale had suggested. As I focused on relaxing each part of my body, a soft numbness came over me. It was peaceful, just listening to Dad's voice and focusing on my breathing. When I was right on the edge of sleep, I heard him settle back into his chair.

"Okay, Braedyn. Tell yourself you're going to have a lucid dream."

My mind drifted as I held onto this thought. I was vaguely aware of a shifting sensation as sleep claimed me. I opened my eyes, and I was back in the field of white roses. I sat up, scared. But I was alone.

I looked around. If Hale was right, this dream was my private haven. I examined my dream world closely for the first time. The first thing that struck me was the strange nature of light here. The sky was dim, like the sky at evening after the sun has dipped beyond the horizon. But the roses gleamed, almost as if they themselves generated illumination. I reached out and touched one of the roses. It felt substantial, soft and cool. I shifted my gaze to the ground.

Karayan had mentioned something about other people's dreams. I remembered the dark water she'd summoned, full of the glowing pinpoints of light. She'd done something to the ground. I tried to mimic what I remembered her doing. I touched the ground. It was solid, like the earth. Yet somehow Karayan had managed to draw a pool out of the dirt. If I wanted to break free of this dream, I'd have to figure out exactly what she'd done.

I tried. I tried everything I could think of. I tried digging. I tried ordering a pool of liquid to form, standing there and shouting down at the ground. Nothing worked. Instinct? If I'd been a newborn depending on that first breath, I'd be dead by now.

Someone touched my shoulder. I jerked—

—And opened my eyes. Sunlight streamed into my bedroom. An entire night had passed, but in the dream it had only felt like an hour.

Dad shook my shoulder again. "Honey, it's time to get ready for school." He read the disappointment on my face. "So, no luck?"

"No."

"I'll tell Hale. We can try again tonight."

I nodded, unhappy. As I stepped into the shower, I felt totally lost.

Maybe I should have taken Karayan up on that lesson after all.

12

Dressing for school, I ended up wearing another tank top under another too-tight shirt, covered by the sweater vest. Looking at the clothes brought on an unwelcome rush of emotion. I'd had such simple plans for the weekend. I should have gone shopping. I should have finished my term paper.

"Getting attacked by a demon really trashes your schedule," I muttered. *And that,* a small voice inside me added, *is only if you're lucky enough to survive.* I glanced out of my window. Lucas's curtains were drawn tightly closed. The memory of our last conversation was vivid in my mind. I opened a dresser drawer and pulled Lucas's note from it's hiding place beneath some clothes. Just holding it made me feel warmer.

Dad knocked on my open bedroom door. "How do you feel about waffles?"

I tucked the note out of sight and turned, smiling. "With or without the carbon scoring?"

"Cute. Maybe I'll try my hand at some scrambled eggs instead." He started to leave.

"Dad?" I asked. He turned back to face me, waiting. "Gretchen—" But I wasn't ready to tell him what she'd said before we'd left her house yesterday. "Are you sure we're safe here?"

Dad saw the angel cameo around my neck and was quiet for a long time. "You're my little girl. My gut's still telling me to take you and run as far away from this as I can. But the truth is, you're probably safer here than anywhere else."

I bit my lip. "What if I can't find Ais? I spent all night trying and I couldn't even break out of my own dream."

"The important point is, you tried." His face creased with concern when I shook my head. "Honey. Honey. No one's going to ask you to do anything you can't handle."

"Are you sure about that?"

"I'll make sure they don't." He said this with such conviction that I actually felt calmer.

"Okay." I took a deep breath. "So what happens now?"

"Right now?" Dad smiled. "You're on toast duty."

When I got to school, I spotted Cassie and Royal on the quad. They were watching a group of teachers huddled together. One of the teachers covered her mouth, horrified. Large signs on the front doors directed students to ASSEMBLY. Groups of students collected across the quad, full of questions. I felt a stone in my stomach. I knew what the assembly was for. Fiedler had to tell everyone that Derek was dead.

Royal saw me first. His eyes narrowed slightly. He wasn't ready to forgive me. I let out a long breath, straightened my shoulders and walked over. Cassie glanced up as I came to a stop beside them.

"Hi," I said.

"Hi," Cassie answered. After a moment, she elbowed Royal. He grunted noncommittally.

"About the party." But the party seemed so trivial compared to everything else. As I struggled to find the right words, Royal gave me a look that was distinctly hostile. Pressure started building up in my eyes. "I'm so sorry," was all I managed to choke out. Cassie had her arms wrapped around me in two seconds. My side gave a small twinge of protest but I didn't pull away.

"So," Royal said stiffly. "She remembers her friends after all."

Cassie spotted something over my shoulder and let out a strangled gasp. I saw Royal's eyes widen in surprise and turned.

Lucas walked toward us, head down. Even wearing sunglasses, the livid patchwork of purple and yellow bruises on his face was clearly visible. He'd replaced the gauze dressing on his hand with an ace-bandage to keep the stitches covered. He joined us, and took my hand in his good hand wordlessly. I felt something lighten in my chest, and the day became a little easier to bear.

"What happened?" Royal said, sounding shaken.

"Lucas." Cassie managed. "Are you okay?"

"I'm not the one with the broken ribs," he said, glancing at me.

"What?" Cassie and Royal turned back to me, eyes searching my face.

Ms. Davies approached us, her eyes red and puffy. "Excuse me, kids. Everyone's meeting in the gym for assembly. Morning classes have been cancelled." She moved on to another group of students a little ways away. Others were already migrating toward the gym.

"Lucas," I breathed. Lucas gave me a worried look, squeezing my hand.

Royal watched us closely.

Cassie started walking toward the gym. "What do you suppose it is?" Lucas and I didn't move. She glanced back after a few steps, confused. "You're not going to assembly?"

"Everyone is going to assembly," Headmaster Fiedler said, approaching behind us. "Assembly is required." But when we turned to face him, he blanched. "Ms. Murphy. Mr. Mitchell." He looked lost for words. "I didn't expect to see you back at school so soon."

"I don't think I can do this," I whispered. The tears I'd struggled to hold back spilled down my cheek. I hurried to wipe them away, but I could feel Royal and Cassie staring.

Fiedler glanced at the gym and softened. "I'll let the faculty know you're sitting this out. Just don't leave campus."

I nodded gratefully.

Curiosity burned in Royal and Cassie's eyes, but Fiedler herded them toward the gym with a stern, "Come along, you two." I watched them walking down to the gym.

"Oh, man," Lucas murmured. I turned to him, my question dying on my lips. Amber crooked her finger at Lucas, demanding he join her with the gesture. Lucas turned his back on her. "I can't deal with Amber right now," he sighed.

"I don't think you have a choice." I gestured with my head and Lucas turned. Amber walked straight for us, eyeing daggers at me.

"What happened to your face?" she asked. Lucas's eyes cut to me. Amber frowned. "Tell me inside. Parker's saving seats for us."

"Go ahead," Lucas said. "I'm sitting this one out."

"Very funny. Assembly is mandatory. So let's move before we end up stuck in the nosebleeds with the freshmen."

Lucas sighed. "Amber, I don't think this is working out."

"Excuse me?" Amber blinked.

"I'm not the right guy for you," Lucas said, quite a bit nicer than I would have been able to manage in his position. Amber opened her mouth to argue, but Lucas cut her off. "And you're not the right girl for me."

Her eyes dropped, noticing our hands twined together for the first time. "You might want to reconsider," she snapped. "I think you're forgetting: all your friends are my friends. You eat lunch with us. You hang out with us. If you want to walk away..." Amber shrugged and her meaning was clear; if Lucas left her, she'd torpedo his social life at Coronado Prep.

"I'm done being your arm candy," Lucas said simply.

Amber stared at him for one terrible moment. Then she turned and walked to the gym.

Lucas let out a sigh. "At least that's over."

We walked down to the soccer field behind the gym. With everyone at assembly, the campus seemed strangely deserted. Lucas led me up the bleachers and we sat together in the empty stands. It was as much privacy as we'd ever had.

Lucas released my hand and lifted his good hand to touch my face.

"Wait," I said, pulling back.

"Hale talked to you, too, didn't he?" Lucas asked.

"What did he say to you?" I asked faintly.

"That if I ever wanted to be in the Guard, I should spend more time thinking about training and less time thinking about girls." Lucas shook his head angrily. "It's not like dating is going to turn our brains to mush."

"Does that mean—?" I started to ask the question, but chickened out.

In answer, Lucas rested his forehead against mine. "It means I don't care what they say." For a long moment we held each other's gaze, then Lucas moved, brushing my lips with his. I pulled back, trying to find the strength to resist.

Lucas caught my hand, pleading with his eyes. "I can't stop thinking about you," he said. "If you still feel—" he swallowed. "If what you told me the night of your party is still true, then I'm not going to let anything keep us apart." He lowered his eyes. "Is it?"

"Yes," I murmured. I brushed my fingers across his uninjured cheek. He leaned into my hand. With my heart hammering in my chest, I kissed him. It was a slow, sweet kiss, and it filled me with a sense of peace. When it was over, Lucas took my hand again. We looked out over campus, waiting. The morning weighed heavily on us both.

I bit my lip. "Cassie and Royal—they're my best friends and I can't tell them anything."

"Sometimes it's kinder to let people believe what they already think is true," Lucas said softly.

"Wouldn't you want to know if a demon was sitting right next to you?" As I said this, the hairs on the back of my neck prickled, as if warning me to shut up.

"If I couldn't do anything about it?" Lucas searched my eyes for a long moment. "No, I don't think I would want to know. And if I remember correctly, you weren't too keen on hearing the truth for the first time, either."

I dropped my eyes. "I'm starting to hate secrets."

"You and me both. Something's going on, but the Guard won't tell me what it is." Lucas's eyes crinkled in frustration. "I could help them, but they still treat me like a child." He sighed. "After this weekend, I'll be lucky if they even let me continue training. Gretchen... every time she sees my face she gets freaked out all over again." He kicked a pinecone off the edge of the metal seat in front of us, turning to me with a bittersweet smile. "Well, at least I have a partner in ignorance." I looked up too quickly. Lucas, watching my face, faltered. "Oh. Right. Being Murphy's daughter would come with some advantages."

I only hesitated for a second. "A Lilitu named Ais is trying to break through the Wall that separates our worlds."

Lucas stared at me, stunned.

"Hale thinks whatever she's doing is going to happen on winter solstice. December 21st," I explained. "That gives us about a month to figure out how to stop her."

"Wow." A wind came up behind us. Lucas absently brushed his hair out of his face, not taking his eyes off of me. "No wonder everyone's freaking out."

"There's more," I said. "Ais killed one of the Three."

Lucas took a long moment to let this sink in. "What..." he swallowed and tried again. "What's the plan?"

"There's only about 100 Guardsmen out there," I said, changing the subject. "Did you know that?"

Lucas nodded slowly.

"Why aren't we recruiting more soldiers?"

"Our recruits are usually related to Lilitu victims," Lucas said. "Like Gretchen and me."

"But there must be thousands of relatives out there."

"They have to believe in Lilitu before they'll be ready to fight. Only, most of them accept the Lilitu cover stories. I almost believed it," Lucas said, frowning at the memory. "Gretchen, she saw what killed Eric with her own eyes. She helped me see the truth. If it weren't for her, I'd still think Eric was killed by a burglar."

I nodded slowly, taking this in. "How do we make them believe?"

"We can't," Lucas said. "We don't have the resources to reach out to the relatives of every victim. But there is a small percentage of people who sense something's off. They can tell that there's been a cover up. It makes them paranoid. Some of them start researching, and if they're determined and persistent enough, their research leads them to the Guard."

"Doesn't sound like a very efficient way of building the ranks," I said.

"No." Lucas's eyes seemed to lose focus. "We'd better find Ais before she tears down the Wall. Because by the time enough people believe in Lilitu for us to recruit a real army, the war will already be over."

The assembly let out an hour later. Lucas and I saw groups of students move across the quad. Some sank onto the grass, crying and holding each other. Most seemed numb. Grief counselors walked among them, stopping here and there to talk. Lucas and I watched it all from the top of the bleachers. We didn't move until the lunch bell rang.

We found Royal and Cassie sitting at our table, subdued. They looked up as Lucas and I pulled out our chairs and sat. The dining hall was unusually quiet. The clink of silverware on china punctuated low, murmured conversations. As I looked around, more than one student snuck a morbidly curious glance in my direction. I turned back to our table, spooning some food onto my plate self-consciously.

"So," I said, trying to sound casual and failing. "How was assembly?"

"Um," Cassie said. She and Royal traded a look.

"Derek," Royal said haltingly. His eyes slid to Lucas's bruised face. "You guys—?"

"We were there? Yeah," I said. Lucas reached for my hand.

"You don't have to—I mean," Royal glanced at Cassie. "We're here for you. But—you don't have to talk about it if you don't want to."

"Thanks," I said, swallowing hard against the lump rising in my throat. Royal nodded. An awkward silence settled over our table. I looked at my plate, but I'd lost my appetite. I pushed it away with a sigh. A strange sound caught my attention. Cassie and Royal were wrestling over something under the table.

"Show them," Cassie whispered.

"I don't think they're in the mood," Royal whispered back.

"Come on. It's funny."

"What's funny?" I asked.

They looked up, caught. Distracted, Royal wasn't prepared when Cassie yanked something out of his hands. She slid a stack of doctor's notes in front of me.

"You look like you could use a distraction," she said.

I glanced at Lucas, who shrugged at me. "Come on. Let's hear 'em," he said.

I picked up the first note and read it aloud. "Please excuse patient from activity. He has tender tootsies."

Cassie snickered. Royal crossed his arms, put out. "He might as well have drenched this in gasoline and lit it on fire. Useless."

"These are from your brother?" Lucas asked. Lucas and I traded a smile.

I picked up another note. "Patient was bitten by a rabid jungle sloth, please limit physical activity to hanging upside down from tree branch." I started grinning and picked up a third note. "Please excuse student from PE. He is experiencing acute PMS."

Lucas snorted in surprised laughter. Cassie looked extremely satisfied.

"Is this seat taken?" Parker said. He touched the empty seat beside Cassie. Cassie flushed bright pink and looked at him with wide eyes.

"No," Cassie said before I could tell him to take a hike. "No one's sitting there."

Parker took the seat. "I heard you guys laughing."

"Sorry," Cassie said, wincing. "We weren't trying to be disrespectful."

"Don't apologize." Parker met her eyes levelly. "You think Derek would have wanted people sitting around moaning about him?" Parker's eyes cut back to his usual table. Several girls were rubbing Amber's back as her shoulders shook. "He wouldn't."

After a moment, Lucas picked up a plate and handed it to Parker. "Here."

"Thanks, man," Parker said, taking the plate and serving himself a generous helping of food.

Cassie snuck a look at Parker as if she couldn't believe he was actually sitting next to her. This would probably make her entire week.

"So, Parker," Royal said stiffly. "What brings you to this neck of the dining hall?"

Cassie smiled shyly at Parker. "Don't mind him. You're welcome to sit with us."

"Actually, I was hoping to get a word with you." Parker turned to Cassie, completely disarming her. "I'm a little lost in pre-calc. I thought, if you had some time, maybe we could—"

"Yes!" Cassie's eyes gleamed. "I mean, I tutor. Math. If that's what you were—what did you have in mind?"

"Well, we've got that test next week, if Mr. Sattler doesn't cancel it."

"I've already got my notes prepared," Cassie said. "I'd be happy to go over them with you. Or—" her smile faltered. "I could copy them for you, if that's—"

"We should study together. Let's call it a date," Parker said, smiling. His eyes flicked over to me briefly, but mercifully he didn't try to talk to me. When Parker reached for the bread, Cassie beamed at Royal and me. I smiled back, and kicked Royal under the table. He flashed a brief smile for Cassie's benefit, but dropped it as soon as she turned toward Parker.

"This feels wrong," Royal whispered into my ear.

"It's just pre-calculus," I murmured, although inside I agreed with him. "Let her have this one moment before you go all psycho on her crush."

"I don't trust him," Royal said. "He might be dressed in sheep's clothing, but underneath all that fluffy white wool he's still an arrogant, entitled ass."

Ms. Davies cancelled dodge ball that day in gym. She had us lie down on the floor instead, and guided us through relaxation exercises. It was obviously meant to help us cope with Derek's death. Lying there, thinking about Derek, I felt the muscles of my back growing tenser by the minute. I was plagued by guilt. Derek would still be alive if it weren't for me. Karayan picked him because she thought he meant something to me. I wasn't able to save him from her.

Finally the bell rang and we got up off the floor.

"Braedyn," Ms. Davies said, pulling me aside. "I'm here if you ever need anyone to talk to."

"Thanks, Ms. Davies." I eyed the door to the girls' locker room. I just wanted to escape this gym, change into my regular clothes, and survive the rest of the school day.

"I lost someone close to me when I was about your age," she continued. She told me some story about a friend of a friend she'd grown up with. I nodded at all the right places, but I didn't really hear her. When I finally made it to the locker room, Amber was waiting for me.

"There's something weird about you."

"If this is about Lucas," I said. "He's allowed to pick his own friends."

"And Greg? And Derek? You did something to them. What was it?" She studied my face intently. "Blackmail?"

"Yes," I said, sarcastically. "I blackmailed the captains of the soccer team and the swimming team." Her eyes narrowed. I shook my head. "Can you even hear how nuts you sound? Derek and I barely knew each other."

"Do you think I didn't notice you two sneaking off for all those private chats last month?" Amber asked quietly. I felt a rush of alarm and I scanned my memory for the few times Derek and I had spoken privately. How closely had Amber been watching me? And what else had she seen?

"Why do you care?" I asked. "You've basically ignored him since Homecoming."

"We dated for almost two years." Amber said. "So we had a fight. We've fought before. We always end up getting back together. We're *supposed* to be together. Only now he's dead." Dark rage swam in her eyes. "Why was he at your house?"

"That's none of your business," I said. I turned my back on her, ready to go to English in my gym clothes if that's what it would take to get away from her.

"Don't you walk away from me," Amber said. She caught my shoulder and pulled, trying to force me to face her. Without thinking, I grabbed her wrist and turned, like Lucas had taught me, sending her face-first into the locker bay with a sharp crack. I was so startled that I released her and stumbled backwards. Amber screamed in rage. The impact with the locker left a pink mark on her cheek. She turned and glared at me, taking a step forward.

Ms. Davies ran into the room, alarmed. "What is it? What's wrong?" She saw us facing one another and stopped. "Who screamed?" Amber and I glared at each other.

"It's nothing, Ms. Davies," Amber said. "Just horsing around. Right, Braedyn?"

"Right," I said hollowly.

Amber left. Ms. Davies looked like she wanted to say something, but she just followed Amber out. I opened my locker with a leaden feeling in my stomach, and changed for class.

Somehow I made it through the rest of the school day. After the final bell had rung, I gathered my things from my locker and headed toward the parking lot. Lucas caught me at the edge of the quad and pulled me close behind a tree.

I gasped, surprised. "What are you doing?"

"These are the last few minutes I'll have with you today," he said. "I don't want to waste one second." I leaned against him, understanding. He enfolded me in his arms. All the noise and chaos of the day swirled around us, but his embrace felt safe and calm. The eye of the hurricane. Gretchen pulled into the parking lot and Lucas's arms tightened around me for a moment. "Until tomorrow," he said.

His lips brushed mine again, and then he was gone, taking the comfort of his presence with him.

I didn't see Lucas in the house when I showed up for practice with Hale that afternoon. I felt my spirits sag a little in disappointment. It was almost a relief to walk down to the basement. I needed something to distract me from the day.

"Your dad told me you didn't have much luck last night," Hale said, looking up as I entered.

"No."

"Thane's going to work with you tonight." Hale smiled in encouragement, but I dropped my eyes. "Don't worry," he said. "You'll get it."

"You sound so confident."

"I have faith in you," he said simply. "All right. We're starting you with a sparring partner today."

"Sparring partner?" I felt a surge of hope, looking around for Lucas.

"Yeah." Gretchen sat against the back wall, taping up her hands. She was wearing slim black yoga pants and a sports bra. Even dressed to work out she looked threatening. I turned to Hale, unsettled, but he just clapped his hands briskly.

"Let's get started." Hale said. "Try out a few punches, Braedyn. We need to get you used to fighting with an opponent." Hale stepped back to watch.

Gretchen moved into the center of the room and faced me. Everything I'd learned over the last month evaporated out of my head. I took a half-hearted swing. Gretchen blocked the punch effortlessly and frowned, glancing at Hale.

"Again, Braedyn," Hale said. "Go ahead and commit. She won't let you hurt her, trust me." I swung, putting some muscle into it. Gretchen swept the punch aside, catching my fist and pulling me off balance. I saw her other fist clench, but she forced it open, her eyes cutting to Hale. If he weren't here, I realized dully, she wouldn't be holding back.

"I don't think I can do this." I said. Gretchen faced me. Her expression was hidden from Hale; he didn't see the hostility burning in the depths of her eyes.

"It takes practice," Hale said. "You'll get it."

I swung for Gretchen again, harder. She dodged the punch. My momentum carried me forward. Gretchen barely moved, but her elbow caught me in the stomach. I let out a whooshing breath, startled.

"Good," Hale said. He walked up to us, excited.

Gretchen calmly helped me right myself, then stepped back. She waited while Hale adjusted my stance and gave me some pointers. I barely heard him. My eyes kept darting back to her face. She wore a small smile. This wasn't sparring practice for her; she wanted to hurt me. I balled my hands into fists as a spark of anger kindled inside me.

"Let me know if you see something I'm missing," Hale said to Gretchen, moving back to watch us.

"Sure thing, boss," Gretchen said, amused.

I launched a fist at Gretchen's half-turned head. She blocked it, but the force rocked her back on her heels. All amusement bled right out of her face. She brought her arms up in a loose stance. Something told me I wasn't going to catch her by surprise a second time.

"Better," Hale said, moving in to adjust my stance again. "Keep your weight on your front foot and watch the angle of your fist." Couldn't he see the hatred in Gretchen's eyes? "Try that one again."

I attacked with another sharp jab. Gretchen blocked, and struck back. I saw her fist coming but couldn't move fast enough to block her. She pulled her punch at the last second, half an inch from my throat. I gasped and stumbled back.

Her smile was icy. "Don't worry," she murmured, too low for Hale to hear. "If I try to kill you, it won't be right under Hale's nose."

I stopped worrying about whether or not I could do this. It wasn't a question of "could" any more. The next time someone tried that on me, I'd be ready. It was a long and grueling practice. When I finally peeled off my sparring gloves, Hale clapped a hand on my shoulder.

"Nice work. See you at dinner."

"Dinner?" I asked. My heart skipped a beat.

Hale glanced at Gretchen out of the corner of his eye. "We need to work on unit cohesion," he said lightly. "We'll be eating dinner together every night." Gretchen glanced at Hale with unhappy surprise, then dropped her gloves in a bin and left.

I went home to shower and change. I picked out one of my favorite non-uniform shirts, a funky long-sleeved t-shirt Royal had picked up for me at a local indie rock festival. I brushed my hair out and put a touch of lip-gloss on, then inspected myself in the mirror. My eyes were shining with eager happiness. A whole meal with Lucas. It was an unexpected gift.

Dad and I returned to the Guard's house as everyone was sitting down to eat. Their round dining room table was worn, but large enough to seat us all comfortably. Gretchen and Thane had taken the chairs on either side of Lucas. I managed my disappointment and took the seat across from Lucas. He shot me a small, warm smile. Hale took the seat to my right and Dad took the last chair between Gretchen and me.

"I have some good news," Hale said. Everyone turned toward him expectantly. "I just got a call from Marx. He's made contact with a unit of 12 Guardsmen in South America. They've picked up the trail of an Ancient Lilitu. They think she's holing up in Ciudad Bolívar, along the Orinoco River. If it's Ais, we've got a real shot at finding her in time."

"That's great news," Dad said. His smile full of relief. I could tell he hoped this meant I wouldn't have to rush developing my Lilitu powers.

Lucas and I stole a glance at each other. When our eyes met, I felt a little charge of energy and my heart seemed to skip a beat. Maybe I'd get to play at being a normal girl for a little while longer.

"It's just a rumor," Thane said quietly. "I suggest we refrain from packing until we've got proof." His eyes cut to me. "In the meantime, we all need to hone our skills. We don't want to be unprepared when the time comes to act."

Thane knocked on our front door later that night. I followed Thane and Dad into the living room. Dad sat beside me on the couch, crossing his arms and watching Thane with a frosty glare. Thane ignored him, sitting on the edge of the coffee table and turning his attention to me.

"You failed to escape your dream last night," Thane started.

"This is how you want to begin?" Dad asked. "By chastising her?"

"I'm merely trying to demonstrate why she needs my help."

"She's sitting here, isn't she?" Dad growled. "You want to help? Give her some useful advice."

Thane pursed his lips. "Very well." He turned back to me, scowling. "Were you at least able to manage a lucid dream?"

"Yes," I murmured.

"Thane," Dad said, leaning forward. "If you can't speak to her politely, this lesson is over."

Thane's eyes tightened. He cleared his throat. "What did you do?" he asked me. "If you don't mind my asking?"

Dad sat back, mollified. I took a deep breath, and told him about the dirt, how I'd tried to dig down for the water like Karayan had done.

Thane stiffened. "Are you telling me," he said quietly. "That you actually witnessed another Lilitu accessing the larger dream world and you still can't do it?"

Shame washed over me. Before I could stammer out a response, Dad was on his feet.

"That's it. Lesson's over," he said.

"Yes, it is," Thane said, standing. "I can't help her until she finds a way out of her own dream. I trust you'll let me know if she ever succeeds."

"I tried," I said.

Thane turned to me. "Try harder. We're running out of time."

My life settled into a strange new normal. Every afternoon, I found Gretchen waiting for me with Hale in the basement. As my ribs healed, our practices got more intense. Fighting with Gretchen was a lot harder than punching and kicking a bag. We didn't become friends. We didn't even grow to like one another. But we did get used to fighting together. Sparring was supposed to be an opportunity for me to practice in a controlled fight. It felt more like an opportunity for Gretchen to work out her aggression on me. I wore padding, but it wasn't exactly body armor. Every once in a while I landed a hit through Gretchen's defenses. I didn't tag her often, but when I did, I savored the feeling.

After each day's practice, I'd shower and head back to the Guard's house for dinner. Dad added himself to the kitchen roster. He was by far the best cook of the group, having had the luxury of time to learn once he'd stepped out of the Guard to raise me. Lucas and I struggled to avoid each other's gaze at the dinner table. But as difficult as dinners were for Lucas and me, they were the one time everyone else seemed to relax. I'd catch Gretchen laughing, and her whole face would transform. Her blue eyes would sparkle, and I felt like I could see the woman she must have been a few short years ago, before Eric's death. Before she'd joined the Guard. She was vibrant and engaging, with a sharp sense of humor. I bet she used to be a lot of fun.

Hale, usually fresh from a shower himself, kicked back and let the rest of us do most of the talking. He spent the meal listening, interested in everything and everyone. He had this way of looking at whoever was speaking as if he had all the time in the world, as if the only thing that mattered to him was what they had to say. When he did speak, it was to offer insight or encouragement. I started to understand why Dad and Thane accorded him so much respect, even though he was younger than they were; he wasn't just a boss, he was a leader.

Eventually, Dad got coaxed into telling tales about the old days, when he was one of the legendary group that tracked ancient Lilitu across the world. Lucas hung on his words, almost star-struck. Whenever someone grew silent, weighed down by the fear and uncertainty of what we might be facing, one of the others would draw them back into the conversation and their troubled expressions would ease. These people really were a family for one another.

But once or twice a night, I'd catch Gretchen or Thane eyeing me. The message was clear; I was tolerated, but I wasn't one of them.

Each night after dinner I would go home, my stomach in knots, to try again. Thane's words taunted me, but as frustrated, angry, or desperate as I got, I couldn't find a way out of my field of roses. I'd imagine shovels and spend all night digging. I'd dream up hoses and create my own puddles of water, but I could never figure out how to fill them with the stars that signified the dreaming minds of humankind. No matter what I tried, I couldn't break through to the larger world of the dream.

I awoke every morning feeling useless. And that became part of my new normal, too.

On Friday night, the week before Thanksgiving, I returned to the Guard's house for dinner after cleaning up. Dad had been cooking since early afternoon, and the savory aroma of green chile stew was making my mouth water. Gretchen, Lucas, and I set the table. Dad emerged with a steaming pot of stew and set it on the center of the table.

"Where's Hale?" Lucas asked.

"Still on the phone," Gretchen answered.

"And Thane?" Dad said. Gretchen shrugged and ladled herself a bowl of stew. "More stew for the rest of us, then," Dad said. But I could see the creases at the edges of his eyes deepen. Something was troubling him.

Lucas passed me a bowl and our hands brushed. I risked a quick glance at him, then noticed Gretchen watching and dropped my eyes.

"I have some news," Hale said, entering. Everyone turned to him and I let out a small sigh of relief. He glanced around the table. "Where's Thane?"

"Out," Dad said. "What's going on?"

"I just got off the phone with the Guard in South America. Their archivist is saying she's certain that the Ancient Lilitu they've been tracking is Ais."

Dad glanced at me, hope lighting his eyes.

"Have they seen her?" Gretchen asked.

"They've closed in on her several times, always just missing her," Hale said. "But the trails they found suggest she's travelling in and around Venezuela."

We all heard the front door open and close. A moment later, Thane entered the dining room, shrugging out of his jacket. He pulled in a draft of icy wind with him; it was cold enough to make me shiver.

"Read." Thane's face was pale, drawn. He slapped a newspaper down in front of Hale. The front-page story was about some local missing men. Hale read the story in silence.

"What does it say?" Gretchen asked when Hale finally looked up.

"12 college kids missing in the last two months, all young and healthy. All men." Thane looked around the room, grim. "They're making more Thrall."

Dad sent me home after dinner. He stayed back to confer with Gretchen, Thane, and Hale. Outside the November air was cold enough to sting my nose and make my eyes water. I smelled the faint scent of firewood burning. As a kid I had always loved that smell. It meant winter had officially arrived, and Christmas was coming soon. This year, the aroma filled me with dread.

When I got home the phone was ringing. I picked up the living room handset. "Hello?"

"Braedyn? It's me." Cassie's voice was tight with excitement.

"Cassie? What's going on?"

"It's Parker. He likes me! He said he thinks about me all the time. He has since we were in geometry together last year." She giggled, thrilled. "Can you believe it?!"

"That's... great, Cassie." I felt like my thoughts were tripping over themselves. I couldn't believe it. Parker hadn't given Cassie the time of day since—ever. The first time he'd shown any interest in her was when he joined us for lunch out of the blue. "What did you say?"

"At first I didn't know what to say, but then, I told him everything." Cassie breathed out a long breath. "It felt so good to tell him."

"Everything? Everything like... how much of everything?"

Cassie laughed at my consternation. "Everything! How I've had a crush on him since middle school. How I've been to every one of his games, even the one they played in Colorado. How I've bought him birthday cards for the last three years but chickened out before I got up the courage to mail them to him. *Everything*, everything."

"Okay," I said stupidly. I wished Royal were here. He'd know how to handle this.

"Look," her voice dropped to a whisper. "Can I say I'm coming over to your place? He invited me to his house, but his parents are out of town and I don't want *my* parents to freak out."

"Cass, I don't know if that's—"

"Please, Braedyn. I *have* to go. He's going to make dinner. They have a grill out back. We're going to eat and hang out and look for shooting stars."

"Isn't it too cold for grilling?" I asked.

"I'll wear a sweater!" When I didn't answer, Cassie made a little sound, half-longing, half-irritation. "Please, Braedyn. I'd do the same for you if it was Lucas asking."

"Um..." It felt wrong, but she sounded so hopeful. "Okay. Don't do anything crazy."

"How about this," Cassie said impishly. "I won't do anything with Parker that you wouldn't do with Lucas. I have to go. He's waiting downstairs!"

"Wait, Cass, before you—" but she had already hung up. I set the handset down slowly. Cassie was fun and smart. Maybe I was worrying for nothing. Parker was going to the trouble of cooking for her. Maybe he really did like her.

I heard a tapping on our new living room window. I turned and saw Lucas peering in.

"What are you doing?" I asked. I started toward the front door to let him in, but Lucas tapped the window again and gestured for me to meet him in our backyard. I slipped through the house and let myself out through the kitchen door. The yard was dark, but my eyes adjusted quickly; I never had trouble in the gloom anymore. Lucas stumbled blindly around the side of the house.

"Lucas," I called quietly. He made his way over to me. I took his hand. He reached for me, burying his face against my neck. My stomach fluttered. I held him tightly.

"I had to see you," he said. "Hale's in there, talking about sending us all out in groups to look for Thrall. I know you're learning to fight, but don't... You have to promise me you'll never go up against one of them. I've been in a lot of fights. I—I had some trouble with authority growing up. But I've never faced anything like Derek in Thrall. We were lucky," he breathed. "Luckier than I think we realized."

"Lucas." Thane stood at the fence, watching us. Lucas and I flew apart, startled. Thane didn't smile. "Gretchen's going to be looking for you soon."

"Promise me," Lucas whispered with an agonized look. I nodded, and he left.

"I thought I might find you two together," Thane said softly. "He's really taken with you, isn't he?" Thane didn't move from his spot at the fence.

A sick dread washed over me. If he told Gretchen what he'd seen... "We were just talking," I said. I forced myself to smile, trying to disarm him.

Thane tilted his head to one side. "It won't work on me, child." His eyes were like steel in the night, cold and hard. "Lilitu only hold power over those who desire them, and there is nothing about you that I find attractive. Every one of us can resist you. Hale is young, yes, but if you try to work your wiles on him, he will know it. Murphy sees you as his daughter, not as a woman. And Gretchen," he said, smiling darkly, "she doesn't fancy girls."

I reeled as his words helped me see something I'd never noticed before. Desire. That explained why boys my age seemed to respond the strongest to me. Girls were mostly unaffected, and teachers— I remembered the day I'd stood on the dining hall table. Fiedler had bent the rules for me, but he never leered at me the way Greg or Parker or Rick had done.

"That just leaves Lucas," Thane said. I realized he was still watching me.

"I haven't done anything wrong," I said, faintly.

"It's not what you've done. It's what you are."

"What I *am?*" I flashed. "I'm trying as hard as I can to help you!"

"And yet you still haven't managed to escape your dream," Thane murmured. "I wonder how long we will be expected to tolerate you if you don't prove useful to the cause?"

"Hale believes in me," I said hotly.

"Hale is playing with fire," Thane answered. "But when your self-control fails, it's Lucas who will get burned." Thane studied me impersonally. "The Lilitu in you will win out eventually. It's just a matter of time."

13

Thane's words haunted me all weekend. I don't know if he told Gretchen what he'd seen, but nothing seemed to change in her demeanor. I couldn't get close enough to Lucas to ask if he'd noticed anything different about her. I tried to keep myself busy with schoolwork. I'd gotten an extension on my English paper, but as I tried to write it, I kept catching myself staring absently out the window for a glimpse of Lucas. When I was away from him, I had this constant nagging sensation that I needed to be somewhere else. But when we were together for dinner at the Guard's house, we had to pretend a distance we didn't feel. We were close enough to touch, and yet unable to talk beyond asking each other to pass the bread. It took an extraordinary amount of effort and energy, and it left us both short-tempered. The whole weekend was an exercise in frustration. By Sunday afternoon I had a throbbing headache.

I was still feeling achy and irritable when I woke up on Monday morning after yet another failed attempt to access the dream world.

I left the house for school, shrugging into a wool jacket. It was Thanksgiving week, so we only had school until Wednesday. Which meant Lucas and I only had three days together this week instead of five. I got the Firebird started and cranked the heat. Cold air blasted me, but as I gunned the engine I felt a hint of warmth. I pulled onto the road.

Lucas was standing on the corner at the end of our street. I stopped for him, my heart giving a little leap.

"Can I bum a lift?" he asked, opening the passenger door.

"Get in," I said, smiling. He sat down and pulled the door closed. I glanced in the rearview mirror. "What about Gretchen?"

"Gretchen left early this morning. Marx's unit needs her. They're on a Lilitu's trail but their spotter's appendix burst. She had to have emergency surgery. Gretchen will be gone for three or four days, at least. Maybe even a week."

"Are all spotters girls?" I asked, pulling out onto the street.

"Most of them, yeah. We don't officially know why, but—"

"Thane has a theory?"

Lucas grinned. "You guessed it. He thinks people share a part of themselves when they have an intimate bond," Lucas said. "So when a Lilitu attacks a guy, she's also attacking the girl who loves him. It's just a theory. But whatever the reason, once you've seen one Lilitu, you can see them all." Lucas turned to me, curious. "You're kind of rare. A natural, I guess. Gretchen, well, you know." Lucas shrugged sadly. He got the same look every time he thought about Eric. "Anyway, I'm glad for Gretchen. She'll get some quality time with Matt."

I noticed a little grin on Lucas's face. "Who's this Matt you speak of?" I asked, smiling.

"He's in Marx's unit. Gretchen hasn't said anything, but it's pretty clear she's interested." Lucas's smile faded. "She needs some R and R. She was out looking for the Lilitu hunting ground until three or four in the morning both Saturday and Sunday night. No luck."

"Hunting ground?" I asked, making the turn into the school parking lot.

"Lilitu typically stake out one or two places for their hunts," Lucas said. "They'll hunt the same spots until they move onto a different city."

I had more questions, but as I shut off the engine, Cassie bounded up to us. Her long black hair hung free, except for two tiny ponytails perched on top of her head. She was so excited, she practically floated above the ground.

"Sorry, Lucas. Can I—?" Cassie pulled me away before Lucas could speak.

"I take it the date went well?" I asked.

"The *dates*." Cassie said, breathlessly. "I saw him every night this weekend! But last night was..." She squeezed my arm, her eyes gleaming. "It was amazing. We bundled up in sleeping bags and watched the sky for shooting stars until midnight, and then he invited me to stay the night." Cassie smiled, an inward smile that hinted at more than she was saying. "It was the most romantic night of my life."

"Unfortunately, the romance ended this morning when she had to call me to come pick her up." Royal joined us, his expression cool.

"He didn't give you a ride to school?" I asked, angry on Cassie's behalf.

"Well, he was already gone when I woke up." Cassie saw me glance at Royal. "No, it's cool. I'm sure he had a morning practice or something and he just didn't want to disturb me." Doubt entered Cassie's eyes for the first time. "I thought it was sweet."

I draped an arm around Cassie's shoulders and warned Royal with a look to keep his differing opinion to himself. "Yeah. I'm sure you're right," I lied.

I spent the morning worrying about Cassie. When we got to lunch, Cassie looked around eagerly. I saw her eyes snag on something and her face clouded over with pain. I followed her gaze and spotted Parker sitting between Amber and Missy. I noticed Royal staring at me. He jerked his head at Cassie as if to say, *distract her or something, will you?*

I cleared my throat. "So, Cassie, am I ever going to see this mysterious present you keep talking about?"

"Hm?" Her eyes focused on my face and she forced a smile. "Oh, yeah. Almost done. Believe it or not, I really am putting the finishing touches on it right now."

"How'd you learn to sew?" Lucas asked. I felt his hand catch mine under the table. He gave it a brief squeeze and released it. So he had caught on. Which meant he knew something was wrong, too. Cassie launched into the story that Royal and I knew inside and out. We'd lived half of it with her; taking trips to fabric stores, haggling for a better price per yard, sitting through epic fitting sessions...

While Cassie talked, I took a bite of mashed potatoes and glanced around. Amber's table was staring in our direction, snickering. It gave me an uneasy feeling. I could tell Royal was burning with the same nervous curiosity I felt.

We were no closer to unraveling the mystery by the end of gym. It was my turn to stay behind and help Ms. Davies put away the equipment. Afterwards, I hurried to change, hoping I might catch

Royal and Cassie before they left for English. They were already gone when I came out, but Lucas was waiting for me outside the doors to the gym.

"Hey, I know this is kind of short notice," he said. "But do you want to go to a movie with me after school? I'm only asking because Gretchen's out of town. You can't have practice without a sparring partner, right? And who knows when we might get another—"

"Yes," I said, laughing. "I would love to go to a movie with you."

By the time I got to English, there was only one available seat left. Right in front of Missy and Amber. With a small sigh, I took it. Missy tapped me on the shoulder about five minutes later. I sighed inwardly. *Here we go.*

"I was wondering if I could ask you for a favor," Missy whispered when Mr. Young's back was turned.

"What?" I meant, *Could you please repeat that, it sounded like you just asked me for a favor.* But she interpreted it as, *What favor?*

"I'm in charge of organizing this year's Winter Ball. We're selling tickets, and the profits are going to diabetes research." I stared at Missy. Her big sister, Carrie, had been born with diabetes. Carrie had graduated last year but I remembered her. She'd been on the cheer squad, and she was down to earth and funny. The kind of girl I would have liked as a friend. I'd never forget the day she slipped into insulin shock. She'd been studying under a tree and she just seemed to go blank. Someone noticed and ran for the school nurse. They called the paramedics, but while we were waiting for them, the nurse got Carrie to swallow some jam and she slowly came back to herself. By the time the paramedics arrived, she was talking again. I'd heard she was studying at Brown now. "I was thinking we could have the dance at the Raven," Missy said.

"Why do you want my help?" I asked bluntly.

Missy gave me a little half-smile. It was like an admission of guilt. "I know we haven't exactly been BFFs," she said. "But I need you. You have a lot of fans at school. If you help us with the Ball, I know it'll be successful." She seemed to be waiting for my answer. When I hesitated, she got worried. "Look, the profits are going to a good cause. My sister—"

"Okay. I'll help." I didn't want her to use Carrie to try to guilt-trip me. "When is it?"

Missy grinned. "December 21st." I felt a chill run over my skin.

"Missy? Braedyn?" Mr. Young said, giving us an irritated glare. "I hope I'm not interrupting your little social hour back there by trying to teach my class."

"Sorry, Mr. Young," Missy said, flashing him a brilliant smile. He frowned and turned back to the blackboard. Missy leaned back to me, keeping her voice low. "I think we should do some kind of winter solstice theme, since Winter Ball is actually *on* the solstice this year. The good news is, we have three and a half weeks to plan."

My mind felt numb. Three and a half weeks. There were only three and a half weeks left to stop Ais before she rekindled an ancient war.

I was still reeling when Lucas found me after school.

"What kind of movie do you want to see?" he asked. I blanched, remembering our plans. Lucas saw my expression and hesitated. "Unless you've changed your mind?"

"No. I just have to call Dad," I said, covering quickly.

When I made the call, Dad assumed this was a group experience, and I didn't correct him. We'd invited Royal and Cassie, but she wanted to get home in case Parker called. So Royal took Cassie home and I drove with Lucas to the movie theater. We got our tickets and Lucas bought a popcorn for us to share. Being an early show on a Monday, the theater was practically empty. We picked a spot near the back and settled in as the trailers rolled onto the screen.

I glanced at Lucas. He caught the movement and smiled at me. I felt a little thrill. No one was going to walk in on us, we weren't late to any classes, and we didn't have any other friends hanging around. This was an honest-to-goodness date. Lucas offered his hand, palm up. I took it, reveling in the touch as his fingers curled around mine with casual familiarity. I was glad for the dark, so he couldn't see the blush spreading over my cheeks.

By the time the movie started, I was relaxing into my chair. It was an action movie, and it was so bad it was funny. We started snickering and couldn't stop. We finally got shushed by a serious-looking guy a few rows in front of us, which just made us shake harder with silent laughter. After we recovered, I found myself watching him, mesmerized, as the flickering light from the movie screen played off his features.

Lucas leaned forward and kissed me. His touch sent jolts of shivery thrills across my skin. After the aching frustration of the weekend, our kiss became urgent, heated. Lucas lifted a hand to my cheek, letting his thumb trace the edge of my jaw. I reached for him, too, resting one hand on his chest, sliding the other up to his face. I felt the pulse of life in his throat, quickening.

But then something changed.

The intense, staccato soundtrack of the movie seemed to fade, slipping into the background of my mind. I was only dimly aware of this. Lucas, and the growing heat of our kiss, filled my head. A strange, surging storm was moving *through* me, wild and powerful and heedless of whatever stood in its path.

Lucas's arm dropped, scattering popcorn on the ground.

With impossible effort, I pulled back.

What I saw in Lucas's face turned my blood cold. His eyes, half-lidded, looked listless and dull. As soon as we broke contact, his eyes closed and he slipped into unconsciousness. The storm within me subsided to a dull roar, receding slowly. My heart thudded painfully. We'd kissed. That was all. What was happening?

I shook him gently, but Lucas didn't stir. His chest was rising and falling with slow, even breaths, but his eyelids didn't flicker. I shook him harder. In front of us, the credits started to roll. They seemed to drag on for hours as I tried to bring Lucas back to consciousness. Finally I saw some movement beneath his lids. Groggily, and with great effort, he opened his eyes.

Relief turned my muscles to jelly. I slumped in my seat, watching as he stirred.

He saw me staring and wiped his eyes, straining to sit up. "Wow, this is embarrassing," he said. "Please tell me I wasn't drooling." He wiped his chin quickly.

I shook my head, still too keyed up to smile. "You feel okay?"

"Actually, yeah. Just a little tired," he said, stretching. "The natural side-effect of spending yet another weekend on home improvement." He saw our popcorn, scattered all over the floor. "Oh man, we made a mess in here."

We scooped up the spilled popcorn and left, tossing the tub in the trash on our way out. Lucas reached for my hand but I pulled away from him quickly. He glanced at me, uncertain.

I used my cell phone as an excuse, pulling it out of my pocket and turning it on. "Dad's pretty insistent. I promised I'd turn it back on right after the movie." As I fussed with my phone, I was screaming at myself internally. Whatever had happened in there could *never happen again.* What if Gretchen was right? What if no matter what I tried to do, I ended up hurting Lucas? If we kissed again? What if I lost control next time? What if I couldn't stop the storm? With a dull realization, I suddenly knew I had to tell him the truth.

"Everything cool?" he asked, worried.

"Actually, there is something I need to tell you," I started. My cell phone beeped, interrupting me. I glanced at it and saw I had 34 missed calls. I lifted the phone up for a closer look. 34?

"What's wrong?"

"I don't know." I hit the speed dial for my voicemail. The first message was from Royal.

"Braedyn, where are you? I need you. Cassie—she slept with that asshole last night. He had friends hiding in his private bathroom, watching the whole thing. It was some kind of bet. The whole school knows. Cassie won't see me. She's locked herself in her room. Her parents don't know, Braedyn. I can't—I can't tell them. I need you. Please. Call me when you get this message." I hung up, stricken. I must have looked faint, because Lucas reached out to steady me.

"What's wrong?" Lucas asked. "Braedyn? What's going on?!"

"I have to go to Cassie," I said, and then a tidal wave of rage choked off my words and I couldn't speak. Lucas grabbed my hand and pulled me back to my car.

"I don't know where she lives," he said.

"I'll drive. You call Royal." I tossed my cell phone to Lucas. He plucked it out of the air and jumped into the passenger seat. I peeled out of the parking lot, ignoring the posted speed limits. Lucas got Royal on the phone. Their conversation was short and grim. Lucas shot a worried look at me while he talked with Royal.

"Yeah, okay," he said finally. "We're on our way over there right now." Lucas hung up and neither of us said anything for a long moment. Then Lucas slammed his fist against the door, furious. "I keep telling myself the Lilitu are the enemy. Sometimes I forget we have more than enough bad guys in our own species."

I didn't take my eyes off the road. Cassie's apartment was on the other side of town. When I finally pulled to a stop in front of her building, the sun was going down. Their complex was old but comfortable, with only four units. Cassie and her parents lived in the top back unit. I ran around the building and up the metal safety stairs that led to the kitchen door. I knocked, frantic, and Cassie's mom opened the door. Her face was wrenched with concern.

"She won't tell me what's wrong," she said. "Braedyn, what happened? Do you know?"

"Can I see her?"

Mrs. Han looked torn between needing to know the truth, and hoping I might be able to reach her daughter. "Go." She stepped aside and I ran to Cassie's room. It was still locked. I knocked softly.

"Cassie, it's me. Are you—?" I cut myself off. Of course she wasn't okay. "Can I come in?" I waited, but heard nothing. "Cass?" After a minute, I heard someone sniffling and saw a shadow moving under the door. I put my hand on the door's smooth surface. I could almost feel Cassie standing on the other side.

"It's not a good time," she said, her voice quivering. "Please leave me alone. And tell Royal—just tell him I need some space, okay?" She flicked off the light and after a minute I heard her bed springs sigh as she laid back down. I tried talking to her through the door, but she didn't answer me again. After half an hour, her mother finally came and pulled me away gently, eyes filled with questions.

"Does this have something to do with that boy she's been talking about?" Mrs. Han asked. I met her eyes and she seemed to get all the confirmation she needed. "I could tell she liked him. But I thought—I thought she would be safe with you."

It was like a knife turning in my gut. I looked at the floor. "She never came over to my place."

Mrs. Han grew very still, and then nodded slowly. "I see. I see."

Lucas and I left. The drive back was nearly silent. He got out of the car and didn't seem to realize I hadn't turned off the engine until I was pulling away from the curb. "Hey," he called after me. "Where are you going? Braedyn?"

I drove straight to Parker's house. I'd been there once before, when we'd had the Progressive Dinner at the end of freshman year.

Somehow I found it with only a few wrong turns. I pulled into his driveway and parked my car, too angry to bother locking the doors. I was marching toward the front door when I heard laughter coming from the backyard. There was a side gate. I threw it open and stormed into the middle of another of Parker's barbecues.

One of his friends saw me and smirked. "Uh oh, vengeance patrol." The guys watched me approach with knowing smiles. I stopped in front of Parker, who was manning the grill.

He gave me an icy grin. "Cassie must have really enjoyed herself if she's sending over referrals." The boys snickered. Parker turned back to the grill, dismissing me.

"I want to talk with you. Alone." I felt something in my voice, a commanding presence. Parker's friends stood. One turned for the door to his house.

"Sit down, guys. She doesn't get to come in here and give orders." Parker's eyes didn't waver. His smile was steely.

"You're sick, Parker. You're—" I wanted to hit him. After sparring with Gretchen, I knew exactly where to strike to drop him. I bet that'd wipe the smirk off his smug face. Somewhere deep inside me, a small voice warned me to hold back. "You made her think you liked her. She trusted you and you—you betrayed her."

"I showed her a good time. I can't help it if she gets all obsessed over me." He shrugged, as though he was the victim, not Cassie. "Besides, wasn't it your idea that I hit on her in the first place? Or don't you remember being too busy to dance with me at that party I threw for you?"

My vision was changing; I felt like I was looking at Parker through a tunnel. I was only vaguely aware of the other boys around us. "You hurt a really good person."

"I didn't force her to go all the way," he said. "She wanted to. And you're trespassing on private property, so if you don't want me to call the cops, you'd better scoot along." He planted a finger in the middle of my chest and shoved me back. I grabbed it and twisted. Parker howled in surprise and anger. I knew if I added even an ounce more pressure, his finger would snap. I really wanted to do it. It would feel like some small measure of justice. But I released him and left, following the path back out to the side gate. His friends were on their feet now, unsure whether or not it was cool to tackle a girl.

"Whatever. Forget her," Parker said, laughing it off. I was no threat to him at all.

I was still seething when I got back to my car. I jerked my door open and slid inside. Someone was sitting in my passenger seat.

It was Karayan.

14

I felt all the air leave my lungs. Karayan reached across me and pulled my door closed. Her silky honey-blond hair brushed past my face. I stiffened. She sat back, and turned to stare out the front windshield. A guy approached us on the sidewalk with his dog. The dog gave a low woof and dipped its tail. It sensed what its master couldn't; we weren't just two girls sitting in a car—we didn't belong in this world. I thought about opening the door, screaming for help. But what could he do? He would be no match for Karayan. I watched them pass, and in a few moments Karayan and I were the only living souls on the street.

"I know you think I'm your enemy. But I'm not." Karayan's voice was quiet. Almost wistful. I glanced at her. She was staring at the house. "He deserves to be punished."

A jolt of surprise distracted me for a moment, but I forced myself to focus. Karayan wouldn't be here without a reason. "What do you want from me?"

"I want you to let me help you." Karayan faced me, and some small part of me was again struck by the perfect beauty of her face. Her rich green eyes held mine, unflinching. "Guys like this? They treat girls like toys. They play with them until they break them, and then they toss them aside. And most of these boys get away with it." Her jaw clenched with real anger. "No one else is going to deliver justice for your friend, Braedyn. It's up to you. You see that, right?"

I looked away from Karayan quickly. I didn't want to hear what she was saying. And it wasn't because I disagreed with her. A different kind of fear took hold of me. Her words wove a terrible kind of logic into my mind, a logic that was hard to argue with. And I did want justice for Cassie.

163

"Let me paint a picture for you of what Cassie's life will be like now," Karayan said quietly. "The boys at school will taunt her, because now they think she's easy. The girls at school will shun her, because now they think she's a slut." Karayan's words were like nails, and she drove them into my heart with uncanny precision. "You and your friends will try to shield her. Don't fool yourselves. You won't be able to make her deaf to the insults they'll shout at her across the quad, or blind to the graffiti they'll scratch into the bathroom stalls." Karayan's eyes seemed to darken, as the ocean does when clouds pass overhead. "If she's brokenhearted today, imagine how she'll feel when her peers get through with her."

I felt a sharp pain in my hand and looked down. I'd squeezed my hand into a fist so tight that I'd driven a fingernail into the flesh of my palm. As I looked at the dot of blood forming in my palm, a drop of water splashed it away. Only then did I realize I was crying.

She stared at me until I met her eyes. "You have the power to make him pay."

"How?"

"By showing him what he's done."

I shook my head, frustrated. And then I voiced what had finally driven me away from Parker and his laughing friends—the awful truth that had kept me in this car, listening to Karayan when I knew I should be running away. "How is that justice? He's—he's proud of it."

"He doesn't know what Cassie is feeling."

"You think he cares?"

"He'd care if he felt it himself."

I looked up at her sharply. "I won't—If you're suggesting I try to do the same thing to him that he did to Cassie—"

Karayan snorted in bitter amusement. "Please. He'd be thrilled to get so lucky." I watched her. Karayan was surprising me at every turn. Her smile faded. "I'm talking about justice. I'm talking about a punishment equivalent to the crime. And I mean it when I say you are the only one equipped to deliver it." I shook my head, but my attempt at denial was so weak that Karayan ignored it entirely. "Your empathy for Cassie—it helps you feel her pain. It's a map of the devastation she's feeling. All I'm suggesting is that you share that with Parker."

I dropped my eyes. "I tried. He won't listen."

"In the waking world, no. But he'll be at your mercy in the dream."

Karayan sat back, waiting for me to make the next move.

I breathed in, trying to calm my racing thoughts. "I don't want to hurt him."

"You don't have to hurt him," she said softly. "You just have to make him see." She gave me a searching look, and then she opened her door, got out of my car, and walked away. It was with shaking hands that I turned the ignition key. I hit the gas, speeding away from Parker's house.

It was much harder to leave Karayan's words behind.

I was still shaking when I changed for bed that night. Hale was counting on me. Cassie needed justice. It felt like all the answers were waiting for me in the dream world. But so was Karayan. I couldn't trust her. She'd attacked Derek so easily, destroyed his life with no more hesitation than I'd have plucking a flower. But what she'd said about Parker... I needed time to think. I lay down to sleep and told myself I wouldn't dream at all. It worked. The morning arrived quickly, but I did not feel rested.

"How did it go last night?" Dad asked me, pouring his morning coffee.

"Um," I turned away quickly, buttering some toast. "Same as the night before, and the night before that," I lied.

"Braedyn." I looked up to find him watching me with a wistful expression. "I know how hard this is for you, but you keep trying. I'm so proud of you."

I forced a smile, feeling sick. "I should get going," I said. Dad glanced at the clock, surprised. "I need to get some last minute studying in," I lied again. "Quiz." Dad nodded and I fled the house, heading to school.

Cassie didn't come to school Tuesday or Wednesday. Neither Royal nor I could get her on the phone. Lucas offered what little comfort he could at school, but knowing what Cassie must be going through, nothing could put my mind at ease.

And then Thanksgiving dawned. The holiday had always meant Dad and I spent most of the day cooking in the kitchen, then savoring our meal together. This year, we were sharing a half-hearted feast with the Guard. We ate at their house around four in the afternoon. Gretchen's absence was unsettling, but everyone else had pitched in. Dad had roasted the turkey, I'd boiled and mashed the potatoes, Lucas and Thane had taken care of the green beans and the yams, and Hale had tackled a pecan pie. It all smelled wonderful, but after a few bites, the food lost its flavor for me. I couldn't stop thinking about Cassie and Parker.

After the big meal, Royal picked me up so we could go visit Cassie. She wouldn't come out of her room to see us. She wouldn't see anyone all weekend. Royal and I stopped by her apartment on Saturday, and again on Sunday. Her mother looked exhausted. She asked us to keep an eye on Cassie at school next week. Only Cassie didn't come back to school on Monday. We didn't know it at the time, but she wouldn't be back for two solid weeks.

The first Monday of December dawned bright and cold. In 19 days, it would be winter solstice. The Guard was depending on me, but I'd spent the previous week avoiding dreams entirely. Every morning I woke up feeling a little guiltier. Hale was starting to worry. In our last practice session he'd asked if there was something else he could be doing to help me. I'd just shaken my head, promising to try harder.

I pushed back the covers and got out of bed. I heard a car pull up outside and glanced out the window, curious.

Gretchen was back. She got out of the passenger's side of a car I'd never seen before. She looked strange, almost hesitant. The driver joined her on the lawn. He was tall and fit, with dark, close-cropped hair. He didn't look much older than Gretchen. He enfolded her in his arms, and they shared a long kiss. I felt uncomfortably voyeuristic.

I glanced away, pulling on my socks. When I looked out the window again, they were walking slowly toward the house, hand in hand. Gretchen stepped onto the first porch step and looked him directly in the eye. She ran a hand along the side of his face, almost gingerly. I had never seen Gretchen look so vulnerable, so soft.

They shared another kiss, and then he returned to his car. Gretchen watched until he was out of sight. I saw her arms curl up to hug herself. A small smile played around the corners of her mouth, and then she straightened and walked into the house.

Lucas was waiting by my locker at school. Since Gretchen was back, she was his ride to and from school again. For a moment, he didn't see me approaching. I let my eyes drink in the sight of him. He wore the uniform of Coronado Prep with a relaxed confidence that made the entire ensemble seem like it was his idea. He looked up and saw me.

"Any word from Cass?"

I shook my head. "We're going to check on her after school. I'll let you know if there's any change." Gretchen would pick Lucas up after school today, so he wouldn't be able to join Royal and me to go visit Cassie.

I opened my locker and reached into my bag for my books. I accidentally dropped a spiral notebook. Someone swept it up off the floor before I could bend to retrieve it.

"Here, I think you dropped this." Greg handed me the spiral with a hopeful smile.

"Thanks," I said, taking it. When he didn't move, I cleared my throat. "See you later." Greg nodded and left. I turned back to my locker and saw Lucas watching me with a faintly amused smile.

"That's what you get for kissing him,"

"I didn't turn him into a drooling idiot," I said.

"Are you sure about that?" Lucas laughed.

The skin on the back of my neck started crawling. I got my books and closed my locker.

We had lasagna again for lunch. Lucas had to leave lunch early, something about a make-up quiz. Royal didn't try too hard to engage me in conversation; we were both lost in our own unhappy thoughts. Missy stopped by our table, interrupting my train of thought.

"Braedyn, we have a problem," she said. Amber followed her stiffly. "I went to pay the security deposit at the Raven last weekend, but they need all the details in advance—how many people, if we're bringing in outside food and drinks. If we lose the Raven we won't have time to find another venue and get it approved by Administration. We'll be stuck in the gym again. I need you for like an hour or two after school to plan."

"I'm sorry, Missy. You should probably count me out," I said. "I've got a lot going on right now, I don't think I can help you with Winter Ball." I had serious problems. Winter Ball wasn't even a smudge on my list of things to worry about.

"Wait, think about it, please," Missy said, her face falling.

"Forget it, Missy. We don't need her." Amber crossed her arms.

"Yes, we do." Missy shut Amber up with a look. "This isn't Homecoming. We're raising money for something worthwhile. I'm sorry if you don't like it, but she only has to snap her fingers and the entire male population of Coronado Prep will line up to buy tickets." Missy turned back to me. "Please. This whole thing is coming apart."

"I'm busy after school today," I said, grasping for an excuse. "I won't be free until at least after five."

"That's fine," Missy said eagerly. "I'll wait for you in the library, just find me when you're done. I don't care how late it is." Missy left with Amber in tow.

Royal watched them go. "If hating Braedyn Murphy was an Olympic sport, Amber would be gunning for the gold."

"What have I ever done to her?" I stabbed a piece of lasagna with my fork.

Royal gave me a level look. "Braedyn, two months ago she was Homecoming Queen, desired above all others, and well on her way to becoming that one girl in our class that everyone sighs over at reunions until the end of time. Then you..." He ran his eyes over me, impersonally. "Blossom... and all that attention she was living on instead of food dried up."

I pushed my food away, exhausted.

After school, Royal drove me to Cassie's house. Mrs. Han ushered us inside. Cassie was sitting in the living room, eating soup. She looked drawn and fragile, but she wasn't crying anymore.

"Hey, guys," she said. "I was starting to wonder if you'd forgotten me. It's been almost two whole hours since one of you called."

Royal sat next to Cassie and curled an arm around her back. "You left your room just in time. I was getting ready to bring in the Jaws of Life." Instead of answering him, Cassie leaned her head on his shoulder and looked up at me.

"I finished your present," she said.

"Cass. You didn't have to—" I started, but Cassie interrupted me.

"It took my mind off of... everything. I'll get it." She put her soup on the coffee table and started to stand.

"No, I'll get it. I'm already up." I moved toward the back hallway.

"My room's kind of a mess," she called.

"You're entitled," Royal said. Cassie looked down, but she nodded. I left them in the living room and went to Cassie's bedroom. Mrs. Han was inside, making the bed. She looked a lot better than the last time I'd seen her.

"Sorry. I was looking for—" I started.

"Your birthday present? It's on the desk." Mrs. Han hesitated before leaving. "She admires you very much. You and Royal."

"Thank you," I said, uncomfortable. She left. I turned to Cassie's desk. It was really more of a table, where she kept her computer, her sewing machine, and any project she was currently working on. The last time I'd been in this room I had been blindfolded so she could do a fitting without "ruining the surprise." I had thought she was making me a blouse, but what I saw took my breath away. It was half-jacket, half-cloak, made of a gorgeous stiff velvet in a green so deep it almost looked black. It was fitted to the waist, but the lower part of the jacket fanned out, sweeping almost to the floor. I picked it up and put it on. It had a comfortable weight.

There was something incredible about the clothes Cassie made. It would be too easy to say they fit like a glove. They were more like a second skin. I could move freely and the jacket didn't pull or bunch the way store-bought clothes always did. Cassie was an artist. I ran my fingers over the lining inside and recognized its feel. This must have been what I'd tried on when she'd brought me in here for the fitting. Somehow, by just measuring the lining, she'd been able to build the rest of the jacket and have it fit me perfectly. I looked at myself in the mirror and saw an elegant, confident young woman.

"Snazzy." I heard Royal's voice and turned. He and Cassie stood in the doorway. There was a new quality to Cassie's smile, a slight twist. I recognized it instantly; it was the same self-loathing I'd seen in Thane's smile that first moment I'd met him. And I knew; every day she'd spent locked in her room, Cassie had driven herself mad blaming herself. One more crime to lay at her tormentor's feet. I chased the thought away, but it left me cold.

"Turn around," Cassie commanded, stepping into the room. I obeyed her and she studied the jacket critically. "Not bad. I was worried about the hem, but it looks pretty decent."

"Um," Royal said, holding up a finger to correct her. "That is something of an understatement. It looks pretty Rock Star." Royal studied me from the other side. "Someone needs to teach this girl how to play the guitar." Shortly after that, Mrs. Han gently but firmly ended the visit. Cassie had to catch up on her homework, she told us. And so Royal and I left.

Royal dropped me back off at school with an arch, "Have fun planning the party."

I locked my gift from Cassie in my car, and then walked through campus to the library. It was the furthest building from the center of campus, but it had the best view. Beyond the library, the land sloped away, dotted with sagebrush and prairie grass. Distant mountains rose up in soft purple folds, their tops edged in white. I slipped around the main stacks to the large picture windows in back, taking a moment to soak in the view. But the peace I was seeking eluded me.

Someone nearby laughed. I froze as I heard Parker's voice. I edged closer and saw him talking with Amber, while Missy tried to focus on her chemistry textbook.

"I'm just saying, a Carnival would be so much cooler than a Ball," Parker said.

"We're trying to raise money," Missy said, with a strained smile. "Not blow it all on rides and cotton candy vendors."

"I don't know," Amber said, giving Parker a flirty smile. "This Carnival thing could be cool."

"You can make money at a Carnival," Parker said. "Like, dunking booths and stuff."

"You have to rent the booth," Missy said.

"We could make a kissing booth," Amber said.

"No—you know what you need to do?" Parker straightened with a wicked grin. "Instead of a kissing booth, set up a *Cassie* booth. Dudes would line up for that, I'm telling you. You'd make a fortune." Amber exploded in laughter.

"Ew!" Missy said. "That's deranged, Parker."

Amber wiped her eyes, grinning. "It's a good thing you're not on the planning committee. You'd get us all arrested."

"You wanted to raise money. I'm just saying." Parker rubbed his hands together, pleased with himself. I felt my feet moving. Missy saw me first and tried to signal them to shut up. Parker noticed her efforts and spotted me. He straightened with a lazy smile. "I'll catch you girls later." Parker turned and walked out of the library.

"Braedyn," Missy started. I silenced her with a look. To her credit, she didn't try to stop me when I walked away.

I felt a steady anger building inside me on the drive home. Hale had left a note for me on our fridge. Practice was back on. I met Hale and Gretchen in the basement five minutes later. For the first time ever, I was eager to throw some punches. Hale gave us the signal to start and I attacked. Gretchen's concentration was fierce. We moved together, jabbing and dodging, kicking out and jumping back. I pressed my attack, focused on burning through the rage in my head. I pictured Parker standing where Gretchen was, and fought forward, trying to land every punch.

Gretchen dodged back and struck out, tagging me hard in the side; it was the exact spot Karayan had hit when she broke my rib. I skittered backwards. My ribs had healed, but a cold fear clamped onto me with the remembered pain. Gretchen shot Hale an unreadable look. Hale considered me, evaluating me with his eyes. I was tired of feeling scared and weak. I squared my shoulders and lunged for Gretchen, fighting against the emotions raging through my head.

"Easy," Gretchen said. She took one step back, then another, blocking my punches.

"Okay, okay. Whoa!" Someone put a hand on my shoulder and I spun to face him, fist raised to strike. It was Hale. I dropped my arm instantly, chagrined. Hale's gray eyes searched my face. He looked unsettled. I glanced at Gretchen. She was bent over, hands on her knees, breathing hard.

"I'm out," she said. "I need to shower. And then pass out." Gretchen looked at me as she straightened. "I'll give her this; she doesn't hit like a girl anymore." Gretchen retreated up the stairs, rubbing her shoulder.

Hale tossed me a towel. I pulled my padding off slowly. He was watching me. "You okay?" His tone was light enough, but I wasn't fooled. I was like a Derby horse; they had to monitor my training carefully so I didn't injure myself before the big race. I nodded, but didn't offer anything else. "You should know—you're learning incredibly fast."

"Right." I finished pulling off all of the protective gear and dumped it on the table, and then grabbed my water bottle and drained it.

Hale gestured at the chair behind me. "Have a seat." I dropped into the chair, bracing myself for another lecture about the mission. He surprised me. "That fear? It's not going to last forever. You're already 10 times as strong as the girl who tried to save Derek that night."

"I don't feel any different," I said, looking at my hands in my lap.

"I see the difference," Hale said. "And Gretchen feels the difference. She's not holding back anymore. Did you notice that?" I looked up, surprised. "It's true. This is as hard as I've ever seen her train." He caught my eye. The look on his face was almost fond. He turned and walked up the basement stairs, leaving me alone with my thoughts.

I went home to shower. As the water ran over my face, I let my thoughts return to the conversation I'd had with Karayan. She said I didn't have to hurt Parker; I just had to make him see. I breathed in the steam and remembered Parker's laughter, his cold, unfeeling smile in the library that afternoon. It didn't seem like hurting him was the worst idea in the world.

I was quiet at dinner. I could feel Lucas watching me, worrying, but I didn't meet his eyes. After dinner, I walked home with Dad. He tried to draw me into watching one of our favorite shows, but I wasn't in the mood for television. When it was finally time to go to sleep, I pulled on an old t-shirt and climbed into bed. I intended to go through the relaxation exercises and spend the night trying to find Karayan.

But as soon as my eyes closed, I saw her standing in my field of white roses.

"I thought I might be seeing you soon," Karayan said, smiling. She picked a rose and ran a finger over the slender stem, playing with the thorns. One of the thorns pricked her finger and she dropped it, irked.

"How do we find him?" I asked.

"Ooo, all business. I like that," she said.

"Just show me."

In answer, Karayan touched the ground. Water seeped out of the dirt to create a mirrored pool. Inside, a dusting of stars twinkled. She made it look so effortless.

"How do you do that?" I asked. Karayan looked up, startled. "I've been trying. I've tried *everything*."

Karayan understood immediately. She moved her hand and the pool vanished. "You're thinking like a human," she said. "They're only aware of the physical world they can see and touch. Don't treat this place like it's real. If you try to touch the ground, all you'll end up with is a fistful of dirt." She waved one graceful hand at the space around us. "This whole dream space is a metaphor. You have to keep that in mind, or your own perception will trap you here. We're inside a bubble of illusion, floating in a vast sea. That sea is the larger dream world. In order to access it, you just have to make a tiny hole in your bubble." She gestured for me to join her. We knelt side-by-side on the ground. "Try it now."

I laid my hand on the ground, but it still felt like dirt to me. I glanced at Karayan, uncertain. She gave me an encouraging nod. I pictured this place like the inside of one of those snow globes they sell to tourists in Old Town. Suddenly, it was like I could sense the curving glass trapping us in this illusion. I visualized the dirt beneath me as being less than an inch thick, and pressed my finger down. I felt something cool and slick under my hand. A pool of dark liquid grew in front of us, full of tiny flickers of light. I met Karayan's eyes, triumphant.

"Nicely done," she breathed, grinning at my excitement. "Now, in order to find someone, you have to picture him in your mind. See his face, hear his voice."

It was too easy; I had been doing that all day. Karayan took my hand and set it onto the surface of the pool. Only it didn't feel like water. It was smooth like glass, even as it flowed around my hand.

Inside the pool, the stars scattered, like dust disturbed by a sudden gust of wind. One of the stars was rising up out of the dark water. It breached the surface, hanging between us like a gleaming seed of light.

"Touch it," Karayan said. I hesitated, but she smiled. "I'll be right behind you."

I touched the glimmer, and was drawn into another field. A soccer field. I turned and saw Derek running toward me. I was so startled, I screamed. Derek didn't stop; he kicked a soccer ball and it sped past my head ferociously. I turned in time to see Parker knock it into the goal with a precise head-butt. Suddenly, the field was surrounded by risers full of screaming fans. As the cheering rose, Derek and the other soccer players faded away.

Karayan joined me. "He dreams of glory. Typical." Parker didn't seem to see us. I glanced at Karayan. "Well?" she asked. "We've found him. What do you want to do?"

"I want to make him feel what Cassie feels. I want him—I want him to hate himself." Even as I said the words, I felt an icy fist close around my heart. I thought about Cassie and her new, bitter smile.

"Then you need to plant that in his mind," Karayan said coolly. She took my hand and cupped it, making a small bowl. "Imagine a seed. All of your friend's suffering, all that agony and pain and humiliation, focus all of it into this seed." I did, and as I watched, a fat, gray seed coalesced in the palm of my hand. "Now picture this seed growing into a tree, every leaf another hated aspect of himself that Parker will have to face. Picture its roots, digging deep into his sense of self, feeding off his arrogance." I obeyed her, pouring these negative thoughts into the seed. It felt heavier and heaver in my hand, and my vision started to blur. I blinked, and found I was woozy, weak. "Almost done," Karayan whispered to me. "Is there anything else you'd like to throw in for good measure?"

I combed through my mind, but the rage I'd started with was gone. I felt empty. Everything was already in the seed. "No." I looked up. "Now what?"

"Now... Plant it." Karayan stepped back, regarding the lush grass of the field. "This is Parker's dream. His mind. Plant the seed anywhere. It will grow."

I hesitated, unsure. Karayan made no move to hurry me. She simply waited. I felt a tugging on my conscience and I almost backed down. But a thought lurked in the shadows of my mind. In the real world, the best thing for Cassie would be for her to get past this pain. To heal. Cassie was too fragile for a direct confrontation, and Parker was too callous to let that kind of thing hurt him anyway. Which meant he would suffer no retribution. Here in the dream, this seed was retribution. It would leave Cassie innocent of any crime. No one ever had to know. And Parker would get what Parker deserved. I drew comfort from this thought, and dug my hand into the thick grass, down into the wet soil of Parker's dream. I dropped the seed inside. Thin roots sprouted from it like hairs, spooling into the dirt around it. I watched in sick fascination for a moment, then covered the rooting seed up.

"Let's get out of here," I said. "This place gives me the creeps." Karayan offered me her hand. I took it. Her fingers were cool and strong. She closed them around my hand and the dream shifted. We were back in my field of roses, only something was different. I tried to place it, but Karayan interrupted my thoughts.

"I wondered when you would come to your senses." She smiled, victorious. "I told them I could save you from the Guard. It would just be a matter of time."

"Told who?" I asked numbly.

"Our sisters. You met them at your birthday party. They were curious about you, but after that night, they didn't think you'd ever leave the Guard. They'll be eager to see you."

I stared at her with a sinking feeling. "I'm not leaving the Guard."

Karayan regarded me for a long moment. "Those men will never accept you for what you are. They are only interested in you as long as they can control you."

"I know how bad it must have been growing up with Thane. But just because he was awful to you doesn't mean everyone in the Guard is cruel."

Karayan stiffened. "Whatever you think you know—"

"I know Thane treated you like a weapon, not a daughter. But my dad is different. Hale is different."

"They have devoted their lives to killing our kind."

"They—They just want to protect people," I said. "Do you really want to start another war?"

Karayan stared at me, frustrated. "Some part of you knows you can't trust them, right?" She scrutinized my face, looking for answers. "If you have even a little doubt, come with me and hear our side." She held out her hand. I didn't take it. She pursed her lips. "Change is coming, and the Guard can't stop it. What do you think will happen when the Wall comes down? If you stand with the Guard, you'll put yourself on the front lines. As soon as our numbers are great enough, the Guard will fall. Stand with them, and you'll fall, too." The look she gave me was full of pity. "It's your choice." Karayan vanished.

I stared at the place she'd been standing for a few long moments before it hit me. I knew what was different about my field. The roses were no longer a pristine white. I grabbed blossom after blossom from the plants, scattering petals on the ground. I lost count of how many roses I tore apart, but every single petal had a crimson stain at its base.

I dropped to my knees, trying to get a grip on this wild fear. Why was I worrying about roses when I had finally found the key to escaping my dream?

With renewed determination, I touched the ground and drew another pool of liquid stars. I meant to seek out Hale, to finally complete that first assignment he'd given me. But when I looked into the pool of stars, a single spark was already travelling toward me. As it emerged from the pool, I felt a little flutter in my chest. This spark felt familiar, warm, safe. I let my hand close around it, ignoring the part of me that urged caution. The world seemed to shift.

I found myself in a deserted parking garage. The skies were murky and dark; there was an ominous feel to this place. Someone grabbed my shoulder.

"What are you doing here?" Lucas pulled me behind a structural support column. "We have to run!"

I felt my eyes widen in understanding. A nightmare. I took Lucas's hand in mine. "It's okay, Lucas," I said.

"No. It's out there. It's coming—"

I leaned forward and kissed him. I felt a rush of sensation, a quieter version of the storm I'd felt in the theater. Lucas's resistance fell away. He curled his arms around me. The dreamscape shifted around us, and I pulled back from the kiss.

We were standing at the edge of an ocean, too beautiful to be real. Water undulated as far as the eye could see, hemmed by a gleaming white beach. As we watched, the sun scrolled through the sky, dropping the day into sunset, bathing this imagined world in russet light.

Lucas brushed my cheek with the backs of his fingers. The sensation was pleasant, but muted. Nothing felt quite real here. Not his touch, not the sand beneath our feet. And yet... I didn't care. Hale had been right. A simple kiss was more than enough.

I opened my eyes to find light streaming into my room. I snuggled deeper into the covers, smiling. What a dream. I felt invigorated. Powerful. I swung my legs out of bed and walked to the window. Lucas's drapes were still closed. The murmur of voices reached me from downstairs. It sounded like Hale was talking with my father. I pulled my clothes on, skipping the shower. I raced downstairs just as Hale and Dad were walking to the front door.

"I did it. I broke out of my dream," I said.

Hale's face transformed with joy. "Fantastic. Fantastic!"

Dad's smile was a little more reserved. "Do you think you can do it again?"

"Yeah. It—I was going about it all wrong before." I took a deep breath, steeling myself. "Karayan showed me how to do it." Their smiles faded. "I need to tell you something else." They listened closely as I told them what Karayan had said about striking at the Guard as soon as the Wall came down. Dad's eyes clouded when I told them how Karayan tried to get me to join her sisters. Hale looked grim when I had finished.

"Thank you. You were right to tell us everything," Hale said. I felt a twinge. I hadn't told them everything. I had made no mention of what I'd done to Parker, or how I'd spent the rest of the night. Hale glanced at Dad. "It sounds like Karayan is deeply involved."

"Thane won't like that."

Hale grimaced. "I don't plan on telling him. I've got Gretchen searching for hunting grounds that may or may not exist. I need Thane focused on his search for minds touched by Lilitu."

My breath caught.

Hale sighed and turned to my dad. "Speaking of impossible tasks, you and I should get started canvassing the city for Thrall."

"Right. We should be back by dinner," Dad said, squeezing my shoulder.

I caught his hand before he withdrew. "Wait," I said. "Can I—" I glanced at Hale, uneasy. "Can I talk to you alone for a second, Dad?"

"Meet me outside when you're ready," Hale told Dad. He walked out, leaving us alone.

"What is it, honey?" Dad asked, concerned.

"What does that mean, minds touched by Lilitu?"

Dad shrugged, surprised by the question. "Whenever Lilitu interfere with someone's sleeping mind, they leave a residual connection behind."

"But, I thought dreams were safe," I said.

"Most of the time they are," Dad said quickly, sensing my anxiety. "We're talking about what happens when a Lilitu wants to hurt someone. But that's a very intentional process," he continued, offering a comforting smile. "Don't worry, honey. You won't accidently hurt someone in a dream."

I lowered my eyes, trying to hide the roiling panic from Dad. "How do you find people after a Lilitu's touched their mind?"

"Thane's very good at IDing victims by extreme or uncharacteristic behavior," Dad said. "Once he finds them, Gretchen can spot the connection and, if it's strong enough, trace it back to the Lilitu responsible. Thane's trying to locate potential victims right now."

"So, Lilitu can hurt people without sleeping with them?" I asked. My voice sounded hollow.

"Yes." Dad looked at me more closely. "Are you all right, honey?"

"Just surprised," I said, forcing a smile. "I keep learning more."

Dad squeezed my shoulder. "Like I said, you can't hurt someone in a dream unless you're trying to. So don't worry so much. Anything else?" he asked. I shook my head. "All right. I'll see you later on tonight." Dad kissed my forehead and left. I sank into the couch.

All day, the gnawing feeling in my stomach grew stronger and stronger. No one had told me Lilitu left traces when they interfered with someone's mind. I'd felt a hesitation before planting the seed in Parker's dream. Why had I gone through with it?

By dinner, I was plagued by an almost constant fear: what would happen if Thane and Gretchen discovered what I had done to Parker?

15

"So," Thane said, sitting down at our dining room table that night. "You're finally ready to begin the search for Ais. You've certainly left little enough time to spare." I felt Dad shift beside me, but he managed to hold his tongue. Hale, who had joined us for this conversation at Dad's request, gave Thane a disapproving frown.

"Just tell me how to find her," I said, trying to keep the hostility in my voice at a reasonable level.

"What makes you think I'd know how to do that?" Thane asked.

"You—you're—?" I stared at him, flabbergasted. "Hale said you were a lucid dreamer."

Hale spoke, explaining gently. "He's human, Braedyn. His abilities are limited to navigating his own dreams."

I turned to Dad. "Then why is he sitting in our dining room?"

"When you escaped your dream, where did you go?" Thane asked, as though I hadn't spoken.

I eyed him defensively. "Into another dream."

"Directly?"

"Yes," I said, trying to figure out where this was going.

"You chose whose dream you wanted to visit." He wasn't asking a question, but I nodded anyway. "How did you find him?"

"I pictured him in my head," I answered. "The dream came to me. But I've never seen Ais. How am I supposed to picture her?"

Thane leaned back in his chair, thinking. "Perhaps you'll have to search for her in the larger dream space."

I felt something shift inside—frustration giving way to curiosity. "When Karayan talked about dreams," I said, noticing Thane's face tighten at the mention of Karayan's name. "She described them as

179

bubbles in a larger sea." Thane nodded gruffly. I swallowed. "So if dreams are bubbles, what is the sea?"

"That," Hale said quietly, "is a great mystery. But if you can explore it, you may find the answer."

Thane regarded me. "And with it, Ais."

My blood-drop roses gleamed pale white in the strange non-light of the dream world. I sat on the ground, staring into another pool of stars. As I gazed into it, I focused on the darkness instead of the glittering lights. The dream-stars scattered out of view, leaving a glassy blackness in their wake. I placed my hand on the surface of the pool, and heard again Karayan's earlier words. *Don't think like a human.* It seemed impossible, and yet—I wasn't human. The closer we got to winter solstice, the more claustrophobic my world had grown. I closed my eyes. I wanted to set these burdens aside, even if only for one night. I wanted to surrender.

I felt the surface of the pool beneath my hand give way, and I opened my eyes.

I was sliding into blackness. The dark was infinite and unrelenting. I felt myself falling away from a gleaming seed of light. I recognized it—even from a distance—as my own dream and reached out for it. In an instant I was speeding toward the dream again. With a thrill of excitement, I realized even the smallest thought was enough to change course. It was better than flying. I had absolute control of my movement. I became aware of more gleaming flickers of light at the edge of the darkness. Once I noticed them, they swirled toward me like tiny fireflies whirling in graceful eddies. I sensed Lucas's sleeping mind as it drew closer, but I didn't reach out to touch it. Instead, I sharpened my gaze and looked farther into the darkness. Lights filled the vast space.

I tried an experiment, focusing on Karayan's face in my mind's eye. Another seed of light drew closer, but this one was haloed by a ring of blue. The color reminded me of the flame of a Bunsen burner in chemistry class. It grew nearer, but I could sense nothing from it. I touched it and *felt* Karayan's attention turning toward me from within her dream. I released the dream—and once more could sense nothing from the haloed seed of light. Was every Lilitu's dream similarly shielded? As I thought this, a smattering of blue-tinged lights lifted out of the swarm and whirled around me in a tight orbit, each one of them a mystery.

I sat up in bed, waking in a slick sheen of sweat.

"Dad?" I said, two minutes later, standing at the edge of his bed. He shifted, saw me, and sat up, turning on his bedside light.

"Braedyn? What is it, honey?"

"Thane was wrong," I said. "I can't find Ais. Not in a dream. Not without giving myself away." I was shaking with adrenaline.

"Slow down." Dad glanced at the clock on his nightstand. It was 3:15 A.M.. "Maybe you'd better start from the top."

I took a deep, steadying breath. "Lilitu dreams are... shielded. You can't sense anything about them unless you touch them. But if you touch them, they know." I shivered in the cold night air.

"Okay." Dad frowned. "No more poking around in the dream space tonight. Let me talk to Thane and Hale. Try to figure out how this changes things. Why don't you just try to get some rest."

I nodded and walked slowly back to my room. I climbed into bed and pulled the blankets up around my chin. But I couldn't shake the chill that had followed me out of the vast darkness of the dream.

With a small twinge of conscience, I slipped back into sleep.

I found Lucas in a dream, and remade the world around us. In a heartbeat, we were curling into a deep loveseat in front of a merrily blazing fire. I leaned against Lucas's chest and he wrapped his arms around me.

"I was hoping you'd come," he said. "I've been waiting for you."

I felt a prickle of alarm. Was this just dream talk, or did some part of Lucas sense I wasn't a regular dream? But when his arms tightened around me, my alarm eased. So what if he remembered this dream? People dream about their friends all the time.

"Nothing could have kept me away," I murmured, and realized it was true. My life had become a long list of obligations and warnings. But in the dream, I could be with Lucas like a normal teenage girl.

Lucas lowered his face toward me and brushed my lips with his. A rosy warmth filled my chest. Whatever guilt I felt, I pushed to the back of my mind. Hale may have forbidden this, but he didn't know how Lucas and I felt about each other. This was the only way I could kiss

Lucas and be sure of not hurting him. Even if it wasn't as nice as reality, it was something. I woke to early morning sunlight streaming through my window.

Dad was eating breakfast downstairs. He looked haggard.

"Dad?" I asked, worried.

"I don't think we should press our luck," he said quietly. "If Ais can read minds, like Thane seems to think she can, then your seeking her out would only alert her to our plans."

I bit my lip. After waking him up, I'd gone back to sleep to spend the rest of the night happily with Lucas. I hadn't given Ais another thought. But Dad... it didn't look like he'd been back to sleep since then. It was now two weeks before winter solstice, and I had just torpedoed the Guard's best hope for finding Ais. No wonder Dad looked wrung out.

"No more waiting around," he said. "It's time for us to act." Dad stood, draining the last of his coffee decisively. "You go on to school, sweetheart."

"What are you going to do?" I asked, suddenly nervous for him.

"I'm going to talk to Hale."

At school, I wandered the hallway, only half-seeing what was in front of me.

"Braedyn," Lucas said. "I've been waiting for you." I turned, my breath catching. But Lucas didn't seem to remember speaking those very words to me in his sleep last night. "Walk you to class?"

"Yeah," I said, forcing my shoulders to relax.

On our way across the quad, we spotted a small huddle of students. Parker stood at the center of the group, leaning against a tree. He looked awful. His usually gleaming black hair was listless. His ice-blue eyes were ringed with deep bags, and his clothes were disheveled. Parker looked up and saw me.

"You need to eat something." I heard Amber's voice from the crowd, then saw her standing by Parker, concerned.

"Braedyn," Parker breathed, looking at me. Amber turned, aggravated.

"What's wrong with him?" I asked. I tried to read Parker's face.

The pain in his eyes was so intense I felt it like a knife in my stomach. Whatever I thought I'd wanted to do to Parker, the results terrified me. He looked like a convicted murderer, stunned and afraid and utterly helpless to take back what he'd done.

"Leave us alone," Amber snapped. "This isn't your problem."

"Come on," Lucas said stiffly. "Let him stew."

Parker's face was a shadow in my mind for the rest of the morning.

At lunch, Royal and Lucas sat on either side of me. They kept up a light conversation, but I was too entrenched in my thoughts to pay much attention. Ten minutes before the end of lunch, Parker approached our table. Royal and Lucas stiffened. Parker stopped at the chair Cassie used to occupy.

"How is she?" Parker asked, hollowly.

"Excuse me?" Royal said, looking up in disbelief.

"Cassie," Parker said.

Royal stood to face Parker. Compared to the soccer captain, Royal looked as slender as a twig. But the anger in his face was real and powerful. "Turn around and walk away," Royal said.

"I—is she okay?"

"She's not okay, man," Lucas said, standing to join Royal. "You should leave."

"Maybe if I could talk to her?" Parker started.

Royal swung out. Parker staggered back, cupping his face in surprise. A shout went up. The soccer team sprang forward to get Parker's back. Royal wasn't a fighter, but he was ready to take Parker on. Lucas stepped in front of Royal, but Royal pushed him aside.

"You never," Royal growled at Parker, his voice quivering. "Never speak to Cassie again."

One of Parker's friends grabbed Royal by his shirt. "You giving orders now?"

"Leave him alone," Parker said. There was no anger in him at all, just misery.

His friend released Royal with a grimace. "Whatever. I don't hit girls."

With the situation diffused, the crowd melted away, somewhat disappointed there hadn't been another fight. Parker hung back. Lucas and I hemmed Royal on either side, ready to keep him from going after Parker again now that the teachers were on alert.

"Tell her I'm sorry," Parker said quietly. Then he left, and the eyes of the school followed him back to his table.

"He's really messed up," Lucas said.

"Good." Royal straightened his shirt. "He should suffer. It's what he deserves."

"No argument here." Lucas glanced at me. I had to force myself to breathe. Parker was losing himself, bit by bit. And it was only going to get worse. I knew this, without a shadow of a doubt, because when I planted that seed in his mind, this is exactly what I had wanted.

"No luck," Gretchen said, answering Hale's question around a mouthful of spaghetti. "I haven't found even a hint of a hunting ground anywhere. I've hit the clubs downtown, the bus station, bars..." she swallowed and sighed. "I even spent a day at the dog track. Nothing."

Thane looked up from scouring the local newspaper. "The police are suggesting the possibility of a serial killer in Puerto Escondido. A serial killer stalking men," he said.

"Sounds like a Lilitu screen," Gretchen mumbled.

"The thing that stumps me," Dad said, grabbing another roll from the basket, "is how we haven't found any Thrall roaming the streets. If that many local men have been attacked, we should have run across at least one by now."

"The Lilitu are being careful," Hale said quietly. "We're going to have to change tactics. I think we should divide the city into grids to help focus the search. Don't rule anything out until it's been examined."

"I can help," Lucas offered. Everyone turned to him.

"Absolutely not," Gretchen said.

"I just want to help you search," Lucas said. "I know the signs. It's not like I'm going to try to take another Thrall on singlehandedly."

"Sorry, Lucas," Hale said. "I'm with Gretchen on this one."

I saw the frustration in Lucas's eyes. He was ready to go to war. Everyone was. Everyone except for me. I was supposed to be their secret weapon, and I had just learned that the one advantage I had over humans, the ability to navigate through the dream world, was useless when it came to finding Ais.

"Murphy," Hale said. "Can I have a word with you after dinner?" Hale might have been talking to Dad, but his eyes cut to me. After dinner, Hale walked us home. He waited until we'd closed the front door before speaking.

"We have to consider the possibility that Karayan knows where Ais is hiding," Hale said. Dad looked at Hale sharply. Hale turned to me. "Braedyn, I need you to tell Karayan you've changed your mind. Tell her you're thinking about joining the Lilitu."

"What?!" Dad and I spoke at the same time.

"If Karayan believes Braedyn is serious about deserting the Guard, she might include her in their overall plan," Hale explained. Dad started to argue, but Hale cut him off. "We have to find Ais, Murphy. I mean, what do we have? A dozen soldiers chasing a ghost in South America? It's not enough."

"You're asking her to walk into the lion's den," Dad said. "She's not ready for this."

"She's stronger than you know," Hale said. "You have to let her grow up sometime."

"No, Hale!"

"I'll do it," I said. They turned to me as one.

"Honey, there's still time," Dad said. "Give it another week before—"

"Dad," I stopped him. "What if this is something only I can do? If I don't help you, and Ais succeeds?" Dad's face was a mask of misery, but I pressed on. "What kind of person would I be if I didn't try?"

Dad turned away from me and sat heavily on the staircase. Hale caught my eye, nodding in gratitude. Then he left us, wordlessly, and pulled the door closed after himself. Dad didn't speak for a long moment.

"You don't have to do this to prove you're good," Dad said quietly.

"Don't I?" A tinge of bitterness entered my voice. "Thane said the Lilitu in me will win out over my humanity. That it's only a matter of time." Dad caught my hand and pulled me down next to him on the staircase. I burrowed against his chest.

"Thane is a bitter old fool," he said. "He can't believe there are Lilitu capable of good." His voice hitched. "But I know there are."

I pulled back and looked up at him. Dad took a deep breath, then let it out slowly.

"It was your father, Paul, who realized the Guard needed a Lilitu ally," he said. "He was only 19 when he convinced the Guard to capture an infant Lilitu to raise. When Leadership handed the baby Karayan over to Thane, Paul was transferred to a unit halfway across the country to keep him from interfering in Karayan's development. Paul resented the move, but he believed in the work the Guard was doing, so he played the good soldier. I joined his unit 10 years later."

"How old were you?" I asked, drinking in the story.

"I'd just turned 20," Dad said. "Paul saw in me the younger brother he had lost to the Lilitu. He became my mentor. My friend. We trained and worked together for six years. When Paul learned that Karayan had run away, he was devastated. By this point, the Guard was in serious decline. We'd lost over two thirds of our forces to old age that decade, and we weren't recruiting fast enough to replace them. Lilitu continued to cross into our world, and it was getting harder to hunt them down. Paul believed, more strongly than ever, that the Guard needed a Lilitu fighting on our side. But Leadership refused to let another innocent man die to try again. Paul knew the key was to raise the baby Lilitu with love—" Dad stopped. I realized he was struggling with emotion.

"Dad," I whispered. He squeezed my hand.

"He suspected there might be Lilitu who didn't want this war any more than we did. I don't know how he did it, but he managed to find one. She agreed to give a daughter to the Guard. But in order for her to have a child—" Dad stopped again, trying to hide the depth of his grief.

"Someone had to die," I said. And then I knew. "It was Paul." Dad nodded.

"He left me a letter asking me to raise his daughter. As soon as I read it I knew what he was doing. I knew he would be dead in three nights. I searched through the city for him but—" Dad closed his eyes for a long moment. "When dawn broke that third day all I wanted was blood. Vengeance. Three weeks later, she brought you to me." Dad looked into my eyes, his face radiant with the memory. "I knew her instantly," he said quietly. "I'd seen her once before in a dream. It was because of that dream I joined the Guard. She'd guided me to Paul's outpost. I never would have met him if it weren't for her. I don't know how but she knew—six years before Paul sacrificed himself to bring you into the world—she knew that I would be raising her daughter."

I watched his face, breathless.

"I don't know anything more about her," Dad said. "But there was goodness in your mother, Braedyn." He tucked a lock of hair behind my ear. "She stayed just long enough to give you your name, and then she passed you to me. When I held you for the first time, I knew I could never trust anyone else to raise you. In his letter, Paul asked me to keep you secret from the Guard until just before your 16th birthday. Over the years, I've grown to appreciate Paul's wisdom. The Guard would never have let me get to know you like I have. You have incredible empathy and courage, and you've taught me more about love than anyone I've ever known. I'm so proud of the young woman you've become."

I felt tears welling in my eyes. "Then you have to let me do this," I said. "For Paul. For my mother. And for you." He looked up, and I saw his eyes were swimming in tears as well. "You raised me hoping I could prevent another war with the Lilitu. It's time to let me try."

Dad squeezed my hand, unable to speak. After a long moment, he nodded.

I felt a growing fear pressing in on me, but I had made up my mind.

Tonight, I had to make Karayan believe I was ready to betray my family.

That night, I laid down to dream.

I turned to study the roses in my garden, and Karayan was there. She simply waited for me to speak.

"I've been thinking about what you said," I murmured. "About picking the right side."

She studied me with a veiled expression. "You seemed pretty adamant about sticking with the Guard. Are you telling me you've had a change of heart?"

"You didn't tell me the Guard could sense the traces I left in Parker's mind," I said, turning on her.

Karayan looked at me, suspicion warring with curiosity in those deep green eyes. "Thane?"

"He hasn't found anything yet," I said. I didn't have to fake the anger in my voice.

"Mm." Karayan said flatly. "Must have slipped my mind."

"Maybe," I said. "Or maybe you figured one way to get me away from the Guard was to force them to drive me out."

"Ooo, yes," Karayan said, smiling. "Let's pretend this was my master plan. It's so Machiavellian, I love it. But I'll need more than your word that you're ready to join our team."

I felt doubt wriggling in the back of my mind, but I kept my voice steady. "Meaning?"

"Meaning you'll have to earn your place." Karayan studied me. "If you're serious about this, I can make sure there's a part for you to play."

"Just tell me what you want me to do."

"Very well," Karayan said, smiling. "I'll be in touch."

"When?" I asked, trying to hide my swell of panic. "Winter solstice is in less than two weeks."

"Be patient," Karayan said. Without another word, she vanished.

I felt weary. I turned and saw a pool of stars at my feet. A parting gift from Karayan? I looked around, suspicious, but I was alone in my field.

The stars within the pool seemed more inviting than they used to. As I glanced into the glassy darkness, I caught a whiff of his scent, felt the lifting power of his laughter. I knew I should be careful, that I couldn't let myself make a habit of doing this. But I let my hand close around Lucas's dream anyway, and his sleeping mind pulled me in.

I found Lucas walking through a deserted carnival. Wind pushed a few papers along the ground. It was oddly lonely. I moved to his side and laced my fingers through his.

"There you are," he said. "You're late." His smile was mischievous.

The carnival lit up, warm lights blazing into life all around us. I grinned, delighted. Lucas drew me toward the Ferris wheel. In moments we were sitting in a car, rising up, rocking more gently than reality would have allowed. As we approached the top of the ride, I saw the city spreading out beneath our feet. It seemed we were higher than we should have been; the view was magnificent. Lucas looked out over the city, the dream wind playing through his hair.

The moment was both too perfect and unreal. I leaned against Lucas, aware that everything I experienced here was born in his mind. He'd created this entire world for us. And it would be extinguished if the Wall came down and Ais's forces began their hunt. I might be all that stood between Lucas and death, and I had no idea what I was doing.

"I'm scared," I whispered.

"Don't be." Lucas's hands curled around me. "I'll protect you."

I felt my stomach turn. It wasn't fair to expect a complicated conversation from dream-Lucas, but I wasn't interested in platitudes. "You can't protect me, Lucas." *You can't even protect yourself,* I wanted to add.

"I'd do anything for you." He caught my chin in one hand and gently lifted it until I was staring into his eyes again. "I love you, Braedyn."

I knew it was a dream, but the words burned into me with the power of 10,000 suns. Lucas leaned forward and kissed me. All my worries were obliterated as we held each other, suspended above the gleaming city, losing ourselves in the shared sensation of our kiss.

I rose from bed early the next morning. I glanced out my window at Lucas's, but his drapes were closed. The giddiness I'd felt last night had faded into a warm glow. He'd said he loved me. Even if it was only a dream.

I went down to breakfast and found Dad waiting for me, eyes ringed with exhaustion.

"You didn't sleep?" I asked.

He shook his head. "Should I call Hale?"

I felt the warmth inside cool a little, remembering what I had done last night. "Yeah."

When Hale arrived, I told them both about my conversation with Karayan, and how she told me I'd have to wait until it was time to bring me in on the plan.

"Then we wait," Hale said. He didn't look happy. "Let's just hope she doesn't keep us waiting for too long."

But she did.

A week passed, each day burning a mark in my mind. 13 days until winter solstice. 12. 11. 10.

Every day I sleepwalked through school, returned home, stumbled through practice, and fell into bed exhausted.

Every night I expected to find Karayan waiting for me in my field of roses. Every night I was disappointed. Each hour became an exercise in patience, until my mind felt frayed under the strain of waiting. My entire life—my entire world—was on hold.

The Guard tried to maintain their duties, focusing on the job at hand. Gretchen continued her search for the hunting ground. Thane kept up his search for victims of the Lilitu's touch. Hale and Dad canvassed the city for Thrall every day. But we were running out of time, and we all felt it.

I started going to sleep earlier and earlier. I'd sit in my rose garden, and when Karayan didn't show up, I'd turn to the tempting pool of stars. Each night I wrestled with myself, but each night I gave in and ended up closing my hand around the gleaming spark of Lucas's dream. We spent the nights together in the landscapes of his dreaming mind, but even my time with Lucas could offer only limited comfort.

On the Friday night the week before winter solstice, Missy dropped by with poster-board, glitter, and glue. She pulled her strawberry-blond hair up into a messy bun and offered to tie mine up, too. She was in a great mood; even my reserved quiet couldn't bring her down. I spent a surreal evening helping her craft five enormous posters for Winter Ball, knowing there was a good chance I'd be somewhere between here and South America on the night of the actual dance.

The next morning I woke up and realized the time until winter solstice was no longer measured in weeks, but in days.

Five days before winter solstice, Hale made everyone pack a bag of essentials and a bedroll so we'd be ready to travel in a moment's notice. Gretchen tucked bug spray and sunscreen into everyone's packs, including mine.

Three days before winter solstice, Hale pulled me aside and thanked me for trying. Neither of us believed any longer that Karayan was going to let me in on the plan. I hoped fervently that the Guard's intelligence was right. Because if Ais wasn't in South America, it seemed unlikely we'd be able to locate her in time to keep her from bringing down the Wall.

When December 19th arrived, I stared at my calendar woodenly. winter solstice was two days away. I moved through my morning routine in a fog. School was a blur.

Royal and Cassie sensed that something was wrong. Royal pulled me aside after lunch and reminded me, "I'm on your speed dial." I squeezed his hand, but there was no way I could tell him what was going on.

That afternoon, I returned home, expecting to find the Guard loading the van for the airport. Dad just met me at the door, shaking his head.

"No word yet," he said.

"So?" I asked, unsure what to do with myself.

"Hale says business as usual," Dad answered. "You'd better go to practice."

When I walked into the basement, Gretchen was warming up.

Hale looked up as I entered. "I'd like to do an hour of sparring, then we'll start you with a sword. Okay?"

"Sure," I said, taking my place on the mat. I was getting so familiar with Gretchen's style that I could watch her and tell what she'd do as she made the decision to do it. A tiny flick of her eyes told me she was going to start with a kick, so I was ready to block her. I countered and she blocked, and we were into another sparring session. We went nearly five minutes before Gretchen managed to land a solid hit. As we squared up again, I decided to attack first. Gretchen misread my move, and I had her on the defensive in a few breathless seconds. She fought furiously, swinging for my ribs again, but I was ready for her. As she whipped close to tag my ribs, I sidestepped her, swept her foot out from under her, and dropped on top of her, fist raised. But I didn't have to take the shot. She knew I had her.

I heard a grunt from the stairs. All three of us turned to see Lucas watching, stunned.

"Lucas?" Hale frowned. "What are you doing in here?" Hale's voice radiated disapproval. Lucas—for once—ignored him.

"She's amazing," Lucas said to Gretchen, accusatorily. Then he turned to me, wounded. "You're amazing. Why didn't you tell me you knew how to fight?"

I glanced at Hale, uneasy. "I—I'm just learning."

It was the wrong thing to say. Lucas flinched. "You know how many of the guys Gretchen used to train with ever knocked her off her feet?"

"She's a fast learner," Gretchen said.

"She's a good teacher," I said. Gretchen's eyes flickered over to me.

"I'll have to take your word for it." Lucas wouldn't meet my eyes. "She won't let me train with her."

"Lucas." Gretchen pulled her gloves off.

"Forget it," Lucas said. He stormed up the steps, and slammed the door.

"Hale?" Gretchen pleaded. Hale waved toward the stairs, and Gretchen ran after Lucas.

I looked at Hale, uncomfortable.

"He'll be okay," Hale sighed. "It's hard for guys his age to see girls that fight better than they do. Though you'd think he'd be used to it, growing up around Gretchen."

"I don't fight better than—" I stared at Hale. "Lucas got into a fight his first day at school." Hale didn't look surprised. "He fought five guys and won."

"Your point?"

"My point—?" I stared at Hale, but he wasn't smiling.

"Did you think I made you train with Gretchen because I thought it'd be easier for you? Gretchen is the best fighter in my unit. She was an alternate for the U.S. Tae Kwon Do team before she joined the Guard. Murphy's got more experience, and I'm stronger, but Gretchen is faster and smarter when it comes to hand-to-hand combat. Get used to it, Braedyn. You're a better fighter than Lucas is. Now you both know it."

I let Hale's words sink in. Strange feelings twisted in my stomach. The glow of pride was tempered with a leaden dread. Lucas had been training for years, learning who knows what from who knows how many soldiers? No wonder he couldn't believe I'd just started learning. No normal kid could have picked this up so fast. Like the dreams and the night-vision, my ability to fight wasn't human.

Hale walked to the weapons rack and drew out a sword.

"Wouldn't daggers make more sense?" I asked. "I can't exactly stash a sword in my backpack."

"You need finer control for the daggers," Hale said. "And the sword has one advantage over the daggers." He lunged, stabbing the sword through the air with precise, lethal energy. "It extends your reach. Keeps the Lilitu from getting too close." He flipped the sword into the air and caught it by the hilt, then offered it to me.

I took the sword gingerly. It was heavy, but balanced—it took little effort to keep the blade parallel to the ground. I made a few half-hearted swings, testing it out. Hale drew a similar sword from the rack.

"Okay. First things first. Let's talk about grip." Hale adjusted my hand on the hilt. For the rest of our session, I practiced lunging with the sword extended. After an hour of this, my lower back was aching, and I was sweating in a way I hadn't since I'd begun sparring with Gretchen. When I finally shelved the sword, my arm was shaking with fatigue.

"Good session," Hale said.

"For what it's worth," I muttered.

"Braedyn?"

I looked up at the sharp tone in his voice. "I just meant," I started lamely. "I mean, there's only two days before—" I swallowed.

"Nothing we do is wasted effort," he said firmly. "And even if—" He looked away from me. "Winter solstice isn't the end of the world, even if it is the beginning of a war. As long as we remain alive, we have to do everything we can to protect the ones we love."

I nodded. Hale turned his back on me, cleaning up from our practice.

I emerged from the basement, and looked around for Lucas. He wasn't in the kitchen or the living room. I left the house and peeked in the Guard's back yard. I saw the shed, but again, no Lucas. I gave up and walked home, the exhaustion of practice finally getting to me. Even my hand felt tired as I turned the doorknob to my house. I took a quick shower and pulled on fresh clothes. I had to tuck my hair up into a wool hat to run back to the Guard's house. It still hadn't snowed, but the nights were starting to drop toward freezing.

An incredible aroma hit me as I entered. Dad had cooked a feast. A gorgeous pork roast shared the table with mashed potatoes, rich gravy, steaming dinner rolls, and asparagus. Lucas was setting the table. He looked a little tense when he saw me.

"I'm sorry," I said. When Lucas didn't answer, I took the forks from him and started placing them around the table.

"I just—I don't know how you learned so fast," Lucas said. "It's like, inhuman." I felt my blood turn to ice in my veins. Lucas looked up, smiling sheepishly. "Seriously, we should get your DNA tested for superpowers."

Gretchen walked in at that moment, toweling her short, dark hair. Her eyes shifted from Lucas to me; she'd heard the last part of our conversation.

"Hit me with the spoons, Mitchell," she said. Lucas handed them over and Gretchen ruffled his hair.

"I told you she still sees me as a little kid," Lucas said. But he didn't look upset.

"You are a little kid," she said, pinching his cheek. "Look at that squishy face."

"Gretchen, please. You're treading on what little masculinity I have left."

"You can take it. You're tougher than you look." Gretchen caught my eye and gave me a small smile. It was over so fast; I wondered if I'd really seen it or had just imagined it.

Ten minutes later, the Guard was savoring Dad's feast. The food went a long way to lifting everyone's spirits. Dad even sang an old Guard drinking song that had the table in fits of laughter.

And then the phone rang.

Hale pushed back from the table and left to answer it. We sat in our chairs, waiting, breathless. After a minute, Hale returned.

"We have news," he said. Everyone listened with bated breath.

"They've IDed Ais in Caracas. Marx's unit will meet us here. They've chartered a plane to take us all to Venezuela at midnight tomorrow night."

I woke up on December twentieth to the phone ringing. I heard the shower running and hopped out of bed to snatch up the receiver.

"Hello?"

"Braedyn." It was Royal; there was an edge to his voice.

"Cassie?" I asked, battling a sudden swell of fear. "Did something happen?"

"It's Parker," Royal said. "He tried to kill himself last night."

I sat down on the edge of my bed. "What?"

"My brother was on shift when they brought him in early this morning. He didn't have any ID on him, but he was wearing his uniform. They called to see if I knew him, so they could reach his parents faster. You should have seen their faces." Royal sounded shaken to the core.

"Oh, Royal," I breathed.

"I thought you should know. I—I have to go."

I hung up the phone, numb. I'd wanted Parker to hate himself. I'd wanted him to feel all the anguish Cassie was feeling and more. I'd fed in my own hatred. Cassie's parent's fear. Royal's helpless fury. It was no different than if I had handed him a loaded gun. I had just finished dressing when Dad burst into my room, a look of horror on his face.

"What is it?! Braedyn? Are you hurt?!" I was only dimly aware that I was sobbing.

"I have to go to the hospital," I choked out.

Dad grabbed his car keys and jacket. We were flying down the road a few minutes later. Dad was trying to get me to tell him what was going on, but all I managed to force out was that I had to see Parker. Dad dropped me off at the hospital entrance and I ran inside. I stopped at the front desk. The duty nurse looked up at me expectantly.

"Parker Webb," I said.

She typed something into her computer and frowned. "I'm sorry, but he isn't allowed any visitors." Dad joined me at the counter. The nurse looked at him, startled.

"Family." Dad said.

"As I was telling your daughter, visitors aren't permitted in Ward B."

"I see. Thank you." Dad pulled me away from the nurses' station.

"I need to see him," I said, struggling in his grip. "I need to see him!"

"This way," Dad murmured in my ear. He was leading me down a hall where a sign directed visitors to Ward B. "You want to tell me why I'm getting ready to break into a restricted section of the hospital?" I glanced at him, startled.

We approached a set of locked doors. The sign for Ward B listed only one department, in small, even letters: "Psychiatric." It turned out to be relatively easy to break into the ward. We only had to wait for a distracted orderly to hurry past, and then slip in before the doors closed behind him. Inside, the patient's names were listed outside their rooms. Parker's room was the third on the left. We scanned the hallway, and then slipped inside.

We weren't the first ones there.

Gretchen and Thane turned as we entered. Thane smiled a chilling smile. Gretchen tensed, but Thane lifted a hand, stopping her from making a move.

"I told you this would happen," Thane said softly. He was standing next to Parker's bed. Parker was unconscious, hooked up to a variety of machines that were monitoring his vitals and administering medication through an IV drip. His skin was pale, almost gray, and covered with a sheen of sweat. His black hair was plastered to his face.

"It was an accident," I whispered. Chaos broke out. Gretchen lunged for me. Dad shoved me behind him, shielding me from her. Gretchen tried to dodge around him, but Dad caught her roughly, pinning her arms to her sides.

"Stop!" Dad said. "What the hell is going on?!"

Gretchen struggled in his arms. "Ask your daughter." Gretchen's eyes found my face. "Just when I was starting to trust you," she spat. Gretchen gasped as Dad's grip tightened on her. She stopped fighting him.

"Braedyn?" Dad's voice was tense.

"It wasn't supposed to go this far," I said helplessly.

"What do you—What did you do?" Dad's composure was starting

to crack as he struggled to keep from freaking out. "Honey? What did you do?"

"He hurt Cassie," I said. My voice sounded weak, thin.

"She pushed this boy to take his own life." Thane spoke matter-of-factly. Dad tore his eyes off Parker's unconscious form and looked at me. I met his desperate eyes but could only shake my head. Dad released Gretchen. She rubbed her arms.

"Karayan said," I started. Thane took a step toward me and I choked. "I didn't know," I managed. "I just wanted him to feel what he'd done to Cassie."

"Go to school," Dad said. "Do not go home. Call Royal for a ride." I opened my mouth to argue but Dad grabbed my arm and pulled me back to the door. "Get away from here."

"No!" Gretchen moved forward. "I'm not letting her out of my sight!"

"You have other responsibilities," Dad spat. "Or do you want to throw everything away to babysit a teenage girl?!"

"She's a demon!"

Dad spun on Gretchen. She darted back, alert. But Dad turned back to me. "Go. I need to find Hale. Explain." He studied me, eyes twisted with worry.

"Dad?" I asked, eyeing Thane and Gretchen. They'd drawn closer together, standing in front of Parker like a shield. Like they had to protect him from me.

Dad lowered his voice. "Let me try to salvage this." He held my eyes, and I nodded. He was on my side.

"I'm sorry," I said, my voice quavering. Dad nodded and gestured for me to leave. Thane glared at Dad coldly. Standing beside Dad, he didn't look like much of a threat. But his wiry frame was rigid with self-righteous anger.

"She's a demon, Murphy. If you let her go, I'll see that you answer to the Field Marshal for it."

Dad opened the door for me.

I slipped out of Parker's room, and found myself face-to-face with Amber.

Her eyes were as wide as saucers. She stumbled away from me, backing into a gurney parked in the hallway.

"Amber."

Amber was rigid with shock. I don't know how much she heard, but it was clearly enough. Without a word, Amber ran to the emergency exit stairs, flew through the doors, and vanished down the stairwell.

16

As I waited for Royal to pick me up from the hospital, fears multiplied in my mind. What would Gretchen and Thane do now? What if Hale thought I was losing control? What if the Guard couldn't stop Ais? My immediate future was a vast, clouded mystery.

By the time Royal arrived, I was a nervous wreck. He pulled to a stop in front of the hospital and I got into the car.

It seemed insane to be going to school at a time like this. I had no idea how much Amber had heard, or what she might tell people. But even if none of her friends believed her, Lucas might hear. With cold certainty, I knew if he heard the truth, he would recognize it. He would realize why I'd featured so often in his dreams. He would see me for what I was. Worse. He would see me as the enemy.

"You look almost as bad as I feel," Royal said. I shook my head silently. "Oh, good," Royal murmured sarcastically. "For a minute I was worried you'd be wanting conversation with your transportation."

I forced myself to meet his eyes. "Thanks for the ride."

"Coronado Prep shuttle, at your service. One more stop before our final destination." He saw my surprise. "Cassie's coming back to school today."

"Today?"

"I haven't figured out how to tell her about Parker yet," he said, gripping the steering wheel.

I nodded, biting my lip. And I'd have to find a way to say goodbye.

We made the drive to Cassie's apartment in silence. Royal put the radio on, but neither of us paid much attention. We let the manic morning banter of radio show hosts wash over us. When we pulled up outside her apartment, a very sedate Cassie came down the stairs, clutching her backpack like a shield. I gave her the front seat. Royal engaged her in light conversation most of the way to school.

As we pulled into the parking lot, Cassie turned around in her seat to study me. "Okay, guys. Seriously, I'm fine. Stop being weird."

Royal caught my eye in the rearview mirror as he parked and killed the engine. Cassie glanced between us, confused. I took a deep breath, trying to figure out the right words, when I saw Lucas. He was standing at the edge of the parking lot, scanning the cars. Searching, I realized, for my Firebird. He looked anxious, but not guarded or angry. Cassie followed my gaze. Lucas spotted her, surprise flashing briefly across his face. He headed toward us.

Cassie was starting to look a little unsettled. "Something's going on."

"It's Parker," I said. Cassie's jaw tightened in anger. "He tried to kill himself last night."

"What?" Cassie's face changed, the tension leaching out of her jaw as this news sunk in.

"He's at the hospital," Royal said. Lucas joined us, catching the last of this. He gave me an urgent look, but didn't interrupt.

"Oh," Cassie said faintly. We all watched her for a moment, then as one, seemed to realize we were staring. Royal got out of the car. Lucas opened the door for Cassie. After she climbed out, Lucas turned to me and lowered his voice.

"I need to talk to you," he whispered. "Thane thinks a Lilitu got to Parker." I stumbled, and Lucas caught me. "Don't worry. They'll find her."

All day I waited for the bomb to drop. Royal and I shadowed Cassie, escorting her from classroom to classroom and making sure she was never alone between periods. I was waiting for her as she came out of second period. Royal and I had agreed to meet at her locker so he could walk with her to the third period class they shared. Before we reached the locker bay hall, a group of guys from the soccer team spotted us. A few of them elbowed each other and pointed toward Cassie. Their cold leers told me they were in the mood to torment someone.

When two of them started forward, I took hold of Cassie's elbow. She glanced at me, alarmed. As the group approached, I felt a wave of defensiveness rising through me. I locked eyes with each of them in turn, and they seemed to falter. They stopped in the middle of the hallway, looking around like they couldn't remember what they were doing. We shouldered past them, and escaped the rest of the dumbstruck soccer team without incident.

Royal, waiting at the end of the hall, looked just as surprised. But when we met up with him, he smiled at Cassie. "Ready for some pre-calculus?"

"You guys don't have to babysit me," Cassie said, giving us both a weary look. "I can take care of myself."

With one last curious look at me, Royal led Cassie away.

I glanced back at the soccer team, unsettled. Lucas found me and I turned to him, desperate to escape. "Ditch morning classes with me," I said.

"I thought you'd never ask," Lucas said. He was just as tense as I was. We waited for the bell signaling the start of class, then edged out of the locker bay and slipped outside. We walked back down to the soccer field, hand in hand.

"I had a feeling you'd come to school today," Lucas said when we'd reached the bleachers. "They're good friends." I knew he meant Royal and Cassie. I nodded, not trusting myself to speak. Lucas read my expression and wrapped both his arms around me. "I know how you feel," he said after a long moment. "I've said more than my fair share of goodbyes."

"You don't think we're coming back here, do you?" I asked, stricken. Lucas didn't have to answer. I felt the sting of tears welling in my eyes. We sat there, holding each other in the cold December light, until the bell rang for lunch.

Cassie and Royal were waiting for us. For Cassie's sake, Lucas and I tried to shed our gloom.

"I can't believe I'm going to say this," Cassie said between bites of grilled cheese. "But it feels good to be back." I could barely smile at her. We'd been through so much together. I wasn't ready to give up this part of my life. I wasn't ready to lose Royal and Cassie. Lunch was over too quickly.

I made my way to the bathroom, looking for a private place to get my emotions under control before gym. Someone followed me inside and locked the bathroom door. I turned around to face her.

"You did something to Parker." Amber said it like a statement of fact.

I felt a thrill of fear, but I kept my face neutral.

"These last three months, I've been looking for anything that could explain how little Mousy Murphy transformed into the five-alarm fire that's burning my life into ashes," she said. "Parker wasn't suicidal until he messed with your little friend. I don't know what you did to him, but I know you're responsible." Amber watched my face for a reaction.

"What do you want from me, Amber?" I said, refusing to give her the satisfaction of showing my fear.

Someone tried the door, discovered it was locked, and knocked. "Hey! Open the door!"

"For starters?" Amber said. "Stay away from my friends." Amber left, opening the door on her way out. I turned to the sink and started washing my hands so whoever entered wouldn't see my face.

I'd wanted to go to gym and English to have more time with Royal and Cassie, but all through English, I could feel Amber's eyes boring twin holes in my back.

It was the longest day of my life.

Dad wasn't answering his cell phone. I spent final period in the grip of my run-away imagination. In some scenarios, I got left behind when the others took the plane out of town. In others, Dad was arrested by the Guard. In still others, Gretchen took Lucas away and I never saw him again. When the end of the school day came, I was sick with anxiety.

I walked to the parking lot with Cassie, looking for my dad's truck. It wasn't there. Lucas and Royal joined us.

"I assume I'm giving you a ride home." Royal said. "Lucas, care to join us?"

"Please. Gretchen isn't answering her phone."

We piled into Royal's car. He dropped Cassie off first. As she got out of the car, I jumped out and caught her hand. This might be the last time I ever saw her. There was suddenly so much I wanted to say. Cassie misunderstood. She hugged me tightly.

"Thanks for being there today," she said. "I don't know what I'd do without you and Royal." Guilt threatened to choke me, but I forced a smile.

"Take care of yourself," I said. Cassie rolled her eyes, and for a moment I saw a hint of her old, mischievous self.

"I'm not a china *doll*," she said. "I'll be okay." She walked up the stairs to her apartment and waved at us from the top of the stairs, then made a *shoo!* gesture and disappeared inside her house. As I leaned back, I felt Lucas's hand on my shoulder. I knew he understood. I felt a cold comfort; if I did have to leave my old life behind, at least Lucas would be going with me.

"Not bad for her first day back," Royal said. "All in all, Parker may have done her a favor. At least she wasn't the current scandal of the day." I nodded, unwilling to contradict him. When we finally pulled up to my house, I couldn't make myself get out of the car. Royal gave me a strange look. "Everything okay?" he asked.

"You know how important you are to me, right? You and Cassie?"

"Of course I do." Royal smiled, but his eyes still held more than a little worry.

I leaned over and hugged him. He squeezed me warmly in return. When I pulled back, I could see all the questions he wanted to ask burning in his eyes.

I got out of the car. It felt like I was looking through a window onto normal teenage life, but I was forever trapped outside of that world now. How could anything ever feel normal again? The world was poised on the edge of a crisis. And only 100 people out of the billions of us who shared this world knew it. Tomorrow. Everything would be decided tomorrow.

"I'm going home to sleep for a short forever," Royal yawned. "See you guys tomorrow." He pulled out of the driveway, leaving Lucas and me alone.

Lucas glanced at his house. "I should see if Gretchen's back."

"Yeah, I'm going to go look for Dad."

We parted ways and I walked up the front steps of my house. I put my hand on the front door and it shifted. The door was unlocked. I edged it open, uncertain.

"Dad?" There was no response. I glanced in the kitchen and the living room; both were empty. I gripped my book bag tightly and walked to the base of the stairs. The phone rang and I almost jumped out of my skin. I picked up a handset in the living room. It was Lucas.

"No one's here," he said. "Did you find Murphy?"

"I don't think he's here," I said quietly.

"You okay?" he asked.

"The front door was unlocked." I hesitated, then bit my lip. "Something's wrong."

"Stay where you are. I'm coming over."

He was by my side 20 seconds later, eyes sharp. We walked upstairs and peeked into Dad's room, the first door on the right. It was empty. So was the upstairs bathroom. My room was the last door on the left. The door was slightly ajar. When I pushed it open, I screamed.

My room was trashed. Empty dresser drawers were jumbled in a pile under one window. Shreds of clothes obscured the floor. The mattress had been upended and slashed, ribbons of fabric and a few bent springs spilling out of it like entrails. My bookshelf had been cleared, the books tossed in a heap alongside the scattered collection of artifacts from my childhood.

Lucas pulled me back down the hall, down the stairs, and out of the house. We ran into the Guard's house and locked the front door.

"Come on," he said, helping me up the stairs. "My room has a good view of your house. We can wait there until your dad comes back."

I nodded stupidly as my reason started returning. My room was the only room in the house that had been trashed. It wasn't a robbery. Someone was looking for something. Something of mine. Or something about me. We got to Lucas's room and I went straight for his window.

I could see my room. The curtains had been ripped off the rod, there was nothing to screen the devastation from view. Who would have done this? Thane and Gretchen? Maybe, if Hale had sided with Dad, they might consider taking matters into their own hands. But why trash my room? Why not just wait for me to return and attack? If not Thane and Gretchen... I drew in a shaky breath. There was one other person who wanted to hurt me. Amber thought I'd done something to Parker. She wouldn't know what she was looking for so she might search everything. And she was mad enough at me for wrecking her life that she might see it as justice to wreck my room.

Lucas put an arm around my shoulder. I turned toward him, and buried my face in his shirt. I felt his arms tighten around me. As he held me, a question burned white hot in my mind.

"What would you do if you found the Lilitu that killed Eric?" I asked. I felt Lucas's back tense. I leaned away from him to study his face. But instead of the anger I expected, I saw uncertainty.

"I don't know. I—" he looked at me, solemn. "I don't know if I have it in me to kill something." I swallowed, hardly daring to believe what I was hearing.

"Maybe," I said, my voice barely a whisper. "Maybe running away is the best option."

"Yeah," he said slowly. "You may be good at sparring, but neither of us are soldiers. All we'd be taking from the Guard is another pair of mouths to feed." I felt a swell of feeling, and tears stung my eyes. Lucas reached up to touch my face. "Hey," he said. "It's going to be okay."

I kissed him, and he responded. As the kiss grew in passion, I felt the swirling, roiling storm rising to meet him. I froze, remembering the kiss from the movie theater. Lucas pulled back, concerned. I felt the storm recede, and could trace the edge of the power inside me. If I could keep it from reaching him...

I leaned back into the kiss. Lucas's arms tightened around me again. He drew me down onto the bed with him. I felt the storm surge. It strained to connect with him like the questing tendril of a tornado seeking the ground. I struggled with it and it fought me, furiously wrestling against my will. I managed to push the storm to the back of my mind, to focus on Lucas and the other—the human—sensations of our kiss.

I didn't hear the front door open, or the footsteps on the stairs. The first moment I was aware that Lucas and I weren't alone was when Gretchen grabbed me by the hair and wrenched me away from him. I was so startled that I didn't have the presence of mind to catch myself. I sprawled on the floor.

"Gretchen? What the hell?!" Lucas was on his feet, furious.

I looked up at Gretchen, sick with dread. I knew there was nothing I could do to stop her. No reason for her to protect him from the truth any longer.

"Look at her, Lucas," Gretchen said, her eyes tight with rage. "She's one of them."

Lucas looked at me, but no flicker of recognition passed over his face.

Gretchen gripped his shoulder, hard. "Braedyn is a Lilitu."

For one breathless second he just stared at her. "No. That's—That's crazy. Braedyn's—" Lucas's eyes swiveled toward me, pleading. "She's one of us."

"If you don't believe me," Gretchen said. "Ask her for the truth." Lucas turned toward me, eyes brimming with confusion.

"I can explain," I said. But even to me, the words seemed hollow.

Lucas shook his head, fighting the dawning comprehension. "But—it can't be true." His eyes searched mine, holding fast to a frantic hope. "Unless—Those dreams—?" My silence confirmed his worst fears. He stepped back, sick.

"I would never hurt you," I said, my voice a hoarse whisper.

As the truth sunk in, I saw him transform into a stranger. Understanding leached all the compassion from his face. A terrible alchemy moved through him, changing his feelings of warmth to hatred, chasing up every tender memory of our time together and poisoning it. I watched it happen in silence. There was nothing I could say to make it better.

And then Lucas moved. I heard the sound of metal sliding free from a sheath.

Gretchen caught Lucas's wrist and I saw the Guardsman's dagger in his hand. "No, Lucas. Not like this." Terror flooded through me like an icy wash. I was on my feet and diving for the door before Gretchen could wrestle the daggers away from Lucas, snatching my bag on the way out.

I stumbled into the hallway and half-ran, half-fell down the stairs. I heard Gretchen race out of the room behind me. By the time I reached the foyer, she was on the stairs, taking them two at a time. I burst out of the house and directly into Hale, who was standing on the porch. He caught me reflexively. The light of the afternoon highlighted the scar on his cheek. We stared at each other for half a second. I don't know what he saw in my face, but he looked haggard.

"Hale! Stop her!" Gretchen was pounding across the foyer behind me.

Hale's head whipped toward her. I felt his hand move for the daggers at his side. But he hesitated.

"I found her with Lucas!" Gretchen screamed. Hale's eyes swiveled back to me, full of pain.

I shoved past him and vaulted over the porch railing. When I hit the ground, I ran flat-out across the Guard's front lawn and hurtled the low dividing fence. I raced to my car, spilling the contents of my bag on the grass until my fingers closed on my car keys. I saw my phone hit the ground and spared a second to grab it. In that second I saw Gretchen leap off the porch steps next door and start racing across the lawn.

Somehow, I got into my car and locked the doors before she made contact. As Gretchen pounded on my windshield, I turned the key and gunned the engine. She fell back as I peeled out. The last thing I saw in my rearview mirror was Gretchen frantically waving Hale toward her car.

The Firebird roared as I hit the gas, desperate to put as much distance between us as possible. I felt the tiny hope I'd been nurturing all day sputter and go out. The Guard might have been willing to forgive me for what had happened with Parker, but Lucas was one of their own.

And every single one of them had warned me to stay away from him.

17

As the adrenaline wore off, I found myself heading toward the freeway and realized I had no idea where to go. I pulled into an empty parking lot to think. I killed the engine and the car shuddered into silence. It was cold outside; the sun was already dropping toward the horizon. Sunset came earlier and earlier as winter solstice drew near, preparing for the shortest day of the year. As I sat in the car, listening to the muffled sound of the passing traffic, my breath fogged the windows. I noticed something in the rearview mirror; a neat bundle of dark green piled on the back seat. I'd never taken Cassie's gift out of the car. I pulled the velvet jacket onto my lap and spread it out over my legs. It kept the chill at bay while I considered my situation. I didn't want to leave town without talking to Dad. Which meant I needed somewhere to wait. Preferably somewhere with heat. I thought about heading to the mall and trying to lose myself in the crowd, but the thought of being around so many strangers made me feel even more lost and alone. I perked up at that thought. I wasn't entirely alone. I turned the key in the ignition, making a decision.

I drove across town, toward the mountains. As the road took me higher, the city opened up in my rearview mirror. When night fell and the streetlights kicked on, it would look like a vast pool of stars. I pulled to a stop at the guardhouse barring entry into the sprawling gated Foothills community. I gave the guard my name and told him where I was heading. He checked his computer, nodded, and let me through.

I drove past mansions with artfully xeriscaped front yards. Prairie grasses stood in elegant contrast to spiky succulents, both nestled among boulders collected from the foot of the mountain. A lot of

Coronado Prep students lived in these houses. I drove higher into the foothills and turned down the last street on the left.

Royal's house looked out over the city below. The entire front portion of the modern adobe house was glass, to take advantage of the breathtaking views. I pulled into the driveway and parked. As I got out of the car, I shrugged into the green velvet coat, grateful for its warmth. By the time I'd walked up the stone path to the front door, the sun was balanced on the horizon like a fat red jewel. Royal came to the door, slightly disheveled. He hadn't been joking when he said he was going home to sleep. For once, his tousled brown hair actually looked like bed head. He rubbed at his eyes, took one look at me, and opened the door.

A few minutes later, I sat curled up at one end of the window seat in his family's kitchen. Royal pushed an oversized stoneware mug into my hands and sat on the other side of the window seat, facing me. Steam curled off the surface of my tea. I breathed it in, taking the spicy aroma into my lungs. Royal leaned back against the curving adobe wall of the window seat and waited.

"I have to tell you something," I said. "It's going to sound crazy, but I need you to listen." I took a deep breath and told Royal everything, starting with the Homecoming dance when I'd first seen Karayan, all the way through the night I'd visited Parker in his dream and how Thane had felt my touch on his mind. I left Lucas out of it, but I told Royal everything else. Ais, the Wall, the coming war. He listened in silence, keeping his face smooth. When I began my story, the sun had just started to dip behind the horizon. By the time I'd finished, the sky was filled with the glimmering pinpricks of stars, which seemed mirrored by the streetlights of the city at our feet. I sat back, my hands trembling around the mug. It wasn't steaming any more, but it was still warm between my palms.

"Hm." Royal said. I stared at him, expecting some further reaction. But he just took another sip of his tea.

"That's it?" I couldn't get a read on his reaction.

"Sorry, did I miss my cue? This is my first 'By the way, I'm a demon' conversation, so if you're looking for the standard response, you'll have to give me some flash cards." Royal's eyes glimmered.

"I'm not kidding," I whispered.

"You're not a demon, Braedyn," he said, his smile fading. "These people who are trying to make you think you're evil, they're—they're sick."

I stood, turning away from him in frustration. "You're not listening to me."

"Because you're talking crazy. Start talking sane, and you'll have my full attention."

I shook my head. The terror and grief of this afternoon were catching up to me. I felt wrung out, as though I'd burned through my lifetime allotment of tears. "I have no place to go."

"Don't be ridiculous." When I didn't answer, Royal walked over to me. He put a hand on my shoulder, turning me to face him. "Come on, Braedyn. If you're not careful, you're going to scare me. Do you really want that on your conscience?"

"Maybe you should be scared."

"We've known each other since first grade!" he said, exasperated. "I know you better than you know yourself." He crossed his arms when I laughed bitterly. "You can't believe this crap. What's your proof? You had a revenge dream about hurting Parker? I've got some news for you, I have multiple fantasies about hurting Parker every single day."

I glanced at him sharply, my breath catching.

His eyes narrowed. "What?"

"You want proof?"

Royal eyed me up and down, unsettled. "Yeah, sure. Hit me with your best shot."

I took a deep breath, letting my mind return to the night of Derek's death. Hale had named it *the call*. I felt a vibrating energy build from a tiny flicker to an almost violent storm with in me. I focused on Royal, desperate to make him hear me.

"I'm telling you the truth. Believe me." As the words left my mouth, I once again felt them pushing forward toward Royal, cracking through the space between us with a delicate ringing. Royal's eyes widened, but in comparison to how it had affected Derek, *the call* had almost no power over Royal. It did seem to impress him, though.

"What was that? I almost—" he shook his head, smiling wryly. "Power of suggestion?"

"It's something Lilitu can do. Only, it's usually a lot stronger than that." I looked at Royal and remembered Thane's words. "But you're not into girls," I said breathlessly.

"This is news?"

"It's desire," I said. "Lilitu only have power over people who desire them."

After one charged moment, Royal sank back onto the window seat. His eyes lost their focus. "When did you say you started feeling... different?"

"On my birthday."

"The day you showed up in your Firebird." Royal's eyes creased uneasily. "Some guy crashed into a post when he saw you. Parker and his friends couldn't take their eyes off of you."

"Yes," I said breathlessly.

"And the entire male population at school showed up after your oh-so-subtle invitation in the dining hall." I saw an expression I'd never seen on his face before—an uneasy awareness.

"Now do you believe me?"

He didn't answer, but I could see the wheels in his head turning. "In the hallway today. When those guys saw Cassie, they saw easy prey. You glared at them and they just... wandered off." Royal's eyes were troubled.

"Are you scared of me now?" My voice was tentative, quivering.

"You're still Braedyn, aren't you?" Royal looked at me, considering. "Aren't you? If everything you've told me is true, it's not like you sought this out. You were born this way. You just know more about yourself now than you did before."

"Parker," I said, as though that explained everything.

Royal's face hardened. "He had it coming."

"You saw him, Royal. You saw what I did to him," I said. Royal turned to look out at the city, but I saw his reaction in the reflection. Whatever he'd seen when they brought Parker in, it hadn't been pretty. "If he dies," I dropped my voice to a hoarse whisper. "It'll be just the same as if I murdered him. Do you still think I'm the same girl you used to know?"

Royal forced himself to meet my gaze. "We all change, Braedyn. It's called growing up. But the core of you, yeah. You're still the same. You're still the same girl who stands up to the bullies and then worries about the consequences. But what I can't figure out is why you care about what happens to that ass, Parker. If I had the power to make him pay for what he did to Cassie, I wouldn't waste one second regretting it."

I shook my head, too weary to argue. The doorbell rang. I looked at Royal sharply. "Are you expecting someone?"

"No." He got up. I followed him to the door. As we entered the foyer, we saw the flashing lights of a cop car through the frosted glass beside the front door. I heard Hale's voice outside.

"Yes, that's her car."

Someone knocked on the front door. "Police. Please open the door."

I shrank back out of the foyer. "They found me."

Royal turned to study me, worried. "The cops?"

"The Guard." The naked terror in my voice galvanized Royal. He grabbed all the cash from his wallet and shoved it into my hand.

"Go out my dad's room. I'll keep them distracted. You can slip over the back wall; follow the foot trail down to the gate. The bus stop—"

"I know where it is," I interrupted him. "Royal—" I wanted to thank him, but he turned me around and shoved me toward the bedrooms. I didn't resist.

As I slipped into Royal's dad's room I heard him open the front door. "Yes?"

I entered the dark bedroom and moved quickly across to the French doors, opening them quietly. The night was getting colder, but Cassie's jacket offered some protection. I slipped up and over the stucco wall. As my feet hit the ground, I heard a door open.

Royal's voice cut across the night, a little too loud. "I told you, she left the car here about an hour ago. Maybe she dropped her cell phone out there and that's why you're picking it up." I scrambled in my pocket for my cell phone. No good taking the battery out now. I dropped the cell phone in a weed and started moving.

I kept low, using the wall as cover, and followed one of the hiking trails that crisscrossed the foothills. In moments I was behind another house, and Royal's father's place was out of sight. I straightened and started running, my feet making soft scuffing sounds in the dry sand of the trail. The moon was rising, casting a silvery sheen on the desert landscape. It was weirdly bright to my eyes. I reached the bus stop in about a half an hour. The hem of my coat was covered with dust and goathead thorns.

I only had to wait about five minutes for the bus. I didn't bother to read the destination; it was going away from here, and that's all that mattered. I paid the fare and slumped into an empty row, staring out the window for any sign of Hale's truck. The bus pulled away from the curb and headed back into the heart of the city. When I was sure no one was following, I glanced up at the front of the bus and read the sign. We were headed to Old Town. Fine. There was a public phone near the bookstore. I could try Dad from there, and just hope he was home. It took about 45 minutes for the bus to make the trip across town. I got off and headed into the Plaza. The coat was drawing stares, but that was fine with me. Neither Hale nor Gretchen had ever seen it, so it might throw them off my trail.

I spotted my favorite bookstore, but hesitated, worried that they might search the places I knew. Instead of heading for familiar comfort, I slipped into a coffee shop I'd never entered before. It was new, capitalizing on the revitalization of Old Town, but it was nice and dark inside. I ordered a simple coffee and found a chair next to a window. I'd had time to think on the bus. I still hadn't come up with a viable plan beyond calling Dad for help. I had a clear view of the public phone outside. I was getting up the courage to call when I saw the Lilitu.

She was strolling down the sidewalk, as though she had all the time in the world. She held the hand of a guy who looked a little star-struck. I recognized her as the brunette Lilitu who'd crashed my party at the Raven. The guy at her side was clearly an intended victim. I studied him a little closer. He still looked alert and aware. It was a safe bet he hadn't been attacked yet. I stood, reaching into my pocket for the cell phone that was no longer there, then, remembering, raced out of the coffee shop. I dropped some change into the public phone and dialed Dad's cell. It went straight to voicemail.

"Dad, it's me," I whispered into the receiver. "There's a Lilitu in Old Town, she's got a guy with her. I don't think she's attacked him yet. Please, hurry. I don't know where they're going." I hung up, feeling helpless. In desperation, I dropped more coins into the phone and dialed our house. It rang and rang, and finally the answering machine picked up. I left another breathless message and hung up, but the urgency I felt kept growing. Who knew when Dad would get the messages? If it wasn't soon, it would almost certainly be too late for the unsuspecting stranger. I hesitated, conflicted, then fed a few more coins into the phone and dialed the number for the Guard's house.

Lucas picked up on the second ring. "Yes." His voice sounded clipped, emotionless. He barely sounded like himself. "Who is this?"

I swallowed, scared. "Don't hang up. There's a Lilitu in Old Town. She has a mark with her, but if you hurry—" There was a click on the other end of the line. "Hello?" He'd hung up on me. I turned back to the street, feeling helpless. The Lilitu and her prey were gone, and for one horrible moment I feared I'd lost them. But then I saw a man craning his neck out of a doorway, and another, and another, all staring in the same direction. I turned to see what they were gaping at, and spotted her. She was leading the stranger into a narrow alley between two buildings. I knew the alley. It let out onto the edge of the park of catalpa trees. Lots of people used it as a shortcut to Old Town's grassy amphitheater. The redevelopment team had paved the alley with terracotta tiles in an attempt to make it feel more like a pathway and less like an alley.

As I watched the Lilitu and her prey disappearing between the buildings, I realized no one was coming. In an hour, it could be too late for him. I slipped after them, only half-sure of what I was doing. I figured that if I could scare her away, I might be able to save him.

I followed them through the alley. As I emerged from between the buildings, I heard the music. The Lilitu was leading her prey toward a low thumping beat. I followed them up the side of a grassy slope, and the music grew louder. As I crested the small hill, I saw the manmade grassy amphitheater, pulsing with young couples. I couldn't see the Lilitu in the crowd. I pressed forward, desperate to find her.

"Braedyn. What are you doing here?" Karayan swept toward me in a white dress. She gleamed in the moonlight, from the tip of her honey-blond head to her gleaming pearlescent toes. The cold night air seemed to have no effect on her. I saw a pair of smoky wings, barely visible, cascading down her back. "No offense, but this is kind of an exclusive party."

A man in his early twenties approached me with a smile. Karayan waved him away, impatient. "Not this one." He glanced at me and I noticed his pupils. They were too wide, even for the darkness of the night. A Thrall. I glanced back at the rave.

The Thrall moved toward another young couple. They looked like students from the local university. Suddenly, a different Lilitu was there, smiling at the college boy. His girlfriend started to object, but the Thrall swooped in with a charming smile and handed her a drink. Distracted, she wasn't watching when the Lilitu unfurled those smoky wings. They curved around the boy, shimmering eerily, cloaking the Lilitu and her prey from human sight. When the girl looked back for her boyfriend, she couldn't see him, even though he was standing only feet from where he'd been moments ago. The Lilitu whispered into his ear. He turned back toward his girlfriend, but the Lilitu caught his face between her hands and kissed him. I saw a glimmer of silvery mist moving from his lips to hers. When she released him, he swayed a little on his feet. She took his hand and led him away.

I stood, rooted to the spot. Karayan watched me, her head tilted to one side. "Don't be shy," she said. She gestured and I saw the Lilitu I had followed here dancing with her mark in the crowd. "I think I see someone looking for a dance partner." She nudged me forward and I saw a kid about my age hesitating at the edge of the rave. I stopped dead in my tracks. Karayan came around to face me with a knowing smile. "First time?" Before I had the chance to answer her, someone spoke over my shoulder.

"Perhaps you were correct after all." I turned, and all thoughts fell away from me. A Lilitu approached, her eyes wide and deep pools of twilight. Her hair was long and so blond it seemed white. I'd seen her once before, briefly, at the Raven.

Karayan straightened unconsciously. "Ais. She surprised me—" The white-blond Lilitu lifted a hand and Karayan fell silent.

"I had hoped you would come around," Ais murmured, studying me.

Ais. I felt a prickle of goose bumps cascading down my neck. Ais was here, and I'd met her without even knowing it! Ais studied me, and once again I saw past her human mask to her Lilitu self. Her eyes might have been beautiful if they weren't so frightening. They glowed faintly, like the blue-purple of the sky half an hour after sunset.

"Still a ward of the Guard?" Ais touched my forehead, her finger leaving another icy chill behind. Her eyes widened a fraction. "Ah. You must question your place in this world." I dropped my eyes, unwilling to let her know how close she was to the heart of my trouble.

Karayan shifted closer to me, linking her hand in mine. "She doesn't know her own strength yet. But she's learning."

"The more she learns, the more fully she becomes herself." Ais murmured. "And the greater the danger she faces at the hands of those who stole her from us. Is that not so?" Ais waited for me to respond, but I could only stare at her, unnerved. "Such potential." A possessive desire glinted in Ais's eyes. "It has been millennia," she said, as if to herself. "And to let you fall into the hands of the Guard. She must have been mad."

"Who—?" My heart lurched in my chest. "Do you mean—? Did you know my mother?"

Ais's eyes hardened. "At one time, I thought so."

"Who is she?" I asked. My mind pored over the story Dad had told me. How she had given me my name. How there had been goodness in her. "Is she still—?"

Ais frowned and I fell silent. "Own your power, or it will own you," she said. Ais turned to Karayan. "Watch her."

Time skipped a beat and Ais was suddenly a dozen feet away, walking back into the crowd of dancing, oblivious humans. Karayan let her breath out slowly.

"She's so—" I started, shuddering.

"Powerful," Karayan murmured.

"Alien."

Karayan glanced at me sharply. "We have more in common with Ais than we do with those creatures." She gestured at the swelling mass of dancers around us.

"Those 'creatures?' Are you kidding me?" I looked at Karayan, really studied her. I could *see* her Lilitu self under her human mask, but they looked virtually identical. The only things that really distinguished the Lilitu part of Karayan were her smoky wings. "No, we don't," I said. "Did you see her?"

Karayan knew exactly what I meant. She crossed her arms defensively. "We'll become like them, but it won't happen overnight. It takes time to grow into our power. Don't be scared." She gestured, and the boy she'd pointed out earlier walked toward us.

"No," I hissed quietly, feeling my face heat up.

"The Guard doesn't own you," she said, coaxing me with a smile. "It's your body, Braedyn."

"Yeah, exactly. And I don't want this." I glanced at the boy as he approached, smiling. His face was open, interested. Human. And Karayan wanted me to break him. He came to a stop beside us. Karayan draped an arm over his shoulders.

"Why? Because he's not Lucas?"

My heart stopped beating for a moment.

Karayan smiled. "I got it wrong the first time, but I've been watching you. And as for Lucas—I think that ship has sailed, sweetie." She watched my reaction calmly. "Yeah, I know all about your little kiss this afternoon. The Guard is hunting you, your guy hates you... Basically, the life you knew is over. So why not drown your sorrows? He makes a cute consolation prize, don't you agree? I guarantee you'll feel better afterwards." She turned to the boy, including him in our conversation. "Her boyfriend just dumped her. Are you any good at cheering girls up?"

"I can try," he smiled at me and offered his hand. "I'm Jesse. You like to dance?"

I pulled him close, hissing into his ear. "Jesse, *run*. You're not safe here."

Without waiting to see if he'd take my advice, I retreated up the side of the grassy amphitheater. At the top of the slope, I glanced back. Karayan was talking with three muscular guys. She flung out her hand, pointing at me. The men started forward. I ran. I found the alley between the buildings and darted inside, risking a look over my shoulder. I could just make out three large silhouettes cresting the hill behind me. They were coming fast.

I reached the end of the alley and was about to step into the Plaza when I saw Gretchen, searching faces in the crowd. I turned and darted back into the shelter between the buildings, my heart leaping into my throat. When I was halfway back down the alley, the three strangers Karayan had sent after me appeared ahead. I saw an opening along one wall of the alley and ran into it. I realized my mistake instantly. It was a blind alley with a trash bin and a pair of metal doors. I tried both doors, but they were locked. No way out.

Panic surged inside me and I turned back to the mouth of the alley, but the men were there, blocking the exit. The first moved forward, and what I saw in his eyes terrified me. I glanced at the others; all shared the same vacant stare. Karayan had sent three Thrall after me.

"*Stop,*" I said, filling my voice with the power of *the call*. I felt the connection, heard the chimes, and the first Thrall stopped. But the other two simply stepped around him. "*Stop!*" I tried to include the others in my command, but as I tried to spread the power, it weakened and snapped, freeing the first Thrall. I panicked, and stumbled up against the back of the alley.

The first Thrall reached for me. He snaked a hand inside my jacket and pulled me close. "A gift from Karayan," he said. His free hand cupped my chin and he forced my face up, leaning in to kiss me. I knew then why they were here. Karayan, trying to help me "feed," had sent these men to be my victims. She'd sent them to die, and they were eager. Revulsion coursed through my veins and I shoved him back, instinctively settling into a fighting stance.

The men ringed me loosely. When they lunged, I moved. It was reflex more than anything else. I sidestepped the first and tried to run, but the second caught me by the shoulder. I grabbed his hand and twisted, running him into the alley wall like Lucas had taught me all those long weeks ago. But the third man kicked my feet out from under me and I fell, hard. As he dropped to pin me, I rolled away. Except Cassie's gorgeous coat gave him something to grab onto. He jerked me back and caught me in a bear hug.

"Let me go!" I cracked my head back into his face and his hold weakened. I ducked out of his arms and sprang to my feet. The second two were flanking me. Terror rose in me, so strong it was suffocating. The man I had driven into the wall was favoring his shoulder. I turned to the other one and attacked. It was different than sparring with Gretchen. Fear and adrenaline lent me an extra boost of speed, but the men were strong, and there were too many of them. All I wanted was to get around them and flee, but they kept moving to block the alleyway. I kicked out, hoping to catch one in the stomach, but my leg got tangled in the coat. It was a fatal mistake. The second man knocked me off balance. I fell and scrambled back, too winded from the fall to stand. They stood, like an impenetrable wall blocking my way to freedom. Fear and rage shot through my scrambled thoughts. But when the first man reached for my ankle to pull me away from the wall, I felt a surge of emotion and a ripping sensation along my spine. I screamed.

The men froze, uncertain. But it wasn't my scream that had

stopped them in their tracks. I realized, as a shimmering cape clamped tightly around me, that they could no longer see me. Slowly, aching, I drew my knees close and got to my feet. The shimmering cape moved with me, stretching to allow me movement but keeping me tightly veiled. Dim realization glimmered in the back of my mind. I reached out and touched my wings. I felt the sensation in my fingers, and an echo of sensation in the wings. They were sensitive, like skin, but tougher.

I faced my attackers, still blocking the alley. I tried to slip between two of them, but brushed one. He struck out, sending me crashing back. My wings snapped open as I struggled to regain my balance. They saw me and moved. I briefly feared the wings would make fighting impossible, but they were insubstantial. I might be able to feel them, but they brushed through my attackers as though they didn't exist. I didn't have time to consider this as I dodged the first man. My attention was divided between trying to figure out how to keep myself cloaked, and fighting the Thralls.

In the end, the wings gave me just enough of an advantage. Half-cloaked, I managed to disorient my attackers. I fought my way free of the alley and ran. When I made it to the Plaza, my body started shaking uncontrollably. I managed to collapse in the alcove in front of a darkened storefront. The trauma of the attack flooded through me, blocking out everything else. I hugged my knees to my chest, kept my wings tightly wrapped around me, and choked out a few ragged sobs before I managed to get my breathing back under control. I sat in the dark alcove for a long time. People walked past me, unseeing, unaware. As my heartbeat slowed and my mind cleared, I was left with one clear thought—I had to warn the Guard before they got on that plane.

Ais was here.

A grizzled old stranger in a worn trench coat stepped into the alcove. I held my breath, wondering if he hoped to hole up here for the night like I had. He stood next to me, and then turned to stare out at the Plaza. I watched him for a long time, but he didn't move. Finally, I eased to my feet, as quietly as possible. I had only taken one step forward when he spoke.

"Who do you fight for, Daughter of Lilith?" he asked.

I turned back. He was staring directly at me, through the cloaking effect of my wings, as though he knew who I was. He must have been some kind of spotter. The recent trauma was still too fresh. I had no fear left in me.

"I'm Murphy's daughter," I said. "Not Lilith's."

He studied me for a long moment, and then drew a sword out of his coat. That was enough to awaken my survival instincts. I tensed, waiting for him to make a move. He handed the sword to me, pommel up. "Take this."

I hesitated, but as I took it, our hands brushed. In that moment, I saw the being beneath this human shell. Or, rather, I saw a blinding figure that gleamed in silhouette against an even brighter light. There was nothing grizzled or old about him; he was ageless and powerful. I squinted against the glare, but as soon as our hands broke contact, he was merely the grizzled stranger again, watching me with inscrutable eyes.

"Who are you?" I breathed.

"That is not important. What is important is that you defeat Ais."

"Defeat? She's—" I shuddered, remembering her from the rave, remembering her touch on my forehead. "She's too strong."

"That is why she must be stopped."

"Stopped?" I had a sinking feeling inside.

"A legion of Lilitu has amassed. Even now, they are preparing to cross into this world. Ais is their doorway. You must prevent her from granting them access to the Earth."

It was then that I realized what he was. "You're one of the Three." I didn't need him to confirm it to know I was right. "You're one of the angels who hunted Lilith."

He faced me, as if considering what to do with me. After a long moment, he answered. "We are Sansenoy."

"Sansenoy. They're going to flip out when they see you. Hale, Dad, everyone. They need you. Badly."

"We are required elsewhere."

"But—you just said a legion of Lilitu are going to come crashing through the gates!"

He faced me directly, his eyes glinting, as bright and hard as steel. "You must stop them or this world will be lost."

"You stop them," I said. "This is what you do, isn't it? Fight the Lilitu? So fight them!"

He gave me a look tinged with pity. "Did you think your Earth was the only battleground in this war?"

It took me a moment to process this. "You're not going to help us?"

"We have already helped you." His eyes dropped to the sword in my hands. It became clear that this was the only answer I would get. As he started to turn away, I felt my panic rising.

"Wait. Can't you take this to the Guard? They don't exactly want me around right now."

His face was impossible to read. "It is in your hands, Murphy's daughter. We can do nothing more in this contest. Be strong, and you will prevail."

"That's great for a bumper sticker," I said, snapping a little. "But I'm telling you, they might not even listen to me long enough to—" I stopped, frustrated. "I just wish—" But again, the thoughts crowded into my head, too many wishes vying for attention. I wished I hadn't messed with Parker. I wished I'd told Lucas my secret. I wished I'd never been born. No. What I wanted, more than everything else, was to be human. To be a normal girl. To grow up and fall in love and get married and maybe someday have kids—and not kill the love of my life doing it. What I wanted was impossible.

"What do you wish?"

"Never mind," I sighed, resigned. "It doesn't matter anyway, unless you're in the business of granting miracles."

Sansenoy studied me for a long moment. "We are not... in the business... of granting miracles," he finally said. The words sounded odd coming from his mouth.

"Then I guess I'll never be a real girl." I smiled humorlessly.

A strange compassion softened Sansenoy's eyes. "If God's favorite angel could be cast down for his acts of evil, perhaps a demon child might be granted humanity for her acts of good." He placed a hand on my shoulder. It felt oddly formal. "All things are possible to those who believe." And then he stepped into the flow of the passersby, and was lost in the crowd.

I stood in the alcove for a long moment, the sword strangely light in my hands. Moments ago I'd been exhausted, desolate. Now, for the first time since the day I'd found out what I was, I felt a swelling hope lifting my heart.

All things are possible.

18

I knew exactly what I needed to do. I would go back to the Guard, tell them about Ais and the travelling raves where the Lilitu were hunting, and hand over the sword. But first, I'd have to get the sword back home. It was a little conspicuous, and I doubted any bus driver in the city would let me carry a weapon like this on board. I glanced down at the full skirt of my coat. It was dirty from the fight, but otherwise not too badly damaged. I tucked the sword under one arm and let the skirt of the coat hide it. Once I had satisfied myself that I could carry the sword like this, I stepped out of the alcove.

"Hey, over here." It sounded like someone was calling to me. I turned and saw a young man leaning against the storefront, like he'd been waiting for me. There was something familiar about him.

"Do I know you?" I walked toward him before I had placed his face. Matt. Gretchen's Matt. The Guard soldier who had driven Gretchen home and kissed her on the front lawn. He tensed, preparing to move. "Wait," I said urgently. "I'm Braedyn." No recognition flickered across his face. Of course. Gretchen would have been forbidden to tell anyone about me.

I didn't see the others coming up behind me. Two of them grabbed my arms. I heard the sword clang to the ground as they hustled me back to the sheltered pathway.

"Stop—the sword!" I shouted. "Someone, please—Grab the sword!" I craned my head around and saw someone pick it up.

"Damn it, Keats, hurry!"

Someone pried my jaws open and forced a cloth into my mouth, gagging me. Then we were in the pathway between buildings, out of sight of the passing crowd. Someone dropped a hood over my head.

Blinded, I panicked and started to struggle. I couldn't see the punch. It took me hard across the cheek, stunning me. I stopped struggling, but another fist drove into my stomach, expelling the air from my lungs. I doubled over in their arms and was only vaguely aware of them dragging me, running now, through the pathway. I heard an engine idling, and the unmistakable sound of a van door sliding open. They threw me into the back. I curled my hands over my head, but before I could pull the hood off, people were piling in around me and someone wrenched my hands behind my back. I felt someone else lean over me, then felt a sturdy band of plastic being slipped over my wrists and tightened.

"Go, go!" The van lurched into motion. I heard someone howl in triumph. "Got one! Not bad for the new kids in town, huh, Matt?"

"Not bad," Matt said. He was sitting next to me. I felt him lean in close to my ear. "Bet you had a different kind of party in mind for tonight. Surprise." The group laughed, giddy with their success. They thought they'd caught a hunting Lilitu. I felt tears of frustration forming in the corners of my eyes. I tried to speak, but the gag reduced me to unintelligible sounds.

Someone else spoke. "Talkative, that's good. But you should save it for the colonel. He's going to have a lot of questions for you." That inspired another round of laughter, but this laughter was darker, knowing.

After that, I was too scared to do anything other than listen. I gleaned they'd only arrived in town a few hours ago, expecting to be on a plane tonight. Gretchen must have told Matt about me, sent him to find me. For nearly 20 minutes I was adrift in an ocean of fear. Then the van stopped. I heard the doors open.

"Wait," someone said in a hushed voice. "Okay. Clear."

I was dragged out of the van and across a lawn. The grass felt crisp with frost beneath my feet. Then I was pulled up a few wooden steps and dragged over a threshold. Inside was warm. Familiar. I knew exactly where I was before they ripped the hood off.

The living room of the Guard's house was packed. Gretchen and Thane sat on the couch, Hale stood by the mantle, and a half-dozen strangers filled the other seats. Dad was deep in conversation with a sinewy old man I'd never seen before. Lucas sat on the staircase, watching the living room. He was the first to see me. He stared, frozen. I thought I saw a flicker of emotion in his eyes, but he looked away before I could be sure.

"Caught one," Matt said. Everyone else looked up as I was shoved forward into the living room. The sinewy man turned around.

"Excellent," he said, eyeing me impersonally. "Take it downstairs. I'll be there shortly."

"Braedyn!" Dad shoved the sinewy man aside and reached me in a heartbeat. He wrenched me out of Matt's hands and shielded me in his arms, backing into the foyer. I felt his hand on my cheek, gently brushing the tender skin. Whoever had hit me must have left a mark.

The newcomers shared a stunned look, and then leapt into action.

"Wait!" Hale shouted above the chaos. "She's on our side!" I felt Dad's arms tighten around me, but we were outnumbered. In another moment, I'd be pulled away from him.

"Enough!" The sinewy man's voice cut through the din like a cannon's crack. The voices died down, but the tension in the room was near the breaking point.

"Hold still," Dad murmured. He used his dagger to cut through the plastic tie binding my hands, and then fumbled with my gag. As soon as it slackened, I pulled it off and threw it across the room, glaring at the newcomers.

"Murphy," Matt said, stunned. "Defending a demon? Now I really have seen everything."

"Stay back," Dad growled.

I studied the sinewy man over Dad's shoulder. He was an older man, with three faint scars travelling down one side of his neck and disappearing under his shirt. He looked hardened, battle-worn. And decidedly unfriendly. He held up a hand toward us, like he was trying to calm a snarling dog, and glared at his soldiers. They gave us some space. Not a lot of space—they still looked ready to attack at one signal from their leader.

"Braedyn." Hale read my panic. "This is Colonel Marx and his team."

The sinewy man, Colonel Marx, turned to Hale. "Explain, Major."

"She's one of us, sir," Hale said, pushing through the crowd urgently. "Murphy raised her. She thought she was human until three months ago. She knows what's at stake, and she's on our side."

"And all of you knew this?" Marx asked, surprised. Thane and

Gretchen shared a tight grimace but nodded.

Hale gestured to the stairs. "All of us except for Lucas." Lucas was staring into the room, his face ashen. Gretchen turned to him, but had to look away from the blame in his eyes.

"So this demon is... safe?" Marx looked uncertain.

"No." A slender, athletic woman glared at me. She had the same edge to her Gretchen had, an outward toughness that seemed to hide the pain of a great loss. Another spotter, I realized. "We followed a residual trace to her room. She's manipulated at least one mind." The newcomers shifted, eyeing me with distrust.

"I have the situation under control, Colonel," Hale said. But he couldn't look at me.

Marx frowned and turned to Matt. "Where did you find her?"

"In Old Town, by the rave, just like we were warned."

"She's the one who called to warn us," Dad said, his frustration erupting.

"What was she doing there?" Marx turned to me. I felt the eyes of the room find me.

"I—I didn't know where else to go." I glanced at Hale. His face tightened, but I didn't read the warning until it was too late. "After everything that happened with Lucas—"

"Lucas?" Marx glanced at Lucas on the stairs, his body tensing. "What happened with Lucas?" His voice was low, steely. I felt Dad's hand tighten on my arm and didn't answer. Marx took a step toward Lucas. "Tell me."

Lucas saw Hale's panic. His eyes darted toward me, scared. Marx followed his gaze, eyes narrowing. I realized it must look to them like I was trying to influence Lucas. By the time Lucas spoke, it was already too late. "It was just a kiss."

That was all it took. Marx only had to nod, and his team piled onto us, pulling me out of Dad's arms. Hale tried to intervene, but Thane, Gretchen, and Lucas stayed rooted to the spot.

"Braedyn, run!" Dad shouted, struggling against the three soldiers who wrestled him back. He was larger than all but one of them, but they outnumbered him.

I twisted against the hands that held me and broke free, but they moved to latch onto me again. I swung out, kicking someone in the side and shoving them away. For a moment, it was just a fit young soldier and me. His eyes were hard, intelligent; he was ready for this fight. I saw the door beyond him and moved, feinting. He lunged toward my feint and I sprinted for the door, feeling my wings snap around me.

"To your right!" The newcomer spotter raced forward, eyes fixed on me. The soldier I'd just dodged was faster than I'd expected. He caught me around the shoulders, spinning me off balance. I hit the floor and rolled back to my feet in one motion, but my wings canted crazily, exposing me. Three of them were ringing me now. I was only vaguely aware of Hale, shouting at Marx over the chaos of the fight.

At that moment, Dad broke free and tackled one of the soldiers. Another turned, surprised. Cloaked beneath my wings once more, I darted for him, sweeping his foot out from under him.

"Sean, left, Caleb, straight ahead!" Their spotter pointed at me, an unerring compass for her unit to follow. I felt my lips pulling back in a snarl of frustration. Her eyes, locked onto my face, narrowed with determination. "Careful!"

I spun to face the last soldier, but found two more backing him. They all had daggers gleaming in their hands.

"No!" Dad's voice was ragged with emotion. "Braedyn, uncloak yourself." I glanced at him. Two of the newcomers had pinned him to the floor. A third was sliding another plastic tie over his wrists to hold him, but he was only focused on me. "Do it! Do it now!"

I did as he asked, willing the wings to retract. The soldiers surrounding me spread out, keeping me in the center of a ring of blades.

"Easy," one of the soldiers said. They advanced, and I retreated. I was dimly aware that they were herding me back into the room, but I couldn't see a way past the daggers. I felt the wall at my back. They pushed forward until I was hemmed into the corner of the living room. By the time I realized there was no way out of this, five of the newcomers had circled me, blades in every fist. It was very quiet.

Marx approached and the soldiers parted for him. He held one of the Guard's daggers loosely in his hand. Hale followed on Marx's heels, but the soldiers ringing me forced him back.

"Don't," Hale said. "Don't throw this opportunity away. We need her, Marx." Hale was focused on Marx, desperate to reach the older man with his words. Marx had his eyes fixed on me. He looked completely calm. I realized with a twisting sensation in my gut that Marx meant to kill me. Hale's voice, already urgent, sharpened. "We need her if we're going to have any hope of stopping this war."

"Give me one reason why." Marx didn't turn to face Hale. He kept his eyes riveted to my face.

"She's one of them," Hale said, scrambling for the right words to reach Marx. "She might be able to—"

But Marx cut him off. "Not you." He pointed at me with the tip of his dagger. "You." I couldn't look away from his eyes. They were crisp, devoid of empathy.

"Ais is here," I said. Hale glanced at me sharply. "She's not in South America. She was at the rave."

"Easy to say and hard to prove," Marx said. "Do better."

"The sword," I said quietly.

"What sword?"

I shifted my eyes to Matt, afraid to move. "One of your soldiers has it."

Marx looked back. Matt nodded and jogged out the door. In a moment he'd returned, carrying the sword. Gretchen and the new spotter reacted as if they'd seen a ghost. Their spotter straightened, flushed.

Marx noticed the movement. "Dina?"

His spotter, Dina, looked unsteady. Instead of answering Marx, she glanced at Gretchen. "The sword. Do you—?" Dina asked breathlessly.

"Yeah. I see it." Gretchen's jaw was tight, her eyes riveted to the sword.

Marx turned back to the sword. "What is it?"

"It has a dream-aspect." Gretchen turned to Hale, dropping her voice urgently. "It has to be one of *theirs*. This sword belongs to one of the Three."

The soldiers traded surprised glances. Suddenly I wasn't the center of attention. I held my breath.

"It's some kind of trick." Thane crossed the distance to Matt in a few long steps. "Let me see that."

"I know what I'm looking at," Gretchen said, snapping.

Marx pushed through the soldiers. "Watch her," he said, gesturing to three of the guards. They turned back to me, laser-focused.

Everyone else was staring at the sword. Gretchen's eyes found me; they were filled with questions. I looked at the sword, and saw what she had seen: the faint haze of another sword. The longer I stared at the hazy image, the sharper it became. It was as though a second sword was sharing the same physical space as the first, in another world superimposed over our own.

Thane took the sword gingerly from Matt and walked to a table lamp. He bent his slight frame to hold the hilt under the light, and then straightened silently.

Marx shifted his weight, uneasy. "Thane?"

"Gretchen's right." Thane was cradling the sword in his hands like a precious thing. "This was Semangelof's. Her name is engraved in the hilt." Thane looked at me. "How did you get this?"

Before I could answer, Marx took the sword out of Thane's hands. "Impossible."

"Unless someone else has figured out how to forge a sword with a dream-aspect, that weapon belonged to one of the Three," Dina said quietly.

"Then how, exactly, did it end up in the hands of a demon?" Marx asked. The room turned back to me. I saw a range of emotions on their faces—suspicion, fear, confusion—and, on Hale's face, hope. They were all waiting for my answer.

"Sansenoy gave it to me so we could stop Ais," I said.

Marx smiled coldly. "You expect us to believe an angel gave this sword to you?"

"I'm telling the truth."

"You're telling us exactly what we want to hear to save your own skin. An angel would never hand over this sword to a demon. And a demon," he smiled at me wryly. "A demon would never *willingly* give an angel's sword to the Guard."

"Colonel," Matt said, stepping forward hesitantly. "She dropped the sword when we caught her."

"Of course she did," Marx said, as though this confirmed everything.

"We almost left it behind, but she shouted her head off until one of us grabbed it." Matt glanced at Gretchen, uneasy. "She told me her name, like that would mean something to me. It took Keats almost half a minute to gag her, but she never tried to use *the call* on us." Matt looked around the room. The newcomers glanced at me, uncertain now.

"Let her go," Hale said quietly.

"She's Lilitu, Hale." But even Marx sounded unsure.

"Let them both go," Hale ordered. The soldiers guarding me stepped back, lowering their weapons. I pushed past them and ran to the foyer. Dad was still lying on the floor. One of the newcomers freed his hands. Two others helped him up. Half a second later, Dad crossed the space between us and caught me in a fierce hug. Judging by the way his arms fastened around me, he was never planning on letting me go. Out of the corner of my eye, I saw Thane take the sword out of Marx's hands.

"You okay?" Dad whispered into my hair. I nodded, not trusting myself to speak. The tension was broken. Several of the newcomers eyed me, curious.

Matt approached us gingerly. "You actually spoke with Sansenoy? Does that mean he's come back to help us?" A thrill of excitement shot through the room. Even Marx turned, waiting for my answer. I looked at the Guard from the safety of Dad's arms.

"No," I said. "We have to deal with Ais on our own." The momentary jubilation faded.

"Winter solstice is tomorrow," Gretchen said, hollowly. "The rest of our forces are in South America."

Hale recovered first. "We don't have any time to waste. I'll call Leadership. Let them know that Ais is here."

I pulled away from Dad to catch Hale's arm. He turned, his attention focused on me. "I know why Gretchen hasn't found the hunting grounds. They move it every night. Karayan called it a travelling rave."

Hale nodded, but he didn't seem surprised. "We figured that out after your phone call. We have a bigger problem now. Gretchen stumbled on to a warehouse the Lilitu are using for a barracks. Thane was right about the Thrall. We're estimating they have somewhere between 20 and 30 men so far." Hale glanced at Marx. "We couldn't figure out why they'd be setting up such a strong force here. But that's when we thought Ais was in South America. If she's setting up camp here... Well, Thane knows more about this than anyone." Hale gestured at Thane.

"I've been conferring with the other archivists," Thane said. "We believe it will take great concentration and power for Ais to force open the Wall. She'll need to prepare the site of the doorway, and she'll do everything she can to ensure she's not interrupted once she's begun."

"That would explain the Thrall," Marx said. "We won't be able to fight through even 20 of them easily."

Thane nodded. "If we want to stop her from breaching the Wall, our best bet is to find the spot she plans to open the doorway and disrupt her preparations."

"Failing that," Hale said grimly. "We'll have to contain the Lilitu she lets into this world."

Thane nodded. "As I said. Our best bet is to stop Ais before she opens the doorway."

"We'll go. We can scout the area Gretchen found. See what we can see." Marx was already gesturing to his team. "Dina, Keats, Sean. You're with me. The rest of you are with Matt." Marx and his soldiers left the house. Before Matt followed them out, he pulled Gretchen close. They shared a kiss. I glanced at Lucas and found him staring at me. His hazel eyes were guarded. My heart lurched painfully. The Guard had forgiven me. That didn't mean Lucas would. I heard Matt and Gretchen talking behind me.

"I'll see you in a couple of hours," Matt said quietly.

"Watch your back," Gretchen said. "I'm getting kind of fond of it. And of the rest of you, too."

"You're going to make me blush," Matt laughed softly. I heard them share another quick kiss, and then Matt was out the door and gone.

"I need a minute, everyone," Hale said. Dad and I followed Gretchen into the living room. "Everyone, Lucas." Lucas walked into the room and perched on the arm of the couch by Gretchen. Hale spoke again. "The war is here," he said. "And humanity needs us to bring our best to the fight." Hale picked up a gleaming set of daggers in an oiled sheath. "Braedyn. We haven't gotten to these yet, but the daggers are more than weapons of the Guard. They're also a symbol. Whether or not you're ready, training is over. Welcome to the Guard."

Hale set the daggers into my hands. They felt heavier than I'd remembered. I caught Dad's eye. He looked torn between worry and pride. Lucas's jaw tightened, he was glaring at the floor. He didn't see

Hale pick up another set of daggers in a sheath.

"Lucas," Hale continued. "You've been telling me you're ready for these for over a year. Now you get to prove it." He tossed the daggers to Lucas, who caught the sheath in one fist.

"Hale," Gretchen said, standing. Her voice was tight with concern.

"We need every soldier we have." Hale silenced Gretchen's fresh protest with a look, and turned back to Lucas. "And Murphy." Hale thrust his hands out to Thane, who still held the sword. Thane transferred it without complaint. Hale turned and presented the sword to Murphy. "Semangelof's sword. This should go to you." Dad accepted the sword, reverently.

Hale glanced at his watch. "We'll know more when Marx's team returns. At that point, we'll start planning our attack. Our best option is attacking at dawn, when she's weakest. In the meantime, try to get some sleep." It was a dismissal.

Everyone stood. Gretchen walked to Hale, pulling him aside to talk. I approached Lucas, hoping for a moment to explain. He was still staring at the daggers in his hands.

"Lucas," I said.

He looked up at me, all warmth evaporating from his face. "There's nothing I want to hear from you."

"Please. Let me explain."

He looked away from me, letting his hair fall over his eyes. "What you did. Trespassing on my dreams. That was a violation." He met my eyes, and I read in them the pain of betrayal. "I don't care why you did it. Those were my intimate thoughts. You had no right." Lucas shouldered past me, and headed straight up the stairs.

I turned to follow him, mortified. "Lucas."

Gretchen stepped in my path. "You're kidding, right?" She frowned and lowered her voice. "The Guard needs you. We both get it. But Lucas doesn't want to see you more than he has to. So do us both a favor and go home."

I looked up the stairs, over her shoulder. Lucas reached his doorway, and disappeared into the darkness of his room.

19

Dad approached and stood by my side. Gretchen's gaze shifted to him. "You protect her, but I have to protect him." He stared her down with a level gaze. Gretchen looked away first, and retreated up the stairs.

When she was out of earshot, Dad turned to me. "You scared the life out of me. If you ever think you need to run, you run *with me*. Do you understand?" He stared into my eyes for another moment, and then pulled me into a rough bear hug.

"I tried to call," I said, tears springing to my eyes.

"That reminds me." He pulled something out of his pocket and handed it to me. "You lost something." My cell phone, adorned with a few new scratches it hadn't had this morning. I read the screen. 27 missed calls. Dad's eyes were a window into whatever personal hell he'd battled for the last few hours.

"I couldn't reach you," I said, the words pouring out in a rush. "And then Hale and Gretchen showed up at Royal's with the police, and I thought— I thought they had decided I was the enemy."

Dad flinched. "This is my fault." As I listened, Dad explained what had happened after I'd left the hospital. They'd called Hale, who ordered an emergency meeting. On their way to meet him, Gretchen spotted a Thrall. She left to tail the Thrall while Dad and Thane went on to explain my situation to Hale. As they had finished telling Hale about Parker, and what I had done to him, Gretchen called. She'd found a few Thrall milling around the warehouse district. It was suspicious enough that everyone joined her to scout the area. They spent the morning searching until they found the warehouse.

While everyone was combing through the warehouse district, Marx's unit had arrived, looking for us. They searched Hale's house first, and then ours. When Dina looked in my room, she saw the residual traces from the night I'd planted that horrible seed in Parker's mind. She flipped out. They had been the ones who'd tossed my room, deeply paranoid that I'd managed to infiltrate Hale's unit. They got a call from Gretchen about the warehouse, but didn't let on what they'd found in my room. They left to join the search in the warehouse district, and missed Lucas's and my return home. Around three, Gretchen and Hale had headed home. Hale wanted to speak with me, to hear my side of the story. He went to our house while Gretchen went looking for Lucas. She found us together.

"She was ready to kill me," I whispered.

Dad's eyes tightened with concern. "She panicked. I'm not saying it was warranted, but with her history... Remember what she's been through. When you ran away, Gretchen called Thane. He drove me back, refusing to answer any of my questions. I thought—I thought something had happened to you." Dad shook his head. "As soon as people calmed down enough to get a good look at Lucas, they realized he hadn't been damaged. Normal pupil reaction, alert, responsive." Dad looked at me, as if he were afraid to ask. "You kissed him?"

I squared my shoulders. "Technically, he kissed me." I didn't want to apologize. I shouldn't have to. If I were a normal girl, getting caught kissing Lucas would have been, at most, embarrassing. "But yeah. I kissed him back. I didn't hurt him. I won't let myself hurt him." *Again,* I added silently. Dad didn't look happy. "I didn't hurt him," I repeated, but it sounded like a question.

"No, you didn't. Once everyone had recovered from the panic, Hale realized we had to find you before you ran off. He called a connection in the police department and asked them to put a trace on your cell phone." Dad smiled wryly. "Which was only useful until Royal tipped you off."

"Royal." My voice caught in my throat. "Dad—I told him."

Dad grew still, a pensive frown drawing down the corners of his mouth. "I suppose you thought you had no other allies. But Braedyn, no one else can know. The more people who do know, the more danger you will be in."

Immediately, I thought of Amber. I still didn't know what she'd overheard at the hospital. But that was a problem for another day.

Dad searched my face again, as if looking for some proof that I was going to be okay. "What you must have been going through," he said. "If I'd known where you were, nothing could have kept me away."

"I know."

A soft pride glowed in his eyes. "But you found their hunting ground. As soon as we got your message, Marx sent two teams out to investigate. Upon reflection, I don't think he trusted our crew to do the job."

"I remember meeting one of his teams," I said, grim.

"Yeah." A muscle along his jaw jumped, betraying his anger. "If you hadn't called Lucas, the other team would never have found the rave. There were at least two Lilitu hunting the crowd. We didn't catch either of them, but we ended the party."

"Lucas?" I felt a sudden lift. He'd hung up on me, but he'd trusted me enough to pass along my warning. I replayed Sansenoy's words in my mind. Not a promise, not a deal, but hope. Hope that some day I might be able to be with Lucas, free from the fear of hurting him.

Dad didn't seem to notice the look I shot up the stairs toward Lucas's room. "Tell me about Ais. You said you saw her?"

I took a shuddering breath and told Dad everything, from when I decided to follow the Lilitu, all the way through when I saw Ais for the first time and felt the icy brush of her fingertip.

"She touched you?" He looked alert.

"Her hand was cold," I said. "Freezing cold."

"Perhaps it was a good thing you thought the Guard was hunting you," Dad murmured. "If Ais is able to read the conscious mind, it might be through that touch."

A sheen of cold sweat prickled across my back as I remembered our conversation.

Dad was impatient for the rest of the story. "Go on. What happened after Ais left?" I continued, and when I got to the part about the Thrall that Karayan had sent after me, Dad unwittingly dug his fingers into my arm. His face twisted into a mask of anguish that only lessened when I assured him I'd escaped unscathed. His eyes changed when I told him about the first time I'd felt my wings.

"Yes," he said, his eyes sharpening. "Show me again."

I concentrated, and as I thought about them, I could feel them, like a shiver in the air behind me. I willed them to enfold me, and they responded. I heard Dad exhale sharply. I lost my concentration and they retracted, fading to the back of my consciousness.

Dad looked unsettled, but he smiled. "That's amazing."

I turned and happened to catch Thane and Hale staring at me, eyes alert. I saw Hale's hand gripping the hilts of the daggers he carried at his side. When he realized I was looking at him, his eyes dropped to his hand. He jerked his fingers away from the daggers as though the hilts had burned him. He looked up and gave me a sheepish smile, as if to say, *Old habits die hard.* Thane gave me a solemn, considered look. He didn't smile, but his customary scowl hadn't returned. He looked... sad.

Dad squeezed my shoulder. "We should get home and get some sleep," he said. "Hale. Thane. Call us when you know anything."

Hale nodded, and he and Thane went back to work pulling bedrolls out of storage and setting them up on the living room floor. I knew Marx and his team would need to crash for a few hours when they returned. How many hours did we have left until dawn? I felt sure that however many there were, we could have used a lot more.

Dad and I went home. I noticed the Firebird, parked out front. Someone had driven it back. As we walked into the foyer of our house, Dad put a hand on my shoulder.

"How do you feel about the downstairs guest room?"

Right. My room currently looked like the target of some tornado that had a personal vendetta against teenage girls. The guest room was cramped and cold, but at least there was a mattress on the bed. I forced a smile. "It's better than the alternative."

Dad helped me change the sheets to a fresh set. While we worked, I caught sight of my reflection in the small mirror over the hutch. An angry red mark had darkened my cheek. I lifted my hand to touch the tender spot and winced. Dad noticed my reaction and straightened.

I didn't think I could take another round of "Let's Make Sure Braedyn's All Right." I cleared my throat quickly. "What was up with Thane?"

Dad bent to straighten the sheets, aware that I was changing the subject but willing to let me do so. "Why, did he seem stranger than normal?"

"He seemed sad." I stuffed the last pillow into its case and dropped it on the bed.

Dad stood straighter, considering. "Despite what he says, I think he did love Karayan like a daughter," he said finally. "When he arrived here, I was convinced he'd driven those feelings out of himself. But now, I'm not so sure. Being around us seems to be getting harder and harder for him."

"You think he still loves her?" And as I said this, I saw Thane's face again, and his deep sadness as he'd watched me reappear from under the cloaking effects of my wings. Thinking about what he'd lost, maybe? Or was he finally acknowledging to himself that if I had committed to helping humankind, Karayan could have made that choice at one time as well?

"I think some part of him knows he drove her away. For as long as he lives, he'll know he destroyed his relationship with the only daughter he'll ever have."

Dad's words were buzzing in my head long after he'd kissed me on the forehead and said good night. I found I couldn't sleep. It was cold downstairs. A thermostat controlled the heater; it was programmed to let the house cool down at night. Before bed, I'd rooted through the pile of clothes on my bedroom floor and found my flannel pajamas. Since it was already bitterly cold, I took my fluffy pink bathrobe out of the upstairs bathroom for good measure and wore it until I climbed into bed. Three hours later I was still cold, and I still didn't feel like sleeping.

I heard Marx's team returning. My mind was plagued with curiosity about what they'd learned, and whether we had a shot at stopping Ais in time. I glanced at the clock. It was 2:12 A.M.. We'd be up and preparing our attack in a little over two hours.

I got out of bed and pulled the robe back on, belting it over my pajamas. I walked over to the hutch and moved my jeans to one side. The daggers I'd left there earlier gleamed in the darkness. I pulled them out of their sheath. With my Lilitu sight, I could make out the play of colors across the metal. I twisted the hilt, and the two daggers sprang apart in my hands, each with one straight edge and one serpentine edge. I walked to one curtained window and pulled the drapes aside. In the moonlight, the colors of the blade, though muted, seemed strangely vibrant against the soft grays of rest of the world.

As I studied the blades, I couldn't help but think about what they meant. I was an official member of the Guard. And so was Lucas. I glanced up at his room, but his drapes were pulled tight shut. He was probably sleeping. Like I should be. I sighed, and was about to put the daggers back when I heard something in the front of the house.

I slipped the daggers into the oversized pockets of my bathrobe and eased into the hallway, thinking I might find Dad in the kitchen, unable to sleep as well. But the front door was standing open, letting in moonlight and the bitter night air. As I edged into the foyer, I heard someone moving in the living room. I turned, and almost screamed. Karayan was standing in the center of the dark room, watching me. Moonlight spilled in through one picture window and pooled at her feet. A glimmer of light caught in her eyes and made them sparkle.

"Shh. Wouldn't want to wake your daddy. I'd hate to turn this into some kind of scene."

"You." My fists curled into tight knots at my sides. "Get out of my house."

Karayan crossed the distance between us in a heartbeat. She caught my face in one hand and turned it into the moonlight. Her brows drew together. "The Guard did this to you?"

I jerked away from her. "You're one to talk. You sent three Thrall to attack me."

"You handled yourself just fine."

"Barely!"

"You didn't have to fight them," she whispered with a small smile. I pulled the robe tighter around me as another wave of revulsion coursed through me. She laughed softly. "Ais was so right about you. Until you own your power, it will own you. I want to help." She reached for me and I jerked back another full step. "You're angry with me." She sounded exasperated.

"Yes!" I spat.

"I'm trying to make it up to you. The Guard will never trust you, even when you've done nothing but try to help them. You must see that now. You're a Lilitu. You belong with us. Ais is ready to bring you in on the plan. I told you there'd be a part for you to play."

I froze, unsure what I should do. The Guard planned to attack the warehouse at dawn. But what if Marx's team hadn't figured out where Ais was planning to open the doorway? I needed time to think. "What plan? What are you talking about?"

"Well, for that, you'll have to come with me." She twined her fingers through my hair, and then let the tips of her fingers trace over my cheek. I forced myself to keep from recoiling. Karayan was looking at the red mark. "No one lays a hand on one of us and goes unpunished," she said softly. "Now." Her eyes locked onto mine, coming back into focus. "Are you with us or not?"

"I should change," I said. If I could go upstairs, I could find a way to alert Dad. Before I had even a preliminary idea of a plan sketched out, Karayan crushed the idea with a small smirk.

"No need to change. I'll have you back here before anyone knows you've gone." Karayan darted out the front door, her feet making almost no noise on the aging wooden floor.

I had to decide: follow her and learn their plan, or stay behind in helpless ignorance. I followed her, pulling the door shut behind me. I only remembered the daggers in the pockets of my robe when they knocked silently into my legs as I followed Karayan down the porch steps and across the lawn to her little black sports car.

Karayan pulled to a stop in the warehouse district on the outskirts of town about 20 minutes later. A late night train rattled past, close by. Huge industrial street lamps hummed overhead. The sound was oppressive, angry. I didn't see a single car anywhere. It was so unsettling that my wings half-expanded, ready to cloak me at the first sign of trouble.

"You won't need those, sweetie," Karayan said, smiling. "You're among friends. This way." Karayan led the way forward, and in minutes we were climbing through a flap of chain-link fence outside an abandoned warehouse. But as Karayan slipped one of the side doors open, I realized it wasn't abandoned after all. Dim light shone through the opening.

I followed Karayan inside. The air was strangely hot, close. Karayan led me through a maze of boxes and sheets of plastic. It finally opened up in the center of an interior room in the warehouse. A dozen young men lounged on salvaged couches and mattresses. I didn't have to examine them to know their pupils were wide and vacant. If they weren't Thrall yet, they would be soon. I was suddenly glad Marx and his team had joined us. These men might bring the number of Thrall closer to 40. Karayan hesitated at the edge of the room. I glanced at her and saw a guarded tension edging her eyes.

Two Lilitu were moving through the room. When they saw Karayan, she forced her face into a neutral mask. The Lilitu changed course, gliding toward us. I recognized them both.

"Welcome," the first Lilitu said. She was the other one I'd spoken to at the Raven, the redhead with the bob. She touched one slender hand to her chest, the action doubled by the Lilitu form within her. "Deliyan." She stared at me, waiting.

"Uh, Braedyn," I said.

"I am Naya." The second Lilitu said. She had darker skin and glossy brown hair. I had followed her and her mark to the rave earlier this evening. I glanced at the young men lounging in the room, looking for him, unsettled. Naya noticed my gaze and shrugged. "These belong to Ais. But tomorrow there will be other, fresher prey."

I forced a smile, remembering why I was here. They had to believe I was one of them, or they would never share the plan. "Yum." I said. I couldn't make my voice sound enthused. Karayan flashed a look full of unexpected understanding at me.

Deliyan and Naya wandered back among the men and Karayan plopped down on a vacant couch. I joined her, watching the other Lilitu nervously. "So when are we having this talk?"

"Soon." Karayan watched me study the Lilitu. They were so strange, enticing and horrifying at the same time. They moved like predators, disarming their prey with those lovely faces. I shuddered. Karayan lowered her voice. "I know how you feel. They take a little getting used to. They grew up on the other side, so they don't see the world the way we do."

"I'll take your word for it." I watched them pass through the men, ignoring them entirely, and come to a stop on either side of a doorway. The opening was obscured with strips of dirty plastic. "They're very... intense."

She shrugged. "They've got incredible control over their powers, and they're not bad teachers. They're just not so good at other things. You know, furnishing a place, cooking, basic conversation. But now we have each other, so, there's that." Karayan smiled lightly, and I realized—*she's lonely*.

Karayan straightened. I turned. Another young man stumbled out from behind the plastic strips. Deliyan caught him and whispered into his ear, sending him toward a mattress against the far wall. He stumbled onto it and passed out. I realized Deliyan and Naya were guarding the door. And not for the boy. At that moment, a slender hand parted the plastic strips.

Ais strode into the room. You would have thought the sun was breaking free from the clouds. The guys stirred, like plants straining toward her. Power radiated off of her, waves of swirling shadow curling around the ground at her feet. The guys fell back into their stupor when she passed them without a glance. They must all be her victims, I realized dimly. So many. She practically glowed with the energy she'd siphoned from them. Deliyan and Naya flanked her, an honor guard. Ais's eyes found my face.

"Karayan tells me you are ready to help us reclaim this Earth," she said.

I stood, a thrill of terror shooting down my spine. Ais. Ais who might be able to read my thoughts with a touch. I turned back to Karayan to buy myself time to calm down. "She helped me see what I was missing."

"Did she?" Ais's eyelashes lowered. I couldn't read her face. I shifted uncomfortably. "Did you tell the Guard you've seen me?"

"I—" I licked my lips nervously. If I lied and she guessed, it was all over anyway. I dropped my eyes. "I had to." I felt Karayan stiffen beside me. I glanced back up into Ais's face, milking the truth for all it was worth. "But they didn't believe me." *At first,* I added silently. "They thought I was making it up to save my own skin."

"And yet, they let you live." Ais's gaze hitched on the mark on my cheek. I touched my cheek self-consciously. My gut warned me to stay silent.

"I told you," Karayan breathed. "They think they can control her. If they've let her live, it's because they still think she might be useful."

"She will be," Ais said. She turned to me. "I have a simple request. Fulfill it, and I will see that you have great riches in the world to come. But if you attempt to betray me, you will pay with your life."

I swallowed and glanced at Karayan. She gave me an encouraging smile. I forced my eyes back to Ais's face. "What do you want me to do?"

Ais's eyes shifted, still gleaming with that odd twilight glow. "Go back to the Guard. Tell them I've disappeared. I've left to return to South America. Confirm the rumors that I plan to take down the Wall in South America, and see that your Guard is on the next flight to Caracas."

I stared at Ais, afraid to blink, trying to keep my face smooth. I nodded.

Karayan linked her hand in mine. "They trust her," she said to Ais. "They'll listen." She gave my hand a squeeze. "Right?"

"Yes," I said. Panic was raging in my mind. Ais would know very shortly that I had turned on her.

Ais misread my panic. "Do not fear retaliation. Within three days, my army will snuff out the Guard, down to the last raw recruit. There will be none left alive who believe in the existence of our kind."

Maybe, if she hadn't been staring directly into my eyes, Ais wouldn't have seen me flinch. I barely felt the movement—it was involuntary. My body reacted the moment my mind's eye filled with images of Dad and Lucas, fighting against overwhelming numbers of Lilitu, falling beneath the onslaught. Ais's eyes narrowed and I knew instantly that I'd given myself away.

Ais shot forward. She caught my throat with one hand and pressed the fingertips of her other hand to my forehead. I felt another icy wash along the skin of my face, but this cold dug deeper. It was as though I could feel freezing fingers raking through my mind. After one breathless moment she shrieked, and her hand tightened around my throat.

"Treacherous child!" Her eyes were dangerous slits. "Like her mother, she means to betray us."

Karayan looked at me, the color draining out of her cheeks. Her green eyes widened with alarm. Deliyan and Naya glanced at her; the threat was clear.

"I didn't know," Karayan said.

"They mean to attack at dawn," Ais hissed. She tilted her head back, eyes half-lidded. "17 soldiers. Go to them now. Kill them in their sleep." Deliyan and Naya bobbed their heads, but I caught a glimpse of fear creeping into those strange, mask-like faces. Ais grabbed Karayan with her free hand. "Do not come back until all are dead."

Karayan looked pale, but she nodded and ran with the others. I struggled to breathe. Ais wrapped her other hand around my throat, tightening her grip and cutting off my air entirely.

"We would have made a place for you," she whispered. "Now you will go down to dust. Just like a human."

Red and gold stars exploded behind my eyelids. I realized dimly that I was losing consciousness.

With a surge of desperate hope, I remembered the daggers.

I reached into the oversized pockets of my bathrobe. My hands closed around the hilts and I slashed upwards. The first blade carved a long line across Ais's torso, from her belly up to one shoulder. Her scream was a guttural snarl of rage and pain. She jerked back, releasing me. Instead of retreating, I drove the second dagger toward her throat, not letting myself think beyond the impact of blade into her gray-white skin.

She was too fast. She caught my wrist and twisted; pain forced my hand open. The dagger dropped with a tinny clank on the cement. I swung the other dagger. Ais dodged back.

"Stay back," I said. My voice was hoarse, but I held onto my remaining dagger tightly. I hoped she hadn't gleaned from my thoughts that I had no idea how to use these weapons.

Her hands curled around her wound and she stepped back. I saw the Lilitu beneath her human features. Her pitch mouth, full of darkly gleaming teeth, opened. "These human feelings will be the end of you." It sounded like a promise. And then the air around her seemed to unfold into 1,000 points of glimmering air and she was gone. I stared at the place she had been standing only moments ago. There was no cloaked Lilitu, no residue of her presence at all.

I heard Hale's voice, as clearly as the night he had told me face-to-face. *There have been rumors for centuries that some of the most powerful Lilitu can use the dream world to make a hole from one physical place to another, in effect folding space... But we have no proof this is possible.*

I had just seen the proof with my own eyes. I knew exactly where she was going.

And my family was completely unprepared for her arrival.

20

Their faces filled my mind, one after the other. Memories of our time together, practice with Hale and Gretchen, sweet, stolen moments with Lucas, and Dad—a lifetime of memories with Dad. The images pressed in on me, threatening to block out reason. I felt a hysterical panic swelling inside, but I clamped it down. My eyes landed on the dagger at my feet. I picked it up. I was a member of the Guard. I was not helpless.

All of this happened in a fraction of a second.

I saw Karayan's couture bag, tossed aside on the couch. She had left it behind as she went to slaughter my family. I upended it and found what I was looking for. A cell phone. I dialed Dad's cell by reflex, my hands shaking on the keys. When it went straight to voicemail I hung up. I was halfway through punching in the next number before I realized it was Lucas's.

"What do you want?" I heard Gretchen's voice and felt a surge of hope.

"They're coming for you now! Get everyone up!"

I heard movement on the other end, then a sharp intake of breath. "I see them. Lucas! Your daggers!"

"My dad," I said. But Gretchen must have dropped her phone; no one responded. Dad was alone in our house. I hung up and dialed our home phone.

It rang only once before he picked up. "Hale?"

"No, Dad, it's me." As soon as I heard his voice, tears blurred my vision.

"Braedyn? Where are you? Are you all right?"

I had to force the words through a choking sob. "Get out of the house. The Lilitu are coming for you right now!"

"What?!"

I heard a crash on the other end of the line. "Dad? Dad?!" And then I realized that alone, without a spotter, he would be as helpless as a gnat. He was blind without me.

The world rocked, and I felt the walls shift around me. I recognized this feeling. I was fainting, pulling the ripcord of reality to escape—another Lilitu instinct, kicking in when I least wanted it. I forced Dad's face into my mind, pictured him alone in his room, unarmed and unable to face what was coming for him. A surge of emotion rose in me, strong enough to clear my vision, even if only briefly. I felt my will kicking into gear, like an emergency brake engaging on a car that's falling off a cliff. Helpless, useless, and yet... something changed.

I held Dad's face in my head; it was the only thing keeping me from passing out. But the walls around me were still shifting, bending in a weird kaleidoscope. I briefly wondered if I was going insane. When the walls of Dad's room seemed to unfold in front of me, I feared I'd lost the battle to sleep after all. But as I staggered forward, my feet catching in the plush carpet, the world resolved. This place felt too solid, too real to be a dream. I was—incredibly—standing in my father's room. And I was alone.

A wave of weakness hit me and I stumbled, catching myself on the edge of the bed and dropping my daggers onto the bedspread. My arms and legs felt like the stuffed and useless limbs of a doll, barely responding to my will. My vision crossed, blurred, and finally cleared. As a child, I'd gotten a flu so serious that Dad had had to take me to the emergency room. They'd hooked me up to intravenous fluids for a day while I battled a fever, delirious and weak. That's what this felt like, only I wasn't delirious. Just thoroughly and completely exhausted.

I heard something from the hallway. I forced myself back to my feet and stumbled through Dad's open door. What I saw stole my breath. Dad stood at the top of the stairs. His daggers had fallen to the floor at his feet. Ais was walking up the staircase, so powerful that she had only to smile to enthrall him.

Ais's eyes shifted from Dad to me, and her smile faltered. Suddenly, her threat became clear to me. These human feelings would be the end of me. She wanted to hurt me. She'd read my thoughts. Nothing she could do would hurt me more than killing my dad.

"Dad!" Dad didn't even flinch. He was completely absorbed by the vision of Ais before him. I ran to him, grabbed his arm, and pulled with all my might. Dad stumbled backwards, and his eyes shifted away from Ais. In an instant, he came back to himself. He glanced at me, turned back, and saw Ais clearly for the first time. He gave a little yell, and pushed me back toward his room. We retreated inside, slamming the door behind us. It wouldn't do much to stop her, but it might buy us a few precious seconds. Dad had lost his daggers. They were sitting out there, useless, at the top of the stairs. I looked around and my eyes landed on Semangelof's sword. "The sword!"

Dad's head snapped up. He ran for the sword and returned to my side. But his eyes snagged on the daggers I had dropped onto the bed. "Are those your daggers?"

I nodded and he picked them up wordlessly. They would do us both more good in his hands than mine. He thrust the sword at me and I took it. But when I started to set it down he caught my arm with his free hand.

"That sword is more powerful than all our daggers combined."

I stared at the sword, and then tried to thrust it back into Dad's hands. "Then take it!"

"No. You keep it."

"Hale said—" I started, but he interrupted me.

"Sansenoy didn't give it to me. He gave it to you. That has to mean something." Before I could argue, Dad put his hand on the doorknob. "Stay by my side. I might need you to snap me out of it again."

And then we were rushing through the door. Ais was waiting for us. Dad lunged, slicing the daggers toward her. She had to jump back to avoid the blades. Her eyes glittered and she smiled. A shadowy mist spooled in the air around her. Dad's movements became less focused.

"Dad!" I screamed. His grip tightened on the daggers as he fought off her influence.

Ais's eyes cut to me, lips peeling back over her teeth in fury. Her wings snapped tightly around her, cloaking her from Dad's sight. She made a move forward, her eyes fastened on me.

"Straight ahead!" I shouted.

Dad moved, his daggers flashing in his hands. It didn't seem to matter that he couldn't see her. His moves were confident and powerful. Ais tried to slip past him but as he flowed through the form one of the blades sliced into her forearm. Ais hissed and jerked back, becoming visible again. The close space of the hall didn't give her much room to maneuver. Dad sensed an advantage and pressed his attack. Ais fell back, eyes calculating. There was no way to pass him in the hallway, and he was gaining ground.

The front door banged open and I heard something that made my blood run cold.

"Murphy? Murphy! Are you okay?" Lucas. He was in the house.

Ais read the horror in my face and turned. Lucas ran into the foyer below, daggers in his fists.

Ais glanced back at me, eyes burning with malice. All pretense of humanity fell away from her. She stood at the top of the stairs, completely revealed in her Lilitu form. Giant bat-like wings snapped into physical existence with a leathery crack. I could just see past her as Lucas looked up at the sound. He gave a strangled yell and stumbled back toward the front door. Ais jumped off the top of the stairs, her wings catching the air like sails. She sped down toward him, a hawk diving for a mouse.

Lucas brought his daggers up reflexively, but Ais knocked them aside. She grabbed Lucas with one clawed hand. He screamed as pitch claws pierced the flesh of his right shoulder. With inhuman power, she lifted him off his feet and leapt through the front door. Lucas's eyes caught mine for a fraction of a second, wide with panic and pain. I scrambled forward, driving my sluggish body with every ounce of strength I had left, but just like that, they were gone. The snapping beat of Ais's thick wings faded into the night too quickly to be believed.

I stumbled down the stairs. By the time I made it outside, Ais and Lucas had vanished into the sky and only the stars remained.

I stared up into the sky, numb. Dad joined me, and we heard a commotion next door—the battle was spilling out of the Guard's house and onto their front lawn. Their overgrown hedges screened most of the lawn from the glow of the streetlights and cast deep swaths of shadow over the battle. Despite the darkness, I could see the fight clearly.

Marx and his soldiers fought seamlessly with Hale's crew. They managed to hem the demons into the center of a circle of soldiers. Dina and Gretchen shouted directions, and the soldiers pressed closer to the enraged Lilitu, seeking to divide them. Deliyan and Naya fought with insane power. I saw one of the newcomers fall as Deliyan struck out. Bright blood coursed over his back as he rolled aside, arching in pain. Naya struck another soldier, raking her claws across his face. He dropped away, momentarily blinded.

I had to pull my eyes away from the fight. I forced myself forward, stumbling, exhausted, to the sidewalk. I scanned the sky, but there was not even a glimmer of Ais or Lucas against the starry blackness. Dad caught me as I fell. The sword clattered out of my hands.

"Lucas," I managed. "She has Lucas."

"I know." Dad's voice sounded tight, thin.

"We have to find them. He's alive." I stared at the sky, eyes wide. I was afraid to blink in case I missed some flicker of shadow that might save Lucas's life. My head seemed filled with a weird static; I couldn't process what Dad was saying. He shook me, hard. I tore my eyes off the sky and stared at him, a numb surprise bubbling up through the shock.

"Focus. We need you."

"But... Lucas."

Dad squared my shoulders to him. "We can't help him if we're dead! You're in no shape to fight, but you can see them. Can you help Gretchen and Dina?"

I turned back to the battle next door. The Guard still ringed the Lilitu in the center of the front lawn. Deliyan and Naya fought back to back. Beneath the cloaking effect of their wings they glistened with the pearly blood of their wounds, but they had given as much damage as they had taken, and the human frame was by far the more delicate. Four soldiers were down in the lawn, which left a dozen others facing the Lilitu. But of those, two favored wounds that were definitely slowing them. Dina was one of the wounded. She and Gretchen had taken opposite sides of the circle to act as spotters, but the Lilitu weren't giving the Guard an opening to attack.

Dad looked at the fight. I could almost feel the pull it had on him. "Braedyn, they need me. Are you strong enough to help?"

"Yes."

He released me and I swayed with exhaustion. Dad reached out to steady me once more. "Are you *here?*" he asked, searching my eyes.

"I'm okay. I can do this."

Dad nodded once, picked up the sword, and then ran to the fight. I followed, slower. It felt like I was forcing my limbs through sludge. Every part of me wanted to lie down and sleep. But we had to save Lucas. And in order to do that, we had to finish this fight.

As I reached the edge of the lawn, Dad was diving through the circle of soldiers, swinging the sword. It caught Naya across the shoulder as she twisted aside, trying to avoid it. As soon as the sword made contact, the shimmering cloak of Naya's wings vanished and she stood revealed in her human form among the soldiers.

Marx sprang forward, daggers in his fists. "We've got this one," he shouted at Dad. The soldiers closed in on Naya, who shrieked in fury. They drove her closer to the hedges on the side of the lawn, leaving the others room to fight the still-cloaked Deliyan.

Dad turned his back on them, trusting Marx to handle Naya. His eyes landed on Dina.

Dina stabbed a finger at Deliyan, who was edging closer to the house. "There!"

Dad moved and Deliyan staggered back, her eyes fixed on the sword in his hand. Dina eagerly stepped forward with the other soldiers as they closed in on the cloaked Deliyan. Deliyan's lips peeled back in a snarl of rage. She lunged for the weakest link of the circle—which was Dina. Deliyan raked a clawed hand down the front of Dina's torso. Dina screamed. Dad, preparing to lunge with the sword, recoiled in horror. To his eyes, it must have looked like the ragged claw marks just appeared across Dina's chest. The closest soldiers reacted instantly, swinging their daggers through the air before Dina and forcing Deliyan back into the circle.

Dina clamped a hand over her wounds and fell back. Her eyes squeezed shut in pain. "We need a spotter!" Dina screamed. "We're blind over here!"

Deliyan turned on Dad, who swung the sword wide, aiming for the place she had been standing moments ago. She slipped around behind him and moved to strike.

"Behind you," I shrieked. Dad heard me and turned. But Deliyan was faster, and still cloaked. She struck Dad with one clawed foot in the chest, kicking him across the lawn. Dad hit the ground and rolled, coming to a stop three feet from the dilapidated mailbox.

Gretchen leaped forward, taking charge. She cried out directions to the soldiers ringing Deliyan as I turned away.

"Dad!" I ran across the lawn, dropping to my knees by Dad's side. I eased him over, terrified at what I might find. He coughed weakly, and then pushed himself up on one elbow.

"I'm okay," he said. "Help the others."

I looked up. One group of soldiers clustered by the hedges at the side of the front lawn. The other was closer to the front porch. Both Lilitu were ringed by five or six soldiers. Naya, near the hedges, crouched in the center of a ring of soldiers that include Marx, Matt, and Thane. She looked ready to snap. Matt dove toward her. Naya turned to face him. She no longer had the claws or wings of her Lilitu form, but she looked fierce and capable nonetheless. As soon as she moved, Marx sprang, driving both of his daggers into her back. I turned away, unable to watch. Naya's scream cut through the night like a siren.

"The sword," Dad coughed, pointing. I saw it gleaming where he had dropped it, steps away. I forced my body to run, willing movement from limbs heavy and sluggish with fatigue. I grabbed the pommel. Hale saw the movement and threw out his hand. I tossed the sword to him. It flipped end over end and Hale plucked it out of the air like a juggler, his hand closing on the pommel with confidence. He turned, gripping the sword with both hands like a baseball bat.

Gretchen stood behind the line of soldiers, calling directions out of reach of Deliyan's claws. Deliyan glared at her, furious. "You want me?" Gretchen taunted.

Deliyan didn't see Hale joining the circle surrounding her. I felt my breath catch as he walked up behind Deliyan. She must have sensed something behind her. She started to turn, claws ready for an attack, just as Hale raised the sword.

"Now!" Gretchen and I screamed the word together. Hale swung out. Deliyan didn't see the blow coming. It struck her head clean off. Her body, instantly uncloaked, collapsed into the grass. The battle was finally over.

I fell to my knees, nausea swelling in my throat. I gripped the grass and drew in long, deep breaths. Someone knelt beside me. It was Dad. I put a hand lightly on his chest, where I'd seen the Lilitu strike him. He winced and caught my palm.

"Just tender," he said, smiling reassuringly. "I'll live."

In moments, Hale and Marx were organizing the soldiers. They dragged the Lilitu back behind the house. Three of the soldiers who'd been downed in the fight were not moving. I saw Gretchen bending over one. She looked up and met Matt's eyes, then shook her head.

Dad stood slowly. "Give me a moment, honey." He walked toward the house.

I turned away, drained. The sudden silence was shocking after the noise of the fight. It struck me then that I hadn't seen Karayan in the fight. I glanced around, wondering if she was still lurking somewhere close by. I noticed a light click on in a neighbor's window. As I watched the window, someone moved the drapes aside to peer out. Half of the soldiers had already disappeared behind the house with the Lilitu's bodies. Several more were kneeling beside the wounded, tucked against bushes or under the shelter of the porch. I doubted the neighbor would be able to see much of anything from his window. In a few moments, I saw the drapes swing shut and the light click off. Like Lucas said, *people see what they want to see.*

Lucas. I felt a roiling anguish spread to fill that part of my mind that had been blissfully numb only moments ago. Lucas was gone.

At that moment, Gretchen made a sound, half-growl, half-moan. I turned. Dad was standing next to her on the porch, one hand resting on her shoulder, his face drawn with anguish. Gretchen doubled over, the news crashing into her like a physical blow. She stood there for a long time, bent over, body wracked with unbearable grief. When she looked up, her eyes landed on me. The intensity of her gaze shot lightening strikes of pain through my heart. She walked toward me, clawing past the hands that tried to stop her.

"You," she said. "You can find him. You can use the dream and find him." She was crying, the words bubbling out of her, unfiltered, unfocused. "You're the only one who can do it in time." She grabbed the front of my robe and hauled me to my feet.

I realized I was shaking my head.

"Damn it, Braedyn, you can do this! Do it! Save him!" Dad and Hale reached us and pulled Gretchen off of me. As soon as she let go, I stumbled back, falling into the frozen grass like a rag doll. Gretchen was wild, fighting them like an animal. "She can do it, I know she can!

She can find him! She can save him!"

A desperate desire raged inside of me. I took hold of Gretchen's wild hope and made it my own. I closed my eyes, willing myself into the dream. I was ready for instinct to take hold of me, to sweep me away from the nightmare of my reality. I wouldn't fight it this time; I would embrace it. I summoned Lucas's face in my mind's eye. Denial thrashed inside of me like a wild thing. I couldn't accept his loss. I wouldn't. Grief overwhelmed me—worse than the night of Derek's death. But nothing happened.

I opened my eyes and saw the assembled Guard staring at me, waiting with bated breath.

"I can't." The truth had slowly dawned on me. The one time I truly needed my full Lilitu powers, they had abandoned me. I had no energy left to dream.

21

"I can't." The words came through dimly, as though someone else had spoken them. Silence crushed over the assembled Guard. Only Gretchen fought it.

"You can," Gretchen said, advancing on me. "You can!"

I tried to stand, but my knees buckled and I fell.

"Braedyn." Dad was by my side in an instant, helping me to my feet. "Easy."

Hale joined us. "What's wrong with her?"

"She stepped through the dream," Dad said. The watching Guard reacted. Half a dozen hushed conversations broke out, adding another layer to the static in my head. I felt hollow—a body taking up space with eyes to see, and ears to hear, but nothing substantial at my core. "She's burned through all the energy she had. And more, by the look of it. She needs to sleep."

"No." Gretchen grabbed for me, pulled me close. "Find Lucas, and then you can rest."

Dad untangled Gretchen's fingers from my robe. "She's got nothing left, Gretchen. Look at her." Gretchen turned her eyes on me. They looked haunted, empty.

Thane put a hand on Gretchen's shoulder. "If Ais has him, it's already too late."

In one moment, we stood as statues in the frozen night. In the next, Gretchen seemed to lose her mind. It took four of them to wrestle her away from me. Her words gave way to horrible, wracking sobs. I watched it all, numb. Some part of me was screaming, too. But it was buried, deep, wrapped in thick blankets of exhaustion.

"Gretchen." Matt tried to reach Gretchen, tried to wrap his arms around her.

She fought him off, inconsolable. "Don't touch me! Why don't you do something?! Why doesn't *anyone do something?!*"

Matt met my eyes. It was as if he were asking permission. I took a step toward him.

Dad reached out to steady me, oblivious of the look that had passed Matt and me, unaware of the bargain we were already forming. "Braedyn?"

Matt crossed the distance between us and took my hands. "You can do this?" he asked. His voice was steady, but his nostrils flared, betraying a shaky fear.

"I don't know," I said. It was the honest truth.

Matt looked back at Gretchen, lost in her wild grief. His shoulders set as he came to a decision. "Try." He caught me in his arms and kissed me. I heard several of the soldiers around us exclaim, but when someone moved toward us, Dad and Hale blocked them. If they spoke, I heard nothing. I was already lost in sensation.

Kissing Matt was entirely different from kissing Lucas. My heart didn't skip a beat. No warmth spread inside my stomach, no shivers travelled down my spine. Instead, all I felt was the stirring of the Lilitu storm. I let it rage, and it connected with that part of Matt that no eye could see. His spirit, his soul, whatever it was, I felt the storm seize on it and pull. This had been the moment I'd broken contact with Lucas when we'd shared our kiss in the theater. But I needed more from Matt. I held onto him, letting the storm ravage through him. I didn't know how much was too much, how much would leave him vulnerable; leave him one strike away from becoming a Thrall. I didn't want to permanently damage him. But for Lucas, I risked it. We dropped to our knees in the grass together. I didn't release Matt until he pitched back onto the ground. He blinked, stunned. His eyes struggled to focus. His pupils were wide and dilated.

The Guard watched us, hands on their weapons. Dina was clinging to another soldier, her mouth frozen in open-mouthed horror. Gretchen's face was a mask of anguish. I met her eyes and saw the conflict that raged within her. She managed a faint nod.

I turned away from them all, feeling a vibrant new energy coursing through my body. I sat on the grass and closed my eyes. I willed myself into the dream, and was there.

I found myself standing in my rose garden. The petals I'd scattered the night I attacked Parker still carpeted the ground, as fresh as if they'd just been plucked, only now the red stain stretched almost halfway across each petal. Dread clenched at my heart, but I pushed it to the back of my mind. I was here to find Lucas. Everything else could wait.

I touched the ground and felt the world beyond the illusion of this dream. I called up a pool of stars, holding Lucas in my mind to the exclusion of all else. A million stars scattered, and one tiny seed of light flickered and rose out of the pool. But it looked different. It was dimmer than it had been before, sputtering with a fitful light. I closed my hand around it, terrified. In that moment, I was certain Lucas was dying.

The dream shifted. I found myself slumped in a chair in a long, cramped room. My shoulder throbbed, and my eyes were fastened on Ais as she paced in tight circles of agitation. I glanced at the door beyond her and saw the logo for the Raven club. A desk beside the door was piled with barstools, and boxes of liquor were stacked on the ground to its right.

Relief flooded through me as I realized what was happening. Lucas was awake. And so his dreaming mind was half-engaged with reality. Unwittingly, he had told me where he was.

Lucas, I thought to him, willing my thoughts to reach his conscious mind. *I don't know if you can hear me, but if you can, I am so sorry I deceived you. I should have told you the truth, but I was afraid of losing you. I'm still afraid of losing you. You told me once in a dream that you loved me. Now I'm telling you. I love you, Lucas. We're coming for you. We're coming. Just hold on a little while longer.*

If he sensed me at all, he gave no indication.

I opened my eyes.

I stood on the lawn in front of Hale's house.

Gretchen's face crumpled in devastation. "It didn't work," she whispered.

"Yes, it did." I met her eyes, steady and confident. "I know where Lucas is."

We were armed and heading to the Raven inside of 10 minutes. I rode with Dad, Gretchen, and half of Marx's team, crammed in the back of their van. Several soldiers were tending wounds they had sustained in the fight. Most were superficial; a few were more serious. But every fighter capable of walking had joined us. All in all, we were only down four soldiers. Two seriously wounded men were laid up in Hale's living room. Matt, still recovering from our kiss, was resting on Gretchen's bed. The last man, who had not survived his injuries, had been wrapped in a sheet, and placed gently on the back porch. The soldier crowded next to me glanced at his watch. I read the face. It was 4:37 a.m.

Gretchen was still watching me. A tight urgency had replaced the bitter hatred I'd always found in her gaze before. She hadn't said anything to me after I'd shared the news of Lucas's location. Dad and I had run home to change into something more suited to fighting. He'd told me Matt was weak but I hadn't taken enough to harm him permanently. When we'd loaded into the vehicles, Gretchen had followed me into the van. The ride had been a silent one, each of us sitting alone with our thoughts of the fight behind us, and the battle to come. Abruptly, the van shuddered to a stop.

Someone slid open the side door. Marx had stopped at the edge of the parking lot, though the entire lot was empty. Hale's truck pulled up next to us, containing the rest of the team. Soldiers unloaded, keeping their eyes on the club.

Dad and I climbed out of the van. The night was bitterly cold. My breath made small puffs of steam in the amber glow of the street lamps. The front door of the Raven club was open, and we could see a pale light shining from within. The light shifted as something inside moved.

"Dad." I grabbed onto his arm.

He nodded grimly. "I saw it."

Marx and Hale moved through their teams, ensuring everyone was ready. The night was strangely silent. A lonely traffic light turned from green to yellow to red, but no cars passed through the intersection. When Marx and Hale were satisfied, the entire team hurried across the dark parking lot toward the club. As we approached, Marx gestured and the team slowed.

Hale approached the club's front entrance, edging the door open farther with the tip of one dagger. He glanced inside and then pressed back against the building, grim. He beckoned the team forward. We grouped close to Hale facing the front entrance.

"We're in trouble," Hale said. "The place is full. If I had to guess? I'd say there's close to 100 Thrall in there."

"But—" I glanced around, stunned. "Lucas is upstairs." I felt Dad's hand tighten on my shoulder. All I'd let myself think about was finding Lucas. Somewhere inside, I'd known we'd have to face Ais in order to save him, but I'd left that thought for later, trusting that the Guard could handle it. We were so close.

"You can talk to them." Gretchen appeared at my elbow, eyes fixed on my face. "Find us a way past. We have to get upstairs."

"Talk to them?"

"Use *the call*," she said. But her voice wasn't tinged with her customary irritation.

Hale nodded at me. "We'll follow your lead."

"Me?" I glanced at Dad, panic driving out all other feeling. I wasn't supposed to be leading this charge. I was surrounded by soldiers who had decades of experience fighting Lilitu and Thrall. Surely one of them could handle this. I expected Dad to fight Hale, but he just stared at the younger man. Dad's jaw was tight with tension, but when he turned to me, he nodded. His eyes were drawn with concern, but beneath that, I saw pride and hope.

"You can do this." Dad placed something into my hands. Semangelof's sword. I heard an unsettled murmur moving through Marx's men, but no one voiced an objection.

Gretchen nodded encouragement, and then turned to the others. "Give her some room."

I gripped Semangelof's sword tightly. Someone pulled the Raven's door open. I took a hesitant step forward, shooting one last look at Dad.

"We'll be right behind you," Dad said.

I entered the club. As I passed through the front lobby and into the club proper, a sea of faces turned toward me. Their eyes were dull, empty. It seemed like they were waiting. For us? I shivered, and then felt the Guard filling the lobby behind me. I took a deep breath. As I envisioned summoning *the call*, I felt the energy I'd gleaned from Matt surging within me.

"*Stand aside,*" I said, raising the sword. *The call* rang out toward the Thrall. They stepped aside to reveal a path to the back hallway. I stared in disbelief.

"Let's go," Gretchen said, nudging me. I walked forward. Gretchen and Dina flanked me. The other soldiers followed on our heels through the mass of Thrall. One hundred pairs of eyes followed us deeper into the club. But why would they stop us? With each step, we were farther from the outside world. With each step, our chances of escaping diminished.

As I reached the back hallway, I could see a set of stairs at the end of the hallway. "That way." I could almost feel Lucas above us. The sensation drove me into the hallway. I was half way to the stairs before I realized only Gretchen and Dina were following me. The rest of the Guard ringed the opening to the hallway, daggers at the ready, facing the Thrall.

"They're not coming?" I asked. My voice squeaked in the silence.

"They can't face Ais," Gretchen murmured into my ear. "You saw what she did to Murphy." I glanced at her sharply. Dad must have told her everything when he'd pulled her aside to give her the news about Lucas. "She has too much power over the men. They'll keep the Thrall downstairs."

"So it's just us." I felt the last of my confidence slip.

"It's nearly dawn," Dina said shortly. "This is our best chance." Dina didn't look so good. The scratches down her chest were deep; she had cleaned and dressed them in the van, but I'd seen the way her skin puffed out, inflamed, around the marks. Every step seemed to hurt her.

I glanced at Dad. He stood shoulder-to-shoulder with the Guard, facing the Thrall.

"Forget them," Gretchen whispered. "It's just us now. Everything else is a distraction."

I nodded, and Gretchen led the way to the stairs. The narrow passageway was dark. A thin wash of light reached us from upstairs. Someone was sitting near the bottom of the stairs. I recognized her by her honey-blond hair. Karayan.

"There!" Gretchen lunged for Karayan, but I grabbed her shoulder, holding her back.

"Wait!" Something was wrong. Karayan hadn't looked up at Gretchen's shout. I edged past Gretchen to face Karayan.

She lifted her face. It was red from crying. "Is Thane dead?"

"Not yet."

Surprise brought a new light to Karayan's eyes. And there was something else, a small knot of hope. I kept a tight hold on my sword; I wasn't ready to trust this show of emotion. Not after everything she'd done. Karayan sensed my hostility.

"Ais is upstairs, in the club's main office. She has Lucas with her."

"I know."

Karayan looked bone tired. "She picked the Raven for you. Did you know that? This place saw your coming-of-age party. Now it will see your death. You shouldn't have come."

As if on cue, I heard a shout of warning, then the sounds of fighting. I jerked around to stare at Gretchen, terrified. The battle had begun. Gretchen looked at me, urgent.

"We have to move. I don't know how long they'll be able to hold them off." Gretchen pushed past us, heading up the stairs. Dina followed, shooting Karayan an icy glare in passing.

I tried to follow but Karayan caught my arm, hissing over the sounds of the fight. "Ais could have run. She could have moved the location of her ceremony. She was willing to sacrifice the rest of us. But you— If she can't have you on her side, she wants you dead."

"Why are you here, Karayan?" I jerked away from her and felt a welcome anger rushing in. It filled the space that had been hollowed out by fear. Anger was better. Anger was fuel.

"I came to tell you not to go up there," she said. "But you're not going to listen to me, are you?"

I pushed past her, following Gretchen and Dina to the top of the stairs. When I glanced back, Karayan was already gone.

"Focus," Gretchen said, calling my attention to the task at hand. I described what I'd seen from Lucas's perspective in the dream. Gretchen and Dina hashed out a quick plan, settling on their attack in a few seconds.

"What about me?"

"You have the sword," Dina said. "What do you think?"

"We'll keep Ais distracted." Gretchen said, shooting Dina a glance. "Try to give you a clean shot at her. Just *make sure you wound her.*"

"But—" The obvious flaw in our plan leaped large in my mind. "She can travel through the dream world. What's to stop her from just escaping if I hurt her?"

Dina looked at Gretchen. "Did you tell her nothing?" Before Gretchen could respond, Dina jerked her head at the sword in my hand. "That's not some random piece of steel you're holding. That sword was forged to fight in this world and the dream. If you even clip her with that sword, you'll cut her off from her powers." Dina snapped her fingers. "They'll be useless until she heals from the wound."

"By the way," Gretchen said with a grim smile. "Don't nick yourself." Gretchen started down the narrow passage, daggers in hand. Dina followed. Gretchen listened at two doors before stopping at a third. She stepped back and pointed. Dina nodded, and then they were bursting into the room.

I heard Dina's attack, crouched in the hallway. Ais's low laugh sent chills down my back. There was a clatter, and a terrible snap. I slipped down the hallway, moving quietly.

By the time I'd reached the open door, Dina was dead—slumped into a little heap by the liquor boxes I'd seen from Lucas's mind. Ais stood over her, in her Lilitu form. By some small miracle, Ais was facing the back of the room; she didn't see me. She was watching Gretchen and Lucas. I bit down hard on the inside of my lip to keep from making a sound. The office was a long, cramped room, extending from the door to a wall of curtains on the far side.

Lucas was slumped in a club chair near the curtained wall. His hair was damp with sweat, his skin pale. Blood had seeped from his shoulder and drenched his shirt, drying into a red-black slick that glistened darkly. His breath came in shallow gasps, but his eyes cut around the room with sharp intelligence. Ais hadn't preyed on him. Yet.

Gretchen was standing in front of Lucas, daggers raised, facing Ais. Lucas's eyes met mine for a fraction of a second—then he shifted them to Ais. Trying not to give me away.

Gretchen's voice trembled. I suspected it was only partly an act. "Let me take him and go. You've already won. We won't interfere."

"No," Ais said. "I need him to make a point."

As I stared at Ais's back, I realized I was burning through this opportunity. I lifted the sword and a surge of adrenaline propelled me forward. But this building was old. As I crossed the threshold, swinging for Ais's back, the floor groaned.

Ais heard me and whipped around. Instead of striking Ais's back, my blade sliced clean through one leathery wing. I had committed everything to the swing, and when it didn't connect as I'd anticipated, it threw me off balance. I stumbled, and the sword clattered to the ground and skidded under the table between Dina's slumped body and the door.

Ais spun to face me, hissing in pain. The sword had sliced a gaping hole through the thick membrane of Ais's wing. For one moment I stared at the ruined wing as the edges of the wound seeped out a pearly ichor. Then Ais's Lilitu aspect vanished, leaving her looking almost vulnerable in her human form. Ais gaped at me, then staggered back, her eyes losing focus. Trying to escape into the dream world. Nothing happened.

Her eyes refocused on my face. Her lips were tight with fury, but she forced a glacial calm into her words. "Clever. You found an angel's sword. You may think you've triumphed here, but I've learned a thing or two about patience. I'll have next winter solstice. You won't."

"Dad!" I screamed out the door, hoping he could hear over the sounds of his fight. "Dad, help us!" I was already moving, racing for the open door. But Ais was faster. She grabbed me at the threshold and threw me deep into the room. I slid along the floor and stopped about two-thirds of the way to Lucas and Gretchen. I saw Lucas's face as the desperate hope in his eyes died a little. His eyes shifted to Ais, over my shoulder. I turned, scared.

Ais closed and locked the office door.

"Such a waste of power." She regarded me coolly, walking across the room toward me. "You have ancient blood in you. You could have been one of our Great Sisters."

Someone pounded on the door from the hallway. "Braedyn? Gretchen?! What's happening?" It was Hale. The door shuddered with an impact. He was trying to break in.

"Hale!" Gretchen's voice was full of urgency. "Get the others! We need you!"

"Hang on! We're coming!" I heard Hale's steps retreating.

I glanced at Gretchen. Her hands were tight fists on her daggers, and her face was pale. When she saw my confusion, she took a step toward me. "Her powers are broken! She can't use the men against us now!" I hadn't thought about what I was doing when I'd called for help. Now my heart swelled with hope.

But Gretchen's words had an entirely different effect on Ais. Ais grabbed a chair and lodged it against the doorknob, then scanned the room for something stronger to barricade the door. Her eyes settled on a bank of heavy metal filing cabinets against one wall.

While Ais was distracted, Gretchen hauled me to my feet and slipped me one of her daggers. I stared at her, numb.

"Just like basement practice," Gretchen said. She held a dagger in one hand, and balled her other hand into a fist. I felt a fierce grin of understanding spread across my face. If nothing else, all those weeks of tense sparring practice had taught us how to anticipate one another, how to move together. We were a perfectly matched fighting team. We turned to face Ais. She was pulling one of the filing cabinets away from the wall.

Gretchen and I launched ourselves across the room toward Ais. Ais turned, surprised. Her eyes narrowed when she saw us. But it worked; she forgot about the door in her effort to defend herself. Rather than get pinned against the wall, Ais charged forward to meet us in the middle of the room.

Ais was fast and strong, even outside of her Lilitu form. But Gretchen and I together were formidable. I heard Lucas give a hoarse yell of triumph. I'd never felt so capable, so powerful. Gretchen and I moved in concert, each of us sensing the other's intentions. The daggers became extensions of our hands as we drove Ais back toward the locked door. Ais fought us, trying to slow our progress. Our blades opened slashes across her arms and shoulders.

Growing desperate, Ais lunged between us. Our blades sliced twin lines along her back and we turned as one, both determined to keep Ais away from Lucas. Though his eyes were still lidded with pain, he leaned forward, focused on every movement of our blades.

As we hemmed Ais into the far corner of the room, she started laughing. I felt Gretchen tense, and we hesitated, wary. Ais's laughter swelled.

"You poor creatures. Fighting so hard for every insignificant victory. The Ancients are reawakening. An army of my sisters is waiting to storm the Wall and reclaim this Earth. Even if you kill me, another will pave the way for their return." She sighed, letting her smile deepen. "But I think if you could kill me, you would have done so already."

Ais's words sent shivers of dread through me, pulling me out of the moment. Gretchen lunged forward, but I hesitated. It was just the opening Ais needed. Ais collided with Gretchen, driving Gretchen past me, back into the center of the room.

"Gretchen!" Lucas tried to stand, but he was too weak from the blood loss. He fell back into the chair, woozy. I felt frozen, watching the fight helplessly from the sidelines.

Gretchen swung her dagger for Ais's face. Ais knocked it out of Gretchen's hand with a powerful backhanded swipe. As Gretchen lost her balance, Ais caught Gretchen's arm and wrenched it painfully behind her. I heard a snap and Gretchen clamped her teeth shut around a growl of agony. Ais grabbed Gretchen by the back of the neck and swung her around with great force, sending her sprawling to the floor. Gretchen slid into a bank of filing cabinets. Her head knocked against the base of a cabinet by Lucas's chair. Lucas forced himself to move, dropping to Gretchen's side. Gretchen was still. Lucas looked up at me, his face ashen. I don't know if there was blame in his eyes. I didn't need to see it to feel it coursing through my veins. We'd been so close. And in one careless moment, our advantage was lost.

Galvanized by horror, I leapt toward Ais. She fell back before my wild swings. But it was panic more than skill that drove me forward. I pressed my attack, pushing Ais closer and closer to the office door. If I could reach it, if I could open it, we might get help. Ais kept dodging back out of reach, gauging my movements. When I finally faltered, she was ready. She caught my wrist and wrenched Gretchen's dagger out of my hand.

I stood face-to-face with her, unarmed. She grabbed the front of my shirt and jerked me off my feet, slamming my back against the office door.

"What am I going to do with you?" Ais leaned in close, giving me a look that would have been almost tender if it weren't for the malice in her smile. I felt more than saw her shoulder move, and my body jerked against the wood of the door.

Pain came crashing through in the next moment—untempered by any relief—so strong my vision doubled. Ais had stabbed me through the left shoulder with Gretchen's dagger. She'd driven the blade through with such force that it had pierced the door behind me, pinning me in place. A hoarse moan clawed its way out of my throat. Ais watched me, unblinking.

"I warned you of the price of betrayal. But before I let you die, it's only justice for you to feel some of the pain you've caused me."

I could see Lucas and Gretchen over Ais's shoulder. Gretchen rolled to one side, and then laid back, hand clamped to her head. Lucas swayed over her, fighting dizziness. I was blocking their only escape. We had come this far, only to fail. Dina's life, snuffed out in less than a second. Gretchen and Lucas, with all their training, still no match for the creature before me. And the Guard—Where was Hale? Where were our soldiers? Unless the Thrall had overwhelmed them? Images spilled into my head of Dad, cornered, fighting for his life.

Ais watched my face for a few moments, and then touched my forehead. But there was no cold spreading through my mind. I smiled hollowly. At least she couldn't read my thoughts.

Ais lowered her hand and tilted her head to one side. "I don't have to read your thoughts to know what you're thinking," she murmured. "You're thinking it can't get any worse. But you're wrong. Just wait and see."

Why had we come here? I rolled my head to the side in defeat, wanting only to escape Ais's stare. Over her shoulder, I met Lucas's eyes and I remembered why.

Lucas held my gaze, steady, determined. He rose to his feet, shaky. Gretchen's dagger gleamed in his hand. His eyes dropped to the ground beside me. I followed his gaze and saw the hilt of Semangelof's sword just peeking out from under the table.

Ais turned to face Lucas. "So fragile," she said. Lucas stared at me, swaying, and I knew what he needed.

"*Fight,*" I said, summoning the last of the strength I'd gleaned from Matt. *The call* came through, weaker than I wanted, but I felt the words, pushing through the air between us.

Lucas was ready, aching for the power of that command. When *the call* reached him, he straightened, eyes sharpening. "You bet your ass I will."

Ais tensed, her attention riveted on Lucas. There was no time to waste. I nudged the chair away from the doorknob with my knee. I tried to fumble with the door's lock, but my left hand was useless—any movement sent searing waves of pain shooting across my shoulder and down my arm. I tried to reach it with my right hand, but twisting my body caused another wave of sickening pain. There was only one thing I could do.

I gripped the hilt of the dagger with my right hand. It didn't budge. I leaned forward, pushing against the searing pain in my shoulder, biting my tongue to keep from screaming out.

Lucas, watching out of the corner of his eye, timed his lunge to the moment the dagger came free from the door. I choked back a gasp of pain and dropped to my hands and knees.

Ais didn't hear me. She was moving to counter Lucas's attack. He dodged back quickly, stumbling, his grip unsteady on the dagger.

My hand closed around the pommel of Semangelof's sword. I pulled it out from under the table. It made a soft whisper as the blade swept against the cheap linoleum floor. The dagger was still embedded in my left shoulder—I didn't trust myself to pull it out without fainting. My left arm hung uselessly at my side, and every movement threatened to blind me with pain. I forced all of this to the back of my mind and rose with the sword in my right hand. I walked toward Ais, forcing myself to place one foot in front of the other. My sense of balance was off. I had to use the sword as a crutch, leaning on it to keep from falling over.

Lucas had dropped back before Ais. When he backed into a wall, he threw his hands up in a gesture of surrender. "Wait."

Ais faced him, confident. "There is no mercy for the sons of Adam."

I planted my feet on the floor and shifted the sword behind one leg, hoping to keep it out of Ais's view for as long as possible. "Don't hurt him," I said. The door behind me opened.

"Braedyn, I'm here!" I heard Dad's voice, but I didn't turn.

Ais's eyes slid past me to the entering Guard. But instead of drawing back in fear, Ais smirked. Something was wrong. "Excellent timing," she murmured.

Ais raised her hands, and two curtains of rippling shadow emerged behind her. Her wings, both whole, extended to the high ceiling. *"Come to me,"* she said.

Her voice shook the air. I heard Dad enter the room. Ais laughed at my confusion.

"I'm nearly 2,000 years old," she said. "Full of the life energy of 100 men. I heal fast." Her eyes slid back to my dad, moving toward her like a puppet. She took a few steps closer, smug with anticipated triumph. "Did you honestly think I would have let your little soldiers in here if there were any chance they might prevail? You've lived too long with the humans, child. You have no instincts, no understanding of your powers, and very soon you'll have no father left to save you."

"I have one thing you don't have," I said, my grip tightening on the pommel of the sword.

"Oh?" Ais flicked an idle glance at me, amused. "What's that?" When I didn't answer, her eyes shifted back to my father, gleaming in anticipation.

I only knew one sword move—the lunge attack Hale had taught me in the last of our practice sessions. It took Ais straight through the heart in one clean motion.

Ten minutes later, I sat on the floor as Lucas knelt behind me and wrapped his good arm across my chest, bracing me. I leaned back against him, letting the pain wash over me, not fighting it.

"I never should have doubted you," he whispered into my ear. "When I felt you in my mind—when I heard you—in that moment I knew you completely. How I ever let myself think you were one of them—" His voice sang with recrimination.

"You heard me?" I asked, feeling a heat rushing into my cheeks.

In answer, Lucas just chuckled softly. Dad stirred in the club chair.

He was still a little out of it, but he was coming around. I could still hear the sounds of a battle downstairs, but it didn't sink in. Ais was dead. Didn't that mean we'd won?

I saw Gretchen across the room, rooting through boxes. Her arm had been dislocated, not broken. With Lucas's help, she'd managed to slam the joint back into place with no more than a hiss of pain.

My whole body tensed as Gretchen returned to us, dousing a clean bar rag with vodka. "Top shelf," she said appreciatively. "But I doubt that will make this any easier."

I felt Lucas's arm tighten around my chest. "I do love you," he whispered.

And then Gretchen pulled the dagger free from my shoulder, and I passed out the good, old-fashioned, human way.

Dad, Lucas, Gretchen and I stumbled down the steps a few minutes later. I had revived quickly, thanks in no small part to the vodka Gretchen had poured liberally over my shoulder. It had sent a stabbing, burning pain to chase me back to consciousness. Judging from the smell rising off of Lucas, she'd treated him in the same fashion while I had been out. As we reached the bottom of the stairs, Gretchen squeezed my good arm gently.

"They'll need your help with the Thrall," Gretchen said. I stared at her, uncomprehending. "Every Thrall will follow the last order Ais gave them until they die," Gretchen explained. "Unless we stop them. You need to use *the call* again. Do you understand?"

I nodded, but the fight upstairs had weakened me. I wasn't sure what I'd be able to do.

We stepped into the hallway. I felt my stomach drop unexpectedly. I couldn't see any Guard soldiers. A handful of Thrall saw us from the club and surged forward. That drew the attention of others. Gretchen stepped in front of us to meet the first attackers, blades in hand.

"Go back," she shouted. "Barricade the door. Don't come out until I tell you it's safe!"

"We're not leaving you," Lucas said. Gretchen ignored him, bracing for the onslaught.

"*Stop!*" I shouted. I felt *the call* forming, but I lacked the strength to force a connection. The Thrall charging for us didn't even hesitate. We retreated up the stairs as the Thrall advanced. I tried to summon *the call* again, but it would not come. There was chaos in the club beyond us. With a sick dread, I knew people were dying.

"*Stop fighting!*" Another voice rang out, clear and powerful. Chimes crackled through the air as *the call* flooded through the cramped club.

On the stairs, Gretchen and I traded a wondering look. I pushed past Gretchen and ran into the hall. I could see the club beyond. The crowd of Thrall had stopped fighting. Their fists had dropped to their sides. Their faces had eased into vacant expressions.

I edged farther into the club, stunned. I could see Guardsmen, grouped into corners and behind the bar. I saw more than one bloody face, but at least 10 soldiers were still on their feet.

Someone opened the emergency exit doors to my right. Crisp dawn light flooded inside.

"*Go home!*" Again, *the call* rang out. The Guardsmen watched, stunned, as the Thrall turned and headed toward the exits. In their wake, a dozen more Thrall lay unmoving on the ground.

I stared. It was Karayan standing by the doors, watching the Thrall trickle away into the dawn. Karayan had just saved all our lives.

Lucas slipped out of the hallway and stood by my side. He watched the retreating Thrall. "That's it? They just go home?" he asked. I looked at him and saw the pain in his eyes.

Karayan turned her green eyes on us, solemn.

It was Gretchen who answered. "They'll return to the lives they remember. But the core of who they used to be is gone. Without Ais, they'll slowly fade away. What she took from them—whether you think of it as the soul or the will to survive—it doesn't grow back. In a few years, they'll all be dead."

Thane pushed through to the front of the crowd. Karayan's eyes met his. He took another step toward her. Karayan flinched, and her wings wrapped tightly around her.

"Wait." Thane couldn't see that she hadn't moved, or the look of pain that laid siege to her face as she watched him. "Karayan?"

Instead of answering, Karayan looked at me. I saw the confusion clear in her eyes. She turned and ran out the doors. I watched her until she had disappeared from view.

I risked a glance back at Thane. He was studying me. My expression told him everything he needed to know. She was gone. Thane turned away from me abruptly.

"We need to clear out," Marx said.

The Guardsmen regrouped. In moments they'd gathered their scattered weapons and were helping the two wounded men out into the dawn light.

Dad scrutinized my shoulder, eyes creased with worry. "You should sit down. Let me bring the truck around. That shoulder doesn't look good."

"I'm okay, Dad." I winced as my shoulder throbbed in protest.

"Tell that to the EMT. We're going to the hospital."

"Probably not a bad idea." The ground seemed to shift, but Dad caught me before I fell.

"What happened?" I heard Dad's voice, hushed and intense. He wasn't speaking to me. Ais had done a real number on him. He didn't remember anything past opening the office door.

"Ais got her with my dagger." Gretchen's voice answered, nearby. "But she did it, Murphy. She killed the demon with Semangelof's sword." Jubilation filled her voice. "That Wall's not coming down anytime soon."

"That's my girl." Dad guided me outside. The cold air felt good on my shoulder. It revived me a little. Dad helped me sit on a step. Lucas lowered himself next to me.

Gretchen studied us, lips tight. "Make that two for the hospital."

Dad nodded. "Stay here. We'll bring the truck around."

Gretchen and Dad headed into the parking lot. Lucas and I had a few moments alone together. He laid his left hand on the step between us, palm facing up, and gave me a small smile. I took his hand with my right hand, and our fingers twined together.

Lucas turned to look at me. I was struck by how calm he seemed. "I've been meaning to ask you about those dreams."

Even with the pain in my shoulder and the exhaustion of the fight, I felt a smile bloom on my face. I didn't fight it. "And what dreams are you talking about, exactly?"

"Well, if you're having trouble remembering, maybe we should try another one."

Hale's truck pulled up. Dad left the engine running as he got out and opened the door closest to us. Gretchen was tossing weapons and gear into the back to clear the seat for us.

"Maybe we should," I said. Lucas's return smile was warm enough to drive everything else away.

EPILOGUE

Snow blanketed the Coronado Prep campus, gleaming brilliantly under a full moon. It muted the winter night, dialing down nocturnal sounds to a whisper. Though it was freezing outside, there was no wind to slip greedy fingers of ice up our sleeves or swirl snow around our ankles. Christmas had come and gone, and school would start again on Monday. As far as the administration knew, Lucas and I had been in a car accident. The "accident" was responsible for our injuries, and bought us all of winter break to study for our exams. Cassie's voice had filled with empathy and concern when I'd called to tell her the cover story. Royal had listened as I stumbled through the same version, but his succinct "yuh-huh" made clear he wasn't buying it. And yet, he seemed to realize I wasn't ready to talk about what had really happened, and didn't push me for the truth.

Cassie and Royal met us in the parking lot. They looked relaxed and happy. Tonight was New Year's Eve, and we were back on campus for the postponed Winter Ball. Dressed in our finery, we turned together and walked toward the gym. As we got closer, we could make out the roiling rhythm thumping inside the building. Lucas opened the door for me with his good arm and I gave him a warm smile. There were a few new rules in place for us at home. The Guard had finally realized that they couldn't keep Lucas and me apart. So instead, they made us promise to keep all the physical stuff to our dreams, aside from holding hands or the occasional hug. When Lucas protested—I had kept the Lilitu storm at bay the last time we'd kissed, after all—Gretchen told him that the alternative was for the two of them to join another unit in another city. And so we both agreed to follow the rules. I know Gretchen keeps a close eye on Lucas, watching him carefully for any signs that we've gone too far. Dreams aren't as nice as reality—not by a long shot—but they'll have to do for now.

As we entered the gym, the music washed over us, along with the heat generated by five hundred dancing high school kids. The Raven had been closed as police were called to investigate the scene. They found 12 bodies. It was considered the worst crime in the city in a decade. The Guard bitterly assured me there was no hope of the police stumbling onto the truth. Ais might be gone, but there were other Lilitu about that would make sure their secret was protected.

Sure enough, days after our fight, the newspapers were filled with the story of a cult of young men, a dozen of whom had taken their own lives at the Raven Club on winter solstice. This story explained in convincing detail what had happened to the missing men. Most returned to their previous lives. A few were even coming forward with stories about their days in the cult—gut-wrenching stories about drugs and psychological abuse that explained why all the returned men seemed like shadows of their former selves. The police department instituted an emergency cult awareness program, and life in the city continued with no one the wiser about what had really happened the night of the solstice.

People believe what they want to believe.

Dina and Alex, the soldier who'd died on Hale's lawn, were buried in a simple ceremony out in the mountains. Ais and her daughters were burned, and their bones pounded to dust. Their ashes had been left in a small hole that Marx's team had dug by the side of the road on their way out of town this morning. Only Matt had stayed behind.

Last night, before they packed for the journey, they'd thrown a party like none I'd ever seen. Hale had enlisted five soldiers to dig a massive fire pit in the backyard. We'd burned a small mountain of wood, trusting the flames to keep the frost at bay. The soldiers of the Guard had finally let loose, cheering the end of Ais, mourning the loss of Dina and Alex, and—to Lucas's immense amusement—outdoing themselves trying to christen me with the perfect nickname. When the hyperbole got too ridiculous, someone hoisted me off my perch on Hale's back porch, and I found myself paraded around the bonfire until Dad ran over and convinced the soldiers (drunk on whiskey and success) that I was still recovering from my wounds.

After that, things settled down a little. Hale and Marx had moved through the crowd, talking with their teams and sharing a drink here and there. There was an undercurrent to the celebration; everyone present now knew Ais's prediction. The Ancients were reawakening. The Lilitu were still massing for another war. And while we may have reinforced the gates for a little while longer, no one believed we'd seen the last of this war.

Lucas and I had watched most of the party from the shelter of the porch, leaning against each other. His wounds had been much more extensive than mine. Ais's talons had wreaked havoc on his shoulder, and he'd been in surgery for close to 12 hours as his doctors fought to mend muscle and tendon. His arm would be in the sling that kept it immobilized across his middle for months. My wound had been cleaner, and the trauma much easier for the surgeons to repair, though I was also ordered into a sling for a few weeks.

But, stepping into the warmth of the gym, I didn't mind. We were alive, and we had won the battle, if not the war.

Lucas held my right hand snugly in his left. "You look amazing."

I smiled. I'd had neither the opportunity nor the desire to shop for something new, and so I was wearing the black floor-length dress I'd worn to Winter Ball last year. But over it, I wore the gorgeous green velvet coat Cassie had made for me. In an act of kindness that had surprised and gratified me, Gretchen had taken the coat and had it cleaned and repaired by an expert tailor in town. It looked as good as new, and Cassie couldn't have been more thrilled when she arrived with Royal and saw me wearing it. Royal was dressed in a black tux with tails, and he knew exactly how good he looked. Cassie had tied her hair up in a simple French twist for the dance. She'd abandoned the fun and crazy hairstyles since everything with Parker had happened. I worried that some deeply hidden part of her self-confidence might never fully recover. She was wearing the same gown she'd made for Homecoming, but she'd added an elaborate boned jacket of the same shimmering material, making the whole thing look vaguely Victorian.

When I complimented her on the jacket, she blushed. "I had so much fun making yours, I wanted to try another one."

We walked through the halls to the main gym, and I spotted Missy taking cash for the last-minute tickets to the dance. She waved us over. After the Raven had been closed, Missy had almost had a nervous breakdown. When I'd recovered from surgery, I'd made a simple video and posted it online, explaining the situation for our classmates. I told them even if it was at the gym, we'd have an amazing time together. I reminded those who knew her of how awesome Carrie is, and the importance of diabetes research. Missy had been flooded with ticket requests a few hours later.

I paused by Missy at the ticket table. "How's it going?"

"We've already made more than I'd hoped," she said, beaming. "Thank you again, Braedyn. I owe you one."

Amber, sitting next to her, eyed me with a tight little smile. It was strangely unnerving.

I dragged my eyes back to Missy's beaming face. "My pleasure. It's for a good cause."

Lucas, sensing Amber's hostility, guided me on. In moments we were stepping into the main gym. I had to hand it to Missy, the gym looked amazing. Silvery white curtains lined the bleachers, complete with great sweeping folds of fabric that screened the basketball hoops at either end. The gym itself was dark, but some kind of light was trained upwards, swirling tiny pinpricks of light across the ceiling. It made it seem as if the stars above us were dancing. I felt Royal stiffen beside me.

Parker had seen us come in. He rose out of a chair against one curtained wall, his eyes fixed on Cassie. Royal took her hand and swept her onto the dance floor before Parker had a chance to approach her. Parker's eyes turned to me. Lucas saw the determination in my face and tensed. I walked over to Parker. He looked better. Stronger. His black hair shone with a healthy gloss again, and his eyes were clear.

"Cassie looks good," Parker said.

"She's doing better," I said. "But your being around her won't help. *Let her go.*" I caught Parker's eye. "Let her go." Parker nodded, numbly, and sank back into his chair.

Lucas's jaw clenched when he heard *the call*, but when I looked back at him, he forced himself to smile. I saw Amber watching from across the room. She turned away quickly.

The music shifted to a slow song and about half the dancers cleared the floor, making more room for the couples. Lucas and I made an awkward dance pair in our slings. I curled my good arm around his neck and he pulled me close with his. We were still dancing when the clock struck midnight. Lucas held my eyes in his steady gaze. Our lips hovered a breathless inch apart as white and silver balloons cascaded down around us. Laughing couples kissed and cheered, ushering in the New Year. With great effort, Lucas and I pulled away from one another, before one of us broke our word. We retreated from the dance floor in silence.

We found Royal and Cassie by the drinks, where Royal had been entertaining Cassie with details about the elaborate vacation his father had taken him on over Christmas.

"This is his way of making up for being mostly invisible the rest of the year," he said. "Because what problem doesn't a villa in the Swiss Alps solve, when you really get down to it?"

I squeezed Royal's shoulder with faux compassion. "The trials of the uber-rich."

"Still. I'm glad to be back."

I saw Amber, standing at the edge of one silver curtain a few feet away. Watching me. There it was again, that unsettling little smile. When she was sure she'd caught my eye, she turned and slipped behind the curtain.

With a twisting sensation in my stomach, I pulled away from my friends. "I'll be right back." They looked surprised when I headed toward the curtain. Amber waited for me in the darkness beyond, leaning against the post supporting the basketball hoop.

"At first I thought that old guy in Parker's hospital room was crazy," Amber said. "We were in the psych ward, after all. But after I had some time to think about it, I started wondering." She held up a small hardback book. It looked old. The cloth cover was stained and dusty. "So I did a little research. The librarians at the University are super helpful. And they've got this killer mythology collection. All kinds of crazy stuff about Mesopotamia." I could see Amber's triumph in the dim light. "I know what you are, Lilitu."

I felt my shoulders tense, and forced them to relax. "I'm not sure what you're talking about," I lied smoothly. "But you might want to know: now *you* sound a little crazy."

Her smile hardened. "I want you to leave Coronado Prep, or I'll find a way to out you."

I drew in a deep breath. I didn't want her to know exactly how frightened I was by her threat. I forced myself to sound bored. "Why are you wasting your time with me?"

"You were there when Derek died. You had something to do with

Parker's meltdown. I don't want you at my school. I don't want you near my friends. I'm warning you. If you stick around, whatever happens next is on your head." Amber watched me for a moment longer, then brushed past me. "Say hi to Lucas for me." The parting curtains let in the soft light from the dance, but as soon as they swept closed I was plunged into darkness again. The space felt claustrophobic, hot and close. I needed to breathe. I turned, saw a glowing green EXIT sign, and headed straight out the door.

The silent chill of the evening hit me with a welcome shock. I breathed deep, and the cold air burned into my lungs. I leaned against the gym, needing time to clear my head.

"You have done well, child of the Guard." Sansenoy joined me. I looked around, startled. We were alone.

"It's just Braedyn," I said, feeling foolish.

Sansenoy smiled, patiently. "We owe you a debt of gratitude."

"Thanks?"

"We have been empowered to grant your request."

I stared at him numbly, running over our last conversation for what he could be talking about. When the realization came, hot tears sprang into the corners of my eyes. "Do you mean—?" I couldn't voice the thought. I was afraid that speaking it aloud would break this spell. To be human—to be free to love without fear or restraint—it was everything I wanted.

"If you still wish it," Sansenoy said, his gaze steady. "The gift of humanity is yours."

I opened my mouth to say *Yes, yes, of course I still wish it! Human me up, baby!* But a prickling thorn of a thought caught in the back of my head.

Sansenoy saw my uncertainty. "Something troubles you."

"Ais." I hesitated. Sansenoy watched me, content to wait for me to find the words I needed. "Could we have stopped her if—if I hadn't been there?" *If I hadn't been a Lilitu.*

Sansenoy's eyes clouded, he seemed to be searching something far off. "It is uncertain," he finally answered.

"Ais said the Ancient Lilitu are reawakening."

"Yes. Lilith's children grow restless across the face of creation."

"Then—" I choked on the next words. I didn't want to say them. I wanted to let this burden pass to someone else. But Hale, Dad,

Gretchen, even Thane—they were counting on me. They believed that I was crucial in this fight. I thought back to that night last week, when Ais had swept Lucas out of our house and into the darkness, as though it meant nothing to rip him away from us. If I hadn't been able to find him...

I realized I was hunched over, one hand clamped to my healing shoulder. Standing in the crisp moonlight, next to the grizzled human mask of an angel, the remembered pain of that night was fresh again. But fresher still was my understanding, finally, of the part I needed to play in all of this. I looked into Sansenoy's face. "I can't. Not yet. Not until I know we're safe."

Sansenoy's eyes widened a tiny fraction. He nodded slowly. "As you wish."

"But later?" I heard the desperate hope in my voice.

It was Sansenoy's turn to hesitate. "Later may be difficult. The stronger your Lilitu power grows, the greater the temptation to abuse it will become. There is a limit to the damage you can inflict on others before doing so corrupts you from within. Know that if you cross this line, there will be no mercy possible."

I swallowed, but nodded. "I understand." I'd learned a lot about the Lilitu storm within me over the last few weeks. *I can do this,* I thought, willing myself to believe it. Another deeper part of me seemed less sure.

Sansenoy placed his hand on my shoulder once more, in that oddly formal gesture. I felt a warmth spreading from his hand throughout my body, driving out the bitter cold that had settled over me as we'd talked. "We wish you wisdom and fortitude, Braedyn, child of the Guard. Until we meet again."

He released me as the gym door opened behind me. I turned to see Cassie, Royal, and Lucas stumble into the cold. They spotted me, their concern melting into exasperation.

"What are you doing out here?" Cassie asked, bounding over.

I turned back to Sansenoy—but he was gone. The soccer field, blanketed in white, spread out before me. I looked down and was only faintly surprised to see no footprints other than my own marring the gleaming snow.

"We saw Amber coming through that curtain you disappeared behind," Royal said, worried. "She looked extremely pleased with herself. It wasn't a pretty sight."

"I tried to tell them you could take care of yourself," Lucas said, smiling into my eyes.

I smiled back, shaking off the unease of the previous moment. I reached for Lucas, and he draped his good arm around my back.

"Aren't you freezing out here?" Cassie was stamping her feet and rubbing her arms.

"Yeah. Let's go back inside."

Cassie grabbed Royal's hand and pulled him back toward the gym. They opened the door and darted inside. I started to follow them, but Lucas held me back. When we didn't follow immediately, Royal and Cassie reappeared in the doorway.

"Are you coming?" Cassie asked.

Royal took one look at us and turned to Cassie. "Let's give them a moment to mack in peace." Royal grabbed the door and pulled it shut. Before it closed, I saw Cassie, trying hard not to laugh. Her eyes twinkled at us. When we were alone, I turned to Lucas.

"Everything okay?" He murmured, pulling me close.

"Yeah." I stared at him, breathing in the scent of him, reveling in his touch. I couldn't know the future, but the possibility of a normal life filled my head with delicious hope. Lucas was studying my face; his eyebrows shot up with interest.

"What's that smile for?" he asked.

"I'll tell you later."

He draped an arm over my shoulders. I felt safe. I felt sure. Whatever was coming, I knew we would find the strength to face it together.

THE FOLLOWING IS AN EXCERPT FROM

INCUBUS

DAUGHTERS OF LILITH:
BOOK 2

Jennifer Quintenz

1

T he late September sunlight had its own kind of magic. Spears
of mid-morning light broke through a heavy bank of clouds to
strike the leaves of an expansive aspen tree, setting each one
aglow with an emerald fire. I tilted my head up, eyes closed, letting the
warmth seep in, welcoming it beyond my skin, through sinew and
muscle, into my bones. Some hidden part of me had been cold since
last December. I lived with this fist of ice around my heart, unable to
pry free from its hold.

Winter solstice.

My eyelids snapped open. I felt the muscles of my back knot up.
With effort, I forced myself to pull in a long breath. As I let it out, I
willed my body to relax.

In answer, I felt his warm fingers lacing through mine. Lucas stood
next to me, distracted by the stream of kids pouring out of the newly
arrived school bus behind us. I don't think he even realized he'd taken
my hand. It was an unconscious gesture, but it did more to warm me
than the sun. I leaned closer, breathing in the subtle spice of his scent.
He sensed the motion and turned to look at me. I smiled but he read
something in my face. Concern clouded his eyes.

"It's nothing," I said, then, tasting the lie, I shrugged. "It's nothing
new."

Lucas nodded. There was nothing else to say. The only reason he
wasn't having sheet-twisting, sweat-drenched nightmares every night
was that I policed his dreams. Even then, more than a handful of
times the Lilitu demon Ais had risen up before us, conjured by Lucas's
sleeping mind. In many dreams we'd battled her together, fighting
teeth and nails that glinted like steel, staring into glassy black eyes.
These fights were always epic and acrobatic—loosed from the laws of

physics that dictate everything in the real world, Lucas and I could run faster, leap farther, and fight tirelessly. Our dream fights were much more glamorous than the actual night we had faced Ais. The night we had nearly died.

Fragmented memories of that night rose up, knife-sharp and aching to shred my forced calm. I turned my attention back to the reason we were all here.

The Mission of Puerto Escondido sat perched in the foothills, about 15 miles away from the center of Old Town. The monks who'd settled here hundreds of years before had picked a beautiful vantage point. Piñon and juniper trees dotted the mountains that enclosed our little valley. Most of the town was nestled comfortably in the lowest dip between the peaks. Standing in front of the mission, I could see across the bowl of our valley, from the glimmering stand of old oaks that edged my neighborhood to the wealthy foothill community on the other side of town.

As if glancing at his neighborhood was some kind of summons, Royal's brand new, platinum two-seater cut across the unpaved parking lot, kicking up a dusty plume in its wake. The kids nearest the parking lot coughed and waved dust away from their faces, irritated. Irritation changed to interest as they got a good look at the car. The Corvette Stingray convertible had been a present from Royal's father. If you asked Royal, he'd say it was an attempt to compensate for being chronically absent—but that didn't mean it wasn't fun to drive.

"Told you." I grinned at Lucas, feeling some of my anxiety melting into the background. Royal was a grounding force in my life. Safe. Familiar.

"You said he'd make an entrance," Lucas replied, unable to wrench his gaze off the gleaming roadster, "but now I'm thinking you left out a few key details."

"What?" I said innocently. "I told you he got a car for his birthday."

"A *car*—?" Lucas glanced at me, incredulous. "That's like calling the Hope Diamond a pretty rock."

"Which is technically true," I shrugged, "depending on your taste in gemstones."

Lucas smiled, shaking his head, then draped an arm over my shoulder. "Okay. Now I'm thinking I put too much thought into your

Christmas gift." I elbowed him in the ribs. Lucas grunted, but his grin deepened.

In the parking lot, Royal emerged from this gleaming work of art, seemingly oblivious to our classmates' stares. He walked around and opened the passenger door for Cassie. She unfolded from the car, smoothing her long black hair back from her face. She was beaming, flushed from the ride, and when she spotted us she waved brightly. We moved forward to meet them at the edge of the parking lot. Royal approached us casually enough, but as he got closer I could see the twinkle of excitement in his eyes.

"Well?" he asked. "First thoughts. Brutal honesty."

"Hm." I said, tilting my head to one side critically. "I thought it'd be more—" I glanced at Lucas.

"Awesome," he supplied.

"Yes. I thought it'd be more awesome," I said. "I mean, don't get me wrong. It's okay, for a car. I'm sure it will get you from point A to point B. Maybe you can upgrade it in a few years. Get something a little—"

"Awesomer," Lucas said.

"Right."

Cassie bit her lip, muffling a giggle.

"It's an incredible ride and you know it," Royal said, unruffled. He held up his car keys. "Just for that, Cassie gets to drive it first."

"Me?" Cassie squealed.

"I'd like to amend my former statement," Lucas said.

"Too late." Royal tossed the keys to Cassie, who plucked them out of the air gleefully. Lucas looked forlorn.

"Although I do need a favor, so if anyone wants brownie points—" Royal jabbed his thumb over his shoulder at the car behind him. "To be clear, brownie points get you behind the wheel."

"Let's hear it," Lucas said.

Royal lowered his voice. "My dad's hired some SAT dude to come over and tutor me three times a week. I could really use some company. This guy is way, *way* beyond plastic. Just watching him smile all afternoon makes *my* cheeks hurt. Isn't there some saying? 'If you're going to suffer, you might as well make your friends suffer, too?'"

"I don't think so, no," I said.

Royal snapped his fingers. "Misery loves company."

"Yeah, that's not exactly the same thing."

"Whatever. My misery basically demands your company. It's the first rule of friendship." Royal turned beseeching eyes on Cassie. "Save me from Academic Ken Doll. You'll have my eternal gratitude."

"All right. I'm in," Cassie said.

"Thanks, study buddy." Royal grinned, catching my eye for the briefest moment. I knew—and I knew Royal knew—that if Cassie was going to go to college, she'd need some serious scholarships. The kind of scholarships that started with an excellent score on the SATs. Which made me suspect that this tutor might not be as lame as Royal would have us believe.

"Count me in, too," I said.

"So these brownie points," Lucas began.

"Don't worry, pretty boy," Royal said, grinning. "There's plenty of road to go around."

Behind us, Mr. Landon clapped his hands together, drawing everyone's attention toward the doors of the old mission. His portly stature and receding hairline—which might have made him the target of students' jokes—were easily overshadowed by a youthful enthusiasm for his subject. He was one of a handful of beloved educators at Coronado Prep voted among the "Best Teachers" year after year. Mr. Landon taught AP History to all the juniors at Coronado Prep, which was the reason for this class-wide field trip.

"All right, kids, I think that's everyone," Mr. Landon said. "Please direct your attention to our fabulous guide for the day, Annie Gerardo. Annie?"

I turned toward the slender, mousy woman standing next to Mr. Landon—but my gaze caught on another figure, hovering at the back of the crowd of students. Almost as soon as our eyes locked, the strange woman slipped through a gate into the mission's garden and was gone. A shivery tingle crept over the back of my neck. I'd only had the briefest glimpse of her, but something about the woman was off. She was human—that much I could see instantly. Approaching middle age, with a wide, kind looking face. But something in her eyes was missing.

"Braedyn?" Lucas looked at me curiously. I noticed the rest of the students were following Annie into the mission's main sanctuary. Royal and Cassie, a few paces ahead, trailed the bunch, waiting for me to catch up.

I turned back to the gate through which the woman had vanished. "Did you see...?"

Lucas followed my gaze, but of course there was nothing to see. "What am I looking for?" he asked, tensing like a coiled spring, ready for release. I realized I wasn't the only one with a hair-trigger these days.

"Nothing," I said, forcing a smile. I squeezed his hand, still laced through my fingers. "Let's catch up before we miss the whole tour. Knowing Landon, this is probably going to end up on a quiz."

Lucas and I were the last of our group to set foot inside the mission. The heavy mission doors swung shut behind us and a sweeping peace enveloped me. The outside world fell away, as though muted by a great distance. The sunlight, which had seemed so harsh moments ago in the parking lot, was at the wrong angle to beam directly into the sanctuary. Instead, fingers of light shot through the high windows to reflect against the painted ceiling, bouncing aimlessly in the vastness above us and filling the cathedral with a reflected glow.

"Come in, everyone. Come on, don't be afraid to scootch a little closer." Annie waved us forward. When Lucas and I edged farther inside, she gestured at the sanctuary around us grandly. "This mission was first established in 1593, by a group of Spanish monks. This room we're standing in was the entirety of the original mission. Everything else—the dormitory, the gardens, the refractory—that was added later." Annie gestured for us to follow her deeper into the sanctuary. I stepped out from under the shelter of the foyer and got my first good look at the simple stained glass windows, depicting the lives and deaths of a variety of saints.

I heard a group of guys muffling laughter from the other side of the sanctuary. I glanced over and saw Dan Buchanan making a lewd gesture while a group of kids surrounding him snickered. One of the girls tossed her icy-blond hair back over one shoulder and noticed me staring. Her smile vanished in an instant.

Amber. She used to brag that she'd grown up getting most of the things she wanted in life. Until I came along, I suppose. She'd made a failed play for Lucas when he started at Coronado Prep, but that wasn't the reason for the icy rage that gleamed in her eyes.

This was about an ultimatum she'd given me last winter.

You were there when Derek died, she'd said. *You had something to do with Parker's meltdown. I don't want you at my school. I don't want you near my friends. I'm warning you. If you stick around, whatever happens next is on your head.*

With some effort, I let my gaze slide away from Amber back to our tour guide. Amber's threats were toothless. If she ran around telling everyone her theory that I was a Lilitu demon, they'd all look at her like she was nuts. Never mind the fact that it was true. Most of humanity wasn't willing to accept that people—things—like me existed. I'd had a hard enough time believing it myself when I'd found out. Steering my thoughts carefully away from this sensitive topic, I sighed. No, there wasn't much Amber could do to me, and we both knew it.

"And now for the *pièce de résistance,*" Annie proclaimed with a wide sweep of her arm. She walked into the small alcove to the left of the altar. "Have you ever wondered why our town is called Puerto Escondido? Well, feast your eyes on this." Placing her hand on a carved wooden rose, she turned her wrist. The rose, which had looked like it was carved into one of the church's pillars, moved. It was some kind of latch. Behind Annie, a section of the rich oak paneling popped open. She pulled it open farther with a flourish.

While Annie was obviously excited about this revelation, the junior class of Coronado Prep did not share her enthusiasm.

Annie, struggling to win back her audience, attempted a "spooky" voice that came off painfully corny. "But why, you may ask, did the monks of Puerto Escondido need a secret door out of their sanctuary?"

"Booty calls?" Dan offered. The sanctuary rang with raucous laughter. Annie's face fell, and my heart went out to her. But seriously, we were in high school, not kindergarten.

"Okay, Mr. Buchanan, you're with me for the rest of this tour," Mr. Landon said. Dan shrugged and moved to join Mr. Landon near the front of the group.

"Um..." Annie struggled for a way back into her tour.

"Maybe the kids could roam a bit? Come to you if they have any questions about the mission?" Mr. Landon offered. Annie's face melted in relief and she nodded. "Okay, kids," Mr. Landon said, taking charge. "Try and remember this is a school field trip. There may or may not be a quiz on this mission so it might behoove you to take some notes." He waved off a chorus groans with good humor.

"Thank the Lord," Royal said, turning around to face us. "That poor woman. I was getting ready to dial emergency services to come and resuscitate her."

I heard someone approaching behind us, but when the newcomer spoke, even Royal's expression blanched.

"Cassie?" Parker's voice wavered. When she saw him, the blood seeped out of Cassie's face. Royal and I had made a pact to keep Parker away from Cassie as much as possible. We'd done a thorough job of it so far this year; Cassie hadn't come face to face with him once since school started. If she guessed why we'd sometimes steer her down a side hall, or forget a textbook and ask her to walk back to a locker with us, she hadn't let on. But here in the mission, outside the confines of school, we'd let our guard down. He'd gotten past our defenses. Royal locked eyes with me and I saw his flash of panic.

"Leave me alone," Cassie said to Parker, her voice suddenly cold.

Royal and I moved at the same time. Royal guided Cassie away. I stepped in front of Parker to block him from following.

"What are you doing, Parker?" I hissed. "She doesn't want to see you anymore, remember?" I felt Lucas move to stand beside me.

"I thought maybe—" Parker ran a shaking hand through his hair.

"Maybe she forgot that little video you made?" My voice crackled with quiet fury. "That's not likely, is it?" It had been almost a year since Parker had seduced Cassie on a dare and shared the videoed evidence of the deed with his friends. She'd never quite recovered. She put on a brave face, hung out with us like old times, but she'd stopped sewing, stopped designing those fashion-forward creations she'd been so passionate about before. And she'd stopped wearing her hair in the quirky twisted knots that had always seemed so *her*. Where she used to radiate her own personal brand of Cassie-ness almost unconsciously, she now struggled to fade into the background. It was the thing I hated most about what Parker had done to her. He'd stolen her from herself.

Parker squirmed miserably. "I made a mistake," he started.

Lucas didn't give him time to finish. "Don't worry. You're not going to get the chance to make another one."

Parker pulled his gaze off of Cassie and glanced at Lucas, as if seeing him there for the first time. "This has nothing to do with you, Mitchell."

"Come on, man," Lucas said, his voice soft and dangerous. "Walk away."

Parker gave Lucas a lopsided smirk. "Or what? You want to take a swing at me? I thought you used up all your second chances with Fiedler last year."

Lucas's shoulders loosened, the way they did before a practice bout with the Guard. I tried to catch his eye. Parker was an arrogant ass, but that didn't make him wrong. Lucas couldn't afford to push things with Fiedler, not after the rocky start he'd made at Coronado Prep last year.

Either Parker couldn't see how close he'd pushed Lucas to the breaking point, or he meant to instigate a fight.

"She's got nothing left to say to you," I said. Parker's eyes shifted to me a half-second before he shook his head and shoved me aside. I stumbled, catching myself on a column.

"Hey," Lucas growled. He caught Parker's arm roughly. Parker spun around, fist clenched, ready for a fight. Behind them, I spotted Mr. Landon wandering through the crowd, eyes peeled for any trouble. If I was going to diffuse this situation, it had to happen now. I fixed my gaze on Parker.

"*Leave Cassie alone,*" I said, willing power into the words. The faint tinkling of chimes echoed strangely around my words as they tunneled through the space between us to settle inside Parker's mind. I saw Lucas tense out of the corner of my eye. I hadn't used *the call* since the night of Winter Ball—the last time I'd told Parker to stay away from Cassie. I shouldn't have had to tell him again, but I pushed that troubling thought down and willed my words to penetrate through Parker's own desires.

It worked. After a second or two he blinked at us, as though startled to see us.

"Um, hello?" Ally Krect snaked her arm through Parker's and glared suspiciously at me before turning an inviting smile on Parker. "Did you get lost, babe?"

"Clearly." Parker seemed to shake the last of his haze off. He looped his arm over her shoulders, turning his back on us.

I could feel Lucas turn to study me.

"I don't know," I said, in answer to his unasked question. I finally met his gaze, and saw my own worry mirrored in his eyes. "Maybe I didn't do it right the first time."

"I was there," Lucas said softly. "You did it right. He's resisting somehow." Lucas turned to stare after Parker, who was ignoring us, arm still comfortably circled around Ally. She flicked a suspicious look over to us, then angled her body so her back was facing us, too.

"Come on," I said, drawing Lucas back to Royal and Cassie, who were studying some old carved panels on the walls. Doing their best to act normal.

"It's so pretty here," Cassie said, glancing up as Lucas and I joined them. "I can't believe this place is over 400 years old."

"All right," Royal said, getting down to business. "I say we split up. You two take that side, we'll take this side, and we can compare notes tonight. Deal?"

I glanced at Lucas, more than a little willing to spend some time strolling through the beautiful mission alone with him.

As if he could read my thoughts, Lucas smiled. "Deal."

Cassie was right. The mission was beautiful. Everything, from the beams in the ceiling to the stones under our feet, had been hand carved by the monks who'd established this mission nearly half a millennium ago. Lucas and I wandered through the sanctuary, letting the peaceful beauty of the space wash over us. As we drifted back to the main sanctuary doors, Lucas spotted a crack in one of the massive columns framing the narthex. He examined it for a moment, then smiled.

"Huh," he said. "Apparently those monks were hiding more than one secret around this place." He hooked his fingers into the crack and what had looked like a carved section of the column turned out to be another concealed door. Lucas opened it, revealing a tightly curved spiral staircase leading up. "Where do you suppose that goes?" There was a decidedly mischievous glint in his eye.

"Well," I said, as if resigning myself to an odious task. "Mr. Landon did give us an assignment."

"True. This might be on the quiz."

The spiral staircase was so narrow you had to watch where you put your feet; each tread narrowed from about eight inches to almost nothing as it connected in the center of the spiral. It took a bit of concentration to walk up, and I knew coming down would be another challenge.

But the climb was worth it. Lucas and I reached the top of the stairs to discover we were in a cozy little viewing balcony overlooking the main sanctuary. Very cozy, actually—we could barely move without bumping into each other. Sheltered in our hiding place, we had the perfect view of the sanctuary. Just above us, a stained glass window depicted a beautiful saint, haloed in light, holding an arrow over her heart.

Something drew my attention back down to the level below. A lone figure stood in the center of the sanctuary. A familiar feeling pulled at the edge of my thoughts, but before I could place it, Lucas spoke.

"Beautiful." He was so close, his breath stirred the hair against my neck. I was suddenly aware of the warmth of his body behind me and ached to lean back into him. My heart quickened. I tried to tamp it down. We couldn't act on these feelings. We had made a promise to the Guard, to our families. But beyond that, I'd sworn to myself to never, *never* let myself risk Lucas's safety again. And yet, right at this moment, none of that seemed to matter.

I turned in his arms.

Whatever reassuring thoughts I might have had about Lucas's and my self-control, I overestimated it.

I don't know which of us moved first. Our lips brushed and I felt the sudden swell of the Lilitu storm inside me, straining forward, waiting for one moment's weakness in my self-control to drain Lucas of his vitality. I pulled back from Lucas as if stung.

"We can't." I cringed at the sound of my voice, hoarse with emotion. "We can't."

"Braedyn," he started. I traced my fingers across his lips, thrilled at the soft warmth of the touch. I bit my own lip and turned aside.

"We promised," I said.

"I know. I just wish—" Lucas pulled away from me, and I could see the struggle on his face. "This would be a lot easier if we knew when the waiting part would end." He smiled, that lopsided smile that made him look in the same moment vulnerable and worldly. "Too bad

Sansenoy didn't leave you his number."

"Right. Because, you know, why not just call and ask?"

Lucas pitched his voice an octave higher than normal, and I realized he was imitating me. "'So, Sans, that whole becoming human thing, when do you figure that's going to happen? 'Cause my boyfriend and I have some plans.'"

"I do not sound like that!" I said, punching him in the arm for the poor impersonation. But I couldn't stop myself from giggling.

"Ouch." Lucas smiled, rubbing his arm, clearly pleased to have won a laugh. "Hey, can I ask you a question?"

"What?"

"Why haven't you told Murphy?"

The question caught me unprepared. When I'd told Lucas of the angel's offer to make me human, he'd been so thrilled, I'd stopped halfway through. There was a part I hadn't told him. I hadn't told him about the caveat. Because if I slipped up, if I used my Lilitu powers to hurt someone badly enough, I would cross a line. My soul would be too tainted to ever be redeemed, and my chance of becoming human would evaporate as completely as a drop of water spilt on the hot desert floor. That was why I hadn't been able to bring myself to tell Murphy, my father. I couldn't bear it if Dad pinned all his hopes on me becoming human, and then I lost control and crossed the line. It would crush him. I'd told myself it was better he not know, but keeping this from him was getting harder and harder. I forced myself to smile. "I just haven't found the right time."

Lucas nodded, but I could tell he didn't believe me. "What exactly constitutes the right time to tell your dad that you might actually get to live a normal, healthy life?"

"It's—" I took a deep breath, then went for a half-truth. "The Guard needs me right now. As a *Lilitu*. I don't want to distract anyone with thoughts of what might happen someday."

"*Might?*" Lucas looked genuinely surprised. "What's this 'might' business? You got a guarantee from an angel that you could be human one day. How does that leave room for 'might?'"

I dragged my eyes back to the sanctuary. "Yeah. No, you're right." I forced a lightness into my voice, hoping that would put an end to the discussion. But Lucas heard the fear behind my words.

"Braedyn?"

I didn't respond, not trusting myself to speak.

"You don't have to hide anything from me."

"I know." Still my words came out too brightly to be believed.

Gently, he cupped one hand under my chin and lifted my face. "What are you not telling me?"

I reached up to take hold of his hand, but I didn't pull it away from my face. After a long moment, I came to a decision. "Okay," I breathed. "But not here."

Lucas's brow furrowed, but he didn't say anything. He simply nodded. I returned to the spiral staircase. I could feel him watching me all the way down.

I emerged from the hidden staircase, trying to get my breath back under control. It would be too humiliating to start crying on a school field trip. I turned to face a row of shadowy statues, pretending to study the carved figures while I quickly thumbed moisture out of my eyes. I turned back to the sanctuary, scanning the room for my friends. If I hadn't been so distracted, I would have seen her sooner. As it was, I only caught the motion of her darting from behind a statue out of the corner of my eye. I barely had time to react, shying to the side as she attacked.

That tiny movement probably saved my life, not that I had time to appreciate my good fortune. One moment I was twisting to shield myself from an unknown attacker, the next I was skidding across the floor, pain lancing through my shoulder, and she was there, on top of me, lips pulled back in a snarl.

I reacted without conscious thought, my muscle memory kicking into action. I drove my knuckles into the woman's throat, which should have flattened her. She barely reacted, but her grip loosened enough for me to plant my feet against her ribs and kick her off of me.

I heard someone scream. Lucas shouted. And then she was diving for me again. I threw my body to one side, rolling onto my feet and spinning around, hands up and ready for a fight. She was already mid-lunge. I was dimly aware that she was the woman I'd seen earlier, slipping through the gate into the mission's inner garden.

She collided with me before I could do more than block her punch.

The force of her blow sent me staggering back a few steps. I faced her, frantic, but hard as I wracked my brain I knew I'd never seen this woman before in my life. Could she be a spotter? Maybe a member of the Guard from a different unit? I held out my hand—a gesture of truce.

"I'm not your enemy."

She lunged for me again, swinging her other arm with more force. I saw the tire iron with just enough time to drop. It sailed through the air where my head had been moments before. Ice gripped my stomach. Whoever this woman was, she was not playing around. That blow was meant to end me. I tried to run past her but she caught me by the scruff of my shirt and jerked me back, hard. I hit the ground with a sickening *thunk*, red and black swirls overtaking my vision. When they cleared, I saw her standing over me, tensing to swing the tire iron for my head.

Lucas hit her like a freight train, bowling her over before the killing blow could fall. A wave of nausea rose in my throat but I pushed it down and forced myself to roll to my knees.

Lucas was wrestling with her for the tire iron beside a bank of stained glass windows. She released the iron suddenly and Lucas, unprepared, lost his balance. Before he could recover, she turned, punching him savagely in the solar plexus. Lucas dropped the tire iron. It struck the ground, impacting with the sound of a clanging bell. Something was wrong—Lucas gasped for breath with a horrible, wet sound. He dropped to his knees, unable to do more than struggle for oxygen.

The woman picked up the tire iron and turned back to Lucas, hunched over on the ground before her.

"No!" My voice sliced through the sanctuary. The woman turned toward me, and I saw again the lifelessness of her eyes. My breath came out in a ragged hiss of realization. "No."

The woman left Lucas, bearing down on me. I realized that I had to end this fight, and I had to do it now. Nothing would make her stop, and the next time I went down, there would be no one there to save me.

I charged toward the woman. She lifted the tire iron to strike, but at the last moment I dropped, skidding toward her across the slick, polished stone, feet first. I connected solidly, the force of my kick shoving her up and back.

No surprised flickered through those dead eyes as she hit the stained glass window. The glass exploded behind her like a shower of multi-colored gems, clearing the way for sunlight to flood the sanctuary with blinding intensity.

I skidded to a stop beneath the window and threw my arms over my head protectively. Tiny fragments of stained glass showered down. The silence was profound, but brief.

Screams sounded inside and outside the sanctuary. I couldn't summon the energy to look up.

"Braedyn!" Lucas called, voice hoarse.

I moved my arms away from my head gingerly, and slivers of glass tinkled to the ground. Glass littered the floor around me. Lucas was half-crawling, half-scrambling forward to meet me. I dragged myself up into a sitting position.

Lucas threw an arm around me. In seconds we were surrounded. Mr. Landon was shouting, his usually jovial face a mask of panic. Annie was screaming into the phone, eyes streaming. And beyond them, a shell-shocked crowd of my classmates watched in horrified fascination.

The only thing that felt real was Lucas's arm around me. I realized I was clinging to him ferociously when Mr. Landon tried to pull us apart.

"Are you hurt?" he was asking. "Braedyn, are you hurt?"

"Don't," I whispered, tightening my grip on Lucas's shirt. Mr. Landon pulled back helplessly.

"How long?" he asked Annie. "How long until the ambulance gets here?"

I didn't hear Annie's response. I was looking at Lucas's face. "Did you see?" I whispered. "Did you see her eyes?" Lucas nodded grimly. So I wasn't crazy. The woman who'd attacked us?

She was a *Thrall*.

We were still clinging to each other 15 minutes later when the paramedics arrived.

End of excerpt.
If you would like to read more, grab your copy of
Incubus (Daughters Of Lilith: Book 2) at Amazon.com.

A NOTE FROM THE AUTHOR

Thank you so much for taking the time to read this book. If you were entertained or moved by the story, I'd be grateful if you would please leave a review on the site where you purchased this book.

Even a few sentences would be so appreciated—they let me know when I've connected with readers, and when I've fallen short.

Reviews are also the best way to help other readers discover new authors and make more informed choices when purchasing books in a crowded space.

Thanks again for reading,
Jenn

ABOUT THE AUTHOR

Originally from New Mexico (and still suffering from Hatch green chile withdrawal), Jenn includes Twentieth Television's *Wicked, Wicked Games* and *American Heiress* among her produced television credits.

Outside of TV, she created *The Bond Of Saint Marcel* (a vampire comic book mini-series published by Archaia Studios Press), and co-wrote *The Red Star: Sword Of Lies* graphic novel with creator Christian Gossett from 2007 to 2009.

She's also the author of the award-winning *Daughters of Lilith* paranormal thriller YA novels, and is currently realizing a life-long dream of growing actual real live avocados in her backyard. No guacamole yet—but she lives in hope.

Follow her on Twitter: @jennq
Visit her blog: JenniferQuintenz.com

You can also sign up for her newsletter at JenniferQuintenz.com to be among the first to hear about new books, deals, and appearances.

18578153R00172

Printed in Great Britain
by Amazon